Gabriel's Salvation

CB Halliwell

Copyright ©2024 by CB Halliwell

All rights reserved.

No portion of this book may be reproduced in any form without written permission from the publisher or author, except as permitted by U.S. copyright law.

Quotes

She was an angel craving chaos, he was a demon seeking peace

H.M Ward

She took my hand and led me out of the darkness and showed me that whatever our souls are made of, hers and mine are the same.

Anna Todd

Important Notes

This book ends on a cliffhanger and is part one of a trilogy.

If you read Forever Entwined, Nate and Izzy's story, you may be expecting another sweet, love conquers all style book, but this is not that book.

Just like Gabe, this book is broken and bruised. It's full of bad language, smut, and morally gray moments. But just like our favorite 'villain,' if you take a chance on this book, it will open your eyes up to a whole new perspective.

Please ensure you read the trigger warnings... unless like me, you are a wild child who thinks trigger warnings are spoilers and prefer to dive in blind.

Trigger Warnings

Child abuse (in flash back memories)

Alcoholism and drunk driving

Physical violence and bullying.

Drug abuse- including potential overdose.

Drugging and attempted sexual assault. (non-graphic)

Lots of smut including some spanking and choking kinks.

Self defense, accidental death and off screen unaliving.

Mild cheating (not between the MC's)

Thug's for hire, who mention rape and abuse (talk only)

Domestic violence (not between MC)

An ex-boyfriend who slaps the MC

Read at your own discretion.

Your mental health matters!

Contents

Prologue   1

1. Chapter One   2
2. Chapter Two   14
3. Chapter Three   19
4. Chapter Four   29
5. Chapter Five   35
6. Chapter Six   52
7. Chapter Seven   63
8. Chapter Eight   73
9. Chapter Nine   86
10. Chapter Ten   96
11. Chapter Eleven   104
12. Chapter Twelve   111
13. Chapter Thirteen   120
14. Chapter Fourteen   129
15. Chapter Fifteen   138

16.	Chapter Sixteen	147
17.	Chapter Seventeen	157
18.	Chapter Eighteen	166
19.	Chapter Nineteen	183
20.	Chapter Twenty	196
21.	Chapter Twenty One	204
22.	Chapter Twenty Two	212
23.	Chapter Twenty Three	226
24.	Chapter Twenty Four	237
25.	Chapter Twenty Five	251
26.	Chapter Twenty Six	256
27.	Chapter Twenty Seven	267
28.	Chapter Twenty Eight	282
29.	Chapter Twenty Nine	296
30.	Chapter Thirty	307
31.	Chapter Thirty One	316
32.	Chapter Thirty two	324
33.	Chapter Thirty Three	335
34.	Chapter Thirty Four	344
35.	Chapter Thirty Five	354
36.	Chapter Thirty Six	362

37.	Chapter Thirty Seven	374
38.	Chapter Thirty Eight	383
39.	Chapter Thirty Nine	398
40.	Chapter Forty	408
41.	Chapter Forty One	418
42.	Chapter Forty Two	425
43.	Chapter Forty Three	433
44.	Chapter Forty Four	439
	Acknowledgments	452
	About the Author	456

Prologue

Every villain's origin story has one thing in common:

A traumatic event that changed the character's life forever.

But I don't have just one traumatic event – I have a lifetime of traumatic events. A loving mother who died when I was just a child, and a father who beat and abused me for most of my life. Then, to top it all off, the one good thing I had in my life, my younger brother, Nate, was snatched away from me when he dared to share our secret with the girl he loved. Only for her to open her big mouth and betray us both.

I'd resigned myself to a life of loneliness, heartache, and isolation. That is, until one day that all changed. She forced her way into my life and made me reevaluate everything I thought I knew about love, friendship, and past mistakes.

For the first time in my life, I was made to feel like the hero rather than the villain. She made me believe that maybe there was hope for me yet.

But I'm getting ahead of myself. Perhaps I should start at the beginning, in a run down house, in the middle of nowhere.

Chapter One

Gabe

My phone rings from the kitchen, and I drag myself off the couch. Just as I reach for it, the annoying sound stops. Looking at the clock on the microwave, I see it's barely 8 a.m. *Who the fuck would be calling me at this time?!* I don't have to wonder for long, though, as my brother's name lights up the screen.

"Hey Na-" I begin before I'm cut off by the annoying sound of singing.

"Happy birthday to you, happy birthday to you...." *Shit, is today my birthday? Surely not,* I think to myself while furrowing my brow. I scroll to the calendar app on my phone while the incessant singing continues, and sure enough, it's my birthday. My 21st birthday to be exact. *How the fuck did that happen? Maybe I should lay off the drinks a bit.*

"Gabe, are you there?"

"Yeah, I'm here. Sorry. I was just getting dressed," I mumble while clearing my throat, trying to get the roughness out of my voice so Nate won't worry about me.

"So, what are you doing later? I know you said you've gotta work today, so ya can't come here, but maybe I could get a flight over to see you? Spend Christmas together?" I can hear the pleading in his voice, and part of me would love nothing more than to accept his offer. Let him come here and finally spend some time surrounded by family. *But what the fuck could I offer him here?*

"Nah, I don't have time. John's got me working nonstop. I try my best to sound cheery. "Have a good Christmas, though." *God, I hope he buys it. Last thing I need is for him to drop everything, catch a flight, and show up on my doorstep.*

"Oh, okay," Nate replies, sounding deflated. *I'm such an ass. He just wants to spend time with me - I don't know why. I can't do this. I'm such an ass. He should just move on with his great, happy life and forget about me.*

"Anyway, I'm at work, so I've gotta go. Speak soon, Nate."

"Wait, don't," Nate starts, but I disconnect the call.

I don't miss the way his voice is laced with hurt and disappointment, but he'd be even more hurt if I said yes and let him come here - back to the house of horrors. Our father may not live here anymore, but his ghost and the memories of him still haunt these halls.

No. Over there, he's living the life of a rich kid. I bet he's got a stack of presents under the tree and a turkey roasting in the oven. Bet he's probably going fucking caroling with the Jacksons or some other shit. Doing all that Christmas movie bullshit.

I look around the rundown shithole I live in — not a single Christmas decoration in sight. Nah, he doesn't need me; he's got his perfect life there. I'd just be holding him back.

I open the fridge to grab myself a beer, but it's bare. *Fuck! Coffee will have to do.*

I grab the milk and a mug from beside the sink, but as soon as I unscrew the lid, I gag as the sour smell assaults my nose. Resisting the urge to throw up, I quickly put the lid back on and throw the carton in the trash.

"Fuck," I huff as I grab my bike keys. I throw on some shoes and a jacket with my joggers and make my way to the store.

"Merry Christmas, that will be $12 please," the pimple-faced asshole at the till whines.

I throw my money down and snatch my beer, milk, and ready meal, not even bothering to give him eye contact.

Grabbing my phone from my pants pocket, I dial John's number. As usual, he answers almost immediately.

"What is it, son?" *Son?!* The sound of that word alone makes bile rise up in my throat, reminding me of exactly whose 'son' I truly am.

"What have I said about calling me that?" I snap back.

As usual, John just ignores me the way he does every time we have this argument. He calls everyone son; I know this. It still doesn't stop me wanting to rip his fucking throat out every time.

"What do you want, Gabe?" I can hear a note of irritation in his voice.

"I was just calling to see if you had any jobs for me today."

"Gabe, it's Christmas Eve! No fucker's working! Not even me. Go fuck off, relax, enjoy the holidays, and try to spread some Christmas cheer."

"Do I look like a fucking elf?" I snap again, the irritation clear in my voice.

"Well, go find some Christmas pussy and fuck that attitude out of ya for all I care. Just get the fuck off the phone. Me and my little angel are making Christmas cookies, aren't we?" he coos in some pathetic baby voice.

"That kid's made you fucking weak man," I scoff.

"Remember who you're talking to. I may not have brought you into this world but I'm more than happy to take you out of it. Now f.u.c.k. off, before I kick your a.s.s.," he spells out because of his granddaughter's proximity to him. *Even that gets on my nerves. Where was that concern for protecting the innocent when I was a kid?*

"Really, old man? I'd like to see you try," I laugh back before hanging up. *Fuck me, what am I gonna do now?*

Ever since his granddaughter was born, she's had him wrapped around her little finger. She's probably only about 4 or 5 but follows him everywhere. She's an annoying little shit, constantly stealing all the donuts or following her grandad around like a bad smell. Usually kids are scared of me, crying when they hear my bike or see my tattoos. But she just laughed when she saw me and demanded I let her sit on the bike. I would never let her, of course. But she's alright I guess.

Climbing onto my bike, I let the sound of the engine coming to life distract me as I drive home. The streets become a blur as I rev the engine, getting faster and faster. It's pretty empty, and the road is clear, so I allow myself to open up the engine and soar.

As soon as I get home, I waste no time popping open a bottle and parking my ass in front of the TV. My phone buzzes in my pocket but as soon as I see who it is, I decline the call.

A few seconds later my phone buzzes, telling me I have a new voice message. I know I shouldn't, but curiosity gets the better of me, so I play it.

"10:30 a.m. on the 22nd of December - Hello Gabe, it's Sarah, erm... Mrs. Jackson. I'm just calling to remind you that you're still welcome here for Christmas. It would mean the world to Nate if you would come. In case you forgot our address, it's- " I hit delete on the voicemail and skip to the next message.

"8:03 a.m. today - Gabe, it's me. Call me back, bro."

"8:07 a.m. - Come on birthday boy, call me back." I can't help but grin as I listen to Nate's voicemails, knowing full well he'd have been bouncing around like an excitable toddler leaving them. Even as a kid, he's always loved birthdays. Even when we both knew our asshole of a father wouldn't get us much, if anything. He'd act like the small handmade gift I made him was better than winning the lottery.

I remember his sixth birthday; mom had passed away a few months before and my father had spent that whole time basically comatose on the couch. So I snuck out and stole a teddy bear for him. Wrapping it in some newspaper and string I found lying around the house. *He carried that teddy bear everywhere with him. Even years later when it started to resemble a dog's chew toy from the years of love and attention he gave it - he continued to lug it everywhere with him. I still remember the hours of inconsolable tears I had to dry when my father ripped its head off in anger one day. I can't remember why he did it though. Knowing that asshole, just because he felt like it or wanted to hurt my brother, just for daring to breathe.*

My smile is short-lived though as the phone automatically skips to the next message.

"9:46 a.m. - Hey Gabe, it's Mrs. Jackson. Nate says you won't be joining us. So I just wanted to wish you a happy birthday and let you know I've sent a little something to you in the mail... it says it was delivered a few days ago. Please let me know if you received it."

Reluctantly, I head down to the mailbox. When I get there I notice it's almost full. I grab everything out and head back inside.

I flip through the pile of mail, which is mostly bills and junk mail, and find three things that aren't. The first is clearly a card of some sort. I open it and straight away cash falls out. Retrieving the unexpected gift from the floor, I count it - fifty dollars.

Who the fuck would send me cash?

Opening the card it reads:

To Gabe, have a great 21st birthday! Treat yourself to something nice. Love from Sarah and Tim (Mr. and Mrs, Jackson)

Well, I never did like the Jacksons, Nate may consider them part of his chosen family, but I never will. But I'll hand it to them, the money they send every birthday sure is a welcome gift.

The next is a package from Nate consisting of a birthday card, some chocolates, an Amazon gift card, and the latest Sons of Anarchy box set.

And finally, there's a Christmas card. This one appears to have been hand-delivered.

Inside, it simply says;

To Nathaniel and Gabe. Merry Christmas, love from the Williams family.

I tear it up into tiny pieces and throw it in the trash. The last thing I want to see is a card from Isabella's family. Back when we were kids and Nate first developed his little infatuation with her and her family, I thought she could be okay. For years I watched their friendship blossom and was dumb enough to believe maybe she could be a true friend to us both. That was until she and her grandparents betrayed us. A betrayal that led to us being removed from the only life we'd ever known and thrown into foster care. And now the mere mention of her name is enough to send my blood boiling.

Yet every year I receive one of these cards- some sort of sick way to torment us further. As if that family hasn't done enough harm to us, they send a card every year just to rub salt in the wound.

My mind transports me back to when I was a child and was dumb enough to believe they actually cared.

6 YEARS AGO

Walking through the forest carrying firewood, I spot a familiar figure heading towards me.

"Gabe, I'm glad I saw you today. I have a bit of a favor to ask," Isabella's grandpa says with a smile. "Would you mind helping me get some stuff out of my car?" he asks, motioning down the path.

Reluctantly, I put down the firewood and follow him.

"So how have you been, young man? Nate's coming over for dinner tonight and Nana is making her famous lasagna. If you'd like to join us, there's plenty to spare." My mouth almost salivates from the thought alone. I can't remember the last time I actually had a meal that didn't come in a box or that wasn't better suited for the trash.

"I can't. I'm sorry, but I'm busy with Dad tonight." *It's not really a lie; I am busy. Busy making sure Dad doesn't choke on his own vomit, busy making sure Dad doesn't get drunk and attack Nate again, and busy making sure everyone is still alive by tomorrow.*

"Oh, okay, maybe next time."

We reach the truck and he hands me two bags to carry. "Are you okay with those?" he asks.

"Yeah, of course." *It's two bags, not even heavy. Surely he could have carried them himself?*

I take in his smaller frame and gray hair and wonder if perhaps they're too heavy for him because he's so old.

"Oh shoot!" he says suddenly as he pulls another bag out of the backseat. "Nana is going to be so cross with me," he sighs as he opens it.

"What is it? What did you do?" I ask, peering into the bag.

"Well, I was supposed to be taking these old clothes to the charity shop, but I forgot. Nana isn't going to be happy if I return home with them. And the shops will be shut by the time I finish work." He begins rubbing his head looking upset, then suddenly gasps. "Wait, I've got an idea! You look about the same size as my grandson. I don't suppose you want these, do you? They've barely been worn."

"Who me? Erm, I'm not sure if–" I begin saying but he cuts me off.

"You really would be doing me a huge favor Gabe, how about we take them with us to the Rangers Office and you can at least try them on. You've got to take the other two bags there anyway."

"I guess," I shrug as I move the two bags into one hand so I can reach for the bag of clothes.

We walk a few minutes to the office and step inside. As usual, there's only Isabella's grandpa and one other person here. Who is this guy? I assess him for a moment trying to decide if he's a threat. *I'm alone now with two fully grown men. Will they try to hurt me?* I take in the other guy and notice he also seems pretty old. I decide it's safe enough. After all, I could take them both if I had to, either that or run. Neither seems fast enough to catch me.

"You can drop the bags just there," he says, motioning to the table in the corner of the room.

"Have you had breakfast yet? I'm starving. I bet you are as well after carrying those heavy bags. Sit down and I'll make us something."

Reluctantly I take a seat. A few moments later he comes over with a warm cup of hot chocolate filled with cream and little tiny marshmallows, and a plate full of toast.

I devour the toast and drink as quickly as I can, just in case he tries to take it away again.

"Wow, you were hungry," he laughs, handing me the half slice left on his own plate. "Now how about we see if those clothes fit."

I open the bag and see what appears to be a brand new thick coat. I try it on and other than being a little big, it's perfect. This will definitely keep me warm all winter, much warmer than the hole covered fleece I'm currently wearing. Next, I find not one but two pairs of jeans, a couple of sweaters, and even a pair of sneakers. All of which look like they've never even been used.

"Are you sure you want me to have these? You're not tricking me, right? We don't need handouts you know," I say, eyeing him suspiciously.

"No, please take them. You'd be helping me so much. I'd never hear the end of it if I went home and Nana realized I didn't do the one job she asked me to."

"Oh okay so, it's like I'm doing a job for you then?"

"Yes definitely, you're helping me stay out of trouble. I'll owe you one."

"Oh, in that case I guess I could, you know, just to keep you out of trouble."

Present Day

Shaking my head to rid it of my memories, I grab another beer from the fridge.

Stupid little Gabe, believing he was actually helping. I bet the old bastard had a good old laugh once I left.

Poor, neglected Gabe, relying on pathetic handouts to survive. Pretending to be a sweet caring family when really they were luring my family into a trap, ready to strike and report us to the authorities.

I will never be weak, afraid, or stupid again. I can take care of myself and I can sure as hell take care of Nate. We only need each other. I make good money and soon Nate will too. We can get all the food and pussy we need when we want it. What else is there to want?

For a moment I feel happy; it's only a few more months till Nate turns eighteen and hopefully moves back home to me. That's been the plan for ages. *But is this enough for Nate? Am I enough for Nate? He's just going to leave me as soon as something better comes along and then it will just be me again. Fuck it! I've done okay since coming back here. I will be okay no matter what.*

These thoughts are going to drive me mad so I grab my beer and park my ass on the couch. Eventually, I grab the DVDs that Nate gave me and lose myself in watching them while I drink my beer and smoke my dope. After a while I look at my phone and of course, there is nothing there from anyone. Everyone has other people that they would rather connect with than me. The only time people contact me is when they need something - a fuck, some dope, a repair, something. People only want me for what I can do for them.

My mind wanders thinking about what Nate's future will be. Even when we were kids he was always the one people liked. Despite everything our father put us through he is someone still encompassed by light and goodness. Not like me who was consumed by darkness.

He will probably find himself some bitch of a wife and a couple of ankle biters running around his knees - make his own family. *Where will I fit in? Nowhere, that's where! I'll be thrown away like last week's trash. I'll be stuck in this house old and bitter just like my father was. Probably right here on this couch and fade into oblivion. No one will miss me when I'm gone. No one will stand over my grave and weep. I'll just be maggot food.*

Trying to distract myself from my downward spiral, I put the next DVD in and try to watch, hoping that the familiar appeal of guns, violence, and motorbikes will make me feel more at home. But of course this episode is all about the biker gang pulling together like a big ass family to try and rescue Jax's baby. *When the fuck did this become some lame ass family show? Why is Jax ready to betray his brothers for some snot-nosed baby?*

At first it makes no sense to me, until I think back to a baby who I would have protected with my life - Nate - he wasn't my kid of course, but he might as well have been. It was me who was there when he took his first steps. It was me who made sure he got food every night, even when my own tummy was empty and hurt. I would have done anything for him. I still would. I'd take a bullet for my brother. *Is that how Jax feels about his kid? Is that how parents should feel?*

A feeling of sadness and yearning settles over me. *Will I ever have that? Would I ever want that?*

Fuck this, I need to stop this before I take a knife and slit my own throat.

Chapter Two

Gabe

I make my way to the kitchen and check the fridge. *Empty.* Check the cupboards. *Bare.* There's officially no food or booze left in the house. Even the bottle of cheap wine I got from one of the customers as a Christmas gift has been drunk. *For fuck's sake!*

Eyeing up the birthday card on the counter, I remember the money. I jump in the shower and quickly throw on some jeans, a shirt, and my trademark leather jacket before grabbing the cash and making my way outside to see my one true love—my Harley— my pride and joy, the only girl I'll ever care about. She's a matte black 2021 Harley Davidson Sportster 1250S. She has black rims, and an exhaust that has the prettiest purr. You definitely hear me coming with that exhaust. *The shit I had to do to get her, but it was worth it*

I somehow make it to town in one piece, despite the fact I'm well over the legal drink and drive limit. As soon as I walk into the first bar I see Declan, the usual bartender. I don't even need to ask before a glass of rum and coke is slid in front of me.

"Run me a tab," I grunt in response.

"Will do," he replies with a thumbs up as he pours a beer for the next customer.

I spend the next few hours silently nursing glass after glass of rum at the end of the bar. That is until someone slides in and sits herself down on the bar stool next to me.

"Hi Handsome, what's your name?" the girl purrs.

I turn my head about to tell her to fuck off but stop in my tracks when I see her. She's hot as fuck with her long blond hair, big tits threatening to spill out of a tight red dress, and legs that seem to go on forever.

"I'm Stacey, how about you buy me a birthday drink?" the girl confidently suggests as she taps the 21 badge on her dress.

"Well, since it's my birthday as well, maybe you should buy me one." I drawl with a cheeky smirk.

"Shots!" she says loudly to the bartender.

"$2 each or four for $5? "

"I'll take eight then," she says, giving me a cheeky wink.

The bartender makes the shots and hands them to her on a tray. She takes one off and places it in front of me.

"That will be $10 then please," the bartender says, handing her the card machine.

"He's paying," she replies, poking her tongue out at me and walking away, swaying her hips and shaking her ass as she does so.

"Man, she played you." Declan chuckles as I nod my head allowing him to add it to my tab. *Damn, I know I should be annoyed but that was sexy as fuck.* I watch her walk over to her friends, all of whom look like they belong in a frat house, laughing and joking.

For the next hour, I can't keep my eyes from wandering over to where she and her friends are partying. She's there with a bunch of girls mostly, and just two other guys. Part of me wants to walk over there, take her by the hand, and lead her into the bathroom to release the frustration currently pitching a tent in my jeans, but I decide against it. I don't like the whole party scene thing. Too..well..peopley.

I head outside for a cigarette to distract myself and it seems to be working. I'm sitting down, eyes closed, enjoying the peace, until I get the feeling someone is too close. I'm about to punch whichever asshole dares to invade my space, but when I open my furious eyes, I am met by a face full of boobs. Stacey, *I believe that's her name, is* standing over me. I don't even have time to speak or process what is happening, because she literally rips the cigarette from my mouth.

I blink, trying to figure out what just happened. *She's casually smoking MY cigarette.*

"Sharing is caring cutie," she grins before removing it from her mouth and placing it back in my gawking one.

She turns away, yet again leaving me to do nothing but stare at her ass as she walks away. *Two - zero to her.*

This doesn't happen to me, like ever. I'm not the sort of guy girls tease. Nope. Never. I'm the sort of guy who picks a girl, gets what he wants, then fucks off. Nothing annoys me more than needy girls trying to get my attention. But fuck me. This girl's confidence is sexy as fuck. Twice now she's run rings around me leaving me begging for more.

I finish my cigarette enjoying the fruity taste of her lip gloss in my mouth.

Nah, I'm not having this, I think to myself. I need to have her now. Fuck her hard and get her out of my head. I rush inside, ready to make my move, but Stacey is nowhere to be seen.

I sit my ass back on the barstool growling out, "Whiskey, neat." *What the fuck am I doing here? I only wanted to get out, have a few drinks, and forget about how crappy my life is. Instead, I'm sitting here with a boner from hell getting more irritated by the minute. I should've just stayed home.*

I'm just finishing my glass when it goes dark. I feel soft feminine fingers cover my eyes as a warm breath whispers into my ear, "Guess who?"

My heart thumps and my dick hardens even more in the hope that it's Stacey, but once the hands are removed I'm disappointed to realize it's only Kelly... Kelly the local whore. I've been fucking both her and her best friend Sophie for months. *Well, that was one way to get my dick to go down I guess.*

I don't actually give a fuck about either girl, but both are easy, sexy, and give great head. Looking around one last time to ensure Stacey really has left, I grab Kelly by the hand and lead her to the men's toilets.

Moments later she's bent over as I fuck her from behind in one of the tiny stalls. Once we're done she attempts to kiss me but I push her back. "That's not what this is, and you know that," I snap back as I tuck myself back into my jeans and open the door.

"Wait Gabe, let's go back to mine. We can finish what we started," she tries to purr seductively but her annoying tone just reinstates my irritation that I finally had gotten rid of. "I'm not interested!" I snap back and I feel a shudder go through me when I envision having to spend more time with this skank.

"Well you sure were a second ago; that's the best sex we've ever had." She whines as she steps forward and attempts to reach down and touch me again but I grab her wrist. "That's because I was imagining fucking someone else!" I snap back, slightly nastier than needed. It's not a lie; it wasn't her I was imagining plowing into, it wasn't her hair I imagined having draped around my fist, or her moans I was dragging out. No, it was another blond-headed beauty I was imagining.

"You're such a fucking asshole Gabe! I wish I'd never met you!" Kelly shouts, and I almost feel guilty when I see the lone tear sliding down her cheek. Almost. *She probably thinks I'm a way out of this dead-end town and life, but what she doesn't realize is that she's better without me. I'll just make her life even worse than it already is.*

I grab my jacket from the stool, pay my tab, and make my way outside. As soon as I do, the cool wind catches me making me feel like I'm going to fall over. Damn, I'm drunker than I thought. No way am I driving home and risking bashing up my bike. So instead I call an Uber.

It drops me off at the beginning of the woods and I stumble through them, stopping a few times to throw up. When I finally make it home I collapse on the sofa and pass out. Nothing but my dreams for company.

Chapter Three

Stacey

6 HOURS EARLIER

Applying one final coat of lipgloss, I can't help but grin. Tonight my boyfriend, Justin, is taking me for dinner and then to the hottest club on campus. He went off to college a few months ago and since school is now over for the summer, this is the first time I'm getting to see him properly. He's usually too busy with basketball playoffs and training. To surprise him I even brought a fake ID as I don't want to embarrass him if I get carded in front of all his college friends.

I grab my handbag and take one last look at myself in the mirror, admiring the way my ass looks in my new jeans. *Thank god the gym squats have paid off.*

My phone pings letting me know my taxi has arrived so I rush out the door, almost bumping into my sister in my rush.

"Sorry," I laugh.

"You will be," she teases back.

I rush out and hop in the back of the taxi. "365 Munro Boulevard, please."

The whole way over I fantasize about what Justin is going to do when he sees me. Sure we chat over the phone, but it's not as much as I'd like. And we Facetime, but mostly in the evenings after practice. But we were inseparable last year before he went off to college, and it's been months since I saw him in person so I bet he's just as excited as I am.

"$22.50," the driver says, snapping me out of my daydream.

"Sorry, keep the change," I say, handing him $25.

I run up the cobbled path to his door and knock a little too loudly out of excitement. I wait a few minutes but no one comes. So I knock again, this time louder. *Perhaps he's upstairs?*

A shout of "come in" sounds from inside, so slowly I push the door open. *Perhaps he's got a surprise waiting for me inside.*

I make my way inside and notice most of the lights in the hallway are out, but I can hear noises from one of the rooms. I walk in and, well, he definitely has a surprise waiting for me, just not the kind I would like.

Inside are Justin and three other friends sitting on the floor in their gym shorts playing FIFA.

"Hey baby I missed you," I say, wrapping my arms around his neck, and placing a kiss on his cheek; but instead of embracing me, he moves his head away so that he can still see the TV.

"Babe, I'm playing. Sit down, I'll be with you after this game," he grumbles.

I make my way over to the recliner and wait...and wait.

"Babe, it's been three games, how about you sit the next one out?" I beg as I again move to try and get his attention by running my hands through his hair.

"Stop being so needy, I'll be with you in a minute," he snaps while pushing my hand away.

One minute turns into one hour, and one hour turns into three.

Justin finally stands up, and I stupidly assume it's to finally come see me, but no. He gets up, walks to the kitchen, and returns a few minutes later with a beer for himself and his friends, but nothing for me.

"I'll go get my own then," I snap.

As I walk into the kitchen I bump into his older sister, Lexi.

"Hey Lex.,"

"Oh hey. Freckles? Didn't even know you were here."

"Yeah, I was supposed to be going out with your dumb brother, but the moron is too busy on his Xbox with his friends to even acknowledge me," I say, trying and failing to hide the sadness and frustration from my voice.

"Well, that's because my brother's an asshole, screw him. Carly and Molly are upstairs, why don't you come join us for a bit?" Lexi offers.

"Nah, it's okay; I don't wanna cramp your style."

"Nonsense, I could do with a change anyway. Molly's complaining about work, and Carly's broken up with yet another love of her life," Lexi laughs as she rolls her eyes dramatically.

"Well, you do sound like you need saving. Poor you." I tease.

"Here, take this," she says, handing me a bottle of prosecco, "and I'll grab the glasses."

"Hey bitches, you remember my brother's girlfriend," Lexi hollers as she swings her bedroom door open.

"Damn! Freckles grew uuuppp!"

"Someone got a 'lil bit sexy!" Carly says, slapping my ass as I walk past.

"We're heading into town soon, you should join us." Molly offers as she takes a glass of prosecco, and offers it to me. "Oh shit, you're not old enough are you?"

"Well actually…" I say, reaching into my jeans pocket and pulling out my fake ID and waving it in the air. "According to this, Stacey Daniels is 21 today," I laugh.

"Let me see," Lexi says, snatching the ID out of my hands.

"This is pretty good actually, where did you get it?" She asked, looking up at me with interest.

"My friend's older brother makes them for cash, so I paid him $30 for it."

"Well then it seems a waste not to use it," Carly says with a wink. " You owe it to Stacey to celebrate her birthday in style."

For the next hour we drink, chat and have fun. After some persuasion, the girls got me to agree to let them give me a makeover to make me look older.

"All done," Molly says, stepping back to admire her handwork.

"What do you think?" she asks, guiding me over to the full length mirror on the back of the bedroom door.

I barely recognize the person staring back at me. My long blond hair cascades down my back in loose curls, and my usual minimalistic makeup has been transformed into smokey eyes and dark red lips. And they've dressed me in one of Lexi's short red dresses. Unfortunately while Lexi is relatively small in the chest department, I'm a little more filled out. I wouldn't exactly say huge. But in this dress, my C cups look more like DDs.

"I can't wear this, Justin will kill me," I gasp, trying to pull up the tight fabric, hoping to hide my now huge chest. *What do I have to lose? Maybe this is what I need to do to get his attention?*

"Screw him, I think you need to show my brother what he's been missing."

"You're right, fuck it," I shrug.

"That's my girl," Lexi says, clapping her hands.

"Now down your drink we gotta go," Carly says, thrusting yet another full glass into my hands.

"One last finishing touch," Lexi says as she opens her wardrobe and removes a shoe box from inside. Rummaging around she finally shouts "Got it!" before walking over to me and pinning a big 21 TODAY badge to my chest.

"Now we can go!"

I walk downstairs and stand in the doorway of the lounge. "Hey Justin, I'm going out with Lexi and her friends, do you want to join me?"

"Fuck's sake, I'm busy," he snaps, not even turning his head to look at me.

"Fine, then I'll go without you," I snap back, slamming the door behind me.

We make our way to one bar, where we meet Lexi's long-term boyfriend, Brett and a couple of his friends. "Wow, is that you Freckles?" Brett says, looking at me wide mouthed.

"Nope, for tonight it's Stacey," both Lexi and Molly giggle.

"Well then, since it's Stacey's 21st, I think we need to celebrate properly," he laughs, throwing his arm around my shoulder.

"Alex, the birthday girl needs a cocktail," Brett proclaims to his friend who heads straight to the bar then returns a few minutes later with a huge fishbowl and eight straws.

Together we down 1…then 2…then 3 fishbowls, before two of the guys say they have to leave.

"Let's move on to another place," Carly suggests, "I know a bar with the hottest bartender."

"Cause that's exactly how I choose my bars," Brett grumbles.

"Come on grumpy pants, it's just round the corner," Carly laughs, poking her tongue out at him.

Once inside we waste no time finding a huge booth in the back.

"I've got an idea, truth or dare," Lexi says cheekily.

We play a few rounds, Carly is made to rub a bald guy's head, Brett is made to find another random guy to swap shirts with, and his friend Alex gets made to get the number of some old cougar. But now it's my turn.

"You've gotta get the hottest guy in here to buy you a drink," Lexi challenges.

"Fine." I look around and there aren't many options. There are a few guys in their mid-twenties near the jukebox, but I quickly decide not to approach them. I'm not shy by any stretch of the imagination, if anything, my friends would say I'm too confident and flirty. But it's one thing being flirty with the dumb guys around school, it's a whole different thing doing it with grown men.

I scan the room some more and spot a couple of possibilities, and am just about to make my way over to two guys sitting a few tables over when Carly suddenly shouts, "Him!"

I look to where she's pointing and he's the hottest guy I've ever seen sitting alone at the end of the bar. *Wow, he looks like he's just stepped out of an episode of Sons of Anarchy. I take in the short brown hair and the way his black t-shirt clings to his broad shoulders. I shuffle slightly so I can get a better view. It's then that I spot the tattoos covering both arms and hands and what appears to be another one, peeking out the top and covering part of his neck. I feel butterflies forming in my tummy from his whole dark and dangerous vibe.*

"No way!!! He's a psycho." Lexi exclaims.

"Yeah, but he's a fucking hot psycho." Molly agrees.

"Seriously, he's a dick. I've seen him around, he's far too much for a girl like you." Brett tries saying but it just frustrates me.

"What do you mean, a girl like me?" I snap, feeling the booze making me even more argumentative than usual.

"I just mean you're nice, he's not. He'll eat you for breakfast," Brett laughs trying to lighten the mood. But it only eggs me on more.

"Fucking watch me!" I demand, as I slide off my seat and straight towards him.

As I get closer, all the sounds of the bar disappear, and all I can hear is the sound of my blood thumping as my heart pounds in my chest. This was a mistake. He looks even more dangerous in person.

My stubbornness refuses to allow me to back down though so instead I sit myself down in the empty seat beside him.

"Hey handsome, what's your name?" I say in my most seductive tone.

If looks could kill, I would have been cremated on the spot, judging by the fiery hatred in his eyes when he first looks up at me; thankfully that look soon morphs into a very different sort of heated look.

"I'm Stacey, how about you buy me a birthday drink?" I purr, trying my hardest to sound confident and sexy. When he doesn't answer right away I tap my fake birthday badge for extra effect.

"Well since it's my birthday, maybe you should buy me one." he replies back with a cheeky smirk. *Damn, those dimples make my knees feel weak.*

I feel myself blushing at his gaze so I turn my attention to the bartender "Shots!"

"$2 each or four for $5?" he asks. *Shit, what do I say? I never order shots. How many are too many? Should I order more or less?*

"I'll take eight then," I say while biting my lip nervously, deciding to just take them back to the group and run.

The bartender makes the shots and hands them to me on a tray. I hand Mr. Sex On Legs one and then rush off before my own legs give way.

"That will be $10 then please," the bartender calls as I try to leave. *Shit! I forgot the dare.*

"He's paying," I reply, poking my tongue out at the guy, internally cringing at my own awkwardness, as I walk away.

"OMG!" The girls all squeal when I make it back to the booth.

"Damn girl, you got bigger balls than me," Brett says, seeming genuinely impressed.

"Yeah, we weren't joking about how nobody messes with Gabe Scott and lives to tell the tale," Carly and Molly both say in unison.

"Damn, you must be some sort of siren or something," Alex jokes before Brett pushes him playfully. "Dude, that fantasy geek shit ain't cool."

We all go back to our game but I can't take my eyes off the guy at the end of the bar. "Earth to Freckles, or should I say Stacey?" Lexi teases.

"It's your turn."

"Dare," I say definitely hoping and praying it will give me another reason to go over to see Gabe.

"I dare you to go back to Gabe and kiss him on the cheek," Lexi challenges, and I can see from her face she doesn't think I'll do it.

"Fine," I say standing again, but as I begin to make my way over, I see him head outside so I follow. When I get to the doorway

I see him sitting with his back to me, smoking a cigarette. *Shit, what do I do now?* I make my way over slowly, and the more I watch him the more I'd give anything to press my lips to his. Instinctively I bend my head down, preparing to kiss his cheek. But as I get closer he looks up at me, and all my confidence disappears.

Shit, he's just caught me staring like a creeper. What can I do now?

Without thinking I take the cigarette from his mouth and put it in my own. Tasting the mint and smoke on my tongue, desperately wishing it was his tongue I was tasting instead. I look down and he's just staring wide-mouthed, looking like he's ready to eat me whole.

"Sharing is caring cutie " I add with a nervous smirk before quickly removing the cigarette from my own mouth and placing it back in his, like some sort of cartoon character about to be eaten by the big bad wolf.

Turning I make my way back inside running straight into the girls who are all watching from the window.

"Oh my god girl, do you actually have a death wish?" one of them says as they all shake their heads in surprise.

"Anyway, our Uber is here. Some of us have work in the morning so we're heading off. Grab your shit and let's go," Molly says, linking arms and leading me back to the booth.

I get my stuff and join the rest of them in the Uber, but it takes all my strength not to turn back around and tell them I wanna stay with Gabe. But I can't. *I have a boyfriend. Lexi's little brother to be exact.* I remind myself. *But damn, how is it that I've felt more in the last hour than I have the whole time since Justin got back home? Someone as hot as him couldn't be interested in boring old me though, could he?*

Chapter Four

Gabe

Every night for the last six weeks I've been here at Saints Bar, desperately hoping to bump into Stacey. I say desperately because that's exactly what I probably seem. Thankfully no one seems to question drinking every night. *Probably because it's normal for you.* My cruel mind reminds me.

But every night I go home alone, more frustrated than the last. I've seen both Kelly and Sophie a few times. But I haven't slept with either of them.

I'm about to leave when I spot her again... like an angel straight from heaven she walks through the doors but she doesn't spot me. I'm about to walk over when one of the assholes she came with grabs her ass and plants a kiss on her lips.

Now I don't have feelings, I don't have a heart, but man if I did, it would have an arrow straight through it right now.

Grabbing my cigarettes from the counter, I storm outside.

Smoking one... two... three in a row to try and calm myself. *This is ridiculous. You don't care about girls, you never have.* I remind myself.

"Can I have one of those?" A voice says from behind me.

I don't even need to turn around to realize who it is, I feel my body heating at her proximity alone. Turning slowly, I offer her my pack, but yet again she takes the one that's already in my mouth.

"So I never did get your name," she says as she continues to smoke my cigarette. I'd be lying if I said I wasn't thinking about what else of mine she could put her beautiful mouth around.

"Hello, earth to hottie," she laughs.

"Erm Gabe... My name's Gabe," I mumble, sounding like some pathetic love-sick fucking teenager.

Before she has a chance to reply, the same asshole she walked in with, is wrapping his arms around her.

"And I'm the boyfriend," he says, giving me a death stare. He might as well get his dick out and piss on her as it's clear to see he's trying to mark his territory.

"Justin," she grumbles, pushing out of his grip, "you weren't saying that five minutes ago when you told me to stop being so clingy, were you?" she snaps before storming back inside.

Thankfully, he follows straight behind her, otherwise, who knows what I would have done. Probably beat his ass just for being there and disturbing us.

Not wanting to see the two of them together, I hop the small gate and leave. Not even bothering to finish the drink waiting for me inside.

I'll pay my tab next time, Declan won't give a fuck.

STACEY

"Who the fuck was that?" Justin huffs.

"No one. I don't know him, he just offered me a cigarette, that's all." I lie. *Well I guess it's not really a lie, I don't know him and he certainly doesn't know me. Yet the connection I feel whenever I'm around him makes me think I do or that I want to at least.*

"Yeah well you're my woman, remember that." Justin snaps back.

"Maybe you should remember that too, next time you reject me in front of your friends." I snap back in return and make my way to the bathroom to get away.

I don't know what happened to us. We've been dating for over a year. The first six or so months were great. We'd laugh and hang around together at school, and despite the fact I was in the year below him, he didn't seem bothered by it. Yet since he went off to college that's all changed. He's become distant and stand-offish. Plus, he's become a real asshole. Suddenly he thinks he's too good for me and that having a girlfriend is some big chore.

I tried to kiss him earlier after he grabbed at my ass but he just pushed me away, yet again. That seems to be all he does lately. Push me away, almost in punishment, every time I say no to taking our relationship to that next step. I'm a virgin. I had planned on giving it up to him now that he is home but all he's done for the last few weeks is treat me like shit so he doesn't deserve it. So when I spotted Mr. Mysterious from the bar the other week, I couldn't resist the urge to see him again.

We spent most of the night getting drunk, even though I switched to plain soda hours ago. I've scanned the bar so many times but it's clear Gabe is no longer here.

The night ends and despite the fact I ask Justin to get the Uber to drop me back at home, he ignores my request and tells the driver we're both going to his place.

We stumble through the door and make our way upstairs. I turn to stay in the spare room as I have many times before when I've stayed with either Justin or Lexi, but he grabs my hand and leads me towards him.

"What are you doing?" I whisper.

"Come on baby, we're not little kids anymore."

"No! Your parents won't like it."

"Oh sorry, I forgot I was dating a baby who's scared of everything," Justin snaps.

"Fine, just to sleep then," I say, not wanting to get into a huge fight right now.

We make our way down to his room and I remove my jeans but leave the rest of my clothes on and slide under the cover.

Justin slides in beside me and almost instantly his hands find their way under my t-shirt.

"Babe, we can't do this here," I whisper, attempting to move his hands, but they don't budge.

"My parents are at some business party and Lexi is probably out with Brett."

"Come on baby, you're my girlfriend. I've missed you. I just wanna be close," he says seductively as he begins kissing my neck. *See here's the Justin I know and love*, I think to myself before rolling onto my back to let him kiss me.

We begin making out, allowing him to remove my top as he kisses and nibbles at my breasts. He then trails his fingers down my mid-section, heading towards forbidden territory. I feel my skin break out into goosebumps and my breath hitches as I feel his fingers slide inside me. I feel my eyes start to flutter close, but before I get the chance to fully lose myself in the moment, he stops. My eyes flicker open, "Justin . . ." *What the fuck is going on? Why did he stop? Did I do something wrong?*

"Put it in your mouth," he demands as he removes his boxers and shoves his dick into my face. *And who said romance was dead aye?*

I do as he says and open my mouth, before he takes it upon himself to essentially fuck my face. Now our sex life, if you can call it that, is never the most exciting, but usually, it's at least mutual. Yet it's clear this is far less about him wanting to be close with his girlfriend and far more about him just being horny. I hear a loud grunt before I feel the disgusting salty liquid invade my throat and he rolls off me. *Geeze, that was so rushed, I didn't even realize he was close.*

I roll over feeling a bit used, so I attempt to kiss him, if nothing else than to bring some intimacy back. But he pulls away. "Eww that's disgusting; I don't wanna taste that shit," he snaps, pushing me away and rolling on to his side. "Go clean yourself up!" he mutters with his back to me.

I lay beside him, as the tears roll down my cheeks. This is not the same Justin I used to know. This Justin is a selfish jerk.

I sneak to his bathroom, use the mouthwash to physically wash him away, and then make my way to the spare room, making sure to set my alarm early enough that I can leave and catch the bus before he wakes up in the morning.

Chapter Five

Stacey

The last few weeks have been a nightmare, Justin has gone from bad to worse, showering me with compliments one minute to ignoring me the next. I'm lying on the lounge chair enjoying the sunshine and reading my book when, out of nowhere, I feel a heavy weight sit on the end of my sun lounger. Looking around I expect to see Justin, but am pleasantly surprised to see it's Lexi holding two bottles of water.

"Hey Freckles, thought you might need a drink. I don't want you burning again and spending the rest of the day in a tomato bath," Lexi laughs. "Your hair was red for days," she teases.

"Yours has been red for years," I joke back.

"Erm, strawberry blonde, actually," Lexi says as she flips her long hair dramatically. "Mine looks great; yours didn't," she laughs.

"I was six," I fake sulk. "When are you going to let me live that down?"

"When the nightmares stop ... even to this day I can't look at a tin of tomatoes without having flashbacks," Lexi cringes and gasps dramatically.

"You're such a drama queen," I laugh.

"Yeah, but I'm still the best damn babysitter you and your sister ever had. Speaking of which, where is she?"

"She didn't want to come," I sigh sadly.

"How come? The two of you are normally thick as thieves?"

"Let's just say her and Justin aren't exactly best friends at the moment." I shrug

"What's my idiot of a brother done now?" Lexi asks, moving to sit on the chair beside me.

"Well..." I begin. "First of all he stood me up when he was supposed to come to family dinner, and you know what she's like. She'd gone all out baking cookies and cakes for us. Then, when he finally turned up the next day saying he'd been in bed with the flu. She gave him the benefit of the doubt until he let slip he was actually playing basketball with a few friends."

"So, that was strike two, as far as she was concerned I'm guessing," Lexi interrupts.

"Yup. And then to top it all off, do you remember my friend? The cheerleader?" I ask.

"Erm, I'm not sure, maybe?"

"Well, she's dating this totally hot jock. He's a great guy, super friendly, super goofy, but also super loyal. Justin saw us joking around outside school while we were waiting for her to get out of practice, and well, Justin got all jealous. Didn't even give either of us the chance to explain. Instead, he punched the boyfriend straight in the mouth. The two of them got into a fight and it took both me and his girlfriend to split them up. So now no one is really talking to me," I admit.

"Damn girl that does sound bad. I'm sure they'll forgive you soon though. It's not your fault my brother's turned into a raging douchebag this year."

"Glad I'm not the only one to notice," I say quietly.

"Believe me, we've all noticed." Lexi reasures, as she puts her arm around me. "And if he's gonna treat you like that you really do deserve better." A single tear runs down my cheek as I think about everything he's put me through these last few months. *Heck even while he was away it was pretty tough.*

"Don't cry, Freckles, You've always been too good for him anyway," Lexi reassures me as she pulls me into a hug. As soon as I feel the comfort of her arms, the floodgates open and I begin to sob. "He's just not the same Lex, I don't even recognize him anymore. He's not the same guy I grew up with." I sob. Lexi reaches out and uses the corner of the towel to wipe away my tears.

"No boy's worth your tears Freckles, especially not my brother. Go fix your makeup in my room, use whatever you need."

I make my way inside and up the stairs, as I do I hear muffled sounds coming from inside Justin's room. I push the door open, expecting to see him working out since that's where he said he was going earlier. But instead, I'm met with a sight that makes me wanna throw up.

Gabe

I do my best to stay away from the bar, but Stacey isn't far from my mind. I hooked up with a few girls trying to get that witchy girl off my mind. I don't know what spell she cast over me, but fuck me, I can't shake it. At best, the randoms keep me entertained for a few minutes. But before I can even tuck my dick away, she's right back there, center stage in my brain.

Monday morning rolls around and I'm at some fancy house working on an extension for some rich lawyer with a few of the guys. The whole time we are working we can hear laughing and squealing from the back garden where the guy's son seems to be having some sort of pool party.

"Rich pricks or what?" I scoff, rolling my eyes in frustration when a scream almost makes me drop my hammer.

"Right! Makes you sick doesn't it," Jack replies.

Next thing we know there's the sound of doors slamming and it becomes apparent that the scream wasn't a playful one.

There's a loud smash sound. One I would recognize even in my sleep. A sound I've heard so many times I could pinpoint its origin in a heartbeat. The sound of glass smashing against a wall.

"You're a fucking psycho, you know that?" a guy shouts as he storms out of the house and straight past us.

"And you're a lying, cheating, mother fucker," an angry female voice screams back from just a few feet behind him.

Jack and I both move, hoping to get a better seat to the shit storm happening just around the corner of the building.

"Wait, it's not what it seems," another voice, a much softer one says, as a girl storms out the door like a fucking hurricane of anger.

"I walked in on my boyfriend with his head between my best friend's fucking legs... pretty sure he wasn't looking for goddamn quarters, Jessica!" the first girl screams. It's then I see the girl's face and realize it's Stacey.

Almost at the same time that I see her, she sees me. She wastes no time marching over to me and kissing me. Just in time for her boyfriend, the same guy who'd virtually pissed on her to mark his claim just a few weeks ago, to walk in and see us.

Refusing to allow her to have all the power, yet again, I wrap my hands under her ass and lift her up into my arms. It's then I realize she's wearing nothing but a skimpy bikini with a thin shirt over it.

"Whore!" the ugly ginger boyfriend shouts before attempting to drag her out of my arms.

I place her down on the floor, step in front of her, and am ready to knock this asshole out. Before I get the chance, Stacey steps around me and swings her fist connecting straight with his nose. Blood starts gushing out everywhere. *Damn, this girl's got some serious fire.*

"Takes one to know one, Justin."

"We're leaving. Go get your shit." I snap, keeping my glare on this douchebag.

I walk her to the back yard and wait while she throws her stuff into her bag. Everyone else either glares in our direction or suddenly decides that the floor is the most interesting thing they've ever seen. So interesting in fact, they can't tear their eyes away from it.

Either way, I stand with arms folded, glaring and warning them with my eyes so they know that I am ready to throw fists at anyone who dares even breathe in our direction.

"Ready?" she asks as she slides her hand around me.

"Oh, and one more thing, Justin, you've got the tiniest dick I've ever seen, and I had to fake it every single time. Enjoy my sloppy seconds, Jess."

The gasps and strained chuckles are just barely heard over the sound of my heart beating a mile a minute in my chest. The anger washes through my veins. *How dare they?*

I turn briefly to look at Jack and a few of the other guys who also have a shit-eating grin on their faces. None of them question me leaving; they wouldn't dare.

Realizing she's walking too goddamn slow in those stupid plastic sandals, I throw her over my shoulder, smack her on her ass, walk us down the path and then plonk her onto the back of my bike.

I hand her my leather jacket since swimwear isn't exactly a great mix on a motorcycle and then climb in front of her.

"Hold on tight, and lean when I do," I say as I grab her hands and loop them around my waist.

I rev the engine and take off leaving the rest of the party in smoke.

"So, where shall I take you?" I shout so she can hear me. But I get no reply back.

"Where do you want to go?" I ask, giving her leg a little squeeze to get her attention. But instead of any words, all I hear is a loud sob.

Shit! Is she crying?

I drive her to the only place I can think of that's close by. A dirt road at the top of a tall hill. It's mostly used as a make out place because it has great views. But it's the only place that comes to my mind.

As soon as I stop the bike, I turn to look at her and it's clear she's been crying. A lot.

"Did I scare you? On the bike?" I ask in confusion as I climb off the bike.

"No, I really liked it, actually." she sniffles, climbing off herself.

"Did I hurt you? Was it too rough? Was the bike too hot on your bare legs?"

"No," she sniffles again, but this time there's a sad smile as well.

"Then why are you crying?"

"Well. I just walked in on my boyfriend with my best friend," she says, this time a loud but angry sob escapes her lips.

"Wait, you're crying because of HIM? The asshole who was screwing your friend?" *Surely not. That makes no sense.*

Why would a girl as smoking hot as her be crying over some pathetic pencil dick cheater? She walked in on him fucking her friend for god sake. So why would she be crying? Girls are weird.

"Well, yeah," she says this time, sounding a little unsure of herself and averting her eyes.

"Why? Does he give you mind blowing orgasms or something?"

"No, he's pretty shit and selfish in bed actually. I wasn't lying when I said I have to fake it," she laughs, wiping away her tears. "He's literally this big," she laughs harder using her fingers to describe what can't be more than about a few inches. "And well, his finger skills leave a lot to the imagination; he might as well be rooting for loose change."

"So why the fuck do you even care then?"

"I don't actually know," she laughs.

She reaches into her bag and pulls out a pair of those stretchy black tight pants, you know the ones that give girls the tight, perky, I've just come from the gym, ass.

Kicking off her shoes she shimmies her curves into them, which just accentuates them more somehow.

"Let's go for a walk," she suggests with her head down as she starts walking away from me.

She finds a big rock to sit on and motions for me to join her. I park my ass next to her and throw a joint in my mouth. Instead of waiting for her to ask for a drag, I grab hold of her cheeks causing her mouth to pop into a shocked O shape, put my mouth just centimeters from hers, and blow the smoke directly into her mouth.

"Next time you want to share my smoke, this is how you do it," I growl, before putting my lips on hers before she has time to blow the smoke back out. Naturally, she begins coughing and choking and pulls away.

"That's what you get for being such a brat," I tease.

"Dick," she coughs.

"What, right here? Whatever you want baby,"I joke, pretending to unzip my jeans.

Catching me by surprise, instead of backing away or becoming flustered she slaps me. Right in the balls. Not hard enough to hurt, but enough to show me who's in charge. If any other girl dared try that they'd be in serious shit. But with her, I kind of like it. I like the fact she's fiery and not in the least bit afraid of me; won't take shit from me. And doesn't cower to me. No, this bitch wants to challenge me.

"Be lucky I didn't mean it." she winks. *Fuck this girl is driving me crazy.*

The minutes turn into hours and before I know it, it is starting to get dark. Looking at my watch I realize it's almost 7p.m. We've been together almost five hours and somehow I'm not bored. Usually, just a few minutes of small talk outside the bedroom with girls is excruciating, yet here with Stacey, I feel at peace. My mind isn't racing, I'm not jonesing for my next drink and I am just... present. As much as I'd love nothing more than to strip her naked and fuck her senseless, that's actually not all I want to do. *Who would've thought this could happen to me. Am I catching feelings for this girl? No, I'm not capable. I just feel bad for her. Yep, that's it. I just feel sorry for Stacey, plus I figure she'll be a good lay.*

"I best get home. My sister will be wondering where I got to," Stacey says looking at her watch.

"Yeah, well I have to go anyway. I wasted my whole day here so I've got shit to catch up with." *Why the fuck did I say that? I'm such a dick. See? I can't do anything right. I always step in shit. Well, better she knows this now.*

I don't miss the hurt that flashes across her face. I look away so she can't see that she's affected me or that I care about the fact I clearly hurt her.

We walk silently to the bike and she doesn't even look at me as she climbs on. Barely holds me as we ride back into town. The whole ride back I'm arguing with my own mind. Part of me wants to pull up on the side of the road, throw myself to my knees and apologize but the other part of me is far too stubborn. Far too scared of being raw and opening myself up to pain. *No, this is the only way I survive. By refusing to allow anyone to see the real me.*

"Take the next left." Stacey finally breaks the silence by saying.

I do as I'm told and again we go back to silence. Every now and then she will shout a word, never a proper sentence, just a 'turn left', 'take the next right' kind of thing until finally "stop here." I pull up to a familiar-looking road and without a word she climbs off and walks into the house. Not looking back once. *Shit! I really screwed up this time.*

I wait a few minutes until I'm sure she's not gonna turn around and say goodbye. Then I drive away.

I'm driving when I feel the vibration of my phone on my thigh so I pull over and answer it. I look at my phone and it's not vibrating and there's no notifications of any missed calls or messages. Then I feel the sensation again and reach in my pocket and realize that it's not my phone vibrating.

three missed calls from Twinnie.

Shit! I didn't realize I had her phone. She must have left it in my jacket pocket.

Turning the bike around, I head back to give it to her. But first, I find an old receipt and write my number on it before placing it inside the phone case.

I pull up outside her house and walk down the driveway. As soon as I knock on the door I'm greeted by what sounds like a pack of vicious dogs.

Shit! I dump the phone on the doorstep and run away. Fast. I have never been a fan of dogs. Not since Dad used to force me to accompany him to those parties. Often I sat in the car with Carl and his two snarling dobermans while dad was inside fucking god knows who or selling god knows what illegal drug. Terrified to even breathe in case they decided to rip my fucking face off.

I arrive home and check my phone desperately praying Stacey has got her phone, and my number. To my shock when I take my phone out there's 1 message from an unknown number. I scramble to unlock my phone to read it. My excitement is short lived when all the message says is a simple thanks and a thumbs up.

STACEY

Rushing downstairs to our basement conversion bedroom, I throw myself onto my bed. Knowing I'm alone, I finally let the weight of today settle over me. As I do, my body begins to shake as the sobs come heavy and hard. I curl myself into a tight ball as I sob and sob. I sob for the boy who broke my heart. Sob for the friend who betrayed me. Sob for the boy I spent the day with, who also rejected me. And sob for the future I had in my mind that's vanishing before my very eyes. My dog jumps on the bed, licking my face. "Honey," I whine as I gently push her away. She curls up beside me and lets me snuggle into her for support. That is until she hears a noise upstairs and runs off to investigate. I don't even have the energy to move, it's probably just an Amazon driver or car passing by anyway. Instead, I stay where I am until I am so dehydrated my body can't even make more tears. Physically holding myself together, but the next thing I know I feel someone crawl in beside me silently. I don't even need to look to know it's my sister, my twin flame beside me. Even before we were born she's always been the other half of me.

"What happened?" she whispers beside my ear as she continues to hold me.

"Justin is fucking Jessica. I walked in on them at it." I sob. *Maybe I wasn't as dehydrated as I thought?*

"That spineless, good for nothing asshole!" she growls. "Just you wait till I get my hands on him."

"He's not worth it." I say, grabbing her before she moves to leave.

"He doesn't get to treat my sister like this and get away with it," she huffs, sounding furious.

"Maybe he did me a favor," I admit as I wipe away the tears.

"You'll find someone better, your prince charming will be around somewhere. You might just have to kiss a few frogs along the way."

"Well, I may have already kissed one frog," I giggle.

"What? When? Who?"

Now that I'm sure it's over between me and Justin and I no longer have to hide the truth from her, I tell my sister all about the night I went out with Lexi. About the handsome stranger I met in the bar. About the exciting day we spent together today and then finally how quickly he'd brushed me off at the end of it.

"Well, he might not be Mr. Right, but he'll definitely do for Mr. Right Now," I laugh.

"Tell me what he looks like," she says with a giggle while poking me in the side.

I squirm away from the offending digit. "He's dreamy," I coo, picturing him today and wishing I knew what he looked like without a shirt on. *I bet he's ripped with hard abs and a six pack. Damn, I bet he's even got those sexy little V dips.*

"That doesn't tell me anything!" she pouts.

"A girl has to have some secrets," I tease back and laugh at her attempt to give me the stink eye.

"There's keeping secrets, then there's joining the next level, CIA secret keeping. You gotta give me something to work with; hair color, eye color, name, age, something at least." I can't help but giggle at the frustration on my sister's face. Ever since we were kids she's always hated feeling like she's missing out on something.

"You're not giving up are you?" I sigh as I reach for a cushion to prop myself up.

"Nope," she replies with an accomplished grin as she flops onto her tummy and places her hands under her chin, preparing to hear the 'latest gossip'.

"Fine, so he's tall, not basketball player tall, but tall enough I have to lift my chin to look at him. His eyes are green, but not like a pale green. More like a bright green that stares into your soul." *I wish I was with him right now staring into those eyes.*

"Damn you've always been a sucker for nice eyes," she coos as she wiggles her feet back and forth in the air excitedly.

"Guilty." I smirk.

"So what else? Where did you meet him? When can I meet him? Does he go to our school?" *Fucking hell I love my sister, but this is starting to feel like a bloody inquisition.*

"That's all you're getting for now," I laugh, "you'll know more when I know more"

"So, you really aren't going to give me anything else?" she huffs before she finally relents and gets up.

"I told ya, a girl has got to have some secrets!" I look her straight in her eye and wink, letting her know I'm done.

"Whatever," she snarks, "I'm going upstairs to study. Oh and I found this on the doorstep," she says, pulling my phone out of her pocket. It must have fallen out of your bag when you were looking for your keys."

I didn't have a bag, last time I saw my phone it was... in Gabe's jacket. Did he bring it back for me? He must have. But why not ring the bell then? Why leave it on the doorstep? All my unanswered questions race through my mind.

I reach out and take the phone from her, desperately wishing I'd been clever enough to have gotten Gabe's number. Even if it was just to say thanks for returning the phone to me.

I open the cover of my phone ready to pass the time with some endless scrolling; if nothing else, it will pull me out of my funk. Videos of random dogs doing silly things might just help. Then I notice a small piece of paper poking out the side of my case. *How did that get there?*

I gently remove the paper and unfold it. *Hmm, it's just a receipt for beer and snacks at a gas station. That's odd.*

I almost crumple it up, thinking it's worthless trash, until I spot Gabe's name and number at the bottom and my heart skips a beat as a flurry of butterflies fly around in my tummy.

Eeeekkkk he left his number!!!

"Twinnie?" I call out as I watch her grab her backpack and head out the door. "I love you, and I promise you I will tell you all the deets when there is actually something to tell. I just don't want to say too much yet because I don't want to jinx it."

She turns and I can see her frustration leave her face and it is replaced with warmth and love. "I love you too, Twinnie. I just want the best for you. You deserve it, especially after all that crap with Justin."

When I know she is gone, I pull out my cell phone and save Gabe's contact.

'Thanks for returning my phone; maybe we could meet again some time.' I type before I delete it, realizing it sounds too desperate.

'I got my phone back, thanks for returning it. It was really nice of you.' *Nah, that's not right either.*

He left it on the doorstep rather than giving it back to me in person. Maybe that was his way of telling me he doesn't want to speak to me anymore. *But if that was the case, why give me his number at all?*

Maybe he just thinks I'm some pathetic girl, desperate for attention. *After all the few times we've seen each other, I've basically thrown myself at him.*

Whatever it is, I refuse to beg for any man's attention or give any man that power over me again, so instead I simply type 'thanks' followed by a thumbs up.

My finger hovers over the button. I think back to today. *He was sweet. And nice. Well, until he wasn't.* I keep replaying the events of the day in my head. *Could he like me? Could I like him? What made me trust him today? Is he just a rebound? Do I want a rebound? Maybe this could be fun! Maybe I'll finally find a man who knows what they're doing in the bedroom.*

I shake my head to clear out the mental spiral and I realize my hand has slipped into my panties. My mind plays out different scenarios: I imagine removing his shirt and kissing all down his toned body. My hand slides further into my panties as my fingers feel my wetness and glide inside my sacred place.

I think about him removing my thin beach dress. The feel of his strong calloused fingers grazing my skin the way they had when he gave me his jacket earlier. My fingers find a steady rhythm and I let out a small moan. Thankfully I can hear the slight sound of soft music playing upstairs letting me know I'm not going to be disturbed.

I imagine him tugging on the straps of my bikini top and releasing my breasts, which he quickly takes into his perfectly dirty mouth. Instantly my other hand begins playing with my nipple, my hips buck up as I begin to chase my release.

I can almost feel that it's his fingers bringing me to orgasm rather than my own, as I see the image of his cocky, bad boy grin appearing on his face. A face, that in this moment, I wish was beside me so that I could turn my fantasy into reality.

My legs start to shake as my orgasm washes over me.

Chapter Six

Gabe

Saturday morning rolls around. I've been waiting for Saturday since me and Nate made our plans back in January. Today Nate is flying into Washington, ready to move back home.

Heck, I've even hired two maids... topless ones, of course, to come and clean the place so it's ready for him when he arrives later today. I get dressed, head to Walmart to stock the fridge, and cupboards full of food and am just finishing a well-deserved beer when my phone pings.

Nate

> Just boarding the plane now. See you in a few hours.

Smiling and resisting the urge to get in my car now and drive to wait at the airport, I head to the kitchen to make myself a sandwich.

I try to stay home and distract myself with TV but the excitement is too much, so after just an hour I jump in the truck John lent me to pick Nate up from the airport. I throw on the stereo, open the windows, and drive.

I have the music blaring and I'm singing along with the tunes. It's not exactly the same as riding my bike, feeling the wind whipping all around me, but it's okay. It's nice to be able to sing along to the radio without getting bugs in my mouth, I guess.

I arrived at the airport shortly before 6 a.m. I check the app on my phone, the one I use to track Nate's flight hoping it's going to be early, but nope, I still have an hour and fifteen minutes until he's due to land.

Finding a cafe nearby, I order myself a coffee. I'd rather have a beer but this is the first time I've seen Nate in almost three years so I want to be at my best.

One coffee turns into two, then three, then four. After drinking all those coffees, I'm virtually bouncing off the walls. Finally though, I receive a "just waiting for my bags" message. So I grab the makeshift sign I made from the chair beside me and head to the gate.

I see dozens of people come out of those gates, most of whom have to take a double look at my well thought out sign. Then, finally, I see him. *At least I think it's him. Although he looks nothing like I remember. . He still has the same dark hair, but it no longer looks dirty and disheveled.*

The last time I saw him he still looked like an awkward teenager, far too skinny and weak for his own good, yet now he's filled out. *He's obviously been hitting the gym.* I watch him scan the room, until his bright blue eyes lock with mine. Yup, it's definitely Nate; I'd recognize his face anywhere.

"Gaaaabbbe!!" Nate shouts before abandoning his bags in the middle of the walkway and running full speed into me. It takes all my strength to stop myself from falling over.

"I've missed you sooo much bro," Nate squeals. That's right, the motherfucker squeals like a ten year old girl.

"I've missed you too," I say, pushing him off of me.

"Shit my bags!" he laughs before running back to the cart.

I can't help but shake my head in shock and disbelief. *I can't believe that Nate is finally home. I better not fuck this up too.*

I can't help but let out a little smile as I see him strutting over with not one but two large suitcases and a duffle bag slung over his shoulder. He's finally here ready to live with me. It makes me happy to know that he's obviously had a good life and has been treated well, hence why he has so many belongings to bring. *The last time I saw him was just a few years ago and we managed to fit all our worldly positions in a single black garbage bag. That garbage bag somehow held over thirteen years worth of memories for us both. Yet, now he looks like a kid who's never wanted for anything.*

I refuse to allow my mind to relive that moment. The moment we were ripped away from the only family we had ever known and were thrown into foster care. I just put on my protective armor, push any feelings I have deep, deep down and lift my sign higher.

As he walks back over I see the recollection on his face. He snatches the sign out of my hands and whacks me over the head with it.

"Really, Gabe? Fucking really?" Nate huffs, as his cheeks turn as red as a tomato.

"It's okay, Nate. I love and support you anyway," I say loud enough to draw even more attention to me and my sign.

"Welcome home from the World's Tiniest Dick Convention - Give a girl your inch, they'll run a mile."

Complete with little squishy dicks stuck on for effect.

I can't help but belly laugh at my own joke, even more so when Nate attempts to storm off while still pushing the cart with the bum wheel through the airport.

Running to catch up, I throw my arm around him. "What's up, Nathaniel? Don't want everyone to know you've got a micropenis?" I laugh again. More so when I see a cute looking girl almost choke on her drink as we walk past.

"You're such a fucking asshole, Gabe," Nate whisper shouts through gritted teeth as he continues trying to storm through the airport.

We finally make it outside and I lead the way to the truck. Popping open the back, I help Nate throw the cases in. Just as I turn to walk to the driver's seat, Nate throws his arms around me and pulls me into a tight hug. "You're a dick, but I've missed you so much, Bro," Nate says. I try to push him away, but he grips tighter. "Enough now. I've missed you too, but get off," I grumble. Still he doesn't release me. "Seriously, get the fuck off me," I groan, trying again to push him off. "Seriously Nate this is your last fucking warning, get the fuck off me!" I push him much harder this time, hard enough that his back crashes against the back of the truck.

"Woah, Gabe, what's your fucking problem? Can't I hug my own brother? The brother I've not seen in years!" Nate snaps, sounding a mixture of hurt, confused and pissed off.

"Not when that bothers me, you can't," I snap, turning round and slamming the driver's side door as I get in.

A few minutes later Nate finally joins me. "Seriously, Gabe, what the fuck's your problem? I gave you a bear hug, and you're acting like I fucking attacked you or something."

"Same thing," I snap. "I don't like being touched."

I see the way he subconsciously rolls his eyes. He may know I don't like being touched, but sometimes I wonder if he understands that it runs so much deeper than not being a touchy feely person like him.

"I know Gabe, but it was a fucking hug. One hug isn't gonna kill you. Is it?" Nate says as he looks out the window.

"I just don't like people randomly touching me, that's all. No big deal."

"No big deal? I'm not some random stranger in the street, Gabe. I'm your goddamn brother," Nate snaps. This time it's clear to see he's hurt by something I said.

"You know the shit we went through; it makes me wary of anyone touching me," I admit.

"Know it? I lived through it, too. Or did you forget that? In case you don't remember, I was usually the one bleeding on the floor."

"Yeah, and I was the one constantly saving your ass. You have no fucking idea what I went through to try and keep you safe, Nate. No fucking idea!" I all but scream back at him. I take a deep breath in, hold it for five seconds and release it, all in an attempt to calm down. *This is so not going the way I thought our reunion would go.*

The next hour of our drive is in pure silence, not even decent music to break up the awkwardness since this piece of shit truck doesn't have a place to plug in my phone to drown out the silence. Instead I'm forced to listen to the shitty ass radio as we drive back to Washington.

My phone beeps in my pocket, so I slide it out. Assuming it will be another job from John. But to my surprise it's not.

> **Unknown number**
> Hey sexy, wanna meet up later? Was thinking you could take me for another ride. *wink emoji*

> **Me**
> Who is this? Stacey?

> **Unknown number**
> Wow! You have so many girls that you can't even remember me? Now there was me thinking saving me from my asshole of an ex and spending the whole day together might have been at least slightly memorable.

> **Me**
> Oh, believe me it was definitely memorable. Maybe next time I'll let you ride more than just my bike. *Devil emoji*

> **Unknown number**
> Who knows, maybe I will.

"Who are you smiling at? Does Gabey have a girlfriend?" Nate teases as he reaches out and snatches the phone from my hand.

"Hmm, Gabe has a naughty girlfriend," he laughs as he reads the last message.

"Fuck you! She's not my girlfriend. She's just some girl I wanna fuck." Even as the words leave my mouth, they leave an uneasy feeling in my stomach.

"Sure sure, I believe you. Many wouldn't, but I do," Nate laughs, handing me back my phone. I tuck it back into my pocket and continue driving.

We make it back to the house and as soon as we pull up I see that uneasy look on Nate's face, the one I had pretty much every day for the first year I lived here alone. That face that lets me know he's got a million memories, none of them good, flying through his mind.

"He's gone, Nate. Gone and never coming back. We're safe," I whisper as I reach out and squeeze his shoulder reassuringly.

"He might be gone, but his memories and the fear live on," Nate replies, more so to himself than me.

Stepping out to give him a moment alone to compose his thoughts, I head out, get the bags and take them inside. Nate follows behind a few minutes later.

"It's so much smaller than I remember," he says as he looks around.

"Wow, this is new," he says pointing to the brand new doors separating the kitchen from the living room.

I don't mention that the reason I swapped it out was because it still had the holes from the times Dad hit or kicked it in a drunken rage.

"And this wasn't this color before... was it?" he asks, pointing to the now gray walls.

"Yeah, thought they could do with some color," I lie. Not revealing the real reason I painted them such a dark color was to hide the many blood stains that were ingrained in the once white walls.

"Where shall I put my stuff?" he finally asks.

"Erm, in there, in your old room. I've bought a new bed for you and new carpet as well."

"Oh? Where do you sleep then?" he asks looking genuinely confused.

"In the other bedroom." I see his eyes widen in surprise, knowing that the only other bedroom in this place used to belong to our father.

"Yeah, it's bigger," I lie again. Refusing to admit the real reason I sleep there is to remind myself he's never coming back. That I'm the man of the house now. I tried sleeping in our old room when I first moved back, but I couldn't stand lying in our old room, falling asleep staring at the same crack in the ceiling I used to when we were kids. Putting my clothes away in the same wardrobe I used to hide in as a child. Or listening to the same creak in the door I used to listen out for as a child knowing it meant danger was on the horizon.

"Oh, okay. That makes sense, I guess." Nate replies with a shrug.

I leave him alone to unpack his things, grab a beer and head outside. Sitting down on one of the old deck chairs, I pull out my phone and find more messages from Stacey. I save her number then begin scrolling through.

> **Cock Tease**
> So is that an invite?
>
> Or perhaps a promise?

I can't help but smirk at her playfulness and confidence. *This girl is hot as fuck.*

That is until I read the next message and almost throw my phone in anger.

> **Cock Tease**
> Or maybe it's neither, maybe I need to find someone with a bigger engine to ride?

Bigger engine? Maybe I should march over there right now and show her exactly how big my engine is!

> **Me**
> Don't you fucking dare!

Immediately another message pings through.

> **Cock Tease**
> Sorry the user you're trying to contact is busy having the ride of her life right now, please try again later.

I hit the call button before I even have time to think about what I'm doing. She answers straight away.

"Who is he?" I snap. *Whoever he is, he's about to become familiar with my fist.*

"Who is who?" she asks, feigning innocence.

"Who are you with?" I snap back feeling frustrated. My heartbeat pounding in my chest, my breathing coming out in short bursts.

"Well, if you were here you'd know the answer now, wouldn't you?" she pokes and I can hear a hint of laughter in her voice.

"You're alone aren't you?" I ask, finally feeling my pulse slowing and my breathing evening out.

"Yep," she replies, popping her lips on the P sound before laughing. "But nice to know you care so much." She replies with sass.

"I don't care," I snap feeling flustered. *Wait, do I care? Why do I care? I don't care about people, especially random girls.*

"Oh? So you wouldn't care if I told you I was here right now with two gorgeous guys who are about to take turns fucking me senseless?" she asks in that annoyingly sexy yet innocent voice.

I can't even speak; instead, I simply let out an agitated growl.

"That's what I thought," she laughs before hanging up.

I pick up my half empty beer bottle and throw it against a tree in frustration. *Who the fuck does she think she is trying to annoy me? And more to the point, why do I care?* Why does the thought of her with another guy fill me with so much rage? I want to charge over there and rearrange this fictional guy's face.

Just at that moment I receive a text from Kelly. I almost ignore it, the same as I do almost every time she messages. After all, she only has one or two uses, and both of them involve some part of my body entering a hole in hers, neither of which I have any interest in right now. But desperate to take my mind off of Stacey and whatever the fuck that girl is doing to me, I open it.

"Hey sexy, my friend is down from New York for the weekend. Wanna meet up for a little fun tomorrow?"

Spending the night with her is the last thing I want to be doing since she bores the fuck out of me, but I need to take my mind off Stacey so I agree.

"Sure, my little brother just got back so I'll bring him along to keep her company."

Chapter Seven

Nate

Walking into the room I can't help but feel a shudder run down my spine. Sure the room looks different from what I remember. The two small beds have been replaced by a double bed in the corner of the room and there's now a small bedside table and lamp. But it's still like walking into a nightmare. One that I know I can't wake up from. I throw open the built-in wardrobe and carefully begin unpacking my bags. As I do, I notice the chipped wood on the inside of the door and the tiny nail marks from the time Dad caught me hiding in there, hoping to escape his drunken wrath. He grabbed me by the feet and dragged me out. I grabbed onto the wood for dear life, but my little child's grip was nothing compared to his drunken, angry strength. Slamming the door and deciding that's quite enough of a journey down memory lane, I head back and start unpacking things somewhere else. I head into the bathroom, take out my toiletries, and begin placing aftershave, hair gel, and other essentials under the sink. Then an idea hits me.

"I'll be back in a bit," I shout as I head out the door. But I see Gabe sitting outside in the backyard. "Oh, you're out here. I assumed you were watching TV or something," I say.

"Nah, there's fuck all on. What's up?" Gabe asks as he offers me a beer from the cooler beside him.

"No, thanks, I don't drink," I reply, the way I have so many times before. But rather than the approving nod or 'if you say so' shrug I usually get, I'm met with what seems like anger. *What the fuck is this about? Is he really angry that I don't want a beer?*

"What do you mean you don't fucking drink? Like legally or at all? Because it makes no difference to me that you're only eighteen, I'm not trying to bust your ass over a number." Gabe laughs.

"No Gabe, it's got nothing to do with my age, I just choose not to drink."

"What? Never or just before noon?" he quizzes

"Ever, like I don't drink at all." I clarify, crossing my arms. *What the fuck is his problem? Why is he so mad?*

"Is something the matter? Are you like dying or on medication or something?" Gabe asks, sounding genuinely horrified.

"No," I laugh. " I just don't drink. I choose not to."

"Why?" he gasps as though I just told him something that is utterly horrifying to him.

"Take a look around Gabe. Ring any bells?" I ask, waving my arms. He looks around but still doesn't seem to be getting it. "Our father was an alcoholic, Gabe. He had problems his whole life with the shit and from what he told us about his father, he probably had problems with alcohol, too. It's not worth the risk." Gabe flinches like I physically punched him.

"Well I drink, all the time, in fact. Doesn't mean I'm an alcoholic," Gabe tries to argue, sounding very defensive. I look past him and into the cooler. I notice at least four if not five of the beers are missing.

"Gabe it's..." I say looking at my watch, "quarter past eleven in the morning, we didn't get back from the airport until just past eight, and it looks like you're already on your fourth beer."

"Who the fuck are you to judge? A man's allowed a beer in his own backyard to unwind, you know." he snaps back defensively. I could feel his anger and something else, perhaps shame, radiating off of Gabe.

"Anyway, I'm going out, I feel like I need a walk to clear my mind. I'll be back later." I say.

"Wait, I've made plans for us. We're meeting some girls at six." Gabe says, looking towards me.

"Gabe, I'm not interested in girls." Gabe looks at me with confusion written across his face.

"Not like that, I am interested in girls. I just meant I'm not interested in meeting random girls."

"Oh good... not that I wouldn't still love ya if you were interested in dudes. Like, it would be weird as fuck, but I'd still love ya," he stutters, a flush creeping up his neck.

"Good to know I guess" I laugh back, enjoying seeing my usually cocky brother, flustered.

"Anyways, as I said, I'm heading out."

"Come on, I already told them we'd meet them," Gabe begs.

"Fine, I'll be back before six then. Friends only, though," I say, giving him my best 'I mean it' face.

"Deal," he agrees, nodding his head.

I leave our yard and make my way towards the woods. It all seems so different, yet oddly familiar. I head through the woods, past the tall trees with a very clear destination in mind. I continue walking until I see it. The cabin. My real home away from hell growing up. My legs begin running like they've got a mind of their own till I reach the wraparound porch. Running up to the door I knock as hard as I can, begging and praying that by some miracle, since it's summer break, she'll be there. Disappointment fills me but not surprisingly, there's no answer. I make my way around, peering in the window. Looking for some sign of life inside. But I see nothing to indicate anyone is even staying there.

I slump down onto the decking and sit, reminiscing about all the other times I was here. I envision me and Bella playing hide and seek around the trees just in front of me. Then I remember how we used to play games and draw right here on the deck. *I wonder...* I crawl around the decking looking, until I spot it. Our handprint. I chuckle to myself remembering the time her pops was varnishing the wood and Bella accidentally put her hand in it. She was so worried they would get mad that I decided to put my hand in it too, so that if they found it they'd realize the mark belonged to me instead of her. But of course, I did it wrong. Instead, we ended up with some strange seven fingered hand print. *I can't believe after all these years it's still here.*

I can't believe her pops never painted over it. Her pops. I suddenly remembered. He worked at the Ranger's station, *I wonder if he's still there.*

I make my way there, knock on the door and am greeted by a guy who looks barely in his thirties. "Hey, I'm looking for Mr. Williams, erm George, I think. . ." I say desperately hoping I got the name right.

"Sorry kid, I don't know him," the guy answers.

"Ignore the newbie, he's barely out of diapers," a voice from inside calls.

"What do you want with George?" the older man asks.

"Hi sir, so my name is Nate. I used to know him and his granddaughter years ago. I've been to the cabin, but they're not there," I say, a little too quickly.

"Yeah, that old cabin hasn't been used in years. Not since the rugrats grew up and moved away."

"Do you have any idea when he'll be here next?" I ask.

"He's gone kiddo, retired a while ago. Had a heart attack you know, or was it a stroke?" He ponders and scratches the top of his head. "You know this old mind ain't what it used to be. I'm only here to make sure Diapers here, doesn't screw up.

"Gramps, I'm almost thirty five," the kid says as he rolls his eyes.

"Do they still live in the same house?" I ask. realizing I must sound like a stalker.

"Who knows kiddo, who knows. I barely remember where I live some days," he laughs.

"Well, thanks for your time anyways, sir," I say as I wave before turning and walking away.

I make my way back to the cabin and lay down on the porch, letting the sun rays hit my face as I take in the peace and quiet, remembering all the happy memories I had growing up here.

Gabe

I'm getting out of the shower when my phone rings.

"Hey handsome. What are you up to tonight? Wanna meet up?"

"I can't tonight, I've got plans with my brother," I say even though I'm now kicking myself, wishing I didn't. *I'd much rather be spending it balls deep in Stacey instead.*

"Oh wow, you've got a brother, how old? Older or younger…"

For almost forty-five minutes our conversation flows easily back and forth.

"Anyway, I've got to go, think about what I said. I've got an extra ticket to the concert tonight. Bring your brother if you want. I'm sure it will be easy enough to get tickets at the door."

"It's not really my thing."

I get off the phone feeling odd. I never talk to girls like that on the phone. Usually, they are lucky to get five minutes, let alone forty five.

I head to the kitchen to make myself a snack when another message buzzes through.

Cock Tease
> Loved chatting with you, miss you already.

Miss me already? How the fuck can she miss me already. We've only just finished talking.

I decide to ignore her message and continue making myself a grilled cheese.

Cock Tease
> You'll never believe it, Justin is still coming. He doesn't even like the band. I had to beg him to come. Yet now when I don't want him there he says he's still coming fml.

Me
> fml?

Cock Tease
> it means fuck my life, grandad. *wink emoji*

> I'd rather fuck something else instead.

> Oh yeah? Like what?

> Well, you for a start.

> So what would you do?

And there goes the next hour, back and forth flirty texting each other driving each other wild.

Cock Tease

> Seriously, I've gotta get ready, before I'm too hot and horny to make it to the concert. Talk soon. I leave at seven and it'll take me three hours to get ready at least.

Three hours! Fuck, girls are hard work. I look at my watch and realize it's already four o'clock. *Where the heck is Nate?* He's been gone all day.

For fuck's sake! Grabbing my shoes I head out to look for him.

NATE

I must have drifted off to sleep as the next thing I know I'm waking to the sound of Gabe bellowing my name.

"There you are," he finally says as I stand up and make my way down the steps. "I've been looking for you everywhere. I thought you'd gotten lost or something. I should have guessed I'd find you here," he says, a little colder than necessary.

"Sorry, I must have fallen asleep, what time is it?"

"It's almost five, we're going to be late," he says. Although it's clear from his voice he's not even remotely bothered about being late.

I head back to the house, quickly take a shower, and change my clothes and I'm ready just thirty minutes later.

"Come on then, Gabe, it's 5:45. Are you ready to go?" I ask, but I notice that the cooler is now empty.

"Give me the keys," I demand.

"Why?"

"Because you've been drinking and I haven't. Now give me the keys," I demand, more forcefully this time.

"I've always been drinking, it's fine," Gabe laughs. *What the fuck? This is no laughing matter.*

"Put it this way, either I drive or I don't come," I snap.

"Fine, you big baby, here," Gabe laughs, taking the keys and throwing them to me.

We get in the car and Gabe directs me all the way until we reach a pub called Saints. "Is this it?" I ask as I park.

"Yeah, they'll be waiting for us at the back." Gabe makes his way to the door.

As he was saying that, some woman waves at us from one of the booths at the back.

"Hi! I'm Kelly," the blonder of the two girls says, leaning over and giving me an awkward hug. "And this is my friend Amy. She's visiting from New York for the week." Amy attempts to lean forward, presumably to greet Gabe, but Kelly puts her arm on her shoulder and pulls her back. "I wouldn't," she whispers.

We spend the next thirty minutes chatting, well, I say we, but it's mostly me and the girls. Gabe adds very little to the conversation. He spends most of his time looking down at his phone. After a while, he gets up and heads outside, not even having the decency to excuse himself.

"I'm so sorry ladies, I'll be right back. I've just got to head to the bathroom."

I'm just washing my hands when Kelly appears near the bathroom door. I quickly glance around praying I've not walked into the wrong one, but the urinals soon confirm I'm in the right room.

"Oh, the ladies is next door, I think" I say as I attempt to walk past her.

"Oh, okay," she says, taking a step back. *Poor girl must be so embarrassed.*

I glance over at the booth and notice Gabe is still nowhere to be seen so I make my way outside. I find him sitting on a wall smoking and looking amused. I walk up behind him and can't help but notice what is clearly sexting judging by the amount of eggplant and fire emojis I see.

"Really, Gabe? You're on a date and you're sexting another girl?" I ask, sitting down beside him, but far enough away that I can't see his phone anymore.

"Nah, it's not like that. She's no one, and Kelly wouldn't give a fuck even if she was," he laughs.

"Well, she's inside alone, maybe we should go back inside, at least pretend you have some manners." I say, standing and reaching out a hand to help him up, which he pushes away.

"Okay. Whatever."

Chapter Eight

Gabe

I head back inside and listen to Kelly's stupid fucking voice drone on about something she and her friend, *I don't even remember her name,* did the last time they met up.

My phone buzzes in my pocket. And I don't even need to look who it is as I know it's going to be Stacey; we've been texting on and off all night.

She's trying to persuade me to join her at some shitty concert later tonight but I'm not interested.

> Cock Tease
> Come on, I'll make it worth your while.

> Me
> I've told you, shitty music is just not my thing.

Nate elbows me in the ribs, clearly trying to get my attention. He nods his chin towards Kelly's friend, umm, Amanda, maybe? No, Anita, I think is her name, nope that's wrong too..

"What?" I bite out.

"Oh, I was just asking if you wanted to meet tomorrow. I was hoping to see some of the highlights from the area, I could do it with some handsome tour guides." Anisha? says. *Seriously, what the fuck is her name?*

"No!" I snap back, having absolutely no interest in playing tour guide to some out of town whore.

"Oh, okay," the friend gasps, clearly surprised by my answer.

"What he means is we're both really busy tomorrow, so can't. Sorry."

Nate rushes out looking slightly embarrassed. *What the fuck does he have to be embarrassed about. I don't give a shit about what these bitches think of me; why should he be concerned about it?*

"Maybe you two would like to take the party back to ours since it's getting late?" Kelly adds in that sickly sweet voice of hers. I cringe, not the least bit interested.

"It's fucking 8:00 p.m." I snap back. "We are off anyway, come on Nate."

"I'm so sorry, I don't know what's gotten into him," I hear Nate saying as I'm walking away. "It's fine sugar, I'm used to him," Kelly replies.

"Nate, hurry up or I'm leaving without you," I shout back. I make my way to the truck and that's when I remember he has the key. *Fuck!*

I have no choice but to wait.

> Cock Tease
> Last chance sexy, we're leaving in ten minutes and I look like fire.

I smirk again when I see the three fire emojis she's used. I've never been a fan of emojis. I kind of think it makes you seem like an idiot using pictures instead of words, but I gotta admit. It does work.

"There you are," Nate snaps as he reaches the truck. I tuck my phone back into my pocket and climb inside.

The whole drive back, all Nate does is complain and bitch about the fact I was rude and disrespectful to the girls. *Does he not realize Kelly and her friend are two cheap, worthless whores?* The only reason they came tonight was because they wanted to get laid.

"I just don't get you," Nate snaps. We pull up at home, he quickly jumps out and slams the truck door behind him.

I walk in, grab a beer and pull out my phone.

> Smoking Little Cock Tease
> Seriously you're gonna make me go alone?

> Well, we're leaving, I can't believe you're making me go with Justin and his friends. Do you have any idea how awkward this is going to be?

> Fuck sake! Jessica is here-the girl he fucking cheated on me with. I need you!

> Please Gabe, I need you here! The address is 57 Hampton Crescent.

> Me
> I'm in bed, I'm not going. Figure it out yourself.

> Fine! I'll just get back with Justin instead. At least he's not ashamed to be seen with me!

I throw my phone onto the bed in frustration. *Who the fuck does she think she is?* She may be hot as fuck, a total firecracker, but she's not my goddamn girlfriend; I've made that clear to her from the start.

I pour myself a glass of Hennessy, followed by another to try and calm my frustration.

Seriously, what's wrong with this bitch? Does she actually think I'm gonna drop everything to go to some shitty ass concert with her and her ex boyfriend? For what? To make him jealous? To prove she's over him? Screw her. I'm fine here.

I switch on the TV and try and distract myself with my favorite show, since Nate's fucked off and left me. I'm just forgetting about her as the second episode starts, that is until I receive another message.

This time it's a picture of her taken in the bathroom mirror, dressed in a short black skirt, fishnet stockings and boots. *Fuck she looks hot. I wanna tear my eyes away but I can't.* Without thinking my hand dips inside my gym shorts and grips my cock, I begin stroking it as I stare at my phone. My hand takes on a life of its own as my mind begins fantasizing about what I'd do to her if I was there right now. I imagine bending her over and ripping a hole in those fishnets so I can fuck her from behind. I imagine what her hair will feel like wrapped around my fist as I thrust into her harder and harder.

I feel the unmissable twitching beneath my hands and the tingle at the bottom of my spine just as the cum shoots out, soaking my shirt. *What the fuck is this girl doing to me?*

I remove my t-shirt and head towards the shower. Once out and dressed in some new jeans, I make my way to the kitchen. I grab the bottle of Hennessy and chug it directly from the bottle, feeling the slight burn as the liquid runs down my throat.

I try to go back to my show, telling myself she can do what she wants. She's single after all. We're not dating. *Hell, I've been balls deep in not one but two different girls this weekend.*

My phone dings again. This time it's a video of Stacey, Justin, and another asshole I don't recognize. Stacey and the guy are singing along to the music while Justin looks furious in the background. *That's not a look I like.* Throwing on a clean shirt and grabbing the keys to my bike, I decide to make my way over.

I arrive less than twenty minutes later, and after paying some punk $20 to look the other way I head inside. I search the dimly lit bar until I spot her a few rows ahead, she's now sitting on the shoulders of who I can only assume is the guy from the video. Swaying along to the music. I grab a beer and watch. Feeling irrationally angry to see her with him.

That is until irrational anger turns into full on fury when I watch Justin grab her by the hips and drag her off the other guy's shoulders. I see Stacey kick and shout as he forces her to her feet on the ground. I can't hear what she says but it's clear from her body language that she's pissed off. Part of me is strangely proud of the way she's holding her own against a guy easily twice her weight. *She's such a little spitfire.*

That is until I see his hand move up and slap her straight across the face, knocking her clean off her feet. I don't even have time to think before I'm there and my fist is connecting with his nose, spraying blood everywhere. I turn around and Stacey is still sitting, dumbfounded on the floor. The asshole she was with is looking at me in shock, so much shock he's not even attempted to help her up. Bending down, I scoop her into my arms, and throw her over my shoulder and carry her straight out. No one, not even her, makes any attempt to stop me.

It's only when we get outside and the cold air hits that she seems to register what's happening.

"Where are we going?" she says in such a soft, almost childlike whisper that all I want to do is protect her. I was never big enough to protect my mother, all those times I watched my father knock her to the floor. But I'll be fucked if I'm not big enough now.

"I'm taking you somewhere safe," I reply back, placing her softly onto my bike. I reach for the helmet but as I go to place it onto her head she cowers away in fear. "I'm not going to hurt you," I say fiercely enough to ensure she hears me, but not enough to scare her more.

I climb on the bike and reach for her arms to wrap them around my waist. She doesn't say anything but grabs on tight.

I begin driving, but soon realize I have no idea where I'm going. I don't wanna take her home in case Justin goes there later. *But she sure as shit isn't coming back to mine.* Instead, I opt for a cheap motel just a few blocks away. One I've used more times than I can count for cheap and easy hook ups.

I pull into the parking lot, help her off the bike, and then lead her inside.

The creepy old guy is on the desk as usual. "Will that be for the hour or the night?" he asks, eyeing up Stacey with far more interest than I'd like. I pull out my wallet and throw the cash on the counter. "The night," I snap. *Heck, I won't be staying the night, I never do. But she can.*

He hands me the key to Room 15 and I snatch it and make my way there.

The motel only has about twenty rooms so it doesn't take me long to find the room. As soon as we get inside I head to the vending machine and buy a cold can of beer, placing the metal can to her cheek, the one that's already a lovely mixture of red and purple bruising. She winces in pain but I hold her head steady, knowing that as much as it hurts now, the cold will help the bruise. After all, I've spent most of my life dealing with the effect of being hit by people much bigger than me. "Hold steady baby, I know it hurts, but I'm helping you." *Baby? Did I just call her baby?*

"Thank you, Gabe" she whispers, as she takes the can from me and places it back on her cheek.

"It's fine, Stacey." I shrug, feeling a bit uncomfortable.

"Stacey?" she repeats like she doesn't recognize the word. *Shit, does she have a concussion or something? Should I take her to the emergency room, maybe?*

"Do you need a doctor?" I ask. Suddenly feeling completely out of my depth. Which makes no sense since I've spent my whole life either causing the injuries or dealing with the aftereffects of other people causing injuries.

"No, I think I just need sleep," she says sleepily as she stands up.

"Can you turn around?" she asks shyly as she begins to undo the buttons on her skirt.

Any other time I'd tell a girl to fuck off. Heck, I'd be the one taking the skirt off. Yet for once I oblige and cover my eyes.

"Ready," she says a few moments later. I half expect to open my eyes to find her naked or in her underwear on the bed, trying to seduce me. But instead, she's snuggled in bed, with the blanket pulled right up to her chin.

I turn to leave, not liking how weird and coupley this suddenly feels. These rooms are not used for cute romantic getaways, they're made for cheap, nasty sex, with cheap, nasty whores.

"Wait, don't go, please." she pleads. I can hear the fear and desperation in her voice. She's not saying it in a way like she wants to get laid. She genuinely needs me to stay.

A feeling in my chest is swirling around, but I don't quite know what it is. I take off my shirt, kick off my shoes, and unbutton my jeans, then lay down awkwardly beside her wondering what the fuck is happening. I don't do this. I don't do cute, and cuddly. I don't do snuggles in bed. I don't do stupid pet names. And I definitely don't do whatever this shit right here is.

She shuffles herself closer so that her head is on my bare chest. I make no attempt to hold her though; instead, I just stare up at the ceiling. *What the fuck am I doing?*

I hear her breathing soften, and soon after soft sleepy snores. Now I know she can't see or feel me any longer, I begin to stroke her hair. The way my mom used to when Nate and I were younger. I hear soft murmurs escape Stacey's lips, so I stop. But once I realize she is still fast asleep, I continue.

I don't know how long I lay there stroking her hair while staring down and watching as that bruise on her cheek gets more and more pronounced. I run my finger over it ever so gently but it still causes her to flinch and suck in a breath.

I may be a selfish, heartless bastard, but even I would never cross the line and hit a woman like he did. My anger continues to rise as I think about what happened until I can no longer keep it in. So carefully I get up from the bed, sneak out the room and onto my Harley.

Unfortunately for him, I know exactly where he lives. I pull my bike off onto one of the bushes nearby, and slowly with the cover of darkness make my way to the house. I sneak past the gate and can hear the sound of a man's voice. I stop to listen, trying to work out how many people are here, and how many I may have to fight. *What the fuck am I even doing here? I'm not some knight in shining armor, the hero, here to rescue the princess.* Heck, normally I wouldn't even care enough about anyone to walk ten steps let alone go across town but this is different. She makes it different somehow.

I try to tell myself it's just because I hate men being violent towards women and not some leftover trigger from childhood. That seeing Stacey knocked to the ground doesn't remind me of what my mom went through at the hands of my father. But deep down, I know there's more to it than that.

I continue to listen and it becomes apparent the asshole is alone and on the phone.

"Where the fuck are you, baby? I'm sorry, I didn't mean to hurt you. It was the booze talking. You know that's not me."

I can't control the way my hands instinctively curl into fists at his words. I've heard those same words more times than I can count.

Flashback- Age Four

Mommy is snoring on the sofa, so I play quietly with my truck. This is my favorite truck, Mommy bought it for me at the store.

I hear a loud noise outside and know that means Daddy is home.

Daddy is home and he's sad. I always know Daddy is sad when his car door makes that big bang.

The door flies open making another bang against the wall behind it. This makes Mommy wake up.

"Sofia? Where are you, woman?" my dad bellows as he storms through the front door.

Mommy stands from the sofa and makes her way to the door to greet him.

"Hey sweetie, we've missed you," Mommy says, leaning up on her toes to kiss daddy.

"What's for dinner?" he demands and pushes past her.

"Erm, I was just about to start it now. What would you like?"

"Start it? It's almost 5p.m. Why the fuck isn't it ready and waiting for me? My father demands, pushing her off him.

"I'm so sorry, I must have fallen asleep. I didn't have a very good night. I'm sorry" she stutters again. "I'll do it right now, though," my mother says. "There's some steak in the fridge, it will only take me a few minutes to fry it up. And there's beer in the fridge. Go sit down and relax, and I'll bring it to you soon."

"That goddamn baby kept you up again, didn't he? I don't know what's wrong with that kid. Always goddamn crying. Gabe was never like that," my father snaps. I peer around the door and watch him walk into the kitchen.

"You need to do something about that little demon spawn; find some way to shut him up or I will," my father snaps angrily with the threat hanging in the air.

"He can't help it, the poor thing has reflux. The doctors sent some new meds and milk. I'm picking it up tomorrow. Maybe that will help," my mother says in a sad voice. I hate that sad voice. She doesn't have a sad voice with me. Only daddy.

"My boy, there you are," he says, bending down and scooping me into his arms.

"You're not a cry baby like your fucking brother, are you?" he asks as he pulls me onto his lap.

"No Daddy. I'm a good boy," I say with a smile as we sit on the big chair. Daddy puts on the tv and we watch some football together.

"Mommy, can I have some water, pwease," I shout.

"Here son, try some of this instead." Daddy hands me his stinky Daddy juice and I take a sip. It tastes disgusting though and the bubbles burn my nose.

Mommy walks in at that moment and takes the bottle away from me.

"He can't have that, he's only little." Mommy says, sounding worried.

"Who the fuck do you think you are talking to?" my daddy bellows as he stands up so fast I almost fly off his lap.

"No, nothing, I'm sorry I didn't mean..." Mommy says quickly but before she has a chance to say anymore, Daddy's big hand hits her face. Mommy makes a strange noise and starts to cry.

Feeling so scared that I think I might be sick, I run into the bedroom to hide. As I do, I see baby Nathaniel fast asleep in the middle of the bed.

I run and hide in the wardrobe, as I hear my daddy shouting.

I hide at the very back, behind the big coats, and pretend I'm in Narnia. The book Mommy has been reading us at bedtime. I sit quietly knowing Daddy can't find me here. He'd tried once before but when he opened the wardrobe he didn't see me.

Suddenly, I hear the baby starting to cry. *No, no, don't cry. Crying makes Daddy mad.* I crawl out from my safe space and open the wardrobe. I rush over to the baby and try to pick up his little basket but it's too heavy. I see the milk bottle on the side and try to give him that but he still cries. *Shush baby, please stop crying!* His crying just gets louder and louder. My heart is beating so hard in my chest I'm almost sure it can be seen through my skin.

I know Mommy said I'm not allowed to pick him up in case I drop him but I have to stop the noise. I carefully pull him out of his basket and hold him close to me like Mommy does. Thankfully, he stops crying as soon as I do. Next, I try to pick up his bottle but I have no hands so I have to bite the nipple with my teeth. Finally, I take us both back into the wardrobe. I place him at the back, behind the coats then quickly turn to close the door behind us. Nathaniel begins to cry again so once the doors are closed and I'm hidden at the back, I pull Nathaniel back onto my lap and begin feeding him. *Please be quiet baby; don't let Daddy find us.* Nathaniel finishes the whole bottle then falls back to sleep. I sit there hiding for a long time. Long after the shouting has finished. I sit there holding Nathaniel even when my arms start to ache, until finally the door opens, and the coat gets moved to the side. That's when I see Mommy's face.

"I'm sorry, Mommy, I know I'm not allowed to hold the baby on my own. But..."

Mommy hushes me, "No, you did a good thing, Gabriel. You kept the baby safe. Mommy is very proud of you! You're the best big brother in the world."

Chapter Nine

Gabe

The sound of a door slamming brings me back to reality.

"This is the last fucking message I'm leaving, I don't know where you are, you fucking whore, probably getting railed by whoever that guy was. The one you're blatantly fucking. So much for being a virgin, yeah? Anyway, we're done. I don't want his fucking sloppy seconds anyway. Jessica gives better blowjobs and puts out. Oh, and while I was at college I fucked two other girls as well, so fuck you!" he bellows into the phone before throwing it onto the ground in frustration.

He bends down to try and find his phone in the dark. As soon as he stands up and turns to walk back inside, my fist connects with his jaw.

"That's for being a pussy who hits women," I growl as I climb on top of him and my fist connects with his ribs. "And that's for being a lying, cheating scumbag," I say as I connect with his jaw next.

"This is because I just really like beating the grin off your cheesy, fucking face," I laugh as I stand and kick him in the ribs once more for good measure before leaving.

I get on my bike ready to go home, but something in me persuades me to go back to the motel to check on Stacey. So against every instinct in my body, that's where I go. I pull up to the parking lot, hop off my bike, and make my way to the room. As I get to the door, though, I realize I don't have the key. *Shit! Why didn't you grab the key?* My brain scolds me. *Perhaps because I never take the key? Because I usually rush out the door as fast as my legs will carry me and never even look back.* I argue back.

I turn to leave just as the door swings open and Stacey envelops me in a tight hug. My natural instinct is to push her away, tell her to get the fuck off me and leave again. But the shining bruise stops me for just long enough that she lets go herself.

"Where have you been?" She says, slapping my chest.

"I went to get ice," I lie. I see her eyes glance down at my empty hands so quickly add, "but I didn't find any." *What the fuck is wrong with me?*

"Well close the door then it's fucking freezing," she laughs as she walks back and climbs back under the covers.

I just stare like a dumbfounded kid, not knowing what to do. *Do I leave? Do I stay? Do I climb in beside her? Do I fuck her?* Who knows.

"You just gonna stare or are you gonna come join me and my boyfriend?"

"Your boyfriend!?!" I snap, kicking the door closed as I quickly scan the room.

"Yeah, my main man, Jax Teller," she laughs, patting the space beside her.

I kick off my shoes and sit down.

"You watch Sons?" I exclaim in surprise. *Maybe tonight won't suck too much.*

"Hell yeah! Motorbikes, check. Family drama, check. Hot guy, double check," she laughs as she fans herself.

"Oh, okay," sounding a little off guard. *How can we both love the same show but see it so differently?*

"What, did you think all girls only watch rom-coms and dream of their prince charming and true love's kiss?" she laughs as she throws one of the obnoxiously small cushions at my head.

"Well yeah, kind of," I reply as I remove my jeans and sit on the edge of the bed, ready to watch my favorite show.

"You're in for a rude awakening then as Jax is the only Prince OF Charming this girl needs." She grins as she makes herself comfy and turns up the volume.

I start off sitting on the edge but before long I'm sitting right beside her under the covers. Neither of us say much other than the odd comment here and there about the show. But it feels oddly peaceful. I can't remember the last time I sat with another person and just relaxed or watched TV.

The show is just coming to an end when she breaks the silence by asking, "Should we watch the next episode?"

"Sure, I gotta take a piss first, though," I reply as I stand and make my way to the bathroom. When I come out she's on all fours with her ass in the air and her head hanging off the bed.

Fuck yes! My cock springs to attention in my boxers and I waste no time walking over and slapping her ass.

"What the fuck?!" she shouts. Lifting her head. "What do you think you're doing?" she demands as she turns her head to look at me.

"Well, I thought... you were on all fours." I stutter as I feel a blush rising up my neck. I rub the back of my neck and look up towards the ceiling.

"What were you thinking? That rather than having a conversation like a normal person, I'd just climb on all fours and present myself to you like a fucking cat in heat?" she snaps again and I can see she's pissed. Which I know it shouldn't but it just makes me harder. Never before have I had any woman, let alone one this goddamn sexy, stand up to me or try and challenge me like this. I moan quietly to myself and have the worst urge to adjust myself in my pants but know that will just add fuel to this fire sitting in front of me.

"Well?" she demands. *I swear I can almost see the smoke coming from her.*

"Well, what the fuck were you doing then?" I ask innocently and try to give her my sexiest smirk.

"Honestly. Men are the worst," she grumbles as she pushes her way past me, walks around to the side of the bed where her head just was, and bends down.

"I was getting this, you fucking caveman," she snaps, holding the remote control in the air.

I move to reach for it but she hides it behind her back. I lunge forward to get it from behind her back but she swaps hands and holds it high into the air. Although, why? I don't know, since I'm easily a foot taller than her.

She obviously registers this at the same time as I do, and just as I get close enough to reach for it she throws it onto the bed.

I'm not letting her off that easily though. I grab her still outstretched hand and use that and my weight to push her backward and pin her hand above her head.

"Well, that didn't work, did it?" I growl, voice laced with desire.

She tries to push me away, but it's clear from the lack of strength she uses she has no intention of actually stopping me. So instead I use my other hand to grab hers and pin them both high above her head.

"Now, what are you gonna do?" I purr against her ear.

I hear her breath hitch and know I've got her exactly where I want her.

"Well, answer me." I snap, as I playfully nip the nape of her neck and feel her body jump in shock.

"I'm... uhm . . ... I'm gonna" she mumbles.

I move my hands so that I can grip both of hers in one, then slide my other hand down her side to cup one of her breasts.

"You're gonna stand there and accept your punishment aren't you," I growl and this time bite her a little harder. A whimper leaves her mouth as I feel her head nod. I turn my head to look at her, for any signs she doesn't want this but her pupils are blown and she looks at me with the sexiest eyes I've ever seen.

I let out a low moan as I slide my hands down into her underwear, which are now soaked with arousal, and insert two fingers inside her. Her eyes drop down so I release her hands to lift her chin. But as soon as I do her hands attempt to wrap around me. So I grab her hands and again forcefully thrust them above her head and against the wall.

"Keep your fucking hands here," I demand. *No fucking way am I allowing her to touch me.* She might not know my rules yet, but she will soon enough. Unless my dick is in her hands, there's no reason for her hands to be on me at all.

I see a glint of fear form in her eyes before it's quickly replaced by desire.

"Now fucking look at me," I demand again, although this time much softer.

She does exactly as I tell her and looks directly into my eyes as my fingers move skillfully inside of her. I watch in her eyes as the orgasm builds higher and higher, but the bitch refuses to make a sound. Instead biting her lips defiantly. *Stubborn little brat.*

Finally, she cries out just as I feel her pussy cum around my fingers.

I take my fingers out of her and bring them to my mouth, not missing the look of disgust on her face as I do so. I moan as I lick my fingers clean and I notice her eyes watching every movement of my face and hand.

"You like that Firefly? because I think you did," I tell her in a deep voice and I hear a whimper escape from her.

"On your knees," I growl.

She drops down almost immediately, surprising both me and herself. *Hmm, does she like it when I am demanding?* I make my way over to the bed and sit down. I crook my finger and motion for her to come towards me.

When she is close, I say, "Now take me in your mouth."

Again she does exactly as I tell her. She releases my throbbing, hard cock from my boxers and begins licking it like a goddamn lollipop before finally taking it into her mouth. *Oh my God! Her wet mouth feels like heaven!* She starts off slow, almost shyly, but is soon sucking it like a pro. Placing my hands behind me, I lean back enjoying the view. That is until there's loud gunfire from the TV and her eyes dart towards it.

I reach out my hand, wrapping it around her throat. I feel her throat bob against my palm as she tries to swallow, so I release my grip slightly, not wanting to scare or hurt her.

"What do you think you're doing, looking at another man while my cock is inside you?" I growl possessively. *What the fuck is wrong with me tonight? I've had blow jobs from girls before that are literally being fucked by someone else at the same time and that never even bothered me.*

Yet the thought of her even looking at another guy, fictional or not, fills me with jealousy and possessiveness.

Releasing my grip on her neck I lift her to her feet.

"Lie down," I demand and I push her slightly so she falls onto the bed.

"I'm gonna fuck you now and make you remember exactly who this pussy belongs to," I say huskily. She moans in response and I feel her hips buck towards me, like a siren's call.

I climb on top of her and pull down her pants, ready to fuck her roughly all the while making her forget all about mother fucking

Jax Teller. That is until I see her perfectly shaven pussy glistening and can't help but lean forward for a real taste.

My tongue pushes through her folds as a moan of pleasure escapes her mouth. *Ha, it's not so easy to be quiet now is it?*

I can't help but feel oddly accomplished knowing my little fire cracker can't control her moans, even when she's clearly trying.

I continue sucking and licking as her body melts beneath me, I slide two fingers in and begin working her with my fingers while my mouth focuses on her most sensitive spot.

"Fuck...yeah...that feels soo....wow," she pants as I work harder and harder, driving her into ecstacy. *Fuck she looks so hot right now, her whole body glistening as she moans and grips the bedsheets.*

"I'm gonna fucking destroy this perfect pussy," I growl as I grab my throbbing cock and line it up with her hole, ready to finally get my prize.

"Wait, wait, stop a sec. Time out," she calls, sounding flustered and out of breath. I look up and I see her uncertainty. "I'm a virgin," she finally shouts just as I'm about to enter.

The words stop me in my tracks, She's 21. How the fuck is she still a virgin?

At first I think it's some ruse, something girls say to make out they're all sweet and innocent, but one look at the embarrassment and panic on her face lets me know she is telling the truth.

"Fuck!" I say as I punch the mattress.

"Don't be angry, you can still do it, just be gentle," she whines, as if she didn't just pour a proverbial bucket of cold water on me.

Does she think that's what's bothering me? The fact she said no? Like an ice bath it cools down my frustration instantly.

"I'm not mad that you stopped me. I'm horny as fuck and my dick is frustrated," I try to joke "but I'm not angry you said stop. You have every right to say stop," I say, trying to speak as nicely as I can.

"We can still do it, if you want, it's fine," she says, she pulls her pants back into place again, looking dejected. But I'm no longer interested in fucking her senseless, even if my dick is screaming for me to continue.

"Firstly, I'm not the kind of guy you should give that up to. Give it to some nice guy, not me. I'm a fucking asshole and secondly, I have no idea how to fuck you softly even if I wanted to. I only know how to fuck fast and hard. I'm a fucker not a lover," I laugh, hoping to lighten the mood, but it's clear there's now a tension and awkwardness in the air that not even a knife could cut.

I see the way she reaches for the blanket and covers up, and I hate the look in her eyes. Gone is the fire and instead it's replaced with an emotion I don't recognize. *Shame, perhaps?*

Either way I hate it, but I don't know how to wash it away. Normally this is the part where the boy would pull her into his arms and hold her, but I'm not that sort of guy.

Instead, I bend down to kiss her which she allows for only a second before she turns away.

"I don't want a pity kiss" she says softly and I can hear in her voice that she's about to cry. I've made enough girls cry in the past to recognize that stupid voice wobble. *This is so NOT the way I saw this night going.*

Rubbing the back of my neck, unsure what to do or how to respond, since unlike every other time before, I don't want her to run away. I do the only thing I know how to do, and that's take control.

I wrap my hand around her throat again and slowly whisper, "I may not be able to fuck you, but I'm still gonna punish you."

Chapter Ten

Stacey

My heart pounds faster at the implication of his words. But before I have the chance to think about what they could mean he's pushing me back onto the bed. He removes his t-shirt showcasing his chiseled abs. I notice a scar running down one side of his hips and reach my hand out to touch his but he grabs my wrist stopping me in my tracks.

"I told you before, don't touch!" he growls, before using the t-shirt he'd just removed to bind my hands together.

"Hold here and don't let go," he snaps as he pulls me up to the head of the bed and encourages me to grip the headboard. Next, he lifts up my own top; I assume he's going to remove it entirely but instead, he only partially removes it. Just enough that my eyes are now covered as well.

He has me completely at his mercy - hands bound, eyes blindfolded, and in the most compromising position of my life. Yet, instead of feeling fear, after all I barely know him and he could do anything to me against my will, I feel nothing but desire and heat pooling. Part of me wants him to do what he wants, use my body for his own pleasure. *What the fuck's wrong with me. I knew Justin for years, thought I loved him, yet not once did he fill me with half the longing I feel right now.*

I feel a breath against my ear just as I hear, "You've been a bad girl. Are you ready for your punishment?"

My body goes into overdrive at his words alone. I nod my head slowly before I feel teeth nipping roughly at my earlobes.

"I didn't hear you, little spark, I need your words," he whispers, again.

"Yes, I'm ready," I answer back while taking in a shaky breath. With that, I feel him remove my pants completely, but then to my surprise he begins to kiss and nibble at my neck instead.

"Mmm," I moan as he continues to bite harder, to the point I know there's going to be a mark. Next, he works his way to my breasts, palming and pinching them. I try to rub my thighs together to ease some of the tension building in my core but to my shock, I feel his strong hands grab at my thighs as he forcefully spreads my legs apart.

"Don't even think about it. You'll get to feel pleasure if and when I decide it," he snaps as he grips my thighs tighter. The pressure tight enough to leave marks. That thought should have me running, but instead I can feel my wetness drip even more down my legs.

My mind is in overdrive; part of me loves what he's doing, the other part of me knows I should hate it. Still, some weird part of me desperately wants to obey.

"Now, you're going to lie here and take your punishment like a good little girl aren't you?" he growls, his voice sounding even more gravelly than it did just a few minutes ago.

Again, I try to nod but he wraps his hand around my throat and squeezes. "What did I tell you about using your words?" he snaps, this time shocking me further by slapping his hand against the inside of my thigh, not enough to hurt but enough to leave a slight sting.

"Fuck!" I shout out in surprise.

"I want to, so fucking bad," he purrs.

He releases his hand on my throat and quickly thrusts a finger inside my now soaking slit. "Hmm, so wet for me already," he says and I can hear the grin in his voice, just before I feel a second finger enter me.

His fingers begin thrusting in and out of me at a quick pace causing me to moan and groan as my orgasm begins to build.

"Yes... yes... oh god," I moan, then suddenly he stops.

"Heey ..." I grumble, feeling all types of frustrated. My frustration is short-lived though, because he lifts my body up by my hips and thrusts a pillow under my ass as he begins expertly fucking me with his fingers all over again. He peppers kisses and bites along the inside of my thighs and onto my mound before sucking and licking my most sensitive spot.

"Does that feel good, baby?" he asks, as I begin to moan out in ecstasy.

"Yes, yes, don't stop," I manage to say. *Fuck me, Justin's gone down on me a couple of times, but it never felt like this. It felt okay, I guess, a little sloppy and rough, kind of like being licked by a cat, but fuck me this feels nothing like that. This feels like the perfect mixture of heaven and hell combined.*

He continues licking and sucking before adding his fingers to the mixture, as well. Before I even have time to tell him I'm going to cum, I'm cumming hard and fast, so fast in fact, that I feel my legs begin to shake.

"Such a dirty, little bitch," he chuckles in a most delicious sounding way.

"My dirty little bitch," he says before he grips me by the jaw and thrusts his tongue deep inside my mouth. I taste a mixture of him, cigarettes, mints, as well as what I can only assume is me on his tongue.

GABE

The plan was just to edge her a few times and then leave her wanting. To punish her by depriving her of the one thing she wanted most in that moment. Have her begging me to let her cum. But hearing her moans and pants, all I could think about was hearing the sound she'd make when I made her cum. Watching the way her chest heaved and her body shook as the orgasm took over her was like my own personal drug. Never in my life have I been more desperate to fuck someone. It took every ounce of strength, strength I didn't even know I possessed, not to fuck her then and there.

"Wow, that was, wow," she moans, still writhing on the bed. I lean over her, take a quick nip at her dusky nipple, and finally remove the t-shirt binding her hands.

She reaches down and removes her makeshift blindfold. I can't help but smirk at the cheesy grin plastering her face. Her hair is a mess and she's sporting the typical just fucked look, and I didn't even fuck her yet.

"I'm so tired," she yawns as she rolls over and curls herself into a beautiful, naked little ball. I kiss her head and tell her to sleep.

Against every fiber in my body, the ones that are telling me to run away, I climb in beside her on the other side of the bed. *I'm just tired, that's all. It doesn't mean anything. Sure, this is the first time since you were sixteen you've let a girl sleep in your bed, but it doesn't mean anything. This isn't even your bed.* I argue with my own mind before I finally drift off myself.

I don't know how long I've been asleep, but I wake with an unfamiliar feeling, the feeling of something heavy weighing down on my chest. Fear takes over as in my sleepy haze I'm transported back to my childhood and the soul crushing feeling I'd get when my father woke me up. My hand flies down, expecting to feel him pushing me down. But I'm surprised when my fingers connect with hair and lots of it. I reach for the lamp beside me, wondering what the hell is on my chest. As the room comes into focus, I realize it's a head, Stacey's head to be exact. She's flung across my chest and her head is resting against my ribs. A small grumble leaves her mouth letting me know she's about to stir. I have two choices here, push her off and run away or turn the light off and lay silently praying she doesn't wake. To my shock, my subconscious chooses the second. I lie there in darkness, holding my breath while I listen to her breathing even back out.

I find myself stroking her hair as I lie there listening to the reassuring sound of the small snores escaping her lips. I stroke her hair, again and again until I feel a strange calmness overtake me as I drift off to sleep myself.

STACEY

I wake up feeling like I've spent the night inside an oven. I try to move, but I'm wrapped in strong arms, arms that are almost impossible to move. The side of my face is hot and sweaty from resting my head against a warm body all night.

At first, I sleepily assume it belongs to Justin. Until I notice the black swirls in front of my eyes. I wriggle enough to break free of the arms holding me and notice more swirls and patterns. Tattoos covering half his chest and arms. I look up and realize it's Gabe. That's when everything from last night floods in like a tidal wave. The concert, Justin's anger, the slap to the face. I reach up and touch my eye and wince at the contact. Rushing towards the bathroom I look in the mirror and gasp. The whole area under my eye and part of my cheek is a mixture of red and purple. That bastard hit me hard enough to give me a black eye!

I rush to find my handbag, hoping to find something in there to cover it up. Thankfully, I find a small concealer which helps slightly, but not enough.

I look over and see Gabe fast asleep, still frowning, but asleep. I contemplate waking him, asking for a ride home again, but what do I say? Hey thanks for saving me from my ex-boyfriend last night, and for giving me the best orgasm of my life, but now let's shake hands and part ways? *I don't think so.*

Instead, I quietly grab my things, get dressed and sneak out the door.

I tried calling my sister, but there's no answer.

Next, I try calling a few friends but they've gone out for the day.

So I have no choice but to ask the front desk to call me a taxi home.

I get home and head down to my bedroom, hoping to see my sister and tell her some of what happened last night. About what happened at the concert. And about the fact I ran into Gabe again. But as soon as I do, I spot a folded up note on my pillow.

"Hey you dirty biatch!

Hope you have a good night, I've been called in to work as Jamie has called in sick again ... shocker!

But I get off around 11 o'clock. If ur back by then come meet me for lunch, I've got loads to tell you before we head to the carnival.

Xoxo

I can't help but smirk as I read the note. I pull out my phone to check the time and realize it's barely even 10 am so I've got a few hours to kill yet, so make my way towards our bathroom. I turn on the shower and allow the steam to fill the room before climbing in.

I enjoy the feel of the hot water cascading down my back as I finally take a moment to think about the last twenty-four hours. I can't believe I left my home to go to a concert, concerned about being forced to share air with Justin and then somehow ended up in bed with Gabe. Gabe, the rough, tough guy from the wrong side of town. The asshole who likes to grumble at people and be a dick towards everyone. The 'bad boy' Lexi and all her friends tried to warn me to stay away from because he's dangerous. *But is he really? Or is that just what he's allowed everyone to believe?*

I reach for the shower gel and begin lathering up my achy body as I continue thinking. I mean, sure he can be an asshole at times, and his potty mouth might not be everyone's taste. *Even though it drives my body wild.*

I finish my shower and step out as I continue thinking about Gabe. I guess to the outside world his tough, no nonsense attitude can seem off putting. But every so often I get glimmers of a guy desperate for a connection. Someone who just needs someone to see through the tough, cocky exterior, to the sweetheart buried inside. *Oh fuck! He's a misunderstood villain in need of redemption*, I suddenly realize. *Of course you fell for him. He's a walking, talking red flag.*

I can't help but laugh at myself. I've never been one for the nice guys, not even in movies or books. I've always fallen for the villain who likes to watch the world burn, rather than the hero hoping to save it.

Chapter Eleven

Gabe

I wake up and at first I'm a little confused about where I am. But looking around the memories soon flood in. Going to the concert, and seeing Stacey, beating up her ex-boyfriend, then coming back here and getting to watch her come undone for me.

Then I remember that we had fallen asleep together. I look around and don't see her. I rush to the bathroom, hoping she's in the shower but she's gone.

Wait, did she leave? What the Fuck?! Did she sneak out while I was sleeping? Did she wake up regretting last night and run?

So many questions run through my mind. *Why do I even care? I leave girls all the time, fuck 'em then chuck 'em, so why does it bother me this time?*

I jump on my bike and head home, back to my own prison in the woods. The home is filled with more nightmares than I can count. I pull up and make my way inside. "Nate?... . Nate...Nathaniel, you here?" No answer.

I rush towards his bedroom and bang on the door. "Nate, you in here?" I push the door open slowly, "If you're wanking in here, say something as I don't wanna see that shit," I call as I head inside.

But his bed is empty too. *Where the fuck is he?*

I'm just about to call him when I hear a door slam. I head towards the front door and see Nate standing in the hallway removing his shoes.

"Where the fuck have you been?" I ask.

"Sorry, I've been up since the early hours and couldn't get back to sleep as I was too nervous and excited for today. So I decided to go for a run to settle my nerves."

"Nervous for today? Why?" I ask, but when I see the smile drop from Nate's face I realize I should know.

"You forgot didn't you?" Nate says sadly.

Shit! What the hell are we supposed to be doing? I rack my brain for an answer but nothing comes.

"Of course I didn't forget," I lie. "I just meant you have nothing to be nervous about; it'll be fine."

"Nothing to be nervous about? You remember how difficult school was for me, when we moved in with the Jacksons because....."

Shit, I promised I'd go with him to orientation day. Fuck! I totally forgot.

".... so that's why I'm so glad you're coming with me." Nate says, finally stopping to take a breath.

"Of course I'm coming with you. I just have to drop some stuff off to John, but I'll meet you outside the main gate in an hour." I reassure him as I tap him on the shoulder and then rush off to get the shit done that I need to do. So that I'm on time to be there to be who Nate needs me to be.

An hour later and I'm standing outside the high school, the last place I ever thought I would find myself again, impatiently waiting for Nate to show up. I specifically told him to meet me at twelve o'clock, yet the little shit is almost fifteen minutes late already. If he knew all the strings and favors I had to pull with the head teacher to get him enrolled here, he'd thank me.

The decrepit old principal here has hated me for months, ever since I started dating some seniors, which apparently led to a cat fight between the two girls I was sleeping with at the time. I don't know why the girls made such a fuss in the first place. I was honest and told both of them from the beginning that we weren't exclusive and that I didn't do girlfriends. So technically, it's not even my fault that they both caught feelings. Stupid girls, they both thought they'd be the one to change this bad boy. *Yeah, right.* I scoff

I'm about to hop on my Harley and ride away when I see a familiar looking lady walking up the stairs toward me. I stop to stare at her, silently hoping it's not Mrs. Williams. I can feel the venom building up in my body at the mere sight of her. And of course, things get much worse when I see a girl walking right behind her. I remember when I was a kid, Nathaniel used to say Isabella was the only girl in the family, and how we used to joke that she was the family princess. So there is no doubt in my mind that the girl has to be Izzy. Although she looks nothing like the annoying little girl I remember Nate sneaking off to meet.

I'm almost tempted to smile at her until I remember that all of this, our move, and the forced separation from Nate are all her fault. It's because of her that I broke my promise to Mom and have been all alone for the last few years. It all started because of her and her big, fat mouth. I look up and realize she's staring at me, so I give her my best *fuck off, before I kick your ass* look until she looks away.

I can't help but wonder what she's doing here and when she came back. I know it must have been recently because I've passed her grandparents' house numerous times on the way through since I got back. At first, I just watched them, then I started playing little tricks on them. I slashed a few tires, smashed a few bottles outside their house, and put weed killer in all their rosebushes. It came to a head on the first birthday without Nate when I went out and got drunk and decided to throw a brick through their front window. Luckily, I missed, but it was enough to bring me back to reality a little bit because if I ended up in jail, I would never see Nate again.

Besides, if she's back in town, that can only mean trouble. I'm going to make it my mission to make sure Nate doesn't see her because I know once he does, it's game over. He's been in love with her and pining after her for as long as I can remember, and I know if she shows up again and plays with his emotions, I'll risk losing my brother forever. I know that even now, he'd follow her to the end of the earth.

NATE

I'm running around like a madman. I was supposed to meet Gabe ten minutes ago, but I've been thinking way too long about what to wear and how to look. Today there is an open house at my new school, Avery High, and they always have a big summer carnival. I remember my brother telling me about it when we were kids. About all the fun things they have there and how it's the place to be for all the popular kids to be seen before school starts. The first time he went, he saved up for weeks to be able to afford the visit.

After getting a glimpse of a girl that I'm sure was Bella just a few days ago but chickening out before I got to confirm my suspicions, I'm more determined than ever not to make that mistake again. If Bella really is in town like I suspect, I know she won't pass up the opportunity to visit the carnival. I have to make sure I make the right first impression. Readying my nerves, I send a quick text to Gabe, grab my keys, and head out.

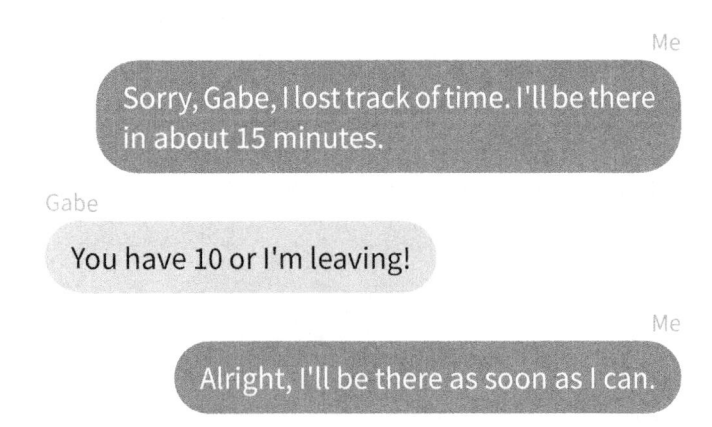

Me

Sorry, Gabe, I lost track of time. I'll be there in about 15 minutes.

Gabe

You have 10 or I'm leaving!

Me

Alright, I'll be there as soon as I can.

A few minutes later, I'm just getting off my bike when I get another text message.

> **Gabe**
> Change of plans, let's meet for lunch instead.

> **Me**
> I'm already here, where are you?

> **Gabe**
> Meet me at the soccer field.

> **Me**
> I don't know where that is, it's my first time at the school, remember? I'm parked near the main office.

> **Gabe**
> Alright, I'll come to you then.

Gabe arrives a few minutes later. "Should we go in?" I ask him, but looking closer, Gabe seems angry. "What's your problem..."

"Nothing." he bites out, "We'll get a drink," he adds, virtually dragging me away. *What the fuck is up with him?* I wonder.

About thirty minutes later, after much pleading, I finally persuade him to go in, and we're greeted by the principal, Mrs. Cross.

"So let's head to my office." The principal suggests.

I follow behind and can't help but hear Gabe grumbling and probably swearing under his breath.

As we walk in, she immediately sits behind her desk, somehow looking even more authoritarian than she did before. I chose the chair directly opposite her desk. I notice how the light from the window behind me seems to glisten against the photo frames stacked on her desk. But Gabe stands, leaning against the door, legs crossed, arms folded, sporting his signature pissed off look.

"Sit down," I mouth silently, but Gabe just flips me off. I whip my head around to the principal, ready to apologize, but thankfully she's busy looking in her drawer of paperwork.

"Here it is," she suddenly says, pulling out a wad of paper.

"So tell me about your last school, so we can figure out what the best fit will be. I know you were held back, but how have things been since?"

"Well...." I begin before explaining all about what I've been doing these last few years and then follow her for a tour around the school.

Throughout the walk, Gabe looks around anxiously. I don't know what's wrong with him. I assume it's just old memories. Although, if I'm honest, he was hardly ever here anyway because of Dad, so I don't understand why he's acting so weird. The tour ends, and Gabe tries to convince me to leave again. I reluctantly agree and tell him I need to go into town, but he insists that he'll accompany me, so I tell him that I have plans to meet a girl for coffee. This seems to satisfy him, and he agrees to leave me alone and go on his way. I start walking towards town, but as soon as I see his bike go by, I turn around and head straight back to school. Part of me feels guilty for purposefully tricking Gabe, but I wasn't exactly lying when I said I intended to meet a girl. I just forgot to mention which girl and the fact that SHE currently has absolutely no idea she's meeting ME.

Chapter Twelve

Gabe

I wake up mid morning with a bit of a start. Listening, I realize the house is quiet – too quiet. I worked really late last night helping John with the books and plans for expansion so by the time I got home, I collapsed in my bed without a second thought. But this morning I figured I wouldn't be able to escape Nate. *Why isn't he making a bunch of noise trying to wake me up? Usually he would be bouncing off the walls dying to tell me about his new school or even his date. What's going on?*

I make my way to his bedroom and notice the door partly open. After getting no reply from calling his name, I push the door open and notice his bed is still made and his clothes are strewn across it from where he obviously tried on multiple outfits before heading out. *Where the hell is he?*

Scratching my head, I head to the kitchen hoping to see his coffee cup in the sink from this morning, but the coffee pot's still full and unused on the side. *How strange.*

Did he not come home last night? The last time I saw him was when I left him at the school fair. He mentioned he was going to see some chick, but did he not come home? *Must have gotten laid.*

I pull out my phone and dial the number but it just rings.

Looking at the clock I realize it's barely 10 a.m., perhaps he's still asleep.

I jump in the shower, grinning when I notice lipstick smeared across my dick and remember how it got there. Knowing I'm alone, I begin pumping my cock to the memories of the other night, how amazing it was watching Stacey come undone for me, watching her body buck and shake as I brought her to orgasm, and how desperate I was to fuck her. My mind then begins fantasizing about what it would be like to fuck her. What positions I'd put her in and what noises she'd make. Finally with one great tug, I spray my load down the drain letting the water from the shower wash it away.

I get out, wrap a towel around myself and head towards the kitchen for a much needed coffee.

I make and enjoy my coffee then try to call Nate again. Once again, all I get is his voicemail.

I try texting him, hoping that if he's too busy to pick up his phone perhaps he'll at least answer my texts.

11:15 a.m.

> Nate, I haven't seen you since last night. Are you still alive?

I make myself another coffee and light up a cigarette in the backyard. When he still hasn't replied by the time I'm finished, I head back into his room. Perhaps he left a note or something.

11:45 a.m.

> Your bed doesn't look slept in, so I'm guessing you slept in someone else's.

I'm sure he's fine; he probably just got lucky with some slut last night. That will be it, I'm sure. I try telling myself, but it doesn't really work. So instead I throw on a hoodie, hop on my bike, and decide to head back into town. Perhaps he left early and is around town somewhere. He did say he was going to look for work. I bet that's what he's doing.

12:30 p.m.

> Text me back bro, I'm getting worried.

I try him twice more over the next hour and by the time the clock hits 1:30 p.m., I'm officially past annoyed, and have fully moved into the panicked stage- *What if something happened? I've only just got him back. I can't lose him again.*

I check online, typing his name into the search engine.

Facebook, nothing. Twitter, nothing. Instagram, nothing. Nate never was big on social media, neither of us are. I'm about to give up when I notice a new friend notification. I click on it and spot some hot little redhead standing beside someone in a football jersey. I don't recognize either of them, but I continue scrolling. There are pictures of the same couple at a party. A video of them dancing to cheesy music. And them sharing some cotton candy. *Well, this isn't much help.* That is until I spot him. Nate, in the background of the picture. I continue scrolling and see more pictures of Nate. Nate with the guy, standing, grinning. Nate and the guy together in the bumper cars. Then I see Nate with his arm around a girl, not just any girl, but Isabella. Issa-fucking-bella, the devil in disguise. Clicking on the picture I see the caption. 'Izzy and her Prince Charming'.

I try calling Nate again, this time leaving him an angry voice message telling him to call me back. I look at the picture again and notice Isabella has been tagged so click it and make my way to her profile next. On it, it's mostly pathetic pampered princess shit. 'Had such a great day with Nana and Pops. Missed them so much.' *I want to vomit.* Next there's a video with Isabella dancing around as she paints some pathetic picture on what I assume is her bedroom wall. I'm about to turn it off when I hear a voice. "Izzy, that looks amazing." I know that voice. My fears are confirmed when I see Stacey come into the frame also holding a paintbrush. "Our girl is a fucking artist," she coos to whomever is holding the camera.

Wait, Isabella knows Stacey? How? Since when? Why?

My mind swirls with all the questions.

Did Isabella put Stacey up to it? Had us meeting all been some sort of trick? Was this all a sick joke? Was this her way of trying to hurt me one last time?

I call Nate again and this time he finally answers.

"Holy shit, man, it's almost two o'clock! Where the fuck have you been?" I roar into the phone. I don't know if I'm relieved, still terrified, or mad with fury. My heart is racing and I have a bad urge to break things.

"I'm sorry, I met some new friends yesterday and went out with them last night. Today we went to a park, and now we've gone out for a drive. I totally lost track of time; no big deal." Nate replies nonchalantly and I feel a mixture of relief that he's safe and annoyance knowing exactly what new friends he's talking about... her. *Yet again she is trying to steal him from me.* "You really scared me, Nate. After what happened, you know it stresses me the fuck out when you're gone too long, especially when you don't even bother to let me know you are alive!"

"Gabe, you seem to forget that I'm almost eighteen. I'm old enough now to make my own decisions. We're not little kids anymore. You're not my parent. No one is going to separate us again. I've got you, and you have me, Gabriel. That's all we need," I hear him say in a soothing voice. I know I'm being completely irrational. I'm not his father; I have no right to dictate what he can and can't do. But I might as well be his father. I was basically the closest thing he had to a loving father growing up. Surely that gives me some right to feel this way.

It really doesn't, you were doing soo much worse when you were his age. My mind reminds me. Still, sometimes I think of him as that little boy who needs protecting. So, like the insecure little boy I once was, I cling to him like a life preserver.

"I know you keep saying that, but I promised Mom on her deathbed that I'd always take care of you and keep you safe, and I never want to break that promise again," I admit, feeling a swirl of emotions brewing as I remember that day so clearly, holding my mother's hand in that tiny hospital room, her whole body covered in tubes and wires. She made me promise to always take care of Nate. I was barely eight years old, and she was making me promise to always protect him. Promise to keep him safe; promise to always look after him. The way I'd always been doing since I was barely out of diapers.

"I know, but like I said, we were kids; that doesn't count. You never broke your promise as far as I'm concerned," he tries to reassure me. We've gone back and forth on this same fight more times than I can count. But as far as I'm concerned mom gave me one job. I made a promise to the most precious and perfect human to ever grace this earth. I couldn't save her but I could do this one thing to make her comfortable enough to finally stop fighting. And I failed.

I hate the feeling it gives me every time I think back to those times. The burn in my chest as I think about all I lost when she died. Even when she was dying and barely had the strength to stand, she found some way to keep my father calm. To take the brunt of his annoyance and keep me and Nate safe. But once she was gone, life became a hell that was beyond anything I could have imagined. *Why couldn't he have been the one to die?* What cruel and sadistic god took away a sweet angel and left us to be raised by a sadistic devil?

"Anyway, did you at least get lucky at that party last night?" I ask, changing the subject. Giving him the chance to mention that he found Isabella again.

"It wasn't like that," Nate snaps back and I know I've hit a nerve.

"That's all it's like, little brother. Girls are only useful for one night. After that, they're just a waste of energy," I sigh as my mind drifts to Stacey. *That is what it is right? They are only good for their hole and a release, and it's time to move on. But why doesn't it feel as right as it did before?*

"Not everyone sees it that way, Gabe. Some see girls are much more than just a place to park your ride." I know now that he's still there, with her. That yet again he's chosen her; he's spending his time with her and leaving me alone in that house. *See! Girls just fuck up everything.*

"Don't tell me, Mr. I'm-too-good-for-a-one-night-stand is still hung up on Princess Isabella," I bite out at him. I can hear the bitterness and condescending tone in my own voice, but I don't care.

"This is none of your business, whether I am or not. I'm just saying that not everyone is a heartless asshole like you," he yells before hanging up on me.

"Fuuuuck!" I scream, kicking the door in anger. *Fuck that hurt. How my foot didn't go through it, I'll never know. Why am I like this? Why is my first instinct to attack anytime I feel hurt or vulnerable? Why can't I just be fucking normal?*

Feeling guilty, I take out my phone again and send Nate a text.

> Me
>
> I'm sorry, bro, you know she's a difficult subject for BOTH of us. I don't want to lose you, especially when I finally have you back.
>
> I know I'm an asshole, but I love you, Nathaniel.

> Nate
>
> And I love you too, Gabriel, but this fucking war you have with Bella and her family has to stop! It's been over five years. You need to let go of the hate now. Just move on with your life.

Move on with my life? How? Not everyone managed to slip into the role of playing the perfect little son to the rich parents like he did. I swear to god he has no idea what the fuck I went through. How fucked up my head is. While his fucked up little life ended the day child protective services came and took us away. That was just the start of my journey.

> **Me**
> It's hard when I lost you in the first place because of her.

> **Nate**
> YOU DIDN'T LOSE ME! I'm RIGHT HERE!!! But if you don't give up this vendetta against Bella and her family, you'll push me away.

Shit! Yet again there's gonna be a choice where he's forced to choose between me and the fucked up family we had together or her and his perfect little fantasy. *It won't be me. I've never been the one people stick around for.*

> **Me**
> I'll try.

I grab myself a bottle of beer and light up another smoke, then find myself reaching to message Stacey.

> **Me**
> Hey, what are you up to?

I internally cringe at how pathetic I sound. I don't text first. I never text first. And definitely not something as stupid as 'what you up to' and certainly not within twenty-four hours of seeing them last.

I'm about to put my phone away and chalk this whole thing up to losing my mind. When my phone buzzes, I can't help but rush to open it.

> **Smoking Little Cock Tease**
> Hey, been thinking about last night all morning. It was so damn hot.

Like a moth to a flame, I feel my body set alight.

> **Me**
> Maybe we should do it again? How's tonight sound.

> **Smoking Little Cock Tease**
> No can do, I'm hanging out with some friends tonight. But I can meet you tomorrow. We can meet for breakfast.

Breakfast? Like a date? I don't do dates. Not even breakfast dates. Are breakfast dates even a thing? Maybe it's not a date. But I do want to see her. An idea hits me.

Chapter Thirteen

Stacey

Sitting in the back of the bus on my way to meet Gabe, I can't help re-reading Gabe's message from last night. 'If you're a good girl, maybe I'll eat you for breakfast.' and then nothing since.

I send him a message letting him know I'm about twenty minutes away.

Taking out the compact mirror, I check my hair and makeup one last time. I don't know if he was serious or joking, but just in case I've thrown some spare clothes into my handbag as well as a toothbrush and a baggy top to sleep in. Although, if I get my way there won't be a whole heap of sleeping.

I get off the bus just as a message beeps from my sister.

Twinnie

> Be safe tonight. You barely know this guy. If you need me, text and we'll swing by and save you.

I roll my eyes but can't help but grin. She's only thirty minutes older than me, but she takes those whole eighteen hundred seconds very seriously and believes it's her role and her right to play the big sister card.

Me

> I'll be fine. Have fun with the gang. I'll see you tomorrow.

I load up my GPS and make my way towards O'Malley's Construction where he apparently works. I see a bunch of guys outside, each one looking more jacked and angry than the last. That is until I see an oddly familiar face making his way over to me.

"Nate? What are you doing here?" I ask as he gets closer.

"Me? I work here. What are YOU doing here?"

I feel my cheeks flush as I admit. "I'm waiting for someone, a guy"

"A guy? As in a boyfriend? You're dating one of the knuckleheads that work here?" he asks, looking around and sounding surprised.

"Well, not dating per se," I hesitate, "more like getting to know." *How embarrassing! I'm literally here to hook up with a guy, and I don't even know what to call us. Are we a couple? Friends? Friends with benefits? Who knows. All I know is I can't seem to stay away.*

"Oh...who? Scotty? Davis? Ryan? Please tell me it's not that loser, Evan, because you're far too good for him; he's a total douchebag."

"Erm, no."

"Who then?" Nate asks, scratching his head.

"Him, actually," I lift my chin as I see Gabe walking out of the door. He clocks me and his face turns to a mixture of confusion and thunder.

"Gabe?" Nate gasps. "You're here to see Gabe?" I can't help but notice how wide Nate's eyes are. *Shit does he know something I don't?* I feel my anxiety bubbling at Nate's comment before the anxiety turns to frustration.

Feeling strangely defensive, I react. "Yes. Gabe. And what's wrong with that? He's actually a great guy if you take the time to get to know him," I snap.

"Woah," Nate says, throwing his hands up in surrender. "Believe me, I know better than most what a great guy he can be, I'm just shocked that you know that too," Nate smirks.

"What? So you think I'm not good enough? You think he's some super hot stud and I'm just boring old me, is that it?" I snap back, feeling all my insecurities come to the surface. *Until now I didn't realize quite how much I liked Gabe.*

"Woah, calm down," Nate laughs, throwing his arm around my shoulder. "First of all, if I thought of Gabe as hot I'd be washing my eyes out with soap. And second, I don't think you're boring at all. You're lovely. My brother would be lucky to have someone as kind, caring, and pretty as you on his arm." *Wait, Nate is Gabe's brother??*

"Did you just call me pretty Nate?" I tease with a smirk.

"No, well yes, but no," Nate stutters, obviously embarrassed. "Pretty in a friend way... pretty for Gabe... not me."

"Haha, don't worry Natey boy, your secrets are safe with me. I won't tell Izzy you want a piece of all this," I laugh as I motion up and down my body.

Nate pushes me playfully just as Gabe reaches us.

"What the fuck?" Gabe shouts, stopping our playful banter in its tracks.

"Take your hands off her, Nate." *Was that a growl? Is Gabe upset?*

"Chill, me and Rilez were just having a laugh, isn't that right?" Nate laughs as he shakes his head at his brother.

"Rilez?" Gabe questions.

"Yeah Rilez, you know, isn't that what they call you, Riley? Nate asks, turning to look at me, with a confused expression.

"Her name's Stacey," Gabe snaps, turning to look at me with a murderous gaze.

"No, it's not." I say in confusion when suddenly it dawns on me. "Oh shit, wait…"

"Damn Gabe, you got given a fake name. That's savage!" Nate gives a full body laugh but it soon becomes apparent this is no laughing matter as Nate's face morphs from playful to panicked in a microsecond.

"Gabe, wait! Let me explain," I call as he turns and storms off.

"Shit, sorry Riley." Nate says as I turn to chase after him.

Nate comes running beside me, "I'll talk to him," he offers.

"No, it needs to be me. I'll explain everything later," I reply, as I try to speed up. Somehow despite the fact I'm running and Gabe is walking, he's still so much further ahead of me.

"Fine, but call me if you need me. Or if you need picking up and taking home. I'm just a call away." he shouts as his voice fades into the distance behind me.

I finally catch sight of Gabe heading into the pub at the corner of the street. I follow him inside and after scanning the bar I find him sitting alone in one of the corner booths.

"Let me explain," I beg as I slide in opposite him.

"What, explain how this has all been some big joke? How you and Izzy thought it would be funny to pretend you were someone special?" he huffs as he takes his drink and downs the whole thing in one gigantic gulp. "Bet you and Izzy had a great laugh at my expense."

"Izzy?" I ask, clearly confused. "What's she got to do with anything?"

"Bet it was her that told you about our father. Bet it was her idea to get that guy to hit you when I was watching to see what I'd do next. Bet you all had a great laugh at my expense," Gabe snaps, clearly spiraling. *What the hell is he talking about?* I stare at him looking at his glass with his chest heaving.

Unsure what to do, my only options are to physically slap some sense into him or to do something to distract him and break the spiral. I decide on the latter. Reaching over the table I grab hold of his face and kiss him. At first he resists, keeping his lips tight in defiance, but soon they open and let me in. Gabe reaches out, grabs the back of my hair, and pulls me tighter against him. This kiss is anything but sweet; it's filled with a mixture of hate, anger, and passion. He kisses me so hard that it almost hurts.

I pull away and run my hand up to my mouth and am shocked when I find that my lip is bleeding. Not a lot, but enough that the metallic taste of blood is present when I swallow.

"You bit me, you bastard." I snap.

"You deserved it." He replies back with a smirk. *At least the anger seems to have subsided slightly.*

"You have five minutes to explain," Gabe informs me.

"Fine but not here. Let's go somewhere else." I suggest.

Gabe throws some money down on the table and we head outside.

"Where to?" Gabe asks.

I realize I have no idea where to go next. *I don't really wanna go for a drive with him in this state, but I also don't wanna end up at another motel, well not just yet.* Then an idea hits me. "Follow me."

I lead him down the road to an old abandoned building, slip through the broken fence, and lead him up the rickety staircase until we get to the top.

"We're here," I finally say, opening the door, and carefully placing a nearby brick to stop the door from closing behind us.

"And where is here?" Gabe asks, looking around with that pissed off look he often has.

"My safe space," I say quietly.

"Really? You call this safe?" Gabe laughs as he takes in the site around us. I look around as well, seeing it the way he must see it. The rooftop is old and bare. There are broken and cracked walls around us. Even the safety rail is hanging off.

"Safer than it is out there," I admit as I sit down and point to the world below us.

I look over at Gabe and he has that 'tell me more' look in his eyes as he sits himself beside me. So I take a huge breath and begin.

"The reason why this is my safe place is because when my world was falling apart I had this place to escape to. When I was ten, my mom was diagnosed with breast cancer. My sister Harper stepped up and took it upon herself to become mom's nurse. Dad was wonderful to my mom. He took care of her and took her to all of her appointments. Dad did so many fundraisers to get money for her to fly all the way to the UK for some experimental treatment. Do you know what I did? I broke down and I didn't know how to cope. I didn't know what to do and I couldn't 'fix' my mom or make her cancer go away. So I acted out, I got into trouble daily, I didn't pay attention or care about school. I became a little shit to everyone."

"And what happened next?" Gabe asks and I can hear the sincerity in his voice.

"Thankfully it worked. She was given some experimental drug that shrank the cancer enough that doctors were able to operate. She had to have a full mastectomy but they say the cancer's gone. She gets checked regularly, but knock on wood, she's been given the all clear for the last five years."

"She was very lucky," Gabe says as he reaches out and wipes away the tear rolling down my cheek.

"Spoken like someone who understands," I say leaning into him.

"Unfortunately, my mother wasn't so lucky. Her cancer was fast and aggressive. She went from happy and vibrant, to a shell of her former self in the blink of an eye." Gabe admits and I can hear how his voice breaks as he speaks.

"How old were you?" I ask.

"Eight, poor Nate wasn't even five," he says, standing and turning away.

Standing to join him I add, "You were only a little kid too, that must have been unbearable."

"You have no idea," he scoffs. Sadness mixed with anger rolling off of him.

We sit back down, letting our legs hang off the edge of the roof as we both sit in silence.

"So you never explained how this became your safe space," Gabe finally breaks the silence by asking.

"This used to belong to my parents. At one point this was the place to be, this whole roof used to be covered in fairy lights." I say as I stand again and begin motioning to different areas of nothingness. "We had a bar here... and over here was a small dance floor. And this here used to have a pool table." I say pointing to the corner of the roof.

"So what happened to it all?" Gabe asks as he comes to join me.

"Well when my Mom got sick, my dad stopped working. Missed a few payments and the bank foreclosed on the business. And it's been sitting empty ever since. When I was a kid I liked to come here and pretend everything was fine. I would just pretend that Dad was still working in the kitchen and Mom was talking to all the customers."

"I get it, kind of. When Mom died I used to spray her perfume on my pillow just so when I woke up I could imagine, even for just a moment, that she was still here." Gabe says sadly as he stares off into space.

"And what about your dad?" I ask, reaching out to touch his hand, but he pulls it away as if I burned him.

"He was a sadistic bastard who died. Hopefully the bastard is rotting in hell," he snaps back his brow furrowing. The change in his demeanor is so sudden it's like he morphed into a whole different person. Two minutes ago he was sweet and caring, now he's cold and distant.

"Anyway can we go, it's fucking freezing up here," Gabe snaps.

"Wait here," I say before running back downstairs. I head towards the old cloakroom that is completely bare. I reach for the light, but of course it's been years since this place had power so I pull out my phone flashlight. Eventually, I find what I'm looking for, the old wooden ottoman. Inside I find the zip locked blankets Mom kept here for emergencies.

Since our parents often worked late, me and Harper would regularly fall asleep waiting. So Mom kept spare pillows and blankets in zip locked bags so we could create makeshift beds on the comfy sofa that was in the corner of the restaurant. Grabbing two blankets and pillows I make my way back upstairs.

"Here," I say, handing Gabe a set, before carefully placing mine down on the floor so I can stare up at the stars.

Chapter Fourteen

Gabe

I wrap the blanket around me and watch as Stacey, or whatever her fucking name is, takes hers and lays it down on the dirty floor. I watch as she stares up at the sky, seeming peaceful. *How the fuck can she be peaceful after just baring her soul like that?* I make my way over and sit down beside her.

She moves to lay her head on my lap, and I let her. She continues to stare up at the sky, neither of us saying a word. But we both seem to enjoy the tranquility. That is until her phone rings, breaking the silence. The first time she allows it to ring out, not even making a move to answer it but when it rings again just a few seconds later she sits up, rummages in her handbag, and pulls it out.

"Hey Nate... no I'm fine... I'm sure."

I feel my blood pulsing, the urge to rip the phone out of her hands and find out why my brother's calling her is overwhelming. I stand up and begin pacing around.

I hear her laughing, and flirting with my brother on the phone so I start making my way over. "Anyway, I've got to go. See you both tomorrow."

"What the fuck Stacey?" I snap. "Oh wait, that isn't even your fucking name is it? What was it? Miley? Or shall I just call you whore?" I scream, so upset that I'm shaking and my heart is pounding.

Her face morphs into a mixture of shock and anger. "What did you just call me?" she demands.

"Whore! It seems fitting for someone who sucks my dick when she has a boyfriend. Then apparently flirts with my own brother in front of me." I shout, letting all the anger inside spew out.

I see the effect my words have on her, she looks like I've physically hit her. *Good, that's what she gets for hurting me.* But then I see that familiar fire behind her eyes, before an almighty 'slap' echoes through the air as I feel the sting on my cheek. The bitch slapped me, and hard.

"You're a fucking asshole Gabe, and I hate you!" she screams as I see her eyes well with tears.

"At least I own who I am. I'm not a fucking liar. Some dirty, little slut who pretends to be 'little Miss Sweet and Innocent'. No wonder your boyfriend didn't want you anymore!" I shout as she storms away.

My words obviously hit a nerve as she spins around and marches right back to the point that I'm forced to look down. She pokes me with her finger. "I'm not a fucking liar!" she shouts back. "Sure, I may have given you a fake name the first time we met, but that was an accident. I was out with friends using a fake name. Playing some stupid game. How the fuck was I supposed to know the stranger at the bar would turn into more?" she says looking sheepish and embarrassed.

"So you admit this whole thing was some pathetic little game then?" I snap again and peer at her.

"NO, you fucking asshole!" she screams, her face so close to mine now that I can feel her breath against my face. "Getting you to buy us a drink was the dare, everything else that's been said or done has been real. I like you Gabe, at least I did before..."

I cut her words off by grabbing her for a kiss. At first, she tries to push me away before giving in. Both of us kiss with so much anger and passion.

Both of our hands begin roaming. I grip her hard by the waist to hold her in place whereas her hands find their way into my hair, pulling and tugging as our kiss becomes more frenzied. I move my hands down to her ass so I can lift her. Her legs instinctively wrap around my waist as I spin us around to pin her against the wall. In this position her dress has ridden up high enough that all that's stopping my raging erection from forcing its way inside is my jeans and her thin, lacey panties.

I thrust myself against her and a breathy whimper escapes her lips. "Do you like that? Do you, my little slut?" I growl as I undo my jeans letting my cock spring out.

"Hmm I've had better," she smirks. But the thought of anyone else fucking her, getting to watch her body shake the way it did last week fills me with a strange jealousy. Without thinking I thrust against her hard, not caring as I feel my cock push against her opening and slide in. That is until I hear a pained wimper. *Fuck!* I pull back so quickly I almost drop her.

"You weren't lying about being a virgin, were you?" I gasp.

"I told you, I'm not a liar," she winces.

Putting her down I force myself back into my jeans and turn to leave, but she grabs hold of my arm.

"Stop shutting me out, Gabe," she whispers as she turns me around so I'm forced to face her.

Avoiding her eyes, I whisper, "I don't know how to do this. Your first time should be with someone you love. Someone who loves you back. Not some dirty fuck on a rooftop, with an asshole like me."

My mind thinks back to my first time with some woman I can barely even picture. High on a mixture of drugs and booze in some dirty basement somewhere.

"What if I don't want love and flowers? What if I just want this? Right here, with you?" she says softly as she reaches up to caress my face.

Leaning down, I take my hand and lift her chin to kiss her. I pull her body against mine to deepen the kiss, before finally lifting her and carrying her over to where the blanket is lying on the ground.

The whole time she makes no attempt to break our kiss or stop me so I carefully lay her down on the blanket. *This is all new to me. I've slept with more girls than I can count. But never like this.* I'm not a soft and sweet kind of guy. I don't do loving and soft kisses. I don't do romance and handholding and I definitely don't do it gently. *Yet for her, I want to do all those things and more.*

I slide my hand up her bare legs which she parts for me instantly, and then begin kissing her neck.

"Mmm, yeah," she moans as I carefully slide my fingers inside of her. I remove the straps of her dress and bra, freeing one breast and I begin kissing and nipping it gently. The moans coming from her may be my undoing. I try to calm myself down because my cock is trying to jailbreak out of my pants and I might blow before this gets much further.

My fingers continue to slip in and out of her tight, moist heat. I can feel how wet she is for me so I undo my jeans, wanting nothing more than to fuck the life out of her.

"Are you sure?" I ask as I remove her underwear and line my thick, aching cock with her opening.

"I'm sure," she confirms.

Slowly I push myself inside, being as slow and gentle as I can. *God this is excruciating.* I begin thrusting ever so slightly, terrified of hurting her any more. This continues for a couple of minutes, but it's almost impossible to hold myself back. A few small moans leave her mouth, but it's clear this isn't exactly going great.

"Gabe, " she finally whispers, as I continue to thrust into her at a snail's pace.

"What?"

"I'm not some delicate doll that's going to break you know. You can move," she laughs.

"But I don't want to hurt you, I'm trying to be gentle. I don't really know how to do this." I reply, pushing back to look at her.

"I never said I wanted gentle. I want you to fuck me like you actually want to. Fuck me like you mean it. Fuck me like I'm yours," she whispers back.

Leaning down so my head is beside her ear I growl, "Be careful what you wish for, because once I fuck this tight little pussy, it will always be mine."

Her breath hitches at my words and I know that she likes that idea. *My dirty little slut likes the idea of being mine. Likes the thought of all the dirty things I want to do to her.*

I wrap my hands around her throat as I thrust inside of her again. A gasp and moan leaves her lips.

"Last chance my beautiful, little slut; last chance to say stop before I destroy you," I growl into her ear.

"Destroy me," she pants back and with that, I thrust into her hard.

"Fuck!" she screams out, just as I feel some resistance.

Pulling back slightly I remove my hand from her throat and instead move it to her cheek. "Do you need me to stop?" I ask softly.

"No," she grunts back but it's clear she's in pain. *Thank fuck! I don't know if I could stop, even if I tried.* So I bend down and kiss her. I start off soft, keeping my lower half as still as possible to allow her to get used to the feel of me inside of her. As our kiss deepens I begin to grind my hips against her.

As we continue to kiss I begin to thrust in and out of her, getting more and more turned on as her moans get louder and louder.

"Fuck Sta..."

"Riley," she moans.

"Fuck, Riley, you feel so good," I grunt.

I break our kiss to lean back on my knees to gain more control. I grab her by the hips, lifting them slightly so I can get even deeper. Gripping her hips, I pull her against me so her body meets mine thrust for thrust. I can tell she's straddling the line between pleasure and pain so I start rubbing my finger on her swollen nub and as soon as I do, she cries out in pleasure. "Oh fuck," she shouts, just as I feel her body begin to convulse and grip me tighter. "Fuuuck," she cries out, as I feel her come. *I can't believe how beautiful she looks coming undone on my cock.*

Watching her in the heat of her bliss is all I need before I'm squirting my load inside her. *Fuck I'm not wearing a condom.* My mind suddenly reminds me. *Fuck!!*

I pull out and roll over beside her. "That was...wow," she sighs from beside me, looking at me with that freshly fucked blush.

"We need to take you to the pharmacy," I snap in reply. Not being able to think of anything other than my own stupidity. *I always make sure to wear protection. ALWAYS.*

"The pharmacy?" she questions, rolling over and leaning up on her elbow to look at me.

"Yeah, for the morning after pill or something," I huff out, feeling the panic rising. *Oh my God! I can't be a father; this can't be happening.*

She leans over to retrieve her underwear and sucks in a slight breath before squeezing her legs together. *Fuck did I hurt her? I know I wasn't exactly gentle but, surely it shouldn't hurt now? Should it?*

But instead of her face morphing into panic like mine probably is, she just smirks. "Don't worry, I'm on the pill. Have been for almost a year."

My worries instantly ease and I almost feel relieved until it dawns on me, "Wait, for him? You went on the pill so you could fuck HIM?!" I shout.

"Well, no, I went on the pill for me. But I guess sure, I also thought he and I would eventually do it," she shrugs.

"Well, did you? Did you fuck him?" I snap. She just stares at me for a moment, before reality dawns on me.

"Oh right," I mumble, feeling my cheeks heat up.

"Jealous much?" she laughs. As she playfully pushes me.

Am I jealous? I fuck girls all the time. And I know they sleep around too, so why am I acting all weird now. It's not like she's my girlfriend or anything.

"I'm not jealous," I snap. " I don't care who you fuck," I lie.

"Oh really?" she asks, eyeing me suspiciously. "You wouldn't care if I touched another guy like this?" she asks as she reaches out and runs her hands over the bulge in my pants.

"No," I snap, stifling a moan.

"Oh good, so it would be fine if I did this too?" she asks as she unzips my jeans and slides her hand inside, and begins to stroke my traitorous dick who's loving every touch.

"No," I growl. *God that feels so good.*

"Oh good, so it would be okay with you if I did this with them too?" she asks as she removes my dick, opens her mouth, and bends down to suck it.

I reach out and grab her hair pulling it back enough that my dick falls from her mouth with a 'pop' sound.

"You dare put another guy's dick in your beautiful fucking mouth and I'll kill him. I'll find him and fucking kill him." I growl as I stare at her, letting her know this isn't some empty threat.

"See, I told you, you were jealous," she laughs. And not just a small smirk of a laugh but a full on 'I know I've got you exactly where I want you' belly laugh.

I release her hair, "You think that's funny don't you?"

"Yep," she giggles, "I do actually."

"You're such a fucking brat, Riley," I answer back, but let a small smile form on my lips.

"Yep, but apparently I'm your brat... or is that your little slut? I lose track," she smirks back as she cocks her head and bites her lip.

Pushing her down so she falls across my lap, exposing her almost bare ass, I swing my hand back and spank her, hard.

"Ouch!" she shouts as my hand connects.

"You're whatever the fuck I tell you to be, Fireball" I growl back as I spank her again, this time slightly softer than before, but enough that I hear her take a sharpe intake of breath. "Enough," she begs, her voice sounding more like a whimper, before I rub my hand soothingly across the part that's now flaming red. This time she moans when I do it and I feel her rub on my leg, trying to get some friction. I sit her up, "Behave," I growl and kiss her softly.

"How about we go for a drink?" I suggest as I carefully move her so I can stand. "Come on, I know just the place."

Chapter Fifteen

Riley

"Come on, I know just the place," he grins. He stretches out his hands and helps me stand. *This guy is a walking enigma; one moment he's sweet and caring, the next he's standoffish and shut down. But my favorite of all is the times in between - when he's dirty, dangerous, and demanding.*

We make our way down and back through the hole in the fence leading to the street. This time though, I'm hyper aware of every bend and movement I make, and the uncomfortable feeling it gives me.

"This way," he says as he walks ahead, causing me to have to speed up to keep up with him. As I do, I feel the material of my dress rubbing against the throbbing pain on my ass. *That spanking was hot and unexpected but damn does it sting like hell now.*

As I get closer I attempt to slide my hand into his, but he pulls it away as if I'd just burned him. I move back in surprise, but he moves his hand, grabs me by the waist, and pulls me back beside him. But he takes his hand away again once. *What's wrong with his guy? He wants me close enough to touch but doesn't actually want to touch me. Is he ashamed of me or something? I know he's hotter than me, but he definitely seemed interested just a few minutes ago.*

We make our way to the pub, the same one we met in for that matter. *Is this his hangout?* As we get to the door, another guy is coming out and politely holds the door open. "Thank you," I say as I attempt to walk past but Gabe loops his arm around me and pulls me back, causing me to almost fall backward.

"I got it," he snaps as he places his hand on the open door and throws daggers at the poor guy who was holding it first.

The guy takes one look at Gabe and then scurries away. "Really?" I say as I roll my eyes and walk in. Scanning the bar I look for a place to sit.

"Over here," he says as he leads me to a secluded part of the bar.

He sits down first and I attempt to sit down beside him but as the wooden stool touches my ass it stings, causing me to suck in air at the pain. *My ass is throbbing.* "I'll be back in a sec," I say, excusing myself and heading towards the bathroom. As I do I run some paper towel under the water, soaking it, and taking it into the toilet with me. Lifting my dress and carefully dabbing it against my sore ass. The whole thing is on fire, I gently run my hand against it and can feel the heat resonating from what I can only assume is a handprint.

"Riley?" I hear from outside the door. I stop and listen. Surely it's another Riley they're calling.

"Riley," the unmistakable male voice says again. I lower my dress and slowly open the door. As soon as I do, Gabe pushes the door open and walks right in, as if this is the men's bathroom, and for a second, I wonder if I made a mistake and went into the wrong one.

I step back to allow him into the tiny stall since it's obvious I have no choice. He takes one look at the scrunched up wet paper towel in my hand and smirks.

"Thought you might want this," he says, holding a towel with what I assume is ice. "Turn around and lift up your dress," he whispers into my ear, causing a shiver to run through my body.

I do as I'm told, turning, lifting my dress, and bending over the back of the toilet. I feel the cold material hit my skin. At first it takes me by surprise, making me jump. "You're fine, trust me," Gabe whispers as he places his hand on my tummy and holds me in place as he pushes the coldness against me again. *It feels like heaven.*

"Does that feel good?" he asks as he leans over and places a kiss just below my shoulder.

"So good," I purr back. I feel his hand begin to slide from my tummy lower. "No, no more" I whine, knowing I can't physically take another pounding tonight.

He removes both his hands entirely for a moment before one makes its way back to my hip. "Gaabe," I warn, as he takes the towel and places it down beside me

"Shhh. Trust me," he whispers. Before I feel a coldness touch my skin. *Ice, he's holding an ice cube.* He runs the ice cube slowly down the inside of my panties and pushes it against my slit. "Gabe, stop," I moan, while secretly praying he doesn't. He begins gliding the ice all around my opening before slowly pushing it inside. He uses his finger to expertly massage and soothe the stinging inside. I feel the other hand snake around under me as he reaches for my throat again. *Damn, I love when he does this.*

He grabs me and pulls me back against him so that I'm standing upright with my whole body pressed against him.

"Let me take care of you," he whispers against my ear before he places a soft kiss on my cheek. *I don't know why but somehow that kiss on the cheek feels more intimate than any of the other things he's done to me tonight.*

"Let's get a drink," he finally says as he removes his fingers and pulls my dress back down as if nothing happened.

He turns and walks out of the stall, not even bothering to look if anyone was around first. I follow behind him and am glad to see that we appear to be alone.

We're about to walk out the door when another girl walks in.

"Oh, hey Gabe," the girl smirks, not seeming even slightly surprised to see him in the women's toilets.

"Kelly," he snaps in a low voice.

"Oh, looks like you've found yourself a new, little bathroom bunny. She's pretty," she says sweetly, while eying me up and down like shit on her shoe.

"Bathroom bunny?" *Shit did I say that out loud?* I know I did when a sadistic smile forms on her lips. "Yep, bathroom bunny. That's what you call us isn't it Gabe? The girls you fuck in the bathroom and then discard like garbage.

"Fuck off, Kelly, you're just some dirty whore," he says as he reaches out and grabs my arm, attempting to pull me out of the room behind him.

"That's not what you were saying when you were fucking me right here last night," she snaps back sounding oddly proud of herself.

Her words feel like a literal punch to the gut. *Gabe clearly has a type.* Like me, she's blonde although her hair is clearly not naturally that color. She's skinnier than me, way skinnier. *Is this what he's into, a walking Barbie doll? Does he think I'm too big? I feel like one of my thighs is probably bigger than both of hers combined.*

"You fucked her here last night?" I gasp, pulling out of his grip.

"Sure did Sugar, and not just me, but my friend, too," she grins. "He fucked me right there in that same bathroom, then we went back to my place where he fucked my friend, too."

The tears pool in my eyes as I run straight out the door.

"Wait, Riley," I hear from behind me but I keep running. I make it outside and realize I have nowhere to go. "Riley!" Gabe shouts again, so I duck down between two parked cars. I watch him run past and then around the corner and out of site. Taking my phone from my purse, I call the only person I can think to -Harper.

"Hey, Rilez," Harper sing-songs.

"Harper, I'm outside Saint's Bar. It's near the old restaurant. Come and get me now," I plead to her on a sob.

"I'm on my way now," she says without hesitation.

She arrives a few minutes later with Izzy and Nate.

"You were quick," I say as I climb into the back of the car. As my ass hits the seat a new wave of discomfort rushes through me. *Seriously, how hard did he hit my ass? It feels like the whole thing is on fire.* I naturally squirm to try and get away from the pressure I'm feeling, having to sit at a slight angle just so I'm not resting all my weight against the side that throbs.

"Yeah, we were just around the corner. Nate wanted to take us to one of the restaurants there," Izzy says as she turns around to look at me.

"Woah, what happened Riley?" Izzy asks, taking in my tear drenched, make-up-smeared, and bruised face.

"Oh nothing, just a crap date," I say, unconvincingly.

"What, with that Justin guy?" she asks. Thankfully, she doesn't know Justin since she and Nate are pretty new to the group. Had she been with Ava like usual though, Ava would have dragged me back inside until I told her exactly which guy made me cry.

I see Nate's eyes staring at me sympathetically in the rearview mirror.

"Err yeah, Justin," I lie and avoid the eyes I feel on me.

Nate drives me and Harper home in silence. "Thanks for the ride, Nate," I say as I climb out.

"Anytime, and I mean that - anytime," he says, emphasizing the last word.

"So, do you want to tell me what really happened?" Harper asks as she throws her arm around me.

"Let's just get inside first," I say quietly in return.

"I'll grab the ice cream," she says as she lets go of me as I unlock the door. "I'll be down in a sec."

I run downstairs to our basement conversion joint bedroom, strip my clothes off, and jump in the shower, letting the water wash away the now dirty feeling I have on my skin. I can't help but wince as the water beats down on my already painful and bruised ass. The tears continue to stream down my face as I scrub and scrub at my skin, hoping to scrub away the feel of his hands. *I can't believe I let him have my virginity. I'm just another notch in his belt. I can't believe he used me. I can't believe I was starting to have feelings for him - I thought he was different, but he's not.*

A knock at the door jolts me from my thoughts and I peer around the shower curtain to see Harper's head peeking through the doorway.

"I'm not looking, my eyes are closed. But I'm just letting you know the ice cream is melting," she shouts, despite the fact there are less than ten steps between the doorway and the shower.

"I'm not deaf Harp, I'm coming out now," I reply, laughing when she attempts to leave and ends up hitting her head on the door frame.

"Oh and Harper," I call just as she's leaving. "Can you grab me an aspirin? I've got a terrible migraine coming."

Painkillers may not be able to ease the emotional pain, but even if they're able to ease some of the physical pain, just enough that I can sleep and hopefully wake up and realize this whole night was just a terrible dream.

I climb out, dry off, wrap the thick purple robe around myself, and head out. I see Harper sitting on my bed with a huge tub of cookie dough ice cream and two spoons.

"So, what happened?" Harper asks, eying me sympathetically.

"Remember that guy I told you about?" I begin.

"Gabe?"

"Yeah." I sigh heavily, "Well turns out Gabe is Nate's older brother," I continue hesitantly.

"Shit, you're kidding me. Did you know? Before today I mean?"

"No, I only found out when I went to meet him tonight."

"Talk about keeping it close to the family," she laughs. But when I don't laugh back, her face drops again. "So what happened next?"

I tell her everything that happened, about the name debacle, about taking him to the restaurant, and that I opened up about Mom's cancer scare. Harper nods along but doesn't say much.

"Okay, so that sounds mostly good," she says cautiously.

"Yeah, it was until..." I continue, telling her about losing my virginity, although obviously, I summarize most of it and definitely don't tell her about the nasty things he did or said to me. I can feel myself blushing just thinking about those things.

"And that's where it all went downhill..." I go on to tell her about the girl in the bar, although obviously I don't tell her we saw her coming out of the toilet together.

"What? That sleazy little shit!" she shouts. "He's the worst. He doesn't deserve you, Riley. Dump his ass and find yourself a new guy! You know Ashton from science has always had a thing for you."

"It's not that easy Harper," I sob. "I think I like him, like really, truly like him." I look at her, pleading with my eyes to get her to understand.

"What's to like, Riley? That guy is a monster," she snaps.

"He's not a monster, he's just... well... a little bit broken," I huff, feeling this unnatural need to defend him.

"You're beyond help, Rilez; first Damon, then Jax, now HIM. You've never found a broken villain you haven't fallen in love with," she says as she rolls her eyes. I could hear the disappointment and something akin to disgust lacing her voice. My stomach drops. *I need to get her on another topic. I can't sit here and listen to her poor opinion of him. It hurts too much.*

"Yeah, but the villains are so much hotter." I grin, ignoring her tone and trying to lighten the mood.

"How about I distract you from this villain with a fictional one, Jax or Damon?" Harper laughs as she walks over and grabs the remote.

"Hmmm, I think a bit of Damon is called for."

"Good, means I get to drool over Stefan then," Harper says as she throws herself onto her own bed.

The intro is just playing when there's a knock at the door. "I'll get it," Harper shouts.

Chapter Sixteen

Nate

I drove Bella home and agreed to have a coffee with her and her grandparents. But the whole time all I'm thinking about is how sad and hurt Riley looked. I knew that her going on a date with someone like Gabe was a bad idea, but I never suspected it would be that bad of an idea. I know Gabe can be an ass and he's always been a bit of a womanizer, but I also know that deep down he's a good guy. *Isn't he?* But that looked like much more than a bad date. *Surely he wouldn't have physically hurt her... would he?*

"I'm really sorry baby, but I've got to go. I've had a great time and I'll see you tomorrow," I say as I lean over, quickly glance around to see if her grandparents are within eyesight, and steal a kiss.

"Oh no! Can't you stay just a little while longer?" Bella whines as she pouts in that cute way of hers.

"I really can't, Princess," I say softly as I brush her beautiful brown locks away from her face, so that I can cup her cheek.

But I'll see you tomorrow, straight from work, and I'll take us somewhere nice."

"Fine," she sulks.

She walks me out to the door and standing up on her toes leans up and gives me another sweet kiss. I tear myself away from her with a moan, my junk aching for me to stay so I force myself to walk to my ride.

I turn and wave goodbye before getting in my car and driving back towards Riley and Harper's house. As soon as I pull up, I make my way to the door and knock. A few seconds later, Harper answers.

"Oh hey Harper, is Riley here, please?" I say. But she pushes me back and closes the front door behind us both.

"Now, I've got no problem with you. And I love Izzy. I think you're both great together. But I suggest you keep that fucking brother of yours away from my sister; otherwise, there's gonna be some trouble," Harper snaps, and I'm shocked. Usually out of the four girls, Harper is the sweetest, calmest, and most laid back, but right now she's more like a mama bear protecting her cubs.

I sigh, "What happened Harper?"

"Let's put it this way, he fooled my sister into giving him something special, and then betrayed her." *What the fuck?*

"Shit, did he hurt her?" I ask, as I think back to the marks I saw on her face that looked like more than just make up.

"Of course he hurt her, she wasn't that upset for nothing," Harper snaps again.

"I mean physically, did he hurt her physically?" *Please say he didn't. Please.*

"No, nothing like that. But I don't want to see him anywhere near her again. She's been through enough shit she doesn't need a jackass like him as well."

I nod my head in agreement, not sure what else to do or say.

"Oh and Nate, if I ever find out you hurt Bella like this, I won't think twice about shooting the both of you... I know where daddy keeps his hunting rifle," she says with an evil smile.

"I can promise you, hand on my heart. I'd give up my life before I ever hurt Bella," I admit, meaning every single word.

"Good" Harper smiles, a more genuine one this time. "Because I kind of like you. Plus it would be a shame to make both Izzy and Riley help me bury the bodies," she laughs playfully.

"What about Ava? Wouldn't she be there too? I joke back.

"Oh yeah Ava would be there too, she's been our ride or die bestie since freshman year. But she'd be loving every minute of it. She'd be the one holding the matches when the fire trucks showed up."

"Damn, you women are crazy," I tease.

"Yep and don't you forget it." Harper laughs. "But I mean it, if I see that brother of yours anywhere near Riley again, he'll be pissing through a straw."

"Hey Nate, is everything okay?" Riley asks as she opens the door.

"Yep, Izzy just thought she'd left her keys in my handbag, but nope, sorry Nate," Harper lies.

"No worries. They're probably in the car somewhere," I reply as I turn and leave.

I drive home, park the car, and make my way inside. "Gabe," I shout, but get no answer. "Gabe, are you here?" I shout louder this time but still get no answer. I make my way to the kitchen and see broken bottles on the floor. *For fuck's sake!* I pick up the bits I can and then get out the vacuum to clean up the rest. I'm just finishing vacuuming and putting it away when I hear the roar of Gabe's bike coming down the path.

"What the fuck Gabe?" I shout as I open the door and see him staggering off his motorbike. "Are you drunk?" I shout as he brushes past, not needing to answer since I can smell the liquor on him.

"Leave me alone, I've had a shitty night," he snaps.

"You've had a shitty night? What about Riley?" I snap back pushing him.

"What do you fucking know?" he slurs.

"I know I had to rescue her after you abandoned her," I snap back.

"Wait, she's okay? She's safe?" he slurs, sounding almost grateful as he grabs hold of my sweater.

"No thanks to you," I say, pushing him. Gabe stumbles back, losing his balance and falling into the wall.

"For fuck's sake Gabe, how much have you had to drink?" I ask, helping him to his feet.

"Get off me," he slaps my hands away as he steadies himself before storming back outside. Lighting a cigarette he slumps down on the grass.

Heading over to join him I sit down. "What happened tonight, Gabe?" I ask, this time much calmer than before.

"Nothing!" he snaps. "Well something happened because Riley called me crying, begging me to come and save her," I reply. I mean that's not exactly true, she called Harper, who just so happened to be with me and Bella. But he doesn't need to know that yet.

"And why the fuck did she call you?" he slurs. "What gives you the right to rescue my girl?"

"Your girl? Really Gabe? That's not how you should treat any girl, let alone 'your' girl," I reply, feeling the anger bubbling back up to the surface.

"What would you know? You're a fucking virgin; you've never even had a girl," Gabe snaps back, voice laced with venom.

"Just because I haven't had sex with anyone doesn't mean I don't know what it means to devote myself to someone."

"Oh yeah I forgot, Princess fucking Isabella." *I hate the way he says her name like it's some sort of joke to him.*

"Yeah, and I've been much more loyal and devoted to her than you could ever be. I'd never make her cry, I'd never hurt her the way you did Riley tonight. Riley's a good girl, she deserves a good guy..." I say before Gabe interrupts.

"And you don't think I know that? You don't think I feel guilty about taking her virginity?" he snaps. "You think I don't realize that's supposed to be something special? Everything would have been fine if it wasn't for that whore, Kelly."

"Kelly? The girl from the other week. The one we went to dinner with? I thought you said she didn't mean anything to you? Wasn't she just a friend?" I ask, feeling confused wondering where she fits into this whole thing.

"Friends isn't really the word I'd use," he admits. "More like an easy lay I call when I'm horny and desperate." He must see my face screw up in disgust because he adds, "It works for us both. Neither of us cares for the other - we fuck each other, and we fuck other people. It works."

"If you say so," I shrug, not really wanting to hear anymore.

"How was I supposed to know she'd go and tell Riley?" Gabe questions.

"Tell Riley what?" I ask, feeling more confused by the minute.

"That I fucked her and her friend just last night," he says matter of factly.

"Wait, you had sex with Kelly? And her friend? Both of them? Last Night? Then you went on a date and slept with Riley tonight?" I gasp.

"Yes, fucking hell Nate, keep up," he huffs, rolling his eyes at me like I'm the problem. "Me and Kelly are… friends with benefits shall we say. We meet up for sex when we feel like it. Last night she invited me out and we went back to her place for a threesome…"

"You're disgusting!" I spit, feeling genuinely disgusted to be his brother at this moment.

"Oh grow the fuck up Nate. As I was saying, I had fun with Kelly and her friend last night. Came home. Then I met Riley, although I thought her name was Stacey at that point, I assumed it would be just sex again but it kind of evolved."

"Evolved?" I ask, confused by his sudden vagueness.

"I don't fucking know what you call it. We met up, had fun, talked, shared shit, laughed..."

"So you went on a date," I clarify.

"Whatever, we went on a date." Gabe rolls his eyes, using air quotes like the word 'date' is completely made up.

"Yeah, then we fucked. Well we didn't really fuck, well I guess we technically did. But we didn't just fuck I guess..." Gabe mumbles as he takes out another cigarette and begins smoking it. "...Yeah, we did that, then I tried to be nice to her - like care for her and shit."

"Gabe, how many people have you slept with?" I question, not really wanting to know the answer. But wanting to confirm my suspicion.

"What like this week or this year?" he asks, sounding confused.

"Okay, how about this, how many people have you dated?" I ask, taking a deep breath.

"Dated? None. I don't date," Gabe says incredulously.

"Gabe, " I say quietly. "You met up with her and spent the whole evening chatting, laughing, and getting to know each other. Then you had sex. And don't even try to lie and tell me she's not the girl I've heard you talking to late at night. Tonight was definitely a date."

"Wait, did she think that?" Gabe gasps as if the idea had never even occurred to him.

"Gabe, she came all the way to meet you from work. You did everything else we spoke about. And then had sex. She one hundred percent thought it was a date." I say, giving him a playful push. *How can he be this clueless?*

"Is that why she let me, you know?... She's a virgin like you, well, I guess she was before tonight," he laughs while shaking his head in disbelief.

"Gabe, I'm not talking about that with you. She's my friend. Plus it's just no," I say, shuddering. *When the fuck did I become the big brother in this family?*

"Fine then, would YOU sleep with someone? Just a random person you weren't dating?" he asks, eyeing me up.

"No," I say, shaking my head. "And neither would most people."

"Ooh," he says, taking out his phone. "Should I call her? Or text maybe?"

"Maybe a text would be better since you're slurring your words," I suggest while rolling my eyes. "But be nice, Gabe. Riley's a good girl and she doesn't deserve to be hurt." I gently remind him.

I watch him text then obviously delete and start again. "Arrgg! I don't know what to write," he says finally.

"Just keep it short, apologize and explain," I suggest.

"Fine, but I need to piss first."

He heads inside, coming out a few minutes later with two opened beers.

"Here," he says, offering one to me while taking a sip from the other.

"I don't drink, remember."

"Oh shit, yeah. Weird. More for me then."

He goes back to messaging while he drinks his beers. I text back and forth with Bella a few times, making arrangements for our date tomorrow. I'm interrupted by Gabe tapping me on the shoulder. "How's this?" he says, thrusting his phone into my face.

"Let's see," I say, taking it from him to read.

-To Riley, Sorry I took your virginity then made you cry. Sorry I made you cum in the same bathroom I've made hundreds of girls cum before, but none of them meant anything. Kelly is just a whore I let suck my dick sometimes when I'm bored. She's a bitch; forget her. Let's meet up soon- Gabe.

I can't believe my eyes. Swinging out my hand, I attempt to punch him in the legs but instead I hit him right in the balls.

"You bastard!" he cries out as he drops down clutching his nuts. "What was that for?"

"Please, for the love of fucking Satan, tell me you didn't actually send that?!" I snap.

"No," he coughs. "I wanted to get you to read it first, why what's wrong with it?" Gabe looks over at me with confusion written all over his face.

"What's wrong with it? What's wrong with it, Gabe? Fucking everything!" I say as I throw the phone at him and walk away. "She's better off without you if you honestly think that's acceptable," I huff, throwing my hands in the air.

"Nate, wait. Wait!" he says as he runs over to me still clutching his balls.

"Help me. I think she might be special.... Well not special but different," he fumbles, clearly embarrassed and seemingly out of his element.

"Special or different? Which one is it?" I say turning to look at what I can only describe as a puppy in the pound sort of look.

"I don't know," he admits, looking down at the floor. "But I want more than just sex . . . I think," he mumbles softly as he kicks up dirt.

"Fine," I say, snatching the phone out of his hand.

"So you'll help me?" he says, sounding unusually hopeful.

"No..." I see his face drop. "...but I will help her. She deserves some sort of apology for tonight. You, you need to decide what the fuck you want and how the fuck to earn back her trust."

–Hey Riley, I'm beyond sorry for tonight. You don't deserve anything that happened. I know I hurt you and for that I'm beyond sorry. But I want you to know that what happened meant something to me. You mean something to me. I'm so sorry for what Kelly said to you. I'd like to say it's a lie, but unfortunately then I'd be lying too. I know I don't deserve your forgiveness but I'm going to try and earn it anyway. -Gabe

"Here," I snap as I thrust the phone back into his hand before heading into my room and closing the door.

Chapter Seventeen

Gabe

I head to bed, re-reading Nate's message again and again. *He made me sound like a pathetic little bitch.*

I drift off to sleep and wake up somewhere around 4 a.m. Reaching for my phone I unlock it and look straight at the messages. No reply.

I call her phone and she answers on the fourth ring "Riley, it's Gabe..." I manage to say before the line goes dead. *Strange.* I try again this time she answers on the second ring. "Riley, it's Ga.." again the phone goes dead. *Wait, is she hanging up on me?* I try one last time and this time she answers straight away. "Gabe, I don't want to talk to you, goodbye." And the phone goes dead again. I try again and it goes straight to voicemail, letting me know she's either blocked me or turned her phone off.

I roll back over and fall back to sleep. When I wake up later I try her again but it's clear she's blocked my number as it doesn't even let me leave a message now; it just tells me the number hasn't been reached.

"Nate?" I call as I make it to the kitchen. "Nate you in here?" I ask as I bang on the bathroom door. But he's nowhere to be seen. Getting out my phone I pull up Facebook, hoping to message her on there. But no matter how many times I type in her name I can't find her. I check out Nate's profile since I know she was tagged in a picture on his, but the tag appears to have left. *Fuck, did she block me from there, as well? Can you even block someone you're not friends with?* I scroll through Nate's pictures. The ones of him and Princess Isabella, and find her page. There are videos taken today of her, Nate, Riley and a few others all at the beach. I look through the pictures and find one of Riley on her own, sitting and reading under an umbrella. She's wearing that same swimsuit she wore the first time we hung out. I take a screenshot of it, then crop out the background and assign the picture to her contact.

Next, I crack open a beer and put on the TV. I try to distract myself with my favorite show but keep feeling this irrational annoyance every time I see Jax mother-fucking Teller, and remember how much Riley liked him. How she turned away from me to him that first night we spent together.

I open my phone again and like some sort of stalker, begin scrolling through Isabella's photos. More pictures at the beach. Pictures of her and Nate building a sand castle, pictures of some guy and girl kissing. A picture of Riley...*what that's not Riley, it looks like Riley, but it's not.* Remembering the fact that the first time I had Riley's phone someone called Twinnie kept calling, and that Riley mentioned she has a sister. I'm assuming this must be her sister... *shit, what was her name? Harley? No. Harpy? Who even gives a fuck?*

I continue scrolling, almost giving up till I see a group picture of people building sand castles. I can see Isabella and Nate beside some random guy. *Who the fuck is he? Riley's new boyfriend?*

He looks kind of familiar, but I don't know from where. Then Riley and her sister. I zoom in and realize it's the sister facing the camera and Riley on her knees digging. I zoom in further and notice an unmistakable bruise poking out of the bottom of her swimsuit. Right on her ass. I feel a mixture of pride and guilt knowing she's walking around with a physical reminder of our night together.

I check the time stamp on the phone. The picture was posted less than twenty minutes ago. I grab my shoes and make my way to my bike. I drive, much faster than legal, to get to the beach. When I get there I make my way down to the beach. I check the phone again. There's a picture posted of them just a few minutes ago and behind them you can see rocks, letting me know they are on either edge. *Shit, which way do I go?* Looking left, I notice the end of the beach is far away, out of eyesight, but on the right, it's not that far, plus there seem to be shops and bars nearby. Taking my chances, I head that way. As I do, I eventually find Riley sitting alone on a rock. I peer around and see the rest of her friends all laughing and squealing in the water, but Riley's all alone.

"Riley," I say softly as I reach her, but as soon as she looks up and sees me she tries to slide off the rock. "Fuck!" she gasps before rubbing her hand against her ass.

"Does it still hurt?" I ask as I carefully lift her off the rock and place her feet back on the sand.

"What my ass, my pussy, or my heart?" she snaps back coldly.

"Erm, all three I guess."

"Yes, they all fucking hurt," she snaps again, as she turns her back on me.

"Riley please, don't be like that," I say, hating how pathetic and whiney my voice sounds.

"Like what? Hurt? Bruised? In pain?" she shouts. "No it's good, now I have a physical reminder of how much you hurt me every time I sit down"

"Riley, it wasn't like that. It means you're mine," I try to explain but she cuts me off.

"Well, if being beaten and bruised, and being in pain is what it means to be yours, then I'm glad I never was," she screams as she attempts to push me.

I reach out to grab her, to shake some sense into her, but instead, I see a fist coming towards my face. I move, but not quite quick enough as it just catches me on the tip of my chin.

"I don't know who the fuck you are, but keep your fucking hands off her!" the asshole from the pictures shouts, "and if I find out you're the same dickhead that left those bruises on her, you'll have more than just me to deal with," he screams in my face.

I swing my fist back ready to attack but Riley jumps in between us both. "Stop it!" she shouts. "You need to leave, now!" *Wait, she wants me to leave?!*

"Come on Rilez, he says, looping his arm around her shoulders." I stand glued to the spot as she walks away, nestled up to him like he's some sort of hero. *Is this her new boyfriend? Really? The blonde haired beach bum is who she traded me in for? Sure, he may have muscles but I'm guessing rather than spending the weekends being thrown around the bed, she'd be forced to watch him throw a football instead.*

I keep staring at them, but she doesn't even look back at me once. *Fuck her.*

RILEY

"Who was that?" Ava asks as she walks out of the water, past me to where she throws her arms around her boyfriend's neck.

"It was nothing, just some drunk asshole," I lie.

"Didn't look like nothing," Izzy adds, walking up to us, holding hands with Nate. I see the worry in Nate's eyes and give a slight nod.

"Hey Ava, how about you and Bella go get some ice cream? My treat." Nate suggests as he bends down and hands Izzy his wallet.

"What do you want?" Izzy asks sweetly.

"You?" Nate jokes back with a cheeky wink. I can't help but smile as I watch the way they both look at each other. If true love were a real thing, these two have it.

"I'm serious," Izzy laughs as she turns bright red.

I can't help but smile at how sweet and innocent she is. A total contrast to Ava who has taken to being glued to her side. Which I guess makes sense since both their boyfriends have a total bromance going on with each other.

"So am I," Nate replies with a wink. "But if we're talking about ice cream, surprise me."

I watch Izzy, Ava, and the other two boys take off to get us some sweet snacks.

"Okay, so now cut the bullshit, who the fuck was that Riley?" Tucker asks.

"Was it who I think it was?" Harper asks as she stamps her feet.

I just nod. "What did he want?" Nate asks but again I don't know what to say so I just shrug and look away. I can feel his piercing gaze linger on me.

"Will someone tell me what the fuck is going on?" Tucker asks with a bite in his voice and sounding nothing like his usual playful, carefree self.

"That was my brother," Nate says as he looks down at the floor, looking almost guilty.

"He's your brother?" Tucker says in surprise.

"Yeah. Look, I'm not trying to excuse what he did..." Nate begins.

"What exactly did he do to you, Riley?" Tucker asks, looking at me with his brow furrowed.

"It doesn't matter. He hurt me, that's all you need to know," I reply, hating the way they're all looking at me like some delicate little angel that needs protecting.

"And you're okay with that, are you? Having a brother that goes around hitting girls?" Tucker questions. I notice that he has his fists clenched and his breathing has gotten a bit faster.

"Woah! It wasn't like that!" I snap, trying to interrupt.

"You don't have to lie, Rilez; we've all seen that big ass bruise. We're not stupid," he growls.

"Okay, so yeah, I guess technically he did give me it," I admit sheepishly. I can feel the heat setting into my cheeks and I blow out a breath. "But it's not like you're thinking; he didn't hit me or anything, it was kind of done, erm, in a different way," I admit, feeling the blush deepen. *Can this be any more embarrassing? How can I tell them, without really telling them that I liked it? That I wanted Gabe to spank me. Am I crazy?*

"A different way? What sort of.... Ooooh, a different way," Tucker says, now looking embarrassed and red-faced himself.

"Yep." Harper laughs.

"But still, there's rough and there's ROUGH, and that's goddamn ROUGH. What was he fucking playing at?" Tucker says as he shakes his head and begins to get angry once again.

"Again, I'm not excusing any of his behavior, not at all. Believe me, I wanted to beat his ass when I heard what he did. Heck, he got a punch to the nuts for it," Nate smirks.

"He did?" Harper gasps.

"Yeah, he did," Nate confirms. "But what you've gotta understand about Gabe is, he's broken. Like I don't know if there's enough glue in all of America to stick him back together kind of broken."

I know it's his brother, but hearing anyone talk about Gabe like this fills me with a sense of sadness. Not for myself, but for Gabe. To know *this* is what people, especially those who are supposed to love him, think about him.

"Don't get me wrong, Gabe can be the greatest person in the world. I've told you about the shit I went through, right?" he asks Tucker, who affirmatively nods at him. Both me and Harper give each other a 'do you know anything' look before we both shake our heads.

"Yeah, well, without him I wouldn't have survived." Nate sighs and I can tell he isn't just talking hypothetically. "He saw and did a lot of bad shit, probably more than even I realize." A visible shudder runs through Nate's body and he has this glazed over look like he's remembering things that weren't pleasant to experience.

"That doesn't…" Tucker begins but is cut off by Nate. "You don't understand," Nate snaps as he tugs on the root of his hair. "He had it hard. Really goddamn hard. I was lucky, I got to know love and kindness with the Jacksons when I moved away. He didn't get that. He spent his time alone in the house where our father abused us. You can't even begin to imagine how much that shit fucks you up. Hell, I don't even know and I was there for most of it," Nate says as his voice begins to shake.

Again, me and Harper share an 'oh shit, I don't think we should be hearing this' kind of look.

"He's got a big heart, bigger than anyone I know. And he will put his life on the line to save you if he cares for you. But dude, that side is buried deep behind hundreds and hundreds of walls. He doesn't know how to love or be loved. Even with me he struggles to connect." Nate turns his attention to me now, "I'm not saying forgive him, Riley. What he did to you, it is unforgivable. But know that I honestly don't think he meant to hurt you."

"Can we talk about something else, I just can't do this now." I sigh as I rub at my temple. *I can't stand listening to this.* I don't know what the future holds for me or Gabe but I know that I can't deal with it now. It's taking all my energy not to either sit and cry or run after him.

"Of course," Nate replies with a sympathetic half smile.

"I got ice cream," Izzy calls and instantly a weight seems lifted from Nate because when he hears her voice, his whole face lights up and he gets a goofy grin on his face.

"And that's why we're going to keep all this to ourselves," I whisper.

"What? Why?" Tucker asks.

I nod my head in the direction of Izzy and Nate who are giggling just a few feet away. "Do you want to be the one who makes either of them choose between the loyalty they have for their best friends and family, and the loyalty they have towards each other?"

"Good point," Tucker says, nodding in agreement.

"What are you guys whispering about?" Ava asks, as she wraps her hands around Tucker's waist.

"Well, it wouldn't be much of a surprise if we told you," Harper answers without missing a beat.

"My birthday? Aww babe, you're the greatest," she says leaping into his arms and kissing him.

"You do realize we're gonna have to help Tucker find the perfect gift now," I laugh with Harper as Ava and Tucker begin making out.

"Who are you kidding? You know we would have had to anyway. If we left it to Tucker he'd get her a football or something," Harper giggles in return as we walk away.

Chapter Eighteen

Gabe

Climbing on my bike, I rev the engine and take off. I don't have a destination in mind; I just know I have to leave. I have to get out of here before I march back down that beach, beat the shit out of her new boyfriend, and throw Riley over my shoulder. The way I'm feeling right now, I'm more than happy to be arrested for kidnapping if it means I get to keep her.

The street signs whiz past me as I get faster and faster. Part of me is tempted to call Kelly and let her work out some of my tension, but since she's the cause, well maybe not the cause, but she's at least partly to blame, I decide against it. Instead, I turn off and drive out onto the open road. I continue driving until I spot a little bar in the middle of nowhere. Pulling up to it, I make my way inside.

"I'll take a beer and a whisky," I say to the woman behind the bar.

She brings the beer and then comes over to pour my whiskey. "Leave the bottle," I say as I reach out and pour myself a larger serving.

"But sir," the shy blond behind the bar tries saying.

"I said, leave the fucking bottle!" I snap. She leaves the bottle and scurries away. I keep drinking and drinking and drinking until the bottle is almost gone.

"Drinking to celebrate or forget?" a woman beside me leans over and asks.

"Both. Drinking to celebrate escaping jail and to forget the things I had to do when inside," I deadpan. I barely manage to keep a straight face when the stupid bitch almost falls off her chair in shock as she scurries to leave. I take out a wad of cash from my wallet and throw it on the counter, grabbing the rest of my bottle on my way out. As soon as the air hits me it almost knocks me off my feet. *Fuck, there's no way I can drive back in this state.*

Staggering back inside I find the quiet bartender again. "Where's the nearest motel?" I slur the words at her.

"Err, turn left, head to the bottom of the road. It's about ten or so minutes walk and then you'll see a side road. It's just down there, you can't miss it."

I throw another $20 on the bar, although I have no idea what for, and head back outside. I do the best I can to follow the instructions but I swear the roads keep moving around me. Or maybe it's the rest of the whiskey I drink as I'm walking. Finally, I find what I'm looking for. I bang on the door, expecting it to be closed, but fall straight through when I realize it's open.

"Fuck," I shout as I fall headfirst.

"Looking for a room?" a guy laughs.

"Yup." I hiccup.

"Follow me," he says, handing me a room key.

When I attempt to grab it but miss, he turns around and picks up a different key.

"On second thought, this may be a better option," he says as he leads me literally ten steps and through the nearest door.

It's a tiny room, barely big enough for the bed and bathroom, but I don't care. I close the door, kick off my boots, and flop on the bed.

I wake up somewhere around 1 a.m. to the sound of god awful singing. Peering out the door, the noise is coming from down the corridor. Not even bothering to try and find my shoes, I grab the key and make my way out to locate the sound.

I don't have to go far; just a few doors down I find it. *great. Fucking Karaoke.* I bang on the door and it's opened by a youngish girl in just some silk pajamas.

"Who ordered a stripper?" she shouts as she pulls me inside.

As soon as I get in I'm greeted by another four or five squealing girls. All around me are penis balloons and banners informing me that it's Lucy's bachelorette party. *Oh great. Just what I fucking need.*

"Who's he?" one girl questions as she pokes at me like I'm some animal in the zoo.

"I dunno, the stripper I guess," shrugs the one who answered the door.

A round of "I didn't order a stripper" can be heard before it finally dawns on her. I'm not a fucking stripper!

"Well, you're here now so entertain us," another woman shouts as she flings herself over me, but I push her, causing her to fall onto the floor.

"Ooof, I like it a little rough," she laughs as she stands back up, but makes no attempt to sit back on my lap.

"So what are you doing here then?" the first girl asks.

We establish that I'm just a guest here, the same as them, and that I only came to ask them to keep the noise down so I could get back to sleep. They apologize and ask me to stay saying they've got enough food and drinks to pacify an army. While the idea of any more alcohol right now isn't the least bit inviting, the idea of pizza and cake, even if that cake is in the shape of a penis, seems too good to pass up.

One of the girls goes and fixes a plate for me, and then somehow I become an unofficial member of the party. By 3 a.m. though, all but me and two of the women have passed out for the night.

"You know," says Blondie. *Pretty sure that's not actually her name but she's blonde, so it'll do.* "I've always fantasized about having a one night stand."

"So have one, one night of wild fun. Never to be repeated again," chimes Big Tits.

"It's just like one of those novels we read at book club isn't it?" chimes Blondie again.

"What do you say, Hot Stuff? Wanna make two college girls very happy?" Big Tits purrs as she rubs her hand across my definitely not-awake cock.

I take one look at them, and it's clear neither of them are college girls, and probably haven't been in at least the last ten years but I let it slide and think, fuck it.

I allow them to guide me across the corridor to their empty room. Once inside, I lock the door and demand they both remove those stupid matching pink pajamas.

They both do as I ask, whispering and giggling amongst themselves.

I take a seat on the bed, undo my jeans, and slip them off my legs.

Both girls make their way over in nothing but their underwear. And begin pawing at me. One attempts to kiss me, but soon changes her mind when I throw her a death stare.

"On your fucking knees," I demand. Both girls oblige even though I was only actually talking to one.

"Put it in your mouth," I groan.

I feel one of the girls remove my dick from my boxers, but rather than spring to attention it just droops down. One of the girls attempts to revive it by stroking her hand up and down repeatedly, but nothing happens, not even a twitch.

"Come here, I'll show you," the other girl says, physically pushing her friend out of the way. She attempts to give it the kiss of life. But still, my traitor of a dick refuses to budge.

"Err, maybe you drank too much," one of them tries to soothe, but it just annoys me more. I bend down to pick up my jeans and spot my phone lying on the floor. As soon as I reach for it I'm greeted by Riley's picture. The one of her reading on the beach. *When the fuck did I set that as my lock screen?*

Like a rocket, my cock suddenly springs to attention. "Oh looks like we have lift off," the girls giggle. I feel one of the girls wrap their lips around me and begin sucking. I continue staring at the picture while this girl goes to town on me. Finally, I squirt my load. Next, the other girl wants her turn. I try. But straight away I know this isn't right. "Get on all fours," I demand. Hoping that if I can't see her face it won't seem like I'm betraying Riley so much. Perhaps I can fool myself into believing this is Riley. Just like I did with her friend's mouth earlier. I try my hardest, but just a few thrusts later and my dick is still as soft and flat as a pancake.

"This ain't working," I say as I push the girl away, pull up my boxers. I grab my trousers and shoes from the floor and walk out the door.

I walk back to my room not giving a fuck that I'm only wearing boxers and a t-shirt and throw myself back on the bed. Once I get comfortable, I pull out my phone, set it to Riley's picture and prepare to finish what I started earlier. I take out my now throbbing, hard as steel dick and pump it to her picture until I'm blowing my load. Then I drift off to sleep.

I don't wake up till early evening by which time I feel sober enough to drive.

As I get near town, I pull up to gas up my bike, and find a voice message from John.

"You're a fucking asshole Gabe, you have put the work back a whole weekend. The boys all had to work overtime. We're all at Saints, I suggest you get your ass here and buy us a drink."

I call John, my boss, apologizing for the fact I've completely skipped two days of work. He's annoyed of course, but knows he can't really say much since I know where the bodies are buried...literally.

"I'll be back at work tomorrow. I'll even work over the weekend to make it up to you," I say begrudgingly.

"Fine, but don't make a motherfucking habit out of it," John replies, "Oh and you still owe us all a drink, so get your ass to Saints, now."

Internally I grimace at the thought of spending my night stuck with the scumbags from work.

"I'm on my way," I say before hanging up. Spending my night with the guys I work with is the last thing I wanna do, but I haven't got much choice in the matter. Some of the guys I work with are okay, especially Jack. He's an annoying prick at times, but I know when we're together on a job it's gonna go quick, at least.

Unfortunately though, I know exactly which 'boys' John will be with, his five goonies. Saints Sinners as they stupidly call themselves. Satan's spawn more like. Each one is more disgusting and devious than the last. I know I can be a dickhead 99% of the time and am known for being kind of heartless with women but these five are something else entirely. They hunt and share women like it's a sport and find some sort of sadistic pleasure in hunting their prey. That's how me and Declan, the bartender in Saints, became friendly in the first place. We both do our bit to minimize their reach in our own ways. Nothing would please me more than to kill the lot of them with my bare hands, but as John's right-hand man I learned young that power and fear work much better to keep yourself safe. While they respect me, they don't fuck with me. I stay quiet and pretend I don't wanna kill every last one of them. It keeps me safe and in control.

I jump on my bike and head straight to Saints. I walk in and see Declan at the end of the bar flirting with some brunette. I eye a half empty bottle of rum still on the side which I grab and head back outside.

"I saw that," Declan shouts from behind me.

"Good, then do your fucking job and put it on my tab," I reply with a smirk.

I push the door open and head outside to the patio. I hear Marko's disgusting laugh and resist the urge to smash the bottle over his head. *No point wasting a decent bottle of rum.*

"Move," I snap, placing my hand on the back of Deeno's chair.

I see Deeno's eyes widen as he turns to look at me. He's a big guy, over six foot tall and built like a boxer. But he's the newest and youngest member of the Sinners and still hasn't quite figured me out yet.

"Did I fucking stutter?" I ask, turning to the group.

"No, sorry man," Deeno stutters as he stands and pulls over an empty chair.

Sitting down beside John, I listen as the group continues excitedly discussing beating some poor guy to a pulp over some debt he owed.

"Gabe, is it true you killed a guy when you were just fifteen?" Deeno asks nervously.

"Sure it is; I was there," John replies as he proudly pats me on the back. I move out of his reach and give him a death glare. *He knows full well I hate being touched.*

"Why do you think I've had this kid working for me since he was in diapers?" John chuckles.

"Thought the old man had gone senile when he told me this lil runt was coming to work with us," Mike replies. Going into detail about what a scruffy, skinny little runt thirteen-year-old me was.

I then listen as John and Mike, both men in their late fifties, talk about me like my shitty childhood is some sort of villain origin story.

"So his dad was a nasty son of a bitch, beat him and his brother constantly..."

"Wait, you got a brother?" Deeno chimes in, as he looks at me.

"Yeah, and mention him again and I'll gut you right there where you sit," I growl back at the piece of shit.

"The brother's off limits, don't even know the kid's name," I hear Marko whisper from beside him.

"So, as I was saying, kid learned how to take a punch young, and was desperate to please his old man, so started working with me when he was just a boy..." John continues as I tune them out again.

".... then one day some punk tried breaking into my van and this goddamn beast, really he was just a kid, had the balls to challenge the punk and beat him over the head with a metal pole killing the bastard right then and there." John chuckles like he's telling a funny story about something stupid his grandkid did.

I take a large gulp of the rum and enjoy the burn as it hits my throat and I shift uncomfortably. What John conveniently leaves out of this story is how it really went down.

Gabe- Age 15

I've been sitting here on this cold, hard floor for hours. My father and his cronies dragged me out of bed at the ass crack of dawn and demanded that I follow them on another hair-brained scheme.

I barely had time to throw on a thin shirt, a pair of jeans and some sneakers before a black balaclava was thrust into my hands. Turns out one of the cronies found out about some big ass mansion being unoccupied from the owner's gardener, and of course that gave them all the bright idea to rob it.

Of course, I was tasked with hopping the fence and shimming my way through a small window because, unlike these fat bastards, I am the only one agile and thin enough to do it.

We wasted no time stealing everything our grubby hands could carry.

The rest of the gang wasted no time, taking their newly found riches to either the local pawn shop or whore house. But me, I've been sitting right here in this shitty ass, abandoned barn, slowly freezing to death, tasked with guarding our share of the loot for hours, and I'm exhausted. I spot a thin piece of tarp and pull it around me, desperately hoping for some warmth as the cold winter air whips and whistles around me.

I must drift off as the next thing I hear is voices and clattering. *Someone's here.*

"The drunk bastard told me the goods are in here," a voice says, just as I see a flashlight illuminate the wall behind me. *Fuck, what do I do?*

I see two dark figures appear and my first instinct is to hide, but I am terrified of what my father will do if he finds out I was sleeping and let someone rob us. I just freeze.

"Looky here, not much of a guard dog are you?" one of the guys laughs when he sees me.

"I have a gun!" I shout back, as I scramble for the gun John gave me for protection. The gun I keep in my belt but have no idea how to shoot.

"Let's go," one of the guys says to the other.

"Nah, fuck him. I'm not running cuz of some punk ass kid," the other replies.

I pick up the gun, and point it at the main guy. "Last chance!" I shout despite the tremble in my voice. The guy laughs so I close my eyes and pull the trigger.

"Fuck this shit!" I hear one of the guys shout as his footsteps get heavier.

I open my eyes to see him running away, while the second guy is glaring right at me.

"Missed me," he taunts as he runs straight towards me. I try to aim again but before I have a chance, I'm being tackled to the floor and the guy is straddling me.

I try to get away, but I'm on my back on the floor, all I see is long greasy hair as the guy's hands find their way around my throat.

"Think you can fire a gun at me, do you? Maybe you should learn how to fucking shoot first," the guy bellows, as his hands get tighter and tighter and dark spots appear in my vision.

All I see is his long hair as my eyes begin to blur. In a panic, I try to push him off, or get his hands from around my throat but he's too strong. I desperately try to buck him off as my body moves and my legs kick but he's too big and heavy. The panic and fear take over. My arms fly out grabbing for something, anything to hit him with. I start to see even more spots and my lungs are on fire. Finally, my fingers connect with something hard. I grab it and with all the strength left in my scrawny, neglected body and I swing it, hitting my attacker straight on the head. He falls off me with a thump.

I release whatever is in my hand and begin coughing and spluttering as the air finally returns to my lungs. I roll over and see my attacker lying beside me. I scramble to my knees to look at him and all I see is a vacant look in his eyes. *Fuck!*

I turn my head and see the blood covered crow bar I'd been holding moments ago. *Fuck, fuck, fuck what have I done?*

I try to shake the guy, praying he's just knocked out. *Please wake up! Please be okay.*

I shake and shake but he doesn't even blink. *CPR! We learned about that last year in health class. What was that goddamn tune?? Staying alive that's it!*

I begin pounding on his chest as I desperately try to get my brain to remember the tune. *That breathing thing!*

I remember you have to give them air sometimes so I pinch his nose as hard as I can and begin blowing into his mouth. *Nothing!* I go back to pounding on his chest again, as hard as I can but still nothing. *Please don't be dead, please! God, if you're real, I know*

I'm not exactly a good kid but if you bring him back to life, I'll be good, I promise. I'll even go to church on Sunday with Nate and his friend. I promise!

I try once more giving him breaths and then I place my ear against his chest praying to hear a heartbeat, but it's silent. The tears stream down my face as reality sinks in. *He's dead. I killed him.* The bile rises in my tummy and I barely have time to move before I'm throwing up all over the floor. The bile mixed with the little bits of undigested food flies out of me like a scene from The Exorcist as my body expels every morsel I've eaten in what feels like my whole life. Once it finally stops, I stagger outside not caring that the rain spills down on me. I flop down on the floor and sit in silence as the rain pours down, soaking me to my very core. I don't know how long I sit there, praying that the water will somehow wash away my sins. But eventually, I feel a hand on my shoulder.

"What the fuck you doing out here, son?" someone says. I look up and see John crouched down in front of me.

Out of instinct I throw my arms around his neck and bury my head in his shirt.

"I fucked up... he's dead... I killed him," I sob.

"Who is?" John asks, as he pulls me up to my feet.

I feel sudden pain in my head as a hand connects with the back of it.

"What the fuck you doing? Men don't hug!" my father bellows as he yanks me away by the collar of my jacket.

"Sorry," I mumble as I quickly wipe away my tears, knowing how much my father hates to see his sons appear weak.

"What the fuck?" I hear from inside.

I turn and run inside just in time to see Mike standing over the body.

"Did you do this?" Mike asks, looking at me. I nod my head.

I wait for the shock, disgust, anger. I expect the men to be just as mortified with the gruesome sight as I am but when I look, my father has the biggest grin on his face I've ever seen. *I didn't even know my father was capable of smiling.*

"That's my boy!" my father beams proudly, pounding me on the back.

"Are you okay, Gabe?" John asks as he places a hand on my shoulder and squeezes it.

"Of course he is, my boy's a goddamn machine," my father beams.

"He's a kid, Scott," Mike says, sounding concerned.

"He's a man!" my father cheers as he throws his arm around my neck and for the first time in my life shows me some real, honest affection.

Present Day

"I'm going for a piss," I announce as I leave the guys all chatting about the worst night of my life.

I head into the bathroom and throw some water on my face. I stare at my reflection for a moment, hating the person staring back at me. I stand there for a moment wondering if this was the monster I was always destined to be. Or if I would have been a different person if that night had never happened. I pull out a cigarette from my pocket and light it right then and there, not giving a fuck where I am.

I continue watching my reflection as my mind heads back to that time in my life. How after that night my father finally seemed to want me. He no longer hit me or treated me like a burden. No, instead, he seemed almost affectionate towards me. He'd often throw his arm around me or pat me on the shoulder. And despite the fact I'd spent most of my childhood praying that one day he'd hug me or hold me, his actions actually made my skin crawl. Even now the idea of anyone holding me, hugging me, or even just brushing up against me gives me that same dirty, disgusting feeling.

Someone walks into the bathroom and breaks me out of my memories. "You can't smoke in here," the guy remarks. I look down at his uptight dress slacks and decide it would be too easy to beat his ass. I just brush past him and leave.

I walk out to my bike but as I reach into my pocket for my phone I realize I don't have it. *Fuck!* I left it outside on the table. Letting out an exasperated breath I make my way back into the bar. I walk past Declan who gives me a confused look.

"There you bloody are! Did you fall down the fucking toilet or something?" John laughs.

"Nah, he probably found a 'lil bathroom bunny to fuck," Marko smirks, as he peers around some drunken whore on his lap.

"Probably Kelly," Deeno laughs. Just the mention of her name would be enough to make my dick crawl back inside my body, but I rather they believe that, than the truth. So I just shrug and look away with a disinterested look on my face.

Declan arrives and begins collecting the empty glasses just as I'm searching the table for my phone.

"More drinks?" he asks. Grumbles of "same" and " another" echo around the table.

"I'll have a Coke to go with that bottle of rum," Marko's lap warmer slurs.

"Give her a beer, one of the cheap ones," I reply, snatching the bottle of rum from the table along with my phone.

"But I wanted rum," the woman whines nasally.

"Cheap beer it is," Declan nods as I place the rum bottle on his tray, letting me know he'll be switching her drink out for water, our little code for 'sober this bitch up and get her outta here quick.'

"See you fuckers tomorrow," I say as I walk off, not even giving them a chance to reply.

I drive home and as soon as I get there, I jump in the shower, doing my best to wash away the memories still desperately swirling around in my mind. Wrapping a towel around my waist, I make my way into my bedroom. As I walk past Nate's room I hear him on the phone to Izzy. *He must have it on speaker.* I stop and press my ear against the door and hear the two of them laughing, joking, and teasing each other.

A bunch of emotions bombard me. Part of me wants to gag at how goddamn cringy and pathetic they both sound. Another part of me is annoyed at the sound of that witch's voice. I know I need to put the past behind us and give her a chance since Nate's made it pretty fucking clear she's not going anywhere, but I just can't forgive her. I hear them laughing again and I feel a mix of sadness and jealousy that I'll never have that.

I head to my bedroom, reach for my phone and I'm again met with that picture. The one of Riley. I know I need to change it, but since she's still refusing to answer my calls, it's the only way I get to see her. For a moment when I wake in the mornings, I get to pretend she's still mine and that I didn't fucking destroy my one shot at happiness.

Feeling unusually hopeful, I try again to call her. But just the same as the last ten times I tried, it just serves to reconfirm that I'm still blocked. So I throw on a pair of boxers and climb into bed.

Chapter Nineteen

Riley

It's been weeks since everything happened between me and Gabe. I've tried everything I can think of to help forget about him, but I can't. I know he's broken and bad for me, but part of me is inexplicably drawn to him. Part of me wishes that like all my favorite fictional men, I'll be able to tame and turn his tortured soul. But this isn't an episode of The Vampire Diaries and I'm no Caroline or Elena.

"Come on, Rilez," Harper calls from down the hall.

"I'm coming, hold your fucking horses!" I shout back as I bend down and pull one of my sneakers out from under the bed.

I race out the door just as the sound of a horn beeps from outside.

"She's so impatient." I laugh as Harper hands me my phone and ushers me out of the door.

"Bout time bitches," Ava sighs as I climb in the backseat.

"Sorry about her," Izzy smiles from the passenger seat as she looks back at us both.

"They're the ones that should be sorry, these nails aren't gonna paint themselves," Ava laughs as she holds up her already perfectly manicured hands. I just shake my head as Izzy rolls her eyes at us in the rearview mirror.

We barely have time to put on our seat belts before she revs the engine and takes off, like the girl racer that we know her to be.

"So, I was thinking about red, to match my dress, or maybe blue, since it's Tucker's favorite color… or perhaps I should go for something a bit brighter to catch his attention," Ava ponders as we make our way to Francisco's, our favorite mani/pedi place.

"Tucker won't give a fuck about the color of your nails, as long as he gets to visit Pound Town," I tease.

"Oh don't worry, he'll defo be visiting Pound Town; it's our anniversary after all," Ava says with a wink.

We pull up outside Francisco's and make our way inside. It's only a small place but we try to come at least once a month, if not for anything more than a little girl time.

"So, who's having hands and who's having feet?" Lexi asks as we walk inside.

"Me and Riley for hands," Ava pipes up.

I give her a confused look. "My treat," she smiles.

"You know the way," Lexi replies.

"Some customer service this is," Ava says, feigning outrage.

"Well, I could always stop letting you use my friends and family discount," Lexi snaps back playfully.

"No we love you, don't we girls!" Ava laughs with a big cheesy grin.

"That's what I thought," Lexi grins back triumphantly.

We head to the back of the salon where Lexi and Jenn are waiting.

I sit down at Lexi's chair since Ava is already rummaging through the nail polishes beside the chair that Jenn usually sits at.

Lexi comes over a few moments later with two small foot spas and places them down in front of the window bench Harper and Izzy are sitting at.

"So what's the special occasion then Freckles?" Lexi asks. Although we come here often, it's usually not me who gets her nails done. Since the salon is owned by Lexi and Justin's mum, Lexi, the girls and I have all been hanging out here for years. So, when Lexi started training a few months ago, she started giving us discounts on things while she got trained. Something Ava in particular enjoys.

"She's been in a funk over some guy and needs a little pick me up," Ava says leaning over to my table.

"Don't tell me you're still hung up on my idiot brother," Lexi says looking at me with raised eyebrows.

"Nah, some sexy older guy," Ava replies.

"Wait. you don't mean G…"

"You don't know him," I interrupt quickly before she has time to name him.

Lexi gives me a suspicious look, but doesn't push it any further.

"So, how about you, newbie? How are things with your guy?" Lexi says changing the subject to talk to Izzy.

"Yeah, it's going amazingly," Izzy blushes.

"She's being modest. She's basically married off to literally the sweetest guy ever," Harper coos from beside her.

"Married off, huh?" Jenn questions incredulously.

"Well, not really, but a little bit, I guess." Izzy mumbles while trying to hide the bright red blush appearing on her cheeks.

"Tell her your story Izzy, don't be shy," I encourage. "It's almost like a story from one of the books we read."

I hope that if everyone focuses on Izzy, Lexi will stop giving me that 'I know you're hiding something' look.

"Okay, so it all started when we were kids..." Izzy begins.

"We met one day randomly when I was forced to spend a week with my Pops and older cousins in their old hunting cabin. As you can imagine, it was the most boring week of my life," Izzy laughs.

"Well that is until I stupidly got lost and decided the best way to find my way home was to climb a huge tree. Then of course, because I'd never climbed a tree before, I fell out and almost crushed poor Nate who was passing by."

"You fell on him?" Lexi laughs.

"Pretty much," Izzy giggles back.

"Okay, so Izzy sucks at telling stories," Ava chimes in, "I've heard this story from Nate and his version is so much more romantic."

"Well go on then, little Miss Theatrical, why don't you tell my story instead?" Izzy says as she gives Ava a playful shove.

"You asked for it." I say as I shake my head at Lexi and Jenn.

"Izzy was right. She did go wandering alone in the woods which looking back was a totally idiotic thing to do, but whatever. She got to meet her prince so it's fine . . . According to Nate, he saw her climbing and was totally bewitched by her but was too nervous to walk over and say hi so he just kind of watched her..."

"Because that's not a little weird," Jenn pipes up.

"Shh, listen," Ava whines. "As I was saying, Nate was watching, trying to pluck up the nerve to speak to her when she got stuck. Nate rushed over like the knight in shining armor he was to rescue her but he was too late. She'd already fallen and was lying on the ground semiconscious. Then their eyes met, the birds sang, and like some sort of Disney movie, they fell head over heels in love right then and there," Ava says with an exaggerated sigh.

"So what happened next?" Lexi says, as she leans closer, fully invested in Ava's dramatic story.

"Well, we stayed friends. We wrote each other letters whenever we were apart, hung out every single moment we could. But then we both moved away so we didn't speak for years." Izzy adds with a sad look in her eyes. I reach over and give her a reassuring squeeze.

"A few years later, fate intervened again and they reunited recently. And since then they've been inseparable. This is why I always say they are basically already married.

"Wow! That's so romantic," Jenn beams. "Don't suppose he's got a brother for me?" Jenn jokes, but her words cut me like a knife. "I could do with finding myself a prince. I only seem to kiss frogs."

"You wouldn't want his brother, he's no prince," Harper snaps, and I can hear the venom in her voice, even if no one else seems to notice. I cringe internally at her tone. *It kills me that she seems to hate Gabe. He's really not that bad, is he?*

"He's not that bad, Gabe's just kind of an acquired taste," Izzy replies. *I can't believe that Izzy keeps trying to see the best in Gabe, even when all he does is treat her like shit.*

"Gabe?" Lexi questions as she eyes me suspiciously.

"Yeah, that's his older brother," Izzy confirms.

I look at Lexi silently begging her not to say anything. Thankfully, she lets it slide and the rest of our appointment goes by incident free. But as we're about to leave Lexi calls me.

"Freckles, any chance you could help me take these spas to the backroom?" she asks, and although I want to refuse, I turn to follow her to the back. I know if I refuse, Lexi may just bring it up right here, in front of everyone.

"Sure," I say with a fake smile.

"How about you girls run and grab me a coffee?" Lexi suggests handing them some money. "I'm dying for a cappuccino too," someone else chimes up.

As soon as the girls leave, I feel like a spotlight is shining on me. "Spill," Lexi demands as soon as we make it to the back room.

"There's not much to...." I begin before I'm cut off.

"Riiiley, spill it!" Lexi says again, this time using that same big sister/babysitter voice she used on me when I was a kid.

"Fine. So, me and Gabe went on a few dates. Well, not exactly dates I guess, but we got closer," I clarify. "At first things seemed to be going great, but then, well, it went to shit. He fucked up. I don't wanna relive it but let's just say he was a complete asshole."

"Okay, so what happened next? Do your friends not know you were seeing each other?" Lexi asks as she rests against the shelving unit.

"Harper knows who he is, Ava and Izzy don't."

"Why? I thought you four were besties? I always see the four of you together and they all seem to adore you," Lexi questions.

"It's complicated."

"What's so complicated about it?" Lexi asks as she sits herself down on a nearby box, and signals for me to do the same.

"Well, Ava is a firecracker with a big mouth, so she'd kick his ass in a heartbeat...." I begin and stop to think about how to explain this.

"Would that be the worst thing?"

"Yes, because of Izzy!"

"Izzy? What about her?" Lexi asks as she furrows her brows in confusion.

"So, you heard Izzy's story right? True love, super cute, and in real life they're even more perfect than the story, if that is possible."

"Okay, so what's that got to do with you and Gabe?" Lexi asks, baffled.

"Gabe is Nate's older brother. He's also hell bent on keeping Izzy and Nate apart for some strange reason. Something to do with some issues he, Nate, and Izzy have from childhood. Anyway, Izzy is doing everything in her power to get Gabe to forgive her and become her friend, but Gabe is point blank refusing. That girl is giving one hundred percent in trying to be nice to him and be his friend, the last thing Nate and her need is me throwing in my drama. If she knew what happened between Gabe and me, that might make her angry with him and cause her to stop trying to make things better between the two of them."

"I guess that kind of makes sense," Lexi admits with a shrug.

"So for now I have to just keep my shit to myself."

"Yeah, but still they are your friends, you're clearly hurting and you need them to be there for you."

"They are there for me. They've been there when I've been upset. They listen to me talk and vent about my older guy. They've also given me tips and ideas on how to get over him. They just don't know who he is. They think he's some guy I met at a concert," I share with a sad half-smile.

"Okay, well if you ever need to talk it out, with someone who you can be fully honest with, you know where to find me. I'll listen anytime," Lexi offers as she pulls me into a hug.

"There you are," Ava says as we both walk out of the storeroom. Harper looks at me with her brow raised and I know she's worried about me. I nod slightly letting her know I'm okay.

"Sorry, that biatch Lexi had me rearranging half the shelf with her," I lie.

"It's true, that room is a mess," Lexi affirms with a shrug.

"Anyway, thanks for the coffee. See you all soon," Lexi comments as she grabs the ice coffee that one of the girls left on her desk.

We leave and get in the car ready to head to the mall so that we can help Ava pick an outfit for her date with Tucker, but on the way there we take a detour.

"Where are we going?" I ask as we turn down a familiar road.

"I said I'd drop lunch off for Tucker on my way, I'll only be a minute," Ava replies as she drives past the old restaurant, past Saints' bar, and pulls up outside O'Malley's.

Harper squeezes my knee and mouths the words, 'Are you okay?'

Unsure of how to answer, I simply shrug my shoulders.

To make matters worse, she pulls up right out front then obnoxiously beeps her horn, causing all the guys outside to turn and stare at us.

Tucker comes running over, quickly followed by Nate.

"Come see what I did," Tucker beams, as he opens Ava's door, kisses her, then tries to persuade her to follow him.

Izzy gets out and hugs Nate. Despite the fact those two are super into each other, they're still at that awkward, not sure what to do in public phase.

"Come see, come see!" Tucker beams again, as he bounces around from foot to foot like an excitable child. "All of you, come see!"

"He's not gonna give up till you do," Ava grins.

Not wanting to cause a scene, I climb out the back seat and follow her, even though everything in my body is screaming for me not to. Especially since Tucker started working with Nate and Gabe at O'Malley's just a few days ago.

Tucker leads us to see something. I don't exactly know what I'm looking at apart from some building structure but he's super excited to show us anyway.

I look up and see Gabe walking towards us from across the yard.

"Do you have a bathroom I could use?" I quickly ask, turning to Nate.

"Yeah, sure. Just walk down that hall, there, past the small office, and it's just there. Want me to show you?" he offers.

"No, I'll find it," I reply, making my escape, while praying that Gabe didn't notice me.

I find the bathroom relatively easily and lock myself inside. I wait long enough that I'm sure everyone will be done with Tucker and ready to leave, so I won't risk running into Gabe. I open the bathroom door ready to leave but as soon as I do, I'm met with those big, green eyes. *Fuck, why does he have to look so good?*

He bends down to kiss me, and for a split second I almost let him, but just as his lips graze mine, I come to my senses and pull away.

"Don't push me away, please, Baby," Gabe whispers, and despite the fact I can hear the sadness in his voice I refuse to look at him. Instead, I attempt to push past him. Rather than moving to let me pass, he puts his hand against the wall beside my head, trapping me.

"Just let me fucking explain," Gabe begins as he bangs his fist against the wall behind me. "I'm sorry, okay?" he whispers when he sees me jump from the sound. "I've been trying to call and text you for weeks."

"I know," I respond, and instantly regret it when a small smirk forms on Gabe's face. "So you've unblocked me now?" he asks with a hint of a smile.

"No," I retort, which is only a half lie. *Technically he is still blocked.* What I don't tell him is that against my better judgement, every now and then, I've been unblocking him to torture myself by reading and listening to his messages and voicemails before reblocking him.

"You need to unblock me, Riley, we need to move past this shit. This is too much! I want you and you want me. There's nothing else that needs to be discussed!" Gabe says in a voice that seems like he's trying to maintain control of the situation, but isn't capable of.

"I'm not one of the guys who you can boss around, Gabe. This isn't a situation where you can just say something and that's what happens. I don't trust you. You hurt me and I don't think I can ever forgive you!" As soon as the words leave my mouth and I see the pain flash across his face, I feel my heart splinter a little bit more. But then I see him steel himself once again and I know that he still doesn't understand, truly understand the hurt he has caused me.

"Forgive me and let's be goddamn friends or some shit. At least for now?" Gabe begs, cocking his brow. Part of me feels a weird satisfaction seeing that he's obviously just as sad as I am, but the other part of me keeps imagining him fucking that whore in the bathroom.

"No, Gabe," I say, trying but failing for it to sound like I'm in charge.

"Come on, I know you want me," Gabe purrs as he bends down and kisses my neck.

"I don't," I say but my voice holds no conviction, it's barely louder than a whisper.

"And I guess this doesn't make your panties wet for me either?" he smirks as he places his hand around my throat, the way he knows I like, and runs his hand down my body until it reaches the waistband of my jeans.

My knees feel weak and again I almost give in, "NO!" I say pushing him as hard as I can. He steps away, giving me enough space to move. But as I go to walk away he grabs my arm.

"Get off me Gabe, I'm serious!" I shout.

"Wait…" he begins but I cut him off.

"I said get off me!" I snap and my voice quivers as I try but fail to hold in all the emotions.

"You heard her," comes a male voice, seconds before I notice Nate appearing in the doorway.

"What the fuck does it have to do with you?" Gabe snaps at his brother.

"She's my friend, now let go of her," Nate says standing his ground.

"And I'm your fucking brother," Gabe snaps back, as he glares at his brother.

"Which is why I'm giving you one more chance to let her go, Gabe."

Gabe looks down at his hand that's still gripping my arm and instantly releases it. "I'm sorry, I wasn't trying to hurt you, I just wanted to stop you. Just wanted you to hear me out, " Gabe mumbles and I can hear the sincerity and uncertainty in his voice.

"I know," I admit with a sad smile before walking out the door.

Chapter Twenty

Gabe

I watch her walk away, and with each step she takes it feels like the weight on my cold dead heart gets heavier.

"You gotta let her go man," Nate tells me as he attempts to pat my shoulder, but I twist my body away to avert his touch.

"I don't know how," I admit. *Shit, did I say that out loud?*

"You gotta try," Nate replies.

"Whose fucking side are you on?" I snarl, barging past him.

"I'm not on anyone's side," I hear Nate state as he follows me. "You really fucked up, though."

"And you don't think I fucking know that?" I spin around to face him, frustrated with myself, the situation, and at Nate.

"You really hurt her Gabe," Nate continues, now using that stupid, pathetic, soft, condescending, goddamn tone of his. I hate when he talks to me like I'm some stupid kid who spilled a drink and now needs to be scolded.

"How would you fucking know? Have you been talking about me behind my fucking back?"

"No, of course not, but we are friends, plus Bella said..."

"Bella said..." I mimic. "Fuck Isabella. Fuck her opinions and fuck you!"

"Don't be like that! I was just saying..."

"Well fuck, don't! What I do or don't do has nothing to do with you or your perfect little Princess Isabella, so keep my fucking name out of both of your mouths." I growl as I feel the rage building up, and without thinking, swing my fist, connecting with a concrete wall. "Fuck!" I yell as I feel the pain in my hand radiate all the way up my arm.

"For fuck's sake, Gabe," Nate huffs as he grabs my wrist and pulls me back into the bathroom to wrap my now bleeding hand in a towel.

"This is exactly what you need to fix before you can get into a relationship," Nate says pointedly while letting out a deep breath. "I don't think it's broken," he finally declares with a sigh as he releases my hand.

"Look, me and a few of the guys are meeting for a poker night. Why don't you join us?" Nate offers.

"Nah."

"Come on, at least consider it," Nate coaxes.

"What's the point? They don't want me there anyway. I don't even fucking know them," I growl at him, even though part of me is a little intrigued.

"You already know Tucker, he will be there. And Davis is also joining us, I think. Also, my friend Danny - you've probably seen him a few times, too," Nate explains.

"Where's it at?" I grumble, half considering it. *After all, maybe it wouldn't be so bad. Plus, I bet none of these chumps have a clue how to play properly, so I could make some money if nothing else.*

"That pub just down the road. Davis said a lot of the guys here go to it."

"Saints? On the corner?" I ask. *If I was a dog my ears would be sticking up right now.*

"Yeah, that's it, I think."

"Fine, I'll come," I reply, feigning indifference. *Free alcohol, check. Easy money, check. My local bar where I can probably score drugs and sex on tap, double check.*

"Really?" Nate asks, sounding surprised.

"Don't make me change my mind."

RILEY

Walking away from Gabe was one of the hardest things I've done. My whole body is screaming at me to turn around and kiss him, put the whole Kelly thing behind us and move on. But my head won't let me. He hurt me. I allowed myself to be vulnerable with him, gave him something special and he betrayed me.

"There you are," Harper says as she appears in front of me. "What happened?" she asks, sounding concerned.

"I'm fine." I lie.

"Tell that to your eyes."

I reach up and feel the wetness on my cheeks; I hadn't even realized I'd started to cry. Rubbing away my tears with the sleeve of my jacket, I try to compose myself. Hating the idea of anyone, even my best friends, seeing me so vulnerable.

"Can you tell?" I ask, looking at her and wiping my eyes again, and praying I don't look like a goddamn panda.

"A little," Harper answers softly. "Here," she says as she rubs her thumb under my eyes, removing the mascara I've clearly missed.

We walk out to the car where both Izzy and Ava are waiting. As soon as Ava sees my face she knows something's up.

"Whose ass do I gotta kick?" Ava demands.

When I don't answer she repeats the question, "Someone made you cry, so whose ass do I gotta kick?"

"Erm, no one, I'm fine, it's just..." I begin.

"It's just that her clumsy ass wasn't looking where she was going and she hit her head on some scaffolding." Harper quickly jumps in.

"Oh my god!! Are you okay? That's so dangerous. You could have been really hurt," Izzy gasps, sounding concerned.

"You know Riley, always on her phone, never looking where she's going," Harper adds.

"Well, I can't exactly fight metal poles for you, can I?" Ava laughs. "As long as you're okay though."

"Yeah, I'll be fine, just a little bump. Maybe it'll knock some sense into me," I add, grateful for Harper's quick thinking.

We head to the mall and I go through the motions -"ooo" and "ahhing" in all the right places as Ava tries on dress after dress, though my head and my heart just aren't in it.

"Are you listening?" Ava asks suddenly. I stare at her blankly, as I have absolutely no idea what she was saying. "Sorry, what did you say?" shaking my head, trying to pay attention.

"I said, do you wanna grab some lunch? Then maybe head back to my place for a movie night?" Ava sighs, clearly annoyed.

"Rain check? I just don't feel good." I admit.

"Maybe you've given yourself a concussion," Izzy pipes up, sounding even more concerned than before.

"I'm sure I'll be fine. I think I just need to head home, turn off the lights, and maybe sleep it off."

"What about you, Harper?" Ava asks

"I think I'm gonna head back and take care of Riley," Harper tells her, and as much as I know she's trying to be nice, I just wanna be alone.

"You can go, honestly, I'm just gonna take a bath and go to sleep." I lie.

Harper gives me that twin look. The one that conveys a whole conversation without barely saying a word, " You sure?"

"Yeah go. Have fun. I'll join you ladies next time." I silently beg that she agrees.

"I'm gonna go grab an uber. See you at school on Monday."

"Don't be silly, I'll drop you home first. I just gotta pay then we'll leave" Ava offers.

Knowing what Ava's like when she's made up her mind, I make no attempt to argue.

I stay quiet and smile politely as I wait for Ava to pay, and I don't say much the whole drive home either. Finally, we pull up outside my house.

"You sure you don't want me to stay?" Harper asks again.

"No, go... please" I whisper.

I wave politely as the girls drive away, unlock the door, and run straight to my bedroom. I throw myself onto my bed and begin to sob. I don't even know why I'm so upset. Gabe hurt me, but so what? I've been hurt so many times before. This isn't me though. I'm not the girl who sits at home crying over some stupid boy. I'm the one who moves on to someone else. Heck, when all that shit with Justin happened, it took me barely any time to get over his betrayal and we were actually a couple. Me and Gabe, we were more of a situationship than anything else. Even so, it doesn't hurt any less.

I change into my favorite fluffy pajamas hoping that the comfy material will somehow offer mental comfort, but when that doesn't help, I attempt to distract myself with TV. I spot Sons of Anarchy, but decide against it since it just reminds me of Gabe.

Then I turn to The Vampire Diaries, but again the tortured bad guy just reminds me of Gabe, too. This is impossible! I eventually settle on a rerun of Friends hoping that it will make me smile at least. But my mind is too distracted to really appreciate it.

Climbing out of bed, I head to the kitchen to make myself a hot drink. I open the fridge to grab the milk and spot a half empty bottle of white wine. I assume it's what's left from the book club mom holds on Friday nights.

"Mom?... Dad?" I call out. Once I'm sure they're not home and likely to catch me, I swipe a glass from the cupboard, grab the wine, and head back to my room.

One glass turns into two and before I know it, my mind convinces me to text him. I unblock his number and as soon as I do my phone begins pinging with notifications.

I head to the bathroom, and when I come back I have 6 missed calls, 4 voice messages, and 3 texts from today alone.

Dark Horse

> Look Riley, I fucked up. I know. Please come back and talk.

> Answer the phone, please.

> Come on, it's been hours! I'm a dickhead, okay. Call me back.

I know I shouldn't but some part of me, the part that seems hell bent on torturing myself, wants to hear his voice so I listen to his voicemails.

1:30pm- Riley it's me, come back and talk to me. Let me explain. I'm sorry.

3:15pm- Riley it's me, erm, Gabe. I know you probably still have me blocked so you might not get this but if you do, call me back.

7pm- Okay I'm a dick. I know that but I've apologized, stop being a bitch and call me back.

7:06pm- I didn't mean to call you a bitch, you're not a bitch, well maybe you're a bitch, who knows. Call me back PLEASE. I'm at Saints thinking about you. How about you come over and I make it up to you.

What sort of asshole thinks I'm going to go back to Saints Bar? The bar he took me to the last time we were together. Does he think that I'm stupidly gonna take him up on his offer? I'm about to block his number again when it begins ringing in my hands. *Shit shit shit.* The ringing finally stops but as soon as it does, it begins to ring again. This time I'm quicker turning my phone off. I open the drawer and throw my phone inside. I pour myself the last little bit of wine and snuggle into bed.

Chapter Twenty-One

Gabe

It rang, the phone rang. I expected it to go straight to voicemail, just like every other call, but this time it rang. *Does that mean she's forgiven me? Is she listening to the messages? What the fuck?*

I hit redial and it rings once before going back to voicemail again. *Fuck!*

I light up another smoke and ponder my options. *Do I keep trying? Pray that she'll answer eventually? Do I give up on her and find someone else who's less of a challenge? Fuck no! I like that she's hard to get and makes me work for it. Fuck knows why, but I do.*

I try calling one last time, but when it still goes to voicemail I decide to give it a rest. At least for now.

"Give me a rum and coke," I bark as I head inside and make my way to the bar.

"Sure thing," Declan replies.

"Actually, hold the rum," I shout, as an idea hits me.

"What? So just Coke then?" Declan asks, clearly confused.

"Yeah. Got a lot of money riding on this next game. Gotta stay sharp," I lie, knowing full well I could beat these chumps with my eyes closed.

Declan pours my drink with a nod, seeming content with my lie. "Cheers man," I say as I grab my drink and make my way over to the table.

I spend the next hour or so playing poker until it's just me and my brother's lackey left at the table. "I raise you $20," I call out as I throw the money on the table.

"You gotta fold, Tuck," Nate says, trying to minimize the shame his lackey is about to feel.

"All in," he replies, as he glares at me.

"Full house!" he calls out proudly.

"Not as good as a straight flush," I laugh, as I see Tucker's eyes widen in surprise.

"Fuck!" he calls out as I begin to swipe the cash, which has to be at least $150, off the table.

I watch Tucker leave and head towards the bathroom, so I follow him.

"Good game," I say as I enter.

"Oh yeah? Tell that to my girl when she realizes I blew our date money on gambling," he huffs. *I've got him exactly where I want him.*

"From what Nate tells me, she's gonna have your balls in a blender when she finds out," I add with a chuckle. *Did I hear him and Nate talking about this super expensive date he was taking his girl on? Yes, I did. Have I already figured out this punk has absolutely zero backbone and is super easy to manipulate? Also yes.*

"I know, she's gonna frigging kill me," he whines, keeping his head down and rubbing the back of his neck anxiously.

"Well, how about we do a 'lil win/ win?" I coax. "How about you lend me your phone for half an hour and I give you back the money I just won? Seem fair?" I ask, cocking my brow.

"My phone? Give me back the money you just won? Why would you do that?" Tucker asks, although I can see on his face he's intrigued.

"Well, you're my brother's best friend, and I know he'd hate to see you upset your girl," I lie. "Plus my phone's broken and I really need to call John about a big job I've got lined up for tomorrow." I lie again.

"Oh yeah? That makes sense. Thanks man, you're really doing me a solid." Tucker's relief is obvious. *It's like taking candy from a baby. I almost feel guilty. Almost.*

"Here," he says, reaching into his pocket and handing me his phone.

"Thanks," I reply with a smirk. I pull out a wad of cash and thrust it at him as I snatch the phone from his hand. "Now fuck off. This is private," I add.

I see a flash of confusion and fear form on Tucker's face as he turns and walks away without saying anything else.

I find the number and dial it.

"Hello," a sleepy, sexy voice at the end of the phone says. I'm speechless for a moment.

"Tucker, is that you?" Riley asks. "I'm not with Ava at the moment."

I don't wanna give anything away so I mumble, "Where are you?" while covering the microphone with my hand.

"I can't hear you very well, Tucker. But I'm not with Ava at the moment, I'm at home. Harper's with her though, if you wanna try her phone." *Jackpot!*

I got all I needed so I hang up and delete the call history.

"I'm off," I announce as I throw Tucker's phone onto the table and grab my jacket from the back of the chair.

"Wait, I'll drive you home," Nate offers, but I just keep walking.

I can hear Nate's footsteps behind me, "It's fine, my Uber is waiting outside," I lie. Not wanting to have another one of Nate's goddamn, 'I'll be the designated driver,' lectures. After all, I've not had a drink in hours. I'm fine.

I hop on my bike and drive straight to Riley's house. I bang on the door, not giving a fuck if anyone else is home or who I might wake up.

"I'm coming, hold your horses," I hear from inside seconds before the door flies open, and I see Riley's beautiful face. As soon as she realizes it's me, she attempts to close the door. But I'm faster than her and I put my foot in the doorway to stop her.

"Fucking move, Gabe. I don't wanna see you," Riley huffs as she continues trying to push the door closed.

"I'm not going anywhere," I reply as I shove the door open.

I feel the door connect with something just as I hear a thud. "Ouch!" Riley cries out and I push the door open slowly to see her sitting in a heap on the floor.

"Shit, did I do that? Sorry! Fuck!" I exclaim. *Why do I keep hurting this girl, even when I don't want to?*

I bend down and carefully lift her to her feet, cupping her cheeks. I turn her head from side to side looking for marks. But thankfully I don't see any. "I'm fine!" she snaps, pulling away from me. "You have to go," she tells me as she attempts to push me backwards out the door, but I refuse to budge.

"I'm not going anywhere!"

"Gabe, please," Riley pleads, and I can hear the sadness in her voice.

"Not till you talk to me," I add, trying to make eye contact with her. *If only she would look at me, truly look at me, she would see how sorry I am; and know that I feel something for her.*

"I can't," she whimpers and I feel my heart splintering a bit more.

I'm unsure what to do; the fiery temper and anger I can take, fuck, I love her spiciness. But the sad, almost broken version of Riley is too much. I have no idea how to make her feel better, how to bring her back to herself. So I do the only thing I know; I lean down and kiss her.

She tries to resist at first, before opening her mouth to give me access.

I kiss her harder, she gives my tongue entry to her mouth and I can feel my cock coming alive in my pants. I get caught up in the moment and I move my hand to slide it under her shirt.

"No!" Riley shouts as she pushes me away forcefully.

"You don't change do you?" she snaps angrily. "You think that after everything you can just kiss me, make me fall for you all over again, just to get what you want. Well, that's not me!" I can feel the anger and frustration radiating from her.

"Well kinda, but it's not like that. I mean yeah, I wanted to make us both feel better. But not in the way you think," I stutter. *What the fuck do I say?* I can feel my anger creeping up within me. She's acting like I was wrong to kiss her, to try to take things a step further. *She was into that just as much as me!*

I attempt to take a step forward, hoping she'll let me inside since I don't really want to air my feelings to the whole street, but she pushes me back again, this time closing the door behind us both.

"Shit, are your parents home?" I say in a hushed voice.

"No, they're at a function," she says, shaking her head. "But that's not the point, you're still not coming inside."

"Why?" I ask, feeling confused. *What is she hiding?*

"Because if you come in we both know how this will end," she says as she places her hand on her hips and gives me that sassy look of hers.

Would that be so bad? I mean, the best way to settle an argument is in the bedroom right? We do our best talking in the bedroom. She usually forgives me when we are alone in the bedroom.

I don't fuck things up there. I know exactly what to do and say to make her smile then.

Riley's words bring me back to the situation at hand. "What do you want from me, Gabe? Do you want to be my boyfriend?

Hold hands in the park, go on fancy dates? Or do you just want to fuck?"

"Err, I don't date. Fuck maybe? No, I don't wanna just fuck, I want..."

"What? You want what, Gabe?" Riley snaps.

"I don't fucking know!" I snap back.

"Well, then there's your fucking problem. Until you do know, you gotta leave me alone. Let me heal. Let me move on." I see the tears making another appearance in her eyes.

"I want YOU, okay. I don't know what that means, but I want you. I can't stop thinking about you." I shout back honestly.

"Fine, then let's go tell the world we're a couple. You call Kelly up right now and tell her you're no longer single, and you don't want to ever see her again."

"I don't care about her. She's a whore, but..."

"But nothing! You've said everything you need to. If you're not ready to shout it to the world, then I'm not willing to be anything more. I've been the secret girlfriend and the long distance girlfriend. I'm not willing to do it again. Either you stand up and proudly tell the world we're together. Or you leave right now."

"It's not that easy. I don't know how to do this. I've never done the whole dating thing before. It's gonna take time. My head is fifty shades of fucked up." I again attempt to reach out and touch her, praying that our bodies can say what my words cannot, but she slaps my hand away.

"No, Gabe, this isn't about fucking sex. I need more!" she cries.

"I don't fucking know how to have a normal relationship," I implore but it's clearly falling on deaf ears. *Why can't this be enough for her? Why aren't I enough for her?*

"Well then I suggest you learn. I suggest you go get some fucking help to deal with whatever the fuck is broken in you and come back to me when you know how to deal with a relationship that's not solely based on sex!" she shouts.

"Don't cry," I beg, as I see the tears begin to run down her beautiful cheeks.

"I'm not crying! I'm just angry!" she screams back, this time so loudly it causes her voice to crack. "Just go!" she says sadly as she turns to walk back inside.

I don't want to, but I know if I don't leave now my own temper is gonna force me to say something, anything to hurt her just so she doesn't see the hurt inside me. I know that if I say or do anything else to hurt her, I'll never win her back.

"Fine!" I snap back as I turn and finally allow her to slam the door behind me.

Chapter Twenty-Two

Riley

Six Months Later

Opening my wardrobe, I pull out the new top I brought for tonight. It's a red corset style top that makes my tits look amazing, and I'm pairing it with my ripped black jeans. The ones that make my legs look like they go on forever. I'm determined to look sexy as fuck tonight. It's Tucker's 18th birthday and he's having a huge house party. But that's not the reason I'm dressing up so much. No, I'm dressing up because I know he's going to be there. Tucker told me he was going to be there. *At least I hope he's going to be there.*

Does he want to see me too? My heart pounds harder in my chest as I think about seeing him again. I know I said that I wasn't willing to be his dirty little secret anymore, but now, after realizing how lost I've felt without him, I'm almost willing to accept anything. Almost. I'm not quite ready to give up the last bit of self-respect I have. *But damn do I miss him. Even if he is a stubborn and infuriating bastard at times.*

It's been almost six months since Gabe turned up at my house and we got into a huge argument. Since then, we've texted occasionally and smiled politely at each other when I've been with Ava to pick Tucker up from work, or when we've passed each other in general.

Gabe's been trying. I know he's been trying. He's started going to therapy with Nate to deal with whatever childhood trauma shit he has. And he's started hanging out with the guys a little more; hence, why I'm hoping he'll take Tucker up on his offer when he invited a few of the guys from work to celebrate with him tonight. But overall, we've tried our best not to be in the same room for too long.

Nate and Izzy are doing great, so I don't wanna cause drama for them if we don't work out. Plus, Harper made me promise not to go back to him. So, I've done my best to keep my feelings bottled up. Not to let it show how my knees go weak and my mouth becomes dry whenever I see him. Or how desperate I am to kiss him or pull him aside whenever I see him hot and sweaty with his top off whenever he's working outdoors and we pass by.

But I'm hoping tonight will be different. Tonight there's gonna be over fifty people there, and everyone is going to be drinking, so hopefully no one will notice if we talk to each other.

"Need some help?" Harper asks as she sees me rummaging around under my bed.

"I'm looking for my other shoe." I hold up one of my red pumps.

"Here." Harper replies as she instantly finds the other one. *I swear this woman secretly has fairy magic or something.*

"What would I do without you, huh?" I laugh.

"Constantly lose everything and be forced to roam the streets with one shoe on and one shoe off probably," she shrugs as she teases me.

"You're so weird," I tell her as I shake my head.

"Girls, are you ready to go?" my father calls out.

"Almost," we both reply at the same time and then giggle.

Harper hands me my shoe and picks my bag up from the bed while I apply one last coat of lipstick before leaving.

"You both look beautiful, girls. Did you remember to bring your stick?" my dad asks as he opens the car door for us to climb in.

"My stick?" I ask, confused.

"Yeah, to beat all the boys off with," he laughs.

"Oh my God, Dad, you're so cringey," Harper replies and I roll my eyes.

"I love your dad jokes," I laugh back. My dad is the biggest dork in the world and he tells the worst dad jokes, the kind that are so bad you can't help but laugh.

"So will you be spending the night or do I need to pick you up later?" my father asks as he drives us to the party.

"Not sure yet, either way, we'll get our own way back. There's no point waiting up for us," Harper offers.

"Yeah, you know what it's like when we all get together," I laugh, but the side eye my father gives me lets me know he'd rather pretend he didn't.

"By that, I mean, it's getting crazy with us all sitting in a big circle studying and drinking tea," I say in my most sickly sweet and innocent voice. Now it's my father's turn to roll his eyes.

"Of course," my father winks at me. "But if those books get a little too scary, you know I'm only a call away."

"Yes, Dad," both me and Harper sing-song in unison.

"Have fun," our father calls as we both get out of the car and make our way towards the gate to the garden.

There's only a handful of people here when we arrive. Tucker, Danny, and Nate are all chatting with a couple of other guys. But I don't see Ava or Izzy anywhere.

Walking over to the boys, I ask, "Where's Ava?"

"Her and Bella are inside making sure we have enough cups or something," Nate informs us.

"Please, for the love of god, try and persuade her to join the party. She's been bossing me, Nate, and Izzy around for hours," Tucker whines. "You'd think this is her birthday, not mine."

"If I don't make it back, tell my family I love them." I joke back as I grab Harper's arm and drag her inside with me.

I adore Ava to bits, she's one of my best friends. But she's the stubbornest, bossiest, most particular person I know. *And, no, I don't care if stubbornest isn't a word. It fits.* She won't be happy until everything is just perfect. I remember her last birthday when she made poor Tucker move the presents table five times before she'd decided it was in just the right space.

"Need a hand?" I ask. When I find Ava, she is pouring a selection of drinks into a huge punch bowl in the kitchen. Izzy looks up from beside Ava, places her hands together in a prayer pose, and mouths the words 'thank god.'

"I just can't get this punch right; it's either too strong or too weak," she huffs as she takes another sip, stamping her feet in frustration. *Guess it's still not right.*

"Let me taste it," I hear Harper say as she takes the cup from Ava's hand and tries some herself.

"It tastes great, Ava, as always."

"You sure? It's not too fruity?" Ava asks.

"No, we don't wanna kill the guests or give them alcohol poisoning," Harper comments while pointing to the array of half empty liquor bottles around the bowl.

"Plus, fruity is good. Means more people will enjoy it and stay longer before passing out," I add.

"Yeah, that's true, I guess," Ava says, finally sounding convinced.

"Can we finally grab a glass and head out to enjoy the party now?" Izzy begs.

"Yep!" Ava replies triumphantly as she begins handing us each a cup.

We head outside and make our way over to Tucker, who's now been joined by a few new faces.

"This is Jack and Luke. They work with us at O'Malley's." Tucker introduces us all to two of the new faces. "And, I think you've seen Davis before, but this is his wife, Amber," he concludes, introducing us to a couple who look to be in their late twenties.

"Don't worry, we're not staying long," Davis replies in the most beautiful Texan drawl. "We just dropped by to give the birthday boy a gift."

"You're welcome to stay," Tucker offers.

"Can I get you a drink, it's yummy," Ava offers, lifting up her cup.

"No thanks. I won't be drinking for a little while." Amber laughs as she rubs what I now notice is a small, round bump.

"It was nice meeting you all. Take good care of these jackasses for us," Davis teases as he nods his head towards the other boys.

"So, is anyone else from your work joining us?" I ask hopefully. Nate gives me a small shrug, while Tucker eyes me suspiciously.

"Like who, Rilez?" Ava teases.

Although neither she nor Izzy know about what happened with Gabe, Ava isn't stupid and says she can feel the sexual tension oozing off of the two of us, so I allow her to believe I have a little crush. It's easier than admitting the whole truth. *Plus, who would believe Gabe cared for silly old me anyway?*

"No one in particular; just wondered if we'd meet any of Tucker's other friends." I slump down beside Nate on the sofa trying to get information nonchalantly.

"I tried; he wanted to come, honestly. Gabe just doesn't handle people well," Nate whispers as the rest of the group all engage in conversations with each other.

The hours tick by, the party fills up, as does my glass. But still no signs of Gabe.

Feeling brave now that the alcohol is cursing through my veins, I decide to send him a message.

> Me
> Thought you agreed to come tonight. It would mean a lot to Tucker and Nate if you came.

Almost instantly, I get a reply.

> Gabe
> Just them? Or does anyone else wanna see me?

My body buzzes with the familiar electricity it gets every time I speak to him.

> Me
> Well I'm sure the other guys from work would be happy to see you, too.

I can't help but smirk, imagining Gabe's face. He pretends he doesn't, but I know he likes my quick wit and attitude.

> Gabe
> I don't give a fuck about any of those pricks. Give me one reason to come, and I'll think about it.

I make my excuses to leave the girls and head to the bathroom. Locking the door behind me, I check my reflection, reapply my makeup, give my boobs a little shuffle in my top to make sure they look as big as possible and begin snapping away until I find the perfect selfie. One that makes me look sexy and inviting and hit the send button.

I wait for a few minutes expecting some sort of flirty reply, but when nothing comes, feeling deflated and stupid I decide to head back to the party.

Before long though, the noise and chaos start getting to me so I step away from the crowds of people to just grab some quiet time out front when suddenly someone grabs me and covers my mouth. I attempt to fight and kick whoever is behind me, but go stiff as a board when a gravelly voice whispers, "Such a fiery little cocktease," in my ear as a shiver runs through my body and I feel my panties going damp. My knees go weak at the dirty words and the voice they belong to.

Releasing his hand from my mouth, he spins me around, kisses me hard, and pulls my body against him.

"What are you doing here?" I pant once his mouth finally releases mine.

"I told you, little flame, I'd come if you gave me a reason to. Now it's my turn to give you a reason to cum," he laughs as he grabs my hand and pulls me to a dark corner around the side of the house.

He pushes me against the wall and begins kissing me hard. My hands naturally find their way into his thick hair. Refusing to allow him to have all the control, I decide to pull it which causes a deep moan to escape his mouth.

"Such a brat," he moans as his hand finds its way to my throat and squeezes playfully.

His lips drop to my neck as he releases his hand and begins kissing and nipping at me, before moving his mouth lower to the parts of my chest still exposed in my corset. He attempts to undo the clasps at the front, but I stop him.

"Not here," I whisper. Despite the fact every part of my body wants to give him exactly what we both want.

"Let's head into the party," I suggest. I attempt to reach for Gabe's hand, hoping to walk in, hand in hand. But he pulls away from my touch. *I don't get this man at all.*

Reluctantly, he follows, but as soon as we get inside, he acts as if I'm invisible. We find Tucker and most of the other guys at the fire pit chatting so we make our way over. But other than pulling me and silently demanding I stand at his side, he makes no attempt to involve me in the conversations.

"So, have you asked out that girl from the coffee shop yet?" Tucker asks one of his friends.

"No, but I swear to god if I buy any more coffee I'll give myself a heart attack," the man, Jack, I think his name was, laughs.

"Fucking pussy," Gabe replies back coldly.

"Oh yeah, and when was the last time you asked a girl out, huh Satan?" Jack jokes back.

"Never, I don't ask girls out; I'm not a pussy. I just fuck 'em," he replies emotionlessly.

His words cut me like a knife. *I'm standing right here, and he has to say this shit?!*

"Oh really? You just fuck them do you, Gabe?" I snap back.

I see the realization finally register on his face, but I don't care. "And that is why you're gonna end up sad, alone, and riddled with STIs," I fire back before storming away. *Don't cry, don't cry. He's stupid and not worth it!.*

I hear quick footsteps behind me and stupidly hope it's Gabe chasing behind to apologize, but when I turn around it's Nate instead. "He's a fucking dick, Riley. I know that you know that, heck, even he knows it. But he does care in his own weird fucked up way. He especially cares about you." Nate offers with a warm smile on his face.

"Well, he certainly has a funny fucking way of showing it," I snap back at him, as I desperately try to hide how hurt I am.

"I know he does. And you deserve so much better. As your friend I should be telling you to forget about him and find yourself a nice guy who will treat you like a princess." He throws his arm around my shoulder and continues. "But as his brother and the only one of us that knows how to use his heart and head at the same time, I gotta tell you that he does care."

"Then why does he pretend I don't mean anything to him?" I snap, the wobble of my voice gives away how hard I'm working to keep the tears in.

How can he be so caring when we're alone, yet so callous when we're not?

"He tries in his own little way. I see how he's a little bit less of an asshole when you're around, and the way his face almost cracks a smile whenever he gets a message that I know is from you as he literally has no other friends. I also think that you know all of this, too, or else you wouldn't have been hoping to see him tonight."

"So then why can't HE say any of that himself?" I sigh.

"Because he's a fucking asshole who struggles with letting his walls down enough to be real and genuine with just about anyone. He's not gonna make this easy. But I promise that deep down there's a good guy buried in there. You just have to help him find him. He's afraid of being hurt and being left behind."

"And what if I'm not strong enough to battle until I reach that guy buried away?" I ask, tentatively.

"Then, I suggest you end whatever the hell you two have now. Because if he falls for you, I mean really falls for you, in the way that I think he is, and then you leave or abandon him, he'll never recover from that. Ever!" I can tell from the sadness in Nate's voice that he truly believes every word he just said to me.

Gabe

As soon as the words leave my mouth, I regret them. "And that is why you're gonna end up sad, alone, and riddled with STIs," Riley snaps, and I immediately see the anger and hurt on her face. I see the way her walls shoot up and I will myself to stop before I say anything more that will hurt her. *It's what I've done so many times before.*

I watch her storm off, and part of me wants to chase after her. Apologize and tell her that's not really how I feel, not about her at least. Because for the first time in my life ending up sad and alone, without HER, is scarier than opening myself up.

"You're a real asshole, Gabe," my brother barks at me, before, like the knight in shining armor that he is, he chases after my girl. My wildfire.

"What was that about?" Jack asks.

"Fuck knows," I reply like the coward I truly am.

I continue drinking my drink pretending to listen to some god awful conversation as I watch Nate catch up with Riley. He throws his arm around her and she leans into him like he's her protector. *It should be me! She's my girl, not his. She should be running to me for salvation, not running from me.*

I try not to let my jealousy rise, knowing Nate has zero interest in Riley. He's head over heels in love with his fucking perfect, princess of a girlfriend. But still, I can't help but feel envious of how easily this all comes to him. *Why can't I be more like him? Everyone loves him. Yet nobody ever loves me.*

He's chatting away to Riley, making her smile, and doesn't seem at all concerned about the fact she repeatedly touches his arm.

I watch the two of them walk away together and go into the house, so I decide to follow.

Riley's alone now, pouring herself another drink.

"Riley, wanna play doubles? I'm getting my ass kicked here," some jock calls from the other side of the room.

"That's 'cuz you suck," Riley calls back as she makes her way over to his side.

I follow but hang back as I watch Riley and Jockstrap line up the beer pong.

He goes first and misses, then she goes second and gets it in the first time. "Drink up loser," she laughs. I continue watching as my girl wipes the floor with the two, big ass men on the opposite team.

"Oooh, last one," Jockstrap announces as he hands the ball to Riley to take the winning shot. She leans over wiggling her ass as she tries to find just the right angle. *What the fuck?? Is he looking at her ass?*

I turn my attention to Jockstrap and sure enough, his eyes are firmly on my girl's ass. *I don't like the guy and it would be so easy to beat his ass for daring to look at what's mine.* But I know I have no right, so I try to compose myself with another beer. *After all, I've already blown it so I might as well drink enough that I forget. It's not like it can make this night any worse.*

"Suck it losers!" Riley calls out, breaking me out of my death stare.

The other team moans and groans as Riley jumps up and down excitedly.

A few others start berating the losers, "Taken down by a girl," another guy cheers.

"Think you can do better, Chad?" Riley challenges.

Chad and what I can only assume is another brain-dead football player step up to the mark and begin setting up.

Every single time Riley takes a shot, Jockstrap's eyes are firmly on either her ass or her tits, and it's taking everything in me not to go beat his ass. But since Riley seems so happy - laughing, cheering, and doing a little dance every time she wins - I hold back and do nothing but seethe. *She deserves to be happy.*

That is until she wins again and jumps up to hug Jockstrap, and the dickhead puts his hands firmly on her ass. Riley pulls away, saying something. I pace over there just in time to hear him say, "Come on, Riley," as he attempts to place his disgustingly drunk mouth on hers. Without thinking my fist flies out and connects with the side of his jaw.

"What the fuck, Gabe?!" Riley screams as Jockstrap falls to the floor.

"We're out of here," I snap as I pick her up and throw her over my shoulder kicking and screaming.

"Let me go!" she insists, but I don't listen - not until I've got her outside, away from the commotion.

"What the fuck do you think you're doing?" she asks in a clipped tone when I finally put her down.

"I was saving you," I reply, just as a hand connects with my face. *She fucking slapped me!*

Chapter Twenty-Three

Riley

"Well, you fucking shouldn't. I'm not one of your dirty whores that you can fuck and then chuck, Gabe. I care about you. And I hope that you care about me, too," I begin, feeling the anger and embarrassment coursing through my body, as I wiggle out of his grip. "You can't say you claim me, then refuse to actually claim me and date me properly."

"Wait, Riley..." Gabe begins, but I cut him off.

"No. You either want me or you don't. You don't get to just have me for sex and nothing else. I'm either your girlfriend or I'm not. And if I'm not then you've gotta let me talk to other guys; to find one who likes me back and isn't afraid to be seen with me."

"I'm not afraid of anyone..." Gabe huffs, voice full of pathetic, male bravado. If I didn't know him as well as I do, I would *almost* believe him.

"You're afraid of your own goddamn feelings!" I counter. "Do you like me?"

"Yeah, but…"

"There are no buts to it. You either like me or you don't. You either want to be with me or you don't. It's that simple." I feel my eyes begin to water. *Fuck, I hate that I cry when I'm mad.*

"Don't get upset," Gabe begins as he reaches out to cup my face, but I slap his hand away.

"No! I'm not upset, I'm fucking pissed off. You said you didn't wanna date. Fine! But you can't now scare every other guy away who I might like because you're too fucking jealous to see me with another guy. You're like a spoiled child - you don't want me until someone else tries to play with me, then suddenly you decide I'm yours, again." I notice that a small crowd is gathering and far too many eyes are on us. But I refuse to let myself care or back down.

"You're always mine. You've always been mine and you'll always be mine!" Gabe growls back as he attempts to kiss me, but again I pull away.

"No Gabe! You don't get to do that. You don't get to confuse me with sex and kisses and think that's okay." *How do I get through to his thick skull??!!*

"I was only gonna kiss you," he replies softly, and I hear a hint of sadness and confusion in his voice.

"It's never just a kiss with you though, is it? We'll kiss, and then fuck. You'll make me believe you care. And then you will reject me all over again. I'm not some doll you can play with when you're bored. You either want me to be your girlfriend and have me all the time, or you have to back the fuck off and let me find someone else who will treat me like I deserve!" I scream before turning my back on him and storming off.

"Riley! Wait!" Gabe calls, but I don't turn around.

I storm past the crowd and head out the gate towards the front of the house. I just need to get away.

"Riley, wait," Gabe calls again from behind me.

I see Tucker's brother having a cigarette with his friends and make my way over.

"Have you been drinking?" I ask, hoping he hasn't. Theo is older than the rest of us and has often played taxi when he's been back from college.

"Sober as a judge," he replies, holding up a bottle of water.

"Take me home, then?" I beg.

Theo takes one look at me and thankfully takes pity. "Be back soon," he lets his friends know. "Car's around the corner," he shares as I follow him.

"Riley!" Gabe bellows from behind me.

"Run!" I shout as I begin sprinting. Thankfully, Theo runs, too, and has the car unlocked and the engine running by the time I get in.

"Riley, get out of there, now!" Gabe orders as he bangs on the window.

"Go, please just go." I plead just as Theo speeds off.

"Wanna talk about whatever the fuck that was back there?" Theo questions as we turn the corner.

"Not really. But thank you for rescuing me," I tell him with an exasperated breath.

"Didn't seem like I had much choice," he laughs back. "Who the fuck was that anyway? Boyfriend? Ex-boyfriend? Goddamn psycho, maybe?"

"All of the above," I laugh, shaking my head.

Gabe

I make my way back inside to grab my jacket and keys so that I can go after her. *Fuck this shit, she needs to hear me out!* On my way back out, I can't resist grabbing a bottle of vodka that was sitting there ripe for the taking.

"Woah, what happened?" Nate asks when he sees the murderous look on my face.

"Who the fuck is the asshole with the red Audi?" I snap.

"What's Theo done?" Tucker smirks. *That's right, fucking smirks like this is the funniest thing ever.*

"Theo, is that the asshole's name? Where does he live? Where can I find him?" I snap as I debate beating that asshole's face in because I'm pretty sure it will make me feel better about the fact he just left with my girl.

"Well, here I guess?" Tucker laughs.

"Theo is Tucker's brother. What the fuck happened?" Nate questions.

"Not here," I grumble as I motion for Nate to follow me.

I take a few steps away from the group, enough that they can't hear us talking, and then ask, "Are Riley and this Theo fucking?"

If I find out they are, I'll fucking kill him.

"For fuck's sake, Gabe, no they're not even DATING as far as I'm aware. He's more like a big brother. He's known the whole group since they were kids. Plus, he's like twenty-five, why?"

"Because he just stole Riley from me and drove her away in his fancy-ass car," I huff.

"Pretty sure he didn't steal her. What happened? What did you do?"

"Why do you assume it's me, that I did something wrong?" I snort.

"Because I know you, Gabe. You act first, think never."

"I did fuck all wrong, well, except maybe punch some kid who was checking her out, but that's all. Then Riley got all pissed, stormed off, and demanded Captain fucking America take her home," I explain.

"For god's sake, Gabe, why can't you just tell her you like her and wanna date her, like a normal fucking person, instead of going all alpha asshole on her ass?"

I round on him stating, "I don't wanna date her!" *How many times do I have to explain that not everyone needs some fairytale romance like he has?*

"Whatever you say. You can lie to yourself, but you can't lie to me. I've seen the way you look at her. You care, even if you refuse to admit it."

"Fuck you!" I toss back as I skulk away. Why the fuck is everyone so adamant that I have to share my feelings like some pathetic, lovesick teenager. Just because I think she's hot as fuck, feel all fuzzy whenever she texts, and the fact that I wanna murder every guy who even looks at her, it doesn't mean I have feelings for her. *Does it?*

Throwing myself back down on the chairs, I reach for the bottle realizing I'm too drunk to ride my bike around town looking for Riley and her 'knight in shining armor', even if I wanted to.

I spot a guy clearly dealing drugs and decide fuck it, I could do with something to take the edge off. As I'm walking over I see him take something out of his jacket, drop it into a bunch of cups, and make his way over towards Izzy and the group of girls she's dancing with. *Oh Fuck no!* I drop my drink and rush over, banging into him causing him to spill the drinks all over the floor and all down Izzy's top. Nate appears from nowhere and grabs the punk by his collar. The girls all try to get in the middle and Izzy pulls Nate away.

"That's right, run away like the little pussy you are," the greasy haired punk calls after him.

"Oh, I'd watch your mouth if you wanna still be able to open it tomorrow," I threaten while getting into his face.

"Screw you!" the guy glares, before turning and walking away. I turn around hoping to salvage the drink I just had, but of course in my haste, I dropped and spilled the whole thing. *For fuck's sake!* Just then I see that same guy throw his arm around Riley's sister's shoulders. I race over but not before she takes a huge gulp of her drink. I knock the cup out of her hands, but it's empty. *For fuck's sake!*

"What the fuck did you just put in her drink?" I demand and push the jackass backwards.

The asshole just smirks at me, an evil, sadistic little smirk. "You fucking heard me! What did you give her?" I repeat, as I grab him by his collar and shake him.

"Just a little something to loosen her up a bit," he laughs. "It's no big deal," he manages to get out as my fist flies, connecting straight with his jaw, knocking him back into the crowd.

"Fucking asshole," the guy mumbles loudly as he spits out a mouthful of blood. He tries to land a punch on me but only manages to miss me.

I'm about to lay into the guy when I hear a small voice, "I don't feel so good." I look over and see that Harpey looks spaced out and her eyes can't seem to focus. *Roofied!*

I pick her up and throw her over my shoulder. "Where's the fucking bathroom," I shout at nobody in particular and someone points me in the direction of the stairs; I run up them.

I see a line forming outside one of the doors so head to the front and bang on it loudly.

"Open the fucking door! Open it now," I bellow.

"There's a line, you know," someone says in a snarky tone, but they soon shut up when I fire them one of my 'fuck with me and you'll regret it' looks. Banging on the door again, I shout. "You've got five seconds to get out!" The door flies open and a terrified girl scurries out.

I go in and kick the door closed behind us, dropping Harpey down in front of the toilet. "Make yourself sick," I command.

"I don't wanna," Harpey mumbles.

"Do as you're told. Make yourself sick," I growl at her.

She puts her fingers into her mouth but barely gets them past her teeth before she's gagging and removes them.

"I can't," she whispers as she begins to slump her head against the toilet seat.

For fuck's sake, I don't have time for this shit. Grabbing her by the hair, I pull her head up and off the toilet seat. Grabbing her hand, I force her fingers down to the very back of her throat until I hear her begin to wretch. I move my hands just in time for exorcist-level vomit to come spewing out of her mouth. *Thank god, I'm still controlling her head with her hair or it would have gone all over her.* Once she stops heaving, I let go of her hair, a little too quickly, as it causes her head to fall down and hit the seat.

"Here, drink this," I offer, filling a cup I found on the floor full of water.

"I wanna go home," Harper grumbles as she sips the water I gave her.

I fling open the bathroom door yelling, "Someone go get Izzy or the Pocket Rocket," to the people still standing outside.

"Who?" a girl asks.

"Isabella or Pocket Rocket." *Fuck, what's her actual name?* "Firey red head, big tits, little ass," I explain to the blank face staring up at me. "Tucker... Tucker's girlfriend, the redhead," I suddenly remember.

"You mean, Ava?" the girl clarifies.

"Yeah, that's her. Tell her to get here now. Riley's sister needs her."

The girl rushes off as does another one standing beside her.

A few moments later the door is pushed open and there stand Firecracker and Tucker.

"What the fuck?" they both say at the same time as they take in a semi-conscious girl on my lap as I'm forcing a drink down her throat.

"She took something. Give her fluids and put her to bed," I order them as I stand up and literally thrust her into Tucker's arms and race out the door.

I head down the stairs and out the door, suddenly feeling more sober than ever. I jump on my bike and spend the next hour driving around hoping to see that wannabe rapist. God, or perhaps the devil himself, takes pity on me as just as I'm about to give up hope, I spot him. I stop my bike and jump off, not even caring as I hear my bike fall to the ground. I tackle the guy to the ground and begin pummeling him, punching him again and again. "You're a fucking scumbag!" I bellow as another punch connects with his ribs. I feel him thrashing beneath me, desperately trying to get me off him, yet I don't move an inch.

"Not so fast, you piece of shit," I say as I press my knee into his chest and my fist connects with his jaw. *Fuck me, it feels good to finally get this pent-up anger out.*

I see a right hook fly towards me, but I block him with ease. *See, growing up with an abusive asshole of a father comes in handy at times. I can sense an attack a mile off.*

"Get off me, man!" I hear him plead but I can't stop because the visions of what this piece of shit could have done to Izzy, Harpey, or even worse, Riley, play through my head like some sort of twisted horror film.

Visions of what could have happened if Riley was still there, play so vividly that I can almost hear her voice begging him to get off of her. All I see is red as I begin hitting him harder and harder.

Next thing I know, there are sirens, and I'm being ripped from my own nightmare by two police officers as they drag me off of him.

"I'll get you for this," the guy manages to whimper while drooling puddles of blood.

"If I ever see you near Izzy, Harpey, or any of their friends again, you're dead!" I growl as I'm thrown in the back of the cop car. The only consolation is that he's thrown into another shortly after.

After being fingerprinted and processed, I'm put in a cell and told to calm down. Not long afterward, the scumbag is thrown into the cell beside mine. His face and mouth are swollen, and his mouth is still bleeding.

"I'm gonna get you for this; just you wait till my cousin hears about this. You're dead! Hope it was worth it to save some stupid slut who wouldn't have looked at you twice if it wasn't for me," he says, words slurred and laced with venom.

"What the fuck are you talking about?"

"I saw the way you looked at that girl. Think you're clever knocking the drink all over her, do you? Jealous I'd get a taste of that sweet pussy before you?" He sneers at me.

"Isabella?" I ask, feeling a mixture of confusion and disgust. "She's basically my sister you fucking sicko and if you had drugged her, not even the cops themselves could have saved you." I feel the anger reaching a whole new level.

"Hope you had fun with the consolation prize; not as hot I know, but a hole is a hole. Heard you had your way with her in the bathroom," he spits.

I lunge forward to try and grab him through the bars, just as someone calls out, "Scott, time for your call."

I considered calling Riley, wanting to let her know about her sister and that she's hopefully safe; but also knowing she probably won't answer the phone. I call my brother, instead. Unfortunately, it's not Nate who answers; but rather the last person I want to speak to right now. *Princess fucking Isabella.*

Chapter Twenty-Four

Gabe

I would recognize that annoyingly cheerful tone anywhere.

"Hello?" *Fuck this. I'd rather spend the night here than beg for her help.* I thrust the phone into the officer's hand and turn my back on him.

"Sit," the officer instructs quietly as he points toward a nearby chair.

"Hello, is anyone there?" I hear a voice say through the phone as I shuffle over to take a seat at the nearby desk.

"Hello ma'am, this is the Avery Hill Police Department. I have a Mr. Gabriel Scott here," the officer says.

I can hear sounds on the other end of the line, but am too far away to make out what's being said.

"Mr. Scott was arrested for assault. Do you want to post bail? Otherwise, he will have to stay here until Monday," internally I roll my eyes. *This is it. This is when Little Miss Perfect's gonna get her chance to be a bitch and leave me here to rot all weekend.*

"She wants to talk to you," the officer says as he covers the receiver.

I shake my head defiantly. No way am I gonna talk to her just so she can have me begging for help. *Fuck her.*

"Unfortunately, he's currently in processing." The officer lies. "Yep, that's correct. If bail isn't posted, he will be spending the night..." The officer stops to listen for a moment before answering. "It's $800, and he can leave once bail is paid and the paperwork is completed....It takes about an hour to file."

The officer hangs up the phone and gives me a strange look.

"Let me guess, the bitch told you to let me rot. She probably laughed and told you I deserved this."

"Actually," the officer says, cutting me off,. "She told me to start the paperwork and that she would send your brother here ASAP, although fuck knows why. If you were my brother-in-law, I wouldn't think twice about making you spend the weekend here. Maybe it would teach you some goddamn manners."

"What? She's actually sending Nate to get me?" *Where is he getting the money? $800 is a hell of a lot of money to find in the middle of the night. Fuck, what if John has him doing jobs on the side? I've worked so hard to keep Nate away from that side of the business.* My mind spirals as I'm escorted back to the cell while my paperwork is filed.

Just over forty-five minutes later, the officer comes and escorts me through the station. I expect to see my brother waiting for me on the other side of the door, but am shocked when I see Isabella's face instead.

"Oh, for fuck's sake, why is she here?" I snap. *Where the fuck is Nate? Did he send her? Is he mad at me? Doesn't he care?* The thoughts run through my mind at hyperspeed.

"I assume she's here to get your sorry ass out of here," the officer fires back at me.

"I don't fucking want her here. Just take me back!" I say feeling angry, hurt, confused, embarrassed and incredibly vulnerable at this moment.

"Well, it's 4 a.m., and I've already maxed out my card to save you. So you might as well come with me," she sighs, sounding exhausted. *Wait? She maxed out her card... to save me? Why?*

"Who says I need to be rescued by YOU?" I spit back. As my walls instinctively fly up. *What the fuck is going on? Is this some sort of trap? What does she want from me for helping?*

"Well, no one, I guess," she stammers and I can hear it in her voice that she's either frightened or nervous, "but I can't just leave you here," she says before giving me a timid looking smile. But it makes me uneasy. Not because it seems disingenuous, but because it reminds me so much of the pitiful smile I saw so many times on Nate's face when we were just kids. The smile he'd give me or Dad when he was trying to be brave, praying that if he was a good boy, Daddy would love him and not hurt him.

"I suggest you leave now before I book you back in," the officer states coldly.

"Are you sure you're okay with him, ma'am? It's not too late to change your mind," the officer proposes, this time looking directly at me.

"Yes, I'm fine. He's family," Isabella says despite the fact it's clearly a lie. Her words take me back for a moment. So much so that

I can't even reply, instead I just rush ahead, needing a moment alone to process the last thirty seconds.

I hear her fast steps behind me, as she desperately tries to match my fast pace. I stop at the bottom of the steps to give her time to catch up, but I must stop too quickly as I hear her stumble on the last one. I reach my hand out instinctively and catch her by the arm just before she falls.

"Should I call us an Uber?" Isabella mumbles as she steadies herself and looks down at my hand that's still on her arm.

"Where's Nate?" I demand as I pull my arm away. *God, I wish Riley were here as well.*

"Well, he's taking care of my friend Harper, who's pretty sick. I got the call and came straight here in an Uber," Isabella explains and I notice that same shit-eating grin on her face as Nate gets whenever he talks about her, too.

Shit, do I have that stupid face when I think about Riley? Shit, Riley! Does she know about her sister? Is she there with her now? Surely she would have come too, if she were. Again, my mind goes into overdrive as I continue walking.

"Wait! Do you want me to call us an Uber or not?" I hear a distant voice say behind me.

"No, I'll walk!" I toss back absentmindedly. I continue walking a few more steps, consumed by my thoughts when it dawns on me - Isabella. *Fuck, I can't leave her out here alone.* I glance back and see her shuffling from foot to foot as she looks down at the floor, mumbling something to herself.

"So, you coming or what?" I call out. Deciding it's the least I can do; to make sure she gets home safe, after all, she did just save me from a weekend in lock-up. I see her head pop up and a grateful little grin forms on her face as she begins running over to me. *What the fuck is she wearing?* Only now do I take in the fluffy, pink trousers poking out the bottom of her coat. *And wait, are those slippers on her feet?*

"Nice pajamas," I tease when she finally catches up to me.

"Oh, I'm so sorry, sir. I should have dressed better for bed, knowing I'd have to bail your belligerent ass out of jail!" she snaps back as she looks down at herself.

"It was a fucking holding cell, not jail," I grumble. *I may be a dick, but I'm not like my father, I don't deserve to end up in jail.*

The thoughts of that bastard, the one I've spent years trying to forget invade my mind. I think about the shit he put us through. About what happened when we moved away, what happened when Nate abandoned me to stay with his stupid foster family.

Why couldn't he have just left with me? I would have taken care of him. But no, his stupid new family and stupid new school were more important. I bet that's why he didn't come tonight. He probably hoped I'd stay in the cell and get sent to prison so he'd never have to deal with me again. After all, I'm nothing but a disappointment to him, and everyone who has ever known me. That's why no one ever stays, not for me. No one cares about me, not really. But then... if he really wanted rid of me, and I'm sure Isabella does too, why did she come tonight?

"Why did you come?" I ask quietly. I see her turn to look at me strangely, like she either didn't hear or doesn't understand the question.

"Why... did... you... come?" I repeat slowly.

"What do you mean, why did I come? They called and said you had been arrested. I couldn't just leave you there to rot," she says with a confused frown, but so matter of fact, like the answer is obvious.

"Why didn't you just leave me in there and pretend you didn't get the call?" I snarl. I just don't understand this girl. Surely this has got to be a trap. I've made her life hell since she started dating Nate. I always thought this nice girl act was just that, an act. Something to make my brother fall in love with her. I was so sure she'd come here to either trick me and watch me squirm, or to demand something in return. But she's done neither.

"Pretend I didn't get the call? Why would I do that? You needed help, so I helped you. I really don't understand the question, Gabe," Isabella snaps and it's clear I've upset her.

"Well, you've already said that Nate doesn't know I called. Why come? Why not just hang up the phone and let me rot in peace?" I ask desperately trying to understand. When she doesn't answer right away, I grab her arm a little too forcefully. I don't wanna hurt her, but I need her to look at me so I can see either the sincerity or the lies in her eyes. If it did nothing else, my childhood made me a human lie detector. I've learned to spot deception a mile away.

She winces under my grip before pulling her arm away with fear in her eyes. "Are you crazy, Gabe? I know you don't like me very much, but to be honest, I don't know why. I've never been anything but nice to you. You're practically family. I love your brother and plan on being with him for the rest of my life. So, sorry, bud, but it means you're stuck with me for the rest of your life," she says as she rubs at her arm before continuing. "You're Nate's big brother, the person he loves the most in the whole world. And whether he asks me to or not, I'll still come and try to save you. I'd never do anything to hurt him. That's why I keep trying to repair this stupid rift between us. You're important to Nate, which means you're important to me as well.

So, just in case it's not fucking obvious yet, I've come to get you and I'm walking the streets at almost five in the morning in my fucking pajamas with no fucking idea where we are or where you're taking me because I care about you, you goddamn psycho!" she screams before physically covering her mouth. *Fuck, she seems like she needed that.*

I can't help but smile at her outburst and the way anger, then shock, then guilt flashes across her face. *Why does it seem like she's just unleashed a lifetime of pent up frustration? And why do I feel oddly amused and proud of her for that?*

I see her looking around nervously, and for some reason want to put her at ease. "I'm taking you home, Princess," I smirk. I see her face screw up at my choice of word. Which just makes me smirk more. That silly stubborn look on her face reminds me so much of Riley. *I guess they are friends after all; but who'd have thought that out of all the big bad people I've met over my years, two stubborn little girls, both barely as high as my chest, would be the only ones brave enough to shout at me like this?*

"What's so funny?" Isabella pouts.

"I like your bitchy side. Who knew the cute kitty had claws?" I say with a mischievous tone.

"I'm not a bitch; you're just an asshole. Besides, you woke me up in the middle of the night. No wonder I'm a little grumpy," she snaps, crossing her arms like a petulant child. It takes everything in me not to burst out laughing then and there.

"Oh no, did I make the little Baby Princess mad?" I tease, nudging her on the shoulder.

"Fuck you," she snaps but lacking conviction, before attempting to storm off in frustration. I watch her take a few steps, then look around before turning left and taking a few more steps in completely the wrong direction. *Stubborn little shit.*

"Wrong way, Princess," I call out before bursting out in hysterics at the frustrated, yet stubborn look on her face as she turns around and walks back to me like a dog with its tail between its legs.

"How do you even know where we're going?! Everything looks the same! You're probably taking me somewhere so you can murder me and bury my body in the woods," she huffs. She looks so much like she's having a tantrum that I half expect her to stomp her foot.

"We're almost there, Princess, and besides, I like this irritable side of you. I'm having too much fun teasing you to kill you just yet. Not to mention, Nate would most likely try to murder me if I let anything happen to his little Bella Boo." I say in my most playfully mocking tone, before laughing loudly at my own joke.

"Wait! What's that noise?" she suddenly gasps dramatically as she whips her head all around quickly.

"What? Where?" I demand as I try to listen for whatever she hears. Instinctively the playfulness I felt just a moment ago is gone, and I'm in full defensive mode. Ready to protect myself, and her, from whatever threat is out there.

"Oh, it's just hell freezing over," she laughs as she tries to poke me. But instinctively I move. It takes me a minute for my adrenalin to ease. *What the fuck is this girl trying to do to me?*

"Who knew the big, bad Gabe Scott actually knew how to laugh?" Now that I'm finally calm and I know there is no imminent threat, I can't help but internally roll my eyes at myself for being so easy to fool.

"It's pretty hard not to laugh at those stupid, fluffy pajamas. What are those anyway, puppies?" I tease, as I try tugging at the sides of her coat to undo the buttons to get a better look at her stupidly childish pajamas. She squirms around as she desperately tries to hold her coat together while I try to open it. I can't help but enjoy this playfulness. It takes me back to the few times we used to all have together. *Back when I could pretend I was young and carefree.*

"You woke me up. I was asleep," she says as she stomps her feet, *ah there it is,* trying and failing to sound frustrated. If anything though, she looks like she's having a toddler tantrum. The way Nate used to whenever I told him he couldn't follow me to school. Back when mom was still alive and times were better.

"So is that your go-post-bail outfit or your special occasion party wear? Or do you always sleep in cute, little puppy pajamas?" I joke as I lead her out of the clearing just a few feet from Tucker's house. I feel relaxed, enjoying this rare chance to be playful. *For once I don't feel like I have to hide my emotions. There's no one here who I need to pretend for, it's nice.*

"It's a good thing I do, or I would be collecting your ass out of jail naked," Isabella replies. *What the fuck? Did I hear that right?* I stop in my tracks genuinely confused. *I should have known!* Of course this was all just some sort of flirty ruse. *How could I have been so fucking stupid!? Of course, all she wanted was to flirt. After all why the fuck would she want to be friends?* She turns around to look at me and I fire her a furious look.

"Wait, I didn't actually mean it," she lies, as she stumbles over her words. *I should have known she was just some dirty whore, just like almost every other girl I've met.* What makes me angrier is that she's my brother's girl. And one of Riley's best friends. *Sure, she may not know that me and Riley are sort of together, but how could she do this to them either way.*

"Whatever, I should have known you were just a slut. Go show that shit to my BROTHER," I snarl viciously as my blood begins to boil.

"Fuck you!" she snaps before the bitch actually swings her hand as if to slap me. ME! When she's the one who essentially just said she wants me to see her naked. I grab her hand a second before it connects with my cheek. "That was the first and last time you ever get to touch me," I hiss through gritted teeth.

"What's your fucking problem, Gabe?! We were just having fun and then you completely switched. Why?" She lies again as she tries to pull away from me but I just grip her hand tighter.

"I have enough girls to have fun with; I don't need you," I say coldly. *Fuck her, fuck these pathetic sluts. At least whores like Kelly admit what they want. They don't lie and try to deceive people like she does. I can't believe I didn't realize this side of her sooner. Nate deserves so much better.*

She continues trying to pull away from me and not wanting to feel her skin on mine a second longer, I release her. Clearly, a bit too quickly as she immediately slips out of my hand and lands on her ass with a thud. She looks back towards the house, where Nate and all her friends are. *What if she tells them? Tries to twist it like I hit her? I'll lose both Nate and Riley!*

"If you tell anyone about this, I'll tell my brother you tried to fuck me, you whore," I threaten as I stand over her in an imposing manner.

"I'm not a whore!" she says as her eyes fill up with tears. "I didn't even mean anything by it. I was just joking around as friends," she looks up at me as she shuffles backwards in fear. *Fuck, this is not how I wanted this to end.*

"We are not friends!" I snap before sprinting off.

I hide behind a tree, just long enough to watch her stand up, dust herself off, and make her way to Tucker's. I stay far enough behind that she doesn't see me, yet close enough that I can see her and make sure she gets back safely. *I hate her right now, but I'd hate myself more, and so would Nate, if anything happened to her because I left her alone in the dark.* Once she makes her way through the back gate, I know she's safe. I run to the nearest pub to drown out the memories of tonight.

When I arrive I realize the door is locked. *What the fuck?*

I bang on the door, once..twice... on the third knock the door swings open. A very rumpled looking Declan stands in front of me in what appears to be an old t-shirt and plaid pants. *Is he in sleep pants? What the fuck is going on?*

"What?" Declan snaps. Before he realizes it's me and his face changes.

"I could have beat your skull in," Declan says as he lets out a deep breath and lowers the baseball bat I now notice in his left hand.

"Yeah, yeah, I'd like to see you try," I joke as I push my way past him. *Where is everyone?*

"We're closed asshole," Declan says on a sigh as he shakes his head and locks the door behind me. *Is it that late?*

"Whiskey, and leave the fucking bottle," I snap to Declan as I slump down at my usual corner of the bar.

"So, business hours clearly mean fuck all to you then," he mumbles under his breath as he makes his way around the bar.

"One of these days I'm gonna get to keep a bottle for my actual customers," Declan jokes as he reaches for the bottle, the one I know he keeps especially for me, on the top shelf.

"Who you kidding, these fuckers..." I say motioning around to the completely empty bar, "...wouldn't know their Bell's from their Macallan's."

"Well, when you start ordering Macallan's, I'll stop complaining," Declan smirks.

"Fine, I may not be getting drunk on $200 whiskey, but I also refuse to drink the cat piss you serve," I groan as I snatch the bottle of Glenfiddich out of his hands.

I hear Declan mumble something in response but instead of listening or answering, I simply flip him the middle finger and go back to drowning my sorrows.

I sit drowning my sorrows as Declan scurries around the place, cleaning up and restocking the shelves for tomorrow.

"Who is she?" Declan asks, suddenly appearing right over my shoulder.

"What the fuck, man?" I slur as I try flipping my phone over hoping to hide the picture, even though it's obviously too late. "Who do you think you are, creeping up on me?"

"Well if you didn't have your eyes glued to the screen, you'd have noticed me, wouldn't you, dipshit," he says, swiping the phone from the bar. I attempt to stop him, but my alcohol fueled reflexes are shit.

"She's hot." Declan says, and I don't miss the way his beady little eyes stare at her. *You think I don't know what your mind is imagining, dickhead!*

A possessive growl leaves my lips. "Don't even think about it," I say through gritted teeth. *I've already been in one fight tonight; I don't need to get in another.*

"Woah, not like you to give a fuck. Who is she?" Declan asks as he pulls up a seat beside me.

"Nobody!" I snap feeling my blood boil at the idea of anyone, even Declan, *who is an alright guy I guess*, looking at my girl like that.

"So does this no one have a number? Maybe I'll give it a call," Declan teases. *I wish I could wipe that stupid shit-eating grin off his face.*

"Relax, tough guy, I'm just joking. No need to try and murder me with your eyes." *Shit, was it that obvious?*

"Just felt like testing out a little theory," he adds, as he looks at me with a raised eyebrow.

Fine, I'll bite, I guess. "What fucking theory?" I toss out.

"Oh just that you're actually human after all. For a while I wondered if you were a robot sent here purely to drink and fuck."

I wish! Life was so much simpler when I had no goddamn emotions. Before Nate came back and before Riley started sending my brain fucking haywire.

"Screw you," I grumble as I stumble off my chair and make my way towards the back of the bar.

"Where do you think YOU'RE going?" Declan laughs.

"To sleep on your fucking sofa!" I shout back, not even turning to look at him as I make my way towards one of the booths, grabbing a discarded coat off the hook to use as a makeshift pillow.

I hear a chuckle leave his lips, but he makes no attempt to stop me. Over the years I've passed out here more times than I can count. Declan doesn't seem to mind, he just closes up around me and tells me to lock up when I leave the next day. His only rule is that I'm not allowed to invite girls for late night parties or fuck anywhere in the bar, which is fine by me as I have no desire to be stuck at some shitty sleepover anyway.

Chapter Twenty-Five

Riley

It's been a couple of weeks since Tucker's birthday. I finally spoke to the girls and told them about what had happened between me and Gabe. Not that I had much choice after half the school saw him punch Chad in the face and then I got carried out like a naughty toddler. Not to mention something going down between him and Harper, although Harper can't remember much other than the fact that Gabe helped her somehow in the bathroom and then made Tucker and Ava take care of her while he disappeared. Thankfully they were all pretty understanding, but all any of them told me was what a mistake I had made getting involved with Gabe. If only I could force myself to feel the same. Despite all the heartache and anger he causes me, I feel drawn to him like a moth to a flame. Ready to fly myself into damnation for a taste of happiness.

Despite my better judgment, I agree to go on a date with Ashton, a guy from science class that Harper set me up with. We head to the movies, the film's okay I guess, but the date itself is kind of bland. "How about we go for a drink?" I suggest.

"A drink? Where?" Ashton asks, sounding kind of sheepish.

"I know just the place, follow me," I say, leading him to the place I would really like to be, hoping to see the guy I really wish I was with.

I walk inside and scan the room, the back booth, and the bar - even standing on tiptoes to try and see out the back door. But nope, he's not here.

"What would you like?" Ashton asks as we make our way to the bar. "A soda? Orange juice? Maybe a mocktail," he suggests.

"I'll take a whiskey," I say to the bartender.

"My kind of girl," a guy a few stools down says.

"Coming right up, I guess," the bartender says, as the other guy steps off his stool and makes his way over to me.

"And what's your little brother having?" the guy teases, "A juice box, perhaps"

"I'll take a beer," Ashton says with a bite in his tone.

The bartender hands us both our drinks, not even bothering to card us.

"How about I introduce you to a few friends?" the guy says as he wraps his arm around my waist and pulls me towards him. "The name's Marko, by the way," he says, taking my hand and kissing it. The feel of his lips on my skin makes me want to hurl. But I don't care. At least it's interesting.

"She's here with me," Ashton states, but even I can hear the way his voice quivers and lacks conviction.

"It's okay baby bro, you can come, too." Marko reaches out and grabs my drink, keeping his arm snaked around my hip as he guides me outside.

When we get out, I'm greeted by at least four other guys, each much bigger and angrier looking than the last.

"Sit," says Marko as his buddy kicks out a chair and Marko basically pushes me into it. "Look guys, I found us a new friend."

Ashton gets a nearby chair and goes to sit beside me. Just then another guy grabs my chair and pulls it beside him just enough that Marko manages to slide a stool in on the other side, splitting me and Ashton up and wedging me firmly between these two strangers.

"You already know me, but that's Deeno, Michael, Phoenix, Christopher, and Johnny Boy, himself," Marko says, pointing around at the different members of this group.

"And what's your name, cutie?" the old man, the one they called Johnny Boy, purrs.

"It's Stacey," I say, holding my own while secretly hoping the name holds as much confidence and luck for me as last time. I see Ashton's eyes widen, but he doesn't say anything.

The bartender comes around soon after and takes everyone's drink orders again.

"I'll take another whiskey, please," I say politely. The men all bark their orders and continue talking. A few moments later the bartender comes back with everyone's drinks, gives them out, then hands me a beer.

"Excuse me," I say, reaching out to get his attention as the rest of the group continue talking, "I ordered a whiskey."

The bartender leans down close enough that only I can hear him and whispers, "You're gonna want a drink you can keep your thumb over the top of, and you're going to want to stay sober, too."

"Is there a problem?" one of the guys bellows.

"No, not all. I was just telling the lady what cocktails we had on offer," the bartender says with a fake smile.

"I think I'll stick to beer, thanks," I reply.

I take a swig of my beer and realize the bartender seems to have replaced it with soda. *Shit! What have I gotten myself into?*

I watch poor Ashton's eyes get wider and wider the more the rest of the group talks. His eyes dart to the door and back into the bar, silently begging for us to leave. "Anyway guys, it's been nice, but we have to get going," I interject into their conversation. I attempt to stand, but the guy on the other side of me grabs hold of my belt and pulls me back down towards my chair.

"Yeah, sorry but we've gotta go. We're catching a movie," Ashton lies.

"Well, fuck off then, she's staying with us." Phoenix, *or perhaps that's Michael,* informs him through gritted teeth.

I see the terrified look on Ashton's face and know that while they might be at least pretending to be polite to me, not one of these guys would think twice about rearranging poor Ashton's face.

"It's fine, Ashton. You go. I'll catch up with you for that movie tomorrow," I tell him, trying desperately to sound calmer than I feel.

"Are you sure?" he asks, eyeing me suspiciously. "Maybe I should stay, too?"

I hear a round of angry noises from the table, so again I try to convince him to save himself. "No, honestly you go. I'm fine, see you tomorrow."

"Erm, okay, see you then," he stammers. I stand up to give him a hug and whisper, "Seriously go, but on your way out tell the bartender to keep the same beer coming."

I see him give me a suspicious look, but when I give a little nod he leaves.

"Thank god he fucked off," says Marko as he pulls me down to sit on his lap.

Chapter Twenty-Six

Gabe

My phone rings and the caller ID tells me it's Declan. "Hey man, this is an unexpected call. What, I miss one night of drinking, and you call to make sure your best customer is alive?" I joke.

"I'm not in the mood for jokes Gabe. I suggest you get your ass down here now. Your girl is in trouble and needs you," he snaps. Normally he's pretty laid back, so I know this is something serious. "Did you hear me?" he repeats angrily.

"Why would I give a fuck if Kelly needs saving? She's a big enough girl; she can save herself," I reply, already done with this conversation. Just as I'm about to hang up, he counters, "No Gabe, not her. She's not who I'm calling about," he pushes out, his voice getting more desperate.

"Then who?"

"I don't know her name, the little blond I've seen you pining over recently. You know the one I definitely shouldn't be serving whiskey to."

"Riley?" I gasp, feeling my heart rate increase dramatically. *What the fuck is she doing there? Was she looking for me? Hoping to run into me?*

"Maybe? I dunno. But I suggest you get here and find out. She's with the rest of your buddies. Alone."

"I'm on my way. Keep her safe," I shout into the phone as I run out of my house.

"I'm trying," he replies before hanging up.

I speed up and make my way over to the bar as quickly as I can. As soon as I get there I park my bike and rush in. "Where is she?" I demand.

"Outside, I've been feeding her soda in a beer bottle. And I've told her not to let that bottle out of her sight. But I can't get her away from them," Declan says.

"Bring another round out," I call as I head outside.

"There he is!" John cheers as I make my way out.

I see Riley sitting on Marko's lap and my heart sinks. Of all the guys he's probably the slimiest. Thankfully, he's still compliant enough to listen to me. I make my way over and see Riley's face morph from fear to relief as she locks eyes with mine. I can see that she is shaken up. *I will kill them slowly and painfully if they have hurt her in any way.*

"So, who do we have here?" I say as I sit down opposite her.

"This is Stacey," Deeno, the baby of the group, says.

"Stacey, huh?" I say with a slight smirk. "How about you come and keep my lap warm for a bit?"

I hear a frustrated growl leave Marko's ugly mouth. "I found her first," he groans.

"And now I want her, so share!" I snap through gritted teeth.

Marko releases her just as Declan arrives with the drinks. Riley makes her way over to me and sits on my lap. I loop my arm around her tightly but can feel her shaking under my touch.

Declan hands her the beer bottle. The sweet smell of soda hits my nose and it now makes sense what he was saying earlier about soda in a bottle.

"She'll have a whiskey, and make it a double," I say, taking the bottle out of her hands and handing it back to him. Declan just looks at me and nods.

Riley continues to shake under my arm, so when no one is looking I lean over and whisper, "You're safe baby; just don't fucking move."

Declan comes back and hands her the double whiskey, which she gulps. "Slow down baby" I say, again, only loud enough for her to hear. She leans forward and places her drink on the table, but as soon as she does I pick it up and place it back in her hand. She looks at me with a smile, like she understands what I'm trying to say.

"So, you still fucking around with that Kelly chick?" Marko asks and I feel Riley stiffen in my lap.

"Nah. She's used goods. I'm done with her, she's all yours man," I say, nonchalantly. *Do I feel guilty feeding Kelly to the wolves? Sure. But is it worth it to keep these savages away from Riley? You bet your ass it is.*

I notice the way both Michael and Deeno keep staring at Riley's bare legs, so looping my arm around them I twist her body so that they are now sprawled over me and the arm of the chair. Deeno looks up like a petulant child, frustrated that I've taken away his favorite toy. But as soon as his eyes catch mine glaring back at him, he turns his gaze away in fear.

While I'd like to think I'm not as depraved and dangerous as the rest of these fuckers, especially when it comes to women, they all know I wouldn't think twice about going toe to toe with any of them. I've been in this business since I was a kid, and I've seen more shit and done more shit than almost all of them combined.

The guys continue to talk shit with each other and since they are no longer paying attention to us, I use the hand that's hidden from them to softly stroke Riley's side, hoping to calm and soothe her.

"I'm going to the toilet," I announce as I lift Riley to her feet.

"I'll watch your lady, while you take a piss," Marko smirks.

"Not that sort of bathroom break, if you know what I mean," I reply with an exaggerated wink and I pull her closer against me.

I lead her inside, past the bathroom, the one I can see by the look on her face fills her with as much disgust as it now does me. I guide her to the end of the bar. "Stay here with Declan. You're safe here," I say as I turn and leave.

"Wait, don't leave me," she says.

"Stay here. I'll be right back," I say as I look over her, to Declan, who nods in agreement.

"What happened to the hottie?" the guys ask when I walk out alone.

"Taking her back to mine to test her out properly," I laugh as I down my drink. "See you tomorrow old man," I joke as I pat John on the shoulder and leave.

As soon as I walk back inside I grab Riley, who is now sitting on a stool behind the bar, and leave.

"You sure know how to live on the wild side," I say as I carefully place my helmet on her head.

"Well, they're your friends," she snaps back.

"Listen here," I say, stopping to ensure she's looking directly at me. "Those animals are not my friends. They are the scum of the earth, and you need to stay far, far away from them." I lift the helmet off her head to make sure she can hear me clearly.

"Well they sure seemed to like YOU," she replies.

"Those animals don't like anyone, not even each other. They'd fuck each other over in a heartbeat."

"Oh," she replies. "But then why..."

"They fear me; they don't like me. There's a huge difference." I say as I put the helmet back on her head. then climb in front of her.

I grab her hands and wrap them around my waist. She settles them underneath my shirt instead of on top. *Her fingers feel amazing as they graze the skin of my abs.*

She squeezes much too hard as we drive away, to the point that her nails sting as they cut into me. Even so, I take the sting with pleasure, not wanting her hands to ever leave me again. *Why the hell am I liking this so much? Normally I'm basically allergic to physical touch. Every moment of it feels like my own form of torture, hell even. Yet the feeling of her skin against mine feels like heaven, not hell.*

The further away from the bar we get, the looser her grasp on me is until she's holding on for comfort.

Not wanting to take her home, I drive us to a nearby hotel. One much nicer than the shitty motel I took us to last time though.

"One double room," I say as we get to the desk.

"Do you require the standard or luxury room?" the guy behind the counter asks.

"Luxury," I reply.

"Sure thing, sir," he responds as he types something on his computer then hands us a keycard. "Third floor, room 308."

I loop my arm around Riley's waist, something I've never done with a girl before, and guide her to our room.

As soon as we get inside I see her eyes widen. "Wow," she says. As she makes her way over to the jacuzzi bath.

"Go run yourself a bath, baby, you need it," I smile and tap her on the ass playfully.

I watch her scurry off to the bathroom and hear the taps turn on.

I pick up the phone and call down to reception. "Hi, I need to order some food to be brought to the room in about an hour - that's okay, right?"

"Of course, sir. What would you like?"

Because I've never shared a meal with Riley and I have no idea what the fuck she likes; I decide to order a platter of different mains and desserts. *She's bound to wanna eat something.*

I push the bathroom door open and am hit with a face full of steam. *Why the fuck do girls have their baths so hot?*

I walk over to the tub and find Riley relaxing with her eyes closed. The bath is so full of water and bubbles that all I can see is her rosy nipple poking out of the water. My first instinct is to let my dick take the lead and walk over there and do whatever I want to her. I want to fuck her so hard that she doesn't remember any other man's touch but mine. But I decide against it. *Riley has already put up with enough shit because of me.*

So I decide to give the whole 'Boyfriend' thing a try and instead sit on the edge of the tub, grip her chin, and give her my best version of the Spiderman kiss, a kiss from above. Riley kisses me back, but as I try to deepen the kiss I realize how fucking problematic this position is. *How the fuck does Spiderman make it look so easy?*

Breaking the kiss only long enough to move, I change positions and then kiss her again, not giving a fuck as I feel the water sloshing and wetting the collar of my hoodie.

"Wanna join me?" she asks with a cheeky wink.

"Abso-fucking-lutely!" I say as I begin removing my clothes. She sits up and scooches back, presumably to make space for me to sit where her legs were. But I have absolutely no desire to sit there, so instead, I coax her forward and climb in behind her. *Fuck me, is this what lobsters feel like when they are thrown into a boiling pot?* I wonder as I sink in behind her and feel at least five layers of skin melt away.

As I sit down, I carefully tuck my dick between my legs, *for once not wanting him to join the party,* and pull Riley back against me. I wrap my arms strategically around her waist, trying my hardest to stop them from wandering either higher or lower.

"I was so scared tonight," Riley admits as she wraps her arms around mine.

"I know, but you're safe now. I'm here." I whisper, kissing her neck.

"Am I?" she questions.

"Are you what?

"Safe. Am I safe; safe with you?" she questions. And my cold dead heart hurts at the uncertainty of her words.

"You're safe baby, I promise," I reply, surprising myself with how much I truly mean those words.

"Am I yours?" she questions.

"Yes, Fireball, nobody else can have you but me," I growl, feeling that possessiveness rise again at the thought of anyone else touching her.

"And are YOU mine?" she asks a little less confidently. *I don't like the insecurity I hear in her voice. I love when she is spitting fire and holding her own.*

This time I didn't answer straight away. *Am I hers? Do I want to be hers? What does it even mean to be hers?*

"Gabe, tell me you're mine or I'm getting out of this bath, walking out that door and you'll never see me again," she says, moving away from me. I grip her tighter, holding onto her like a lifeboat out at sea.

"I'm yours," I whisper as I turn her face to the side so that I can kiss her.

"Then prove it," she mumbles into my mouth.

I grip her throat gently, feeling her pulse, and not missing the small moan that leaves her lips when I do. I push her back so her head rests against my shoulder. Then I slide my hand down her breasts, stopping only to give a quick hard pinch to one of her rosy nipples then slip my hand under the water and between her legs. Her moans fill the room. I start rubbing little circles and with my other hand, I palm her tit and pinch her nipple.

"Oh fuck...yes...Gabe....fuck," she pants as I feel her body begin to shake, but I don't let up. I put more pressure on that hard nub and slip a finger deep into her slick hole. I can feel the wetness inside of her and it's not from her bath. She's close, very close so I pull back a moment and I hear her whine, "Noooo, Gabe, don't stop!" I use my thumb to press down on her clit and pump three fingers into her. On my third pump, I whisper in her ear, "Come for me, my dirty little slut." *Shit, is this okay to say to a girlfriend? She liked it before? But is it different now? Fuck, what if I've ruined the mood again?*

Thankfully I haven't as I feel her body grip my fingers as she comes undone. Her body goes limp in my arms, so carefully I lean her forward so I can climb out, I then lift her up and carry her to the bed.

"I'm all wet; get a towel," she squeals as I place her down on the mattress, not giving a fuck if there's a towel there first or not.

"You'll be even wetter in a minute," I grin as I pull her ass to the edge of the bed, drop down to my knees, spread open her legs, and eat like a starved man, not stopping till I get to taste her on my tongue.

"Wow," she pants when I finally come up for air.

I hear a knock at the door. Picking up my discarded boxers I throw them on and walk to the door while adjusting my hard as steel cock.

"Don't move," I call as I close the bedroom door behind me.

I grab the trolley from an uncomfortable looking guy and push it inside. I make my way back to the bedroom where I see Riley wrapped in the most obnoxiously thick white robe I've ever seen.

"It's so soft," she groans happily, as she rubs the material against her cheeks.

I can't resist pulling her towards me by the tie of that ridiculous robe and giving her a kiss. It was supposed to be just a peck, but it deepens quickly. *Fuck, if I don't stop now, she won't get fed.* Groaning, I force myself to pull away. "Come, be my good girl and eat some food," I force out.

"What if I don't want to be your good girl?" She grins, looking me up and down seductively. "What if I want to be your dirty little slut instead?"

"Even sluts need to eat, baby," I grin back. She lets out a carefree, playful giggle. And *god, do I love that sound. Maybe I should record it to set as my alarm tone? Actually, on second thought, better not, otherwise not only will I be waking up grumpy, I'll also be insanely horny.*

We both make ourselves a plate and climb into bed to eat and watch some reality show on television. We're almost done when I hear, "Oops!" I look over and watch as Riley tries to wipe some cream off the top of her chest that must have fallen while eating her cake. I place my plate down on the floor and lean over. "Here, I'll help," I say, intending to lick the cream off, but as I lean down to do so, I realize that under her robe, she's completely naked. I tug on the rope, causing the robe to fall open exposing the most beautiful sight I have ever seen, and want to see every day for the rest of my life. I carefully lick up the cream, before using my tongue to slowly lick her, starting at her neck. At her collarbone, I suck a bit longer, not quite marking her but enough to let her know that I want to. From there, I move down to one breast where I lick the outline of her nipple before sucking it into my mouth and giving it a bit of a bite. I hear her gasp then moan so I repeat the same to the other breast. Just when I hear her breathing really start to quicken, I move my way down to her bellybutton, lick around it then stop. "Gabe," she moans, pouting her lip like the little brat she is.

"You've had enough," I laugh as I pull the robe back together and carefully re-tie the belt.

"You're mean," she sulks, trying to relax her breathing.

"And don't you forget it," I growl, gripping her by the throat and squeezing slightly. I feel her body quiver under my touch as her breath hitches. But I quickly release her, give her a gentle kiss, then reach for my plate and continue eating, loving the little frustrated look on her face. *I may no longer have the desire to physically punish her. But this is just as much fun.*

Once we're finished eating, we curl up in bed together and I fall asleep, with her nestled in my arms.

Chapter Twenty-Seven

Riley

I wake up still curled up in Gabe's arms and for the first time ever, I feel truly happy. *Sure, I have a good family and great friends, but something has always been missing. He's my missing piece.*

"Morning," Gabe yawns.

"Morning," I reply as I nuzzle into him more. Gabe wraps his arms tightly around me and pulls me in so that I'm trapped against him, listening to the gentle thumping of his heart.

"What do you want to do today? Gabe asks.

"Just this," I sigh contently as I slide my hand down his abs.

"Damn, I've created a monster," Gabe jokes. "How about we have some breakfast first?"

I try to protest but the rumble of my tummy gives me away.

"I'll take that as a yes," Gabe laughs, as he leans over and picks up the room service menu.

We both spend the next few minutes perusing the menu.

"I can't decide what to have; it all sounds so good," I whine. Gabe reaches over and snatches the menu out of my hands and for a second, I worry I've done something wrong. That is until his signature frown turns into a slight smirk.

He picks up the phone and calls down to reception, "Can I place an order for room 308? Yeah, I'll take the pancakes with a side of syrup, chocolate sauce on the side, some strawberries, and uh, yeah, some cream. I also want a portion of the poached eggs on toast with bacon... yes for two, my girl is hungry. You got a fucking problem with that?"

I internally cringe at how rude and snappy he's being to the poor person on the other end of the phone, but something about being called 'his girl' does things to me. *I can't explain what exactly it is, though.*

"Yeah, we will also take a pot of coffee, apple juice, and orange juice..."

He turns to me and whispers, "Wine?" but I shake my head. *It's barely 10 a.m.*

"...and I'll take a bottle of bud... I don't care what time it is....well then I suggest you find one!" Gabe snaps before slamming the phone down.

"Gaaabe, there's no need to be so rude," I yell at him in a half playful, half serious tone.

"Stupid douchebag, trying to tell me they don't serve alcohol at 10 a.m. Who the fuck does he think he is?" he huffs as he takes out his cigarette and attempts to light it, still sitting in bed.

"Gabe, do that on the balcony…please," I add when he throws me a pissed off look. *Heck, if looks could kill, I'd be dead twenty times a day with this guy.* I add a little smile, which seems to do the trick because he shrugs and makes his way outside.

Once he's out of the room I make my way to the bathroom. *For some strange reason, despite everything else we've experienced together, the idea of him hearing me pee just fills me with embarrassment.*

I finish up, making use of the free toothbrush and mouthwash, then head back to the bedroom.

I expect to see Gabe back inside by now but realize he's still outside smoking.

I take my opportunity to stare at the hard ridges of his shoulders, the huge tattoo of angel wings that cover his back, and how cute his butt looks.

I make my way over to him, expecting him to turn around, but when I get near him, it's clear that he is in his own world. As I get closer, I notice he's staring at people who are passing by on the street below. I quickly throw my arms around his waist from behind.

"I got you!" I laugh. "Good thing I'm not a bad guy sneaking up ready to push you off this balcony," I joke as I give him a slight nudge.

A slight scoff leaves Gabe's mouth as he quickly maneuvers so that I'm now the one in the front, trapped within his arms.

"Baby, you couldn't sneak up on me if you tried," he says in that sexy, growly voice he has while he plants little kisses on the side of my neck.

"You had absolutely no idea I was here. I totally snuck up on you," I laugh, giving him another playful push.

"That's cute, Little Spark" he says sarcastically. "I heard you flush the toilet, and turn on the tap. I heard the bathroom door open." I *internally die knowing that if he heard the toilet flush and the water running, he likely heard me pee as well.*

"I heard the floor creaking as you stood perving on me at the door. And I heard all seven steps it took for you to reach me. So remind me again Sparky, at which point you thought you were being so stealthy?" He continues to tease me.

"What the fuck, you heard all that? Who are you, Spiderman?" I laugh.

"Nah, I'm just used to listening for danger," Gabe says nonchalantly.

"And counting footsteps keeps you safe from danger, does it?" I joke, "What danger do your spidey senses protect you from then, I wonder, Mr. Super Hero?"

But his response kills my playful mood instantly.

"I pray you never have to find out."

Even though he only said eight words, he said them in such a raw way that it fills me with so much sadness. *I don't know everything he went through in his life, but from the few small things either he, Nate, or Izzy have let slip, I know it was fucking shitty.*

Unsure of what to do or say, it's clear that whatever he's talking about is no joking matter. Part of me wants him to open up more and let me see the side of him he keeps buried, but from the little I've figured out about Gabe so far, sitting and discussing our innermost thoughts and feelings is a form of torture in his eyes. Instead of asking him the questions I have whirling around in my brain, I just hold him and hug him tightly.

A knock at the door breaks up the silence, so I quickly head inside. I am almost glad for the distraction.

"Hello ma'am, where would you like me to put this?" the porter asks as he motions to the trolley.

"Here, I'll take that," I offer, then quickly state, "the room is kind of messy."

"It's fine ma'am; it's kind of heavy. I'll bring it in for you," he offers with a kind smile, but before I even have a chance to thank him, I sense Gabe behind me.

"She said we've got it. Now fuck off!" Gabe growls, making me jump slightly.

"If you're sure," the guy replies as he turns and leaves so quickly that had this been a cartoon, he would have left a person sized cloud of smoke behind him.

"Really! Was that necessary?" I complain, turning and walking back into the room, leaving him to bring the trolley in himself.

"It was when that creep was undressing you with his eyes."

"He was not. He barely even looked at me," I argue.

"Riley, I know men. He was thinking about all the ways he wanted to fuck you." Gabe huffs as he pulls the trolly into the room and kicks the door closed.

"You're such a...well...man," I toss back, feeling even more exasperated now. "Not every man wants to fuck every woman they see."

"Yes they do," he states in a matter of fact way, "and I'm not having some greasy haired punk, staring and fantasizing about my girl," he snaps back.

Feeling defiant and kind of stubborn, I walk closer to him and point my finger, "And who said I was YOUR girl anyway? Maybe I have a thing for greasy haired punks? Maybe I should head out and see if HE'S single?" I see Gabe's eyes turn to thunder and his whole face morphs in frustration. He pushes the trolly away, not caring as it bumps into the wall and lunges forward, grabbing me and pinning me against the wall.

"You..are...MINE!" he growls possessively.

"You say that, but you haven't even asked me to be your girlfriend yet," I point out in more of a pouty voice than I intended.

"Fuck labels. You. Are. MINE." he says through gritted teeth. "This is mine," he says, running his thumb roughly against my lips. "And these are mine," he says as he grabs hold of my boobs. "And this, this is definitely mine," he growls as he leans over me, spreads my legs with his knee, then takes his hand and possessively grabs hold of my crotch.

"You are so fucking jealous!" I say pushing him back.

"I'm not jealous; I'm possessive, there's a difference," he growls.

"It's the same difference," I grumble back. *Damn, he's so easy and fun to wind up.*

"No. Jealous means I want what is his. Possessive means, I'd kill any man who tries to take what is mine!" he growls back as he kisses me. Hard. *Fuck, his words alone fill me with so much desire.*

I kiss him back with a moan. Just as I'm about to lose myself in him, he ruins everything by muttering the words "I own you," into my mouth.

I push him away, slipping out of his grasp. "You're such an asshole. I'm not some piece of property you can just claim," I huff.

Gabe grabs me by the hand and pulls me back closer to him.

"I claimed you the first time I saw you!"

"You're such a goddamn caveman!" I yell just as he picks me up, carries me over to the bed, and throws me down on it.

"You're such a brat," Gabe laughs back.

"Yep, but I'm your brat," I reply with a smug grin.

"Lucky me," Gabe replies with a sarcastic eye roll.

"Oh shut it, you love it. Now go make me a coffee, slave," I giggle as I use my foot to push him away as I shuffle up the bed to sit against the headboard.

GABE

The defiant look on her little face as she pushes me away fills me with a mixture of emotions. Part of me is turned on by her bratty behavior and wants to fuck the attitude right out of her. Another part of me wants to laugh and enjoy the fact that she's brave enough to have such an attitude toward me. *It's rare to find a girl with some fire; one who doesn't cower down and do whatever I say.* The last part of me wants to cringe and kick my own ass for allowing her to turn me into such a little bitch.

"I'm waiting," her singsongy voice reaches me as I make my way over to make her the fucking coffee she asked for. "And bring some food! I'm wasting away over here."

"Then get your ass over here and get yourself something then," I shout back.

I hear her climb out of bed and make her way over. She comes up beside me and bumps me out of the way with her hips.

"Sorry, fat ass coming through" she smirks.

"Good thing I like this fat ass then isn't it," I joke back as I give it a playful slap.

Riley surprises me by breaking out in song, "he likes big butts and he cannot lie…"

I can't help but laugh out loud as she continues singing and shaking her ass in the silliest, most unsexy, yet strangely attractive way ever.

Moments like this, I can't help but feel carefree. *I don't know what a real relationship would be like. I never spend more than a night with girls, and even then, it's more like a couple of hours. But if I did ever have a relationship, I'm guessing this would be it.*

I imagine these are the moments Nate talks about with Izzy. Like his dates sound boring as fuck, trips to animal farms, cinemas, bowling, and walks in the woods… *snore fest. But the playful moments he describes, I wonder if this is what they feel like.*

"What ya thinking?" Riley singsongs, as she tries to tickle me.

"Just about work," I lie.

"So work has you grinning like the Cheshire Cat does it? Strange. I sure don't have that feeling when I think of work or school," she smirks, and it's clear she's calling me out.

"Here, Pinocchio," Riley grins, as she hands me a coffee. I take a sip and it tastes perfect.

"Did you add sugar?"

"Yep, three, why?" Riley replies with a raised eyebrow.

"How did you know I take three sugars?" I ask in surprise.

"Err, because this is like the third time we've had coffee together, duh."

"And you remembered how I liked it?"

"Well, yeah, of course... I don't know anyone else who would have three sugars, it must be sickly sweet though. Why? Don't you know how I take mine?" Riley asks as she stares at me waiting for me to clearly read off her preference like the local fucking barista.

"No. Erm....wet?" I shrug.

"Really? Wet? You're shit!" Riley says, shaking her head. "I take milk and half a sugar."

"Half a sugar? What's the point of that?"

"Duh, because I'm sweet enough already," she grins as she places her hands in a little V under her chin and tries her best to look angelic.

"Parts of you sure are sweet to taste," I smirk back, letting my eyes drop to exactly the parts I wish I was tasting as I lick my lips hungrily.

"You're such a perv," Riley laughs as she covers that area with her hand. Even though it's already plenty covered with the stupid fluffy robe she's been wearing all morning.

"Here greedy, eat this instead," she laughs as she shoves a piece of bacon into my mouth.

"I'd rather…"

"…eat you instead," she finishes in a mocking, masculine tone.

We both prepare ourselves a plate of food then make our way over to the bed to enjoy it. I flick through the limited channels looking for something to watch.

"Stop, stop," she calls out. "Go back one."

I do as she said just as a bunch of characters come on screen. I don't even have a chance to figure out what it is before Riley begins narrating along with the screen.

I just stare at her as she pretty much recites word for word along with each character.

"How many times have you watched this?" I ask, looking at her in fascination.

"What? Friends, or this episode?"

"Either."

"Friends, every single episode multiple times. This particular episode, at least ten times," she laughs as she continues to eat her breakfast.

"And you're not sick of it yet?"

"NEVER!!" she gasps in mock disgust.

We continue to watch TV and eat our breakfast. I don't say much, but every now and then Riley will pipe up with a random fact, or explain who someone is, or why the fact they're clearly on a break is such a big controversy.

"Can we go out somewhere...together?" Riley eventually asks.

I feel my pulse quicken at the thought. Sure I'm enjoying our time together, but I know we have to check out in a few hours. *Am I ready for us to go out together?* Like what if she wants to hold hands or walk down the street being all sickly sweet and coupley? *Do I want that? Am I ready for that?*

"Never mind, you can just drop me home I guess," she says, but I can hear the sadness and insecurity in her voice. *Why does it bother me so much?*

"No, it's fine, let's do something. What do you want to do?" I ask, still unsure why I'm agreeing to this.

Her whole face lights up which makes my grinch sized heart grow. "I don't mind. Can we pop into Target or Walmart first though, as I need to get a few things?"

She bounces off the bed and heads into the bathroom. I hear the shower running and after waiting a few minutes, I get bored and follow her.

"Don't even think about joining me," she warns as she peers around the shower curtain. "Otherwise, we'll never make it out of this room," she adds as she disappears from sight. *Would that be the worst thing?*

I close the lid, sit down on the toilet, and just enjoy the view. Even if it is partly obstructed by the shower curtain. Luckily it's thin enough, especially now it's wet, that I can see enough to imagine what's behind it.

"I was thinking...." Riley begins as she continues chatting away while she showers.

"Hand me a towel," she instructs.

I look around and see a gray towel sitting in the sink so I hand it to her.

She wraps it around herself and steps out.

Then she spends the next twenty minutes walking back and forth to the bedroom where all her stuff is and the bathroom where the mirror is. *Why doesn't she just grab all of her things and bring them in here? Girls are so dumb.*

I spend my time following behind her like some little lap dog as every time I walk away or attempt to sit down she calls me back into whatever room she's in, then fucking walks off again.

"You're giving me motherfucking whiplash," I reply as she brushes past me for the hundredth time, this time to pick up a hair band from beside the bed.

"What? Why?" she asks, sounding genuinely bewildered.

"Back and forth, back and forth. You're like a goddamn yo-yo"

"You should see what it's like sharing a room with Harper then," she laughs back. "Two girls, one room...not so much fun in the morning."

"You and your sister share a room?" I ask.

"Yeah, kind of weird, I guess," she says as she shrugs her shoulders. "We have the space for us to have different rooms, but neither of us want that. She's my twin and she's always been there. We had separate rooms for a few years when we were younger but it just felt..."

"Lonely?" I finish, knowing exactly how it felt for her because that's how I felt when I stopped sharing a room with Nate.

"Exactly. Lonely. Don't get me wrong, we still both like our space sometimes, and the room is big enough so that we both have our little areas, but it's kind of nice knowing she's there. That if I need her, she's just a few steps away. Does that make me sound like a total codependent freak?"

"No, I get it. Me and Nate shared a room for years. Pretty much our whole lives, actually. When I moved out of the Jacksons' home, that was one of the hardest things to get used to," I admit.

"The Jacksons? Who are they?" Riley asks and instantly I feel my walls shoot up in defense.

"Nobody, just fucking drop it," I bark at her a little more harshly than intended. I don't miss the shock and panic that briefly flashes over her face before it's replaced with a fake grin. *Fuck! Why do I have to ruin everything?*

"I'm going for a smoke," I announce and turn to leave, not even waiting for a response. *Why the fuck did I mention the Jacksons?*

"All ready to go?" Riley eventually asks from the doorway.

"Yeah, let me just grab my shit."

I brush past her and put my boots and jacket on. I grab her small bag from the bed and hand it to her.

"You know you can talk to me about anything, right?" she says softly as she takes the bag from my hand.

"Just fucking drop it, *please*," I reply, silently begging for her to listen to me for once.

We walk down to reception, hand back the keys, sign off all the extra charges and then hop on my bike in silence. She doesn't say a word as I take her bag and place it into my seat or as I put the helmet on her head. She doesn't say a word as she wraps her arms around my waist. We drive in silence for a while until she finally squeezes me to get my attention and shouts, "Pull into Target." I drive in and park near the front door. She climbs off and removes her helmet.

"I need my purse," she says, sounding unusually timid.

I climb off the bike and hand her the small black purse which she takes, and then heads inside without saying another word. I stand outside waiting, half tempted to head inside and grab a beer since I haven't had one since last night but decide against it. For some reason the idea of drinking then driving when I've got her on the back just doesn't sit right with me.

She comes out no longer wearing the dress from last night. She's now wearing jeans and a simple top that makes my mouth water and my dick start to rise. She could wear a burlap sack and it would look amazing on her.

"You changed?" I say without thinking.

"Yeah, I can't exactly ride a bike in a short dress can I?" she laughs. "Unless you wanna just take me home and call it a day."

"No," I say before she has a chance to finish that thought.

"Look I'm sorry for earlier. I didn't mean to push you into talking about something you obviously didn't want to," she says, and again there's that hint of sadness in her voice I hate.

"It's fine. Let's just move on," I suggest pulling her against me. She wraps her arms around me and buries her face into my chest.

"You alright, Gabe?" Lucas, one of the guys I work with, says as he comes out of the store and walks past us. Instinctively, I push Riley away.

"Let's go," I snap. *Shit, I hope Lucas doesn't tell anyone he saw me hugging Riley. Damn. Who am I kidding, that boy is so scared of his own shadow he wouldn't have the guts to spread shit around work.*

Either way, I'm not risking anyone else seeing us, but I also don't want our time to end. "Hold on tight. I'm taking us somewhere out of town," I call back. The truth is I've no idea where I'm taking us. I just know it needs to be somewhere no one knows us.

Chapter Twenty-Eight

Gabe

I rev the engine and head out. Driving and driving until the town is behind us and all that can be seen is the open road. Unsure where to go, I continue driving till we get close to the town I visited before, although this time I have no intention of wasting my time with a drunken hen party.

I pull up to the vaguely familiar bar and after parking we head inside.

"What do you want to drink? Wine?" I suggest.

"Wine? No. It's like lunchtime." Riley laughs. "I'll take a Coke and a bag of chips, please."

"And for you, sir?" the barman asks.

"Er, I'll have a beer," I shrug. I see Riley's disapproving look and decide to change my mind. "Actually, on second thought, I'll take a Coke as well."

"Two Cokes coming right up," the bartender says as he turns to grab two glasses.

"I'm so glad you changed your mind. I don't like the idea of you drinking when we're on your bike," Riley shares with me as she wraps her arm around my bicep and rests her head on me.

"Riley, I've always been drinking, one beer is nothing," I scoff.

"I know, but please, for me? Don't drink and drive. It worries me so much that one day you'll crash and I'll lose you," she sighs.

And for a moment I'm transported back to when I was a kid, and used to think the same when my dad used to go out drinking then drive home. *The difference was I'd pray he'd crash.*

"I'll try," I whisper.

"That'll be $4.50 please," the bartender says as he hands us our drinks and chips.

I see Riley take out her purse from the corner of my eye but reach out and stop her. "I got it," I say as I hand my card to the barman.

"You can't pay for everything Gabe. You already paid for the hotel which couldn't have been cheap." Riley sounds concerned.

"Don't worry, I can afford it," I laugh as I open my wallet to place my card back and flash her the wad of bills inside.

I see her eyes widen. "Did you rob a bank or something?" she jokes.

"Or something," I mumble under my breath. *Shit! Why did I have to even say anything?*

"Still, I don't care how much money you've got, the next round is on me," she says defiantly as she takes a sip of her drink.

This girl amazes me. Normally girls have no issues with me paying for everything. They see the fancy bike I drive and the money I blow on booze and think I'm a cash cow. Yet Riley is arguing over me spending $4 on pop for us.

"Are you coming or what?" she asks as she makes her way over to a table.

We spend the next few hours sitting here. Chatting about nothing in particular.

"How about some food? I'm starving again," I suggest.

"Good thinking," Riley smiles as she reaches for the menu.

"What are you having?" Riley asks after spending far too long flipping from page to page.

"Gonna go for a burger and fries. I think. Those are usually safe bets."

"See, I don't know if I should have the lasagna and salad or chicken and waffles."

I look up at Riley, expecting her to make a decision so I can go order, but instead she's just staring at me expectantly. "Well, what should I choose?" she says finally.

"How would I fucking know? What do you want?" I ask.

"Weren't you listening? I can't decide between chicken and waffles or lasagna," She huffs like *I'm* the one having trouble making a decision.

After having the most annoying debate over the merits of the two dishes, she finally makes her choice.

"I'll go order then," she states. "Do you still want the burger?"

"It's fine. I'll get it, it's my round anyway." I *may be no gentleman, but I'm still not gonna expect her to pay.*

"Is it? I thought it was mine?" she asks, furrowing her brows.

"Nope, you got the last one," I lie.

I head off to order our meals and get another drink. Although this time I switch to water since all the carbonated drinks are making me feel bloated.

"Did you order extra fries?" Riley asks as I return to the table.

"No, was I supposed to?" I ask while trying to rack my brain to see if I forgot her fries. *I'm sure she only asked for salad with her lasagna.*

"No, it's fine. I didn't know if you ordered any for the table?"

"For the table? Why? Is the table hungry too?" I joke.

"Don't be silly. No, it's just people usually order fries to share." *Is that what people do? Normal people? People who actually socialize with others rather than heating up TV dinners at home alone?*

"If you want fries, I can go order fries. It's fine." I offer.

"No, I'm fine," she replies, and I assume that's the end of it. That is until the food arrives and before I can even decide where to start, I see a hand fly over and grab some of my fries.

"I thought you didn't want fries?" I laugh.

"Just one," she says and flashes me an over exaggerated cheesy grin.

"Here take some," I offer, grabbing a handful.

"No, it's fine. I just wanted one," she says as she pushes my fry filled hand back towards my own plate.

"Okay." I shrug and continue eating, but a few minutes later that little hand is back stealing another fry.

"Just take some fries, if you want some, take a handful. Just stop eating them off my plate." I say, shaking my head, feeling a bit irritated but also a bit of something else - like a warmth almost- but can't explain what it is.

"No, it's fine. I just wanted one little one," she replies again flashing that toothy grin.

"Are you sure?"

"Yep," she replies, popping her mouth on the p like a child.

I'm almost finished with my burger when, yet again, she steals a fry.

"Fuck sake, here," I snap, grabbing a handful and dropping them onto the side of her plate. "Just take some!"

"Thanks," she grins as she wiggles in her chair doing some sort of happy dance. I can't help but grin as I watch her. It takes me back to the way Nate used to wiggle around as I read Izzy's letters to him when we were kids. *I swear to God, if I smile any more, either my jaw is going to break or my cheeks are gonna split open. I can't remember the last time I felt this genuinely happy and at peace. Come to think of it, I don't think I've ever felt this content.*

I watch as Riley devours her whole plate, including all of the fries. "That was soo good," she groans as she leans back in the chair and unbuttons her jeans. "I'm stuffed though."

"I'm not surprised! You ate yours and some of mine," I tease.

"Hey, sharing is caring. I always steal food, that's the rule," she pouts playfully.

"Oh yeah, and who exactly do you share food with then?" I joke back. Even though the idea of her sharing food with other guys makes me feel oddly jealous. *What the fuck is wrong with me? This girl has got me fucking whipped!*

"Well, Tucker always orders way too much, and he's gotta stay in shape for football. So I'm doing him a favor, really. Harper just shares instinctively so she doesn't count, and Nate, well, you know Nate, he's a total feeder so he and Izzy give me some of their food anyway."

"So basically you just eat everyone's food then, yeah?" I laugh.

"Noooo! I don't take Ava's food."

"Ava, which one is she again?" I ask. I'm *shit with names. I only know who Tucker is, since he follows my brother around like a goddamn shadow.*

"Ava, Tucker's girlfriend, has red hair. Don't let her size fool you though. She looks cute and sweet but she's a total pocket rocket"

"Pocket rocket? I like that."

"Yeah you see this scar," Riley says pointing to the tiniest little white mark on the back of her hand. "Bitch stabbed me with a fork back in the second grade all because I tried to share some food."

"You mean steal?" I correct

"Yeah yeah, same thing. Sharing, stealing. Same thing, really." Riley shrugs.

"Oh yeah, sorry Officer I was just sharing with the bank. I'll have to try that one day." *Honestly this girl is crazy.*

"Judging by your wallet you already have," she fires back with her eyebrow arched. She doesn't miss a beat. I love that she's happy to call me out on my shit and give it back to me.

"Shit! Is that the time?" Riley asks suddenly. "We gotta get back."

"What's the rush?" I ask, feeling kind of sad at today being over and having to go back to reality.

"I've got a huge final on Wednesday, and me and the girls are gonna study together at Izzy's tonight," she explains, but just the mention of Izzy's name and the fact that yet again she's taking away something precious to me, makes me angry.

"So what, Izzy's more important than me? Good to know." I snap. I feel my heart racing and the urge to go get drunk is overshadowing any other thoughts in my brain. *See, I'm never first for anyone. There will always be someone more important, more exciting for her to be with. I'm always just a second thought or someone who's around when there's nothing better to do.*

"Don't be so silly," Riley says, reaching and grabbing my hand. "It's not like that at all. Izzy is my friend, sure, but you mean more. Isn't today proof of that?"

"I guess," I shrug, still feeling doubtful.

"How about we head home, and on the way you can think about where you're taking me next weekend," Riley suggests with a cheeky wink.

Riley

Gabe drops me off just outside Izzy's. I get off his bike and remove the helmet. The one that he always gives to me and then hand it back to him. I lean in for a kiss, but he just looks towards the house. My stomach rolls and my heart cracks because I guess we are now back to hiding and any hope of acting like a regular couple is now long gone. He places the helmet on his head, gives me an intense look, and then drives off. Feeling sad, but not really surprised, I make my way to the door and knock. Izzy's Nana answers. "Hello Riley, don't you look beautiful with a little rosiness to your cheeks. Have you been out in the sun?"

"Erm, yes Nana," I lie. Not wanting to admit I've spent the weekend surrounded by a completely different type of heat.

"The girls are upstairs. Wait here I've got cookies that you can bring up with you," she says before disappearing off towards the kitchen. I follow her and in true Nana style, she hands me a plate full of cookies to take up with me.

"Thanks Nana," I say as I give her a little squeeze before making my way upstairs.

As soon as I walk through the bedroom door, Ava begins the third degree,. "Was that just a motorcycle we heard?"

I must have a guilty look as Harper lets out an exasperated groan. "For fucks sake, Rilez." Irritation settles through me quickly.

Who is she to judge? She just doesn't understand Gabe the way I do.

"Seriously, does that man have a magical penis or something?" Ava laughs.

"Well," I smirk.

"Eww eww eww! I don't wanna know," Izzy groans while covering her ears.

"What happened to Ashton? I thought things were going well last night," Harper asks as she takes a cookie from the plate in my hand and throws herself onto the bed.

"It was okay, I guess, but he's just not for me. He's kind of boring and predictable and, well, scared of his own shadow," I whine as I put the plate down on the side table and throw myself down beside my sister.

"I just can't help it," I groan, "I know I shouldn't but I really think I might love him." Saying it out loud feels right. I know it's actually true.

"He's a selfish, egotistical, dickhead," Ava chimes. "What's not to love?"

"Not when we're alone, he's not. When it's just us, he's completely different. You wouldn't understand." I sigh as I lie back and look up at the ceiling.

"I get it, kind of," Izzy says quietly.

"How would you know? He's horrible to you constantly. Just look at Tucker's birthday," Ava says.

"What happened at Tucker's birthday?" I say sitting up.

"Nothing," she says, firing daggers at Ava. "It was a big misunderstanding," Izzy replies.

"Why do you always defend him? If Nate knew half the shit that man's said to you he'd kick his ass, I'm sure." Ava replies as she shoves a cookie into her mouth.

"Which is exactly why you'll keep your big mouth full of cookies and not tell Nate or Tucker," Izzy tries to say in a joking way but I can tell there's some seriousness in it.

"This needs milk," Ava grumbles with a mouth full of cookies.

"I'll get some," Izzy offers kindly.

"I'll come help you, I could do with a drink too," I lie.

As soon as we're away from the door, I pull Izzy aside.

"Hey, what happened?" I ask.

"Nothing," she says but it's clearly a lie. *That girl can't lie for shit.* I give her my best 'you better tell me' look.

"Fine, follow me," she says as she pulls me towards the bathroom.

"Spill," I say once the doors shut.

"Okay, so the girls don't know the whole story, and I don't intend on telling them. But if you're going to get serious with Gabe you deserve to know." Izzy begins before she tells me about bailing Gabe out of jail, about the fact they had lots of laughs and she got to see the kid she grew up with briefly before a miscommunication led to everything turning to shit. She also told me that she's since spoken to Gabe, who told her that he'd gotten into a fight that night after watching someone try to spike her and Harper's drinks.

"And then he took Harper upstairs and made her throw up until most of the drugs were out of her system," she finishes and I can see by the look on her face she deeply cares about Gabe, too.

"So yeah, Riley, he can be good. He has the potential to be a real protector, just like his brother. But he also has soo much darkness in him. Darkness that spills out to everything and everyone he touches. Now I'm not going to say don't be with him, but please be careful, Riley. I love you, and I don't want to see his darkness destroy your light."

I hug her tightly. "I think I can heal him. Somehow, I think I can save him," I admit. Hoping that my words carry enough conviction to cover up the doubts I have myself. *Sure, I care for him, I'm pretty certain that I love him.* But I'd be lying if I didn't wonder at times whether I would be the one to save him or be destroyed by him.

"You've been gone forever," Ava whines once we finally make it back with the drinks.

"Yeah you know Nana, she kept us talking for ages," Izzy lies, giving me a sneaky wink. Thankfully, neither girl pays enough attention to see the way Izzy's face turns as red as a tomato whenever she's lying or trying to hold in a secret.

Soon the whole group is distracted with studying and quizzing each other using the little study cards Izzy made for us. The minutes turn into hours and before I know it, it's almost midnight. "Damn, is that the time?" I ask, looking at my watch and yawning. "We gotta head home," I yawn.

"Want me to ask Pops to drive you home?" Izzy asks.

"We'll be fine, it's only down the road," I laugh, but Izzy is having none of it. "No, I'm sure Pops will drive you back. If not I'm sure he'll let you sleep over on the sofa, or something."

Before I even have a chance to disagree she's up and out the bedroom door.

"Come on you two," she shouts a few minutes later.

We pack the last of our things and make our way downstairs, where a sleepy looking, pajama and robe wearing Pops is waiting for us.

"I'm so sorry, we can walk," I offer guiltily.

"Nonsense! What sort of man would I be if I left two damsels in distress in danger?" Pops laughs. Just like Izzy, her grandparents are sweet but kind of goofy.

Pops drives us home but as we are pulling into my drive I see an unfamiliar dark coloured pick up just opposite. I get out of the car and make my way toward the front door with Harper. As I'm waiting for Harper to unlock the door, I turn and glance over at the pickup, but it drives off. *That's strange.*

"Finally," Harper says as she manages to unlock the door. "Next time we pull a late nighter, remind me to leave the porchlight on before we leave."

"There you both are," my mother says as she walks towards us. "You could have called to say you were going to be late. Your father and I were worried," my mother scolds, as she scowls at us both.

"Sorry mom," we both say in unison as we give her our best puppy dog eyes.

"Well thankfully you're safe, that's the main thing." she replies as she shakes her head. "I hope you didn't walk home." she scolds again as she walks towards the kitchen still reading us both the riot act.

"No, Izzy's grandad drove us home." I add.

"With the amount of time you're spending at their house I'm surprised they're not charging you rent yet," she teases. *I feel bad lying to her all the time, telling her I'm sleeping over at either Izzy's or Ava's when really I'm out with Gabe. But at the same time, it's worth all the sneaking around, to get to be spending all my time with Gabe.*

"I know," I reply, unsure what else to say. "How about tomorrow I stay home, we can have a game night like we used to?" I offer feeling guilty.

"That sounds great, except that me and your father are out at another business dinner tomorrow. How about Monday though, we'll pick you up from dance and we can all go to Nona's. We haven't been there in years and it used to be your favorite little italian restaurant. On the way back we will grab snacks and have either a movie or games night? Just the four of us?" I don't miss the excitable glint in my mother's eye.

"That sounds perfect," I reply.

"Can't wait!" Harper adds.

"Anyway, now I know you're both home safe and sound, I'm off to bed," my mother yawns, before reaching out and grabbing us both, placing a small kiss to our foreheads.

"Night mom, love you," we both call as she turns to leave.

I make my way to our bedroom, throw on some pajamas, and curl up in bed. I fall asleep pretty much as soon as my head hits the pillow.

By the time I wake up the next morning, or should I say afternoon since it's almost twelve o'clock, Harper has already left.

"Mom? Dad?" I call out as I head towards the kitchen to pour myself a very strong cup of coffee.

When no one answers me the third time I call, I decide it's safe to assume everyone has gone about their day without me. I've always been the odd one out when it comes to sleep. Harper and both my parents have always been the type to wake up bright and early and be ready to start their day a few minutes later, me on the other hand, could sleep for eighteen hours straight and still be tired, and even when I do wake up, it takes thirty minutes and two cups of coffee before I even partly resemble a human.

Even as a baby, I was grumpy. My parents used to joke that I was part sloth. That and the fact that I didn't bother learning to crawl till I was almost one, preferring to be carried everywhere. Not like Harper who was the queen of the bum shuffle.

Grabbing my coffee and rummaging in the fridge for some snacks, I make my way back to my room ready to spend the last few hours of my weekend with my favorite vampires.

Chapter Twenty-Nine

Gabe

"I swear the clock is moving backward." Nate complains as we load yet another bag of bricks onto the back of the van.

"Fucking tell me about it," I groan as I use the bottom of my t-shirt to wipe away the sweat from my forehead. "Two more hours and counting."

"Technically..." Nate replies looking down at his watch, "... it's only one hundred and thirteen minutes."

I playfully slap him around the back of the head.

"What?" he laughs. "I'm counting down the minutes. I'm taking Bella on a hot date tonight, so the sooner I get home the better," he laughs as he rubs the back of his head.

"Again?" I question as I think about the fact I've not seen Riley since last weekend. "Didn't the two of you go out just a few days ago?

"That wasn't a date," he laughs, shaking his head at me like I'm a complete idiot. "We literally met up at the library to study."

That's the same thing, isn't it? They went to the same place and spent time together. What makes that any different from when they meet for shitty walks in the woods?

"Wait, you do know what a proper date is, right?" Nate questions as he stops what he's doing and leans against the van.

"Yeah, of course," I lie.

"You sure, dude? You have that same confused look on your face, as I have a calculus problem I have to work out."

Shit, am I that obvious?

"Oh fuck off and get back to work," I snap as I turn away and go back to what I was doing.

Me and Nate don't really say much for the rest of the shift, as we're both racing to complete everything on time so we can start our weekend. Before long, it's time to finish and head home. I went in to work with Nate this morning, seeing no point in us both driving the two hours to get here and then doing it again on the way home when we obviously live together.

I do my rounds quickly ensuring everyone has packed up properly and that nothing is being missed then head over to find Nate.

"Yes Princess, I can't wait to see you either," Nate coos in that sickly sweet voice he uses whenever he's talking to Isabella. "I know, but I'll be there soon, and then we can grab the late showing."

I make my way towards the driver's side out of habit but Nate shakes his head and points towards the passenger's side. *For fuck sake!*

Reluctantly, like a scolded child I do as I'm told, knowing I'm never gonna win this argument. I drop myself into my seat just as Nate gets into the driver's side. *Why the fuck does this asshole always insist I ride shotgun? Sure, I've had the odd beer here or there before work but so what? It's not like I'm drunk! But no, this ass seems resigned to demanding I stay a fucking passenger whenever we share a ride.*

I sulk in my seat and as soon as Nate climbs in, his phone connects to Bluetooth.

Princess fucking Isabella's perky as fuck voice beams through the speakers. "So there's this super romantic movie playing at ten, it's from a book me and the girls have been reading." I can't help but roll my eyes at the thought of that. "Or we can watch an action or a horror movie if you'd prefer," she offers.

"No baby, that movie sounds great. You might have to explain it to me a little though," Nate chuckles softly, and I notice a cheese eating grin on his face, but have no idea why.

The conversation goes back and forth for a couple more minutes before he finally hangs up. We drive for a few more minutes, listening to the radio before the questions in my mind get too much for me. I turn down the radio, earning me a raised eyebrow and a side glance from Nate.

"You okay?" he asks.

"Why the fuck did you agree to watch some shitty chick flick? She literally offered you an out and you didn't take it. And even worse, it's a book chick flick. You don't even read, do ya?"

My mind briefly transports me back to the days when Nate truly couldn't read, back in the days before we realized he was dyslexic. The hours I'd spent trying to teach him how to break down those words. How to recognize which letters were silent. And the many failed attempts he'd have trying to read and write his little letters to Isabella when we were young.

"No, but she does. And whatever this book is, it obviously means something to her if she wants to see the movie, so as her boyfriend, that's what we're gonna do," Nate says casually.

"Yeah, but why? If she wants to watch it, she can watch it. Why would you watch a movie you have no interest in? One that's gonna be all mushy and shit?" I ask, generally confused and kind of horrified by the notion.

"You really are a clueless asshole aren't ya, Gabe. She's my girlfriend, which means whatever makes her happy, I'll do. I don't know the movie or plotline, that's true. But I know it will make Bella happy. I know she'll sit there with a huge smile on her face the whole way through the movie and I know that by the end of the night, I'll probably get to kiss my girl a few times," he says with a smile.

Really a kiss? The boy is putting himself through a few hours of boredom and annoyance for a kiss?

Nate looks over again shaking his head at me. "So what would YOU usually do then, oh wise brother of mine?"

"Nothing. Just do whatever I want I guess," I shrug.

"I pity your girlfriend, you self-centered ass," he laughs, as he takes his hand off the steering wheel ever so briefly to give me a little shove.

We sit in silence for a couple of minutes before I pipe up again.

"So are all dates supposed to be cheesy and boring? Can't you just meet up and do shit and that's a date?" I ask as I think about Riley and the fact I'm seeing her tomorrow.

"Honestly Gabe, I swear you're an alien sometimes." Nate sighs." Okay, what do you usually do then? What's your idea of a date?"

"Well, until Riley, I've never dated anyone. Just met up for sex. Does that count? People fuck on dates don't they?" I ask honestly as I scratch my head.

"No... well, I guess technically, yes... but that's not the date part." Nate mumbles, sounding a little flustered. "The date is what happened before. It's the planning, the attention, the romance. That's what makes the date a date. Anything else is just, well, extra. But you don't need it," Nate blushes and I can't help but smirk.

"So you don't like to fuck on your dates then, no?" I tease. Knowing full well this question will fluster him even more.

"No." Nate mumbles before I cut him off.

"So you're saying you don't want to fuck your girlfriend? That's odd," I add.

"Urgh ... ah, I do..." Nate starts, sounding expectantly flustered.

"So you don't find your girlfriend sexy? You don't think about ripping her clothes off and having your fun with her?" I tease.

"That's more than a little odd."

"Well, of course I do but..."

"But what, Natey boy?" I laugh. "You're a pussy that still hasn't figured out how to close the deal yet?"

"It's not like that," Nate says as his whole face goes as red as a tomato. *Man, it's so much fun to tease him.*

"Tell that to your poor blue balls," I laugh again, as I reach for the radio and turn it back up with an accomplished grin.

We drive for a while longer and I can't help but smirk as I see Nate continually giving me the side eye. I hear a buzzing from beside me and look over at Nate's phone on the dashboard. Every couple of seconds it keeps going off.

"Do us a favor and see what that is," Nate asks.

I reach for his phone and notice it says it's from Isabella.

"It's just her," I say, placing the phone back down.

"What did Bella say?" he asks.

"What? You want me to read it?" *No way in hell would I let anyone read my messages.*

"Well yeah, I can't I'm driving, duh"

I reach for the phone again and read the first message out loud.

"Hey baby," I read before clarifying, "she said baby, not me."

"Yeah, no shit Sherlock. What else did she say?"

"Hey baby, I can't wait to see you. Pops says he will drop me at the movie theater so you don't have to drive all the way over here to pick me up. The film starts at ten but I'll meet you about 9:45 p.m. if you want so we have time to grab snacks." *What a boring ass message. Literally no sass or anything. If that was Riley, she'd at least have made it flirty.*

Another message buzzes through as I'm reading. "What's that one say?" Nate asks. *When the fuck did I become a fucking personal assistant?*

"It says.. I got this for you, what do you think?" I reply feeling confused. That is until it buzzes a second later telling me it's a picture. I quickly cover the screen before I see something I REALLY do not want to see.

"It's a picture!" I gasp. *Shit, now I'm the one who's flustered and embarrassed.*

"A picture of what?" Nate asks, still not taking his eyes off the road.

"A..picture.. from your girlfriend," I say slowly as I exaggerate each word to drive my point home.

"A... picture...of...what?" Nate replies in a mocking tone. *Seriously, is this boy an idiot? A picture from his girlfriend. It's blatantly gonna be naughty. And the last thing I wanna do is see a naked picture of my brother's girl by accident.*

"I don't know," I say in frustration. *What sort of weirdo is my brother that he wants me to look? Does he have some weird fetish or something?*

"Well then, looook," Nate replies with a shake of his head.

"O-kay" I reply hesitantly as I remove my hand from the screen and peer at the photo nervously. *What the fuck?!?* It takes me a second to properly grasp what I'm looking at. "It's a picture of candy... on a bed," *What the heck?*

Nate peers over for a microsecond before telling me to hit voice note.

"No way, where did you find those?" he says excitedly. "You're so adorable; bring them with you. Can't wait to see you. Love you, baby," he then hits the send button.

"What was that all about?" I ask as soon as he's done.

"When we were kids her grandparents used to take us to a little sweet shop and she always chose those swizzle sticks. But the shop closed down years ago and we've not seen them anywhere since," he explains.

"Ohh," I sigh. "I really thought it was gonna be something else," I laugh as I shake my head.

"What was?" Nate asks, sounding confused.

"The picture. I really thought it was gonna be some naked picture or something. I just saw the bed and panicked," I say as I continue to laugh.

"Duude?" Nate laughs. "I did wonder why you were being so weird."

"Well yeah. A girl sends you a picture of a bed; what else am I supposed to think?"

"I guess, but no, I can 100% guarantee Bella isn't the sort to send me those kinds of pictures. And if she did, there's no way in heaven or hell I'd be letting anyone else see." He's still laughing but I can hear a little seriousness in his voice as well as he says the last part.

"So, like never?" I ask. "You just know her pictures are going to be safe for anyone's eyes?" I question.

"Well yeah."

"So you never sext?" I ask. Feeling unusually inquisitive.

"I guess sometimes we flirt, yeah. But no, I don't expect to just receive those kinds of pictures or messages, especially without some warning"

"What do you talk about then?" I quiz.

"I dunno. We talk about school and things we like. Or dates we're going on. Or we send each other pictures of things we think will make the other smile. You know, just normal boyfriend and girlfriend stuff."

"Oh," I say quietly.

"There's more to relationships than just sex, Gabe. Surely even you realize that," Nate finally says after a few minutes of silence.

I spend the rest of the car journey thinking and looking through my own phone. I click on Kelly, Sophie, Lucy, and a few other girls on my phone and after a quick scroll realize there's nothing in any of the threads that are about anything other than sex. Sure there are lots of pictures, great pictures in fact. *Although they no longer excite me as much as they used to.* But nothing of any substance, that is, until I get to Riley's. There's a mixture of morning messages from her. Or random ones telling me about her day or asking about mine. And a few pictures, which are sexy but not half as revealing as the other photos I've looked at. Yet these are the ones that make my heart pound and my dick start to swell. I click out of the messages quickly, not wanting to spend the last of my car ride beside my goddamn brother sporting a semi.

We finally pull up at home and both head inside. Nate rushes into the shower as I head to the kitchen to get a much needed beer. I hear Nate moving around in his room, then about half an hour later he disturbs me by rummaging around behind me.

"What the fuck you doing?" I finally ask.

"Looking for my wallet," he replies, in a panic. "I think I might have left it in my coat at work."

"Here," I say, taking my wallet out of my back pocket and throwing it at him. "Take what you need."

"I can't do that," Nate replies, handing it back to me.

"Nathaniel, take the goddamn money. You can pay me back Monday if it bothers you that fucking much." I huff. *Seriously, will he fuck off already so I can get back to my show.*

"Thanks, bro. Love you," he replies as he carefully takes out just a few bills. "I took $50. I'll pay you back Monday, I promise," he adds as he rushes out the door.

I continue watching TV until I receive a text message.

> Smoking Hot Cock Tease
>
> Hey, are we still on for tomorrow? It's fine if not.

I read her message and for some reason feel slightly guilty. Me and Riley arranged to see each other tomorrow. *A date, I guess you'd call it.* Except I made no plans whatsoever for what we'd do on it. I was just gonna pick her up and then drive. Or she could come with me while I went to get a few parts for my bike as it needs a quick once over after I scratched it the night I got arrested.

> Me
>
> Yeah, I'll pick you up around 10 a.m.

Pulling out my laptop, the one I hardly ever use, I begin looking for ideas. I try googling, 'What do girls like to do?' and get a bunch of random shit like 'Get their hair and nails done' or 'go shopping' pop up. *Well that's not helpful.*

Next, I try searching 'What can I do with a hot girl' thinking maybe that will give me a better idea of things to do that don't include trying to make them look better. And of course all I get is a bunch of sex tips. *Pretty sure that's not a problem we have.* I can't help but smirk as I think of all the different ways I've made Riley moan.

Finally, I search, 'Fun things to do with a girl you like.' Underneath a suggestion for 'Top twenty romantic date ideas' pops up.

I click on it, not expecting much, but am pleasantly surprised when I find what I'm looking for. I scroll through the list: picnics in the park. *Lame.* Painting and pottery making. *Boring.* Horseback riding. *Weird.* Hot air balloon rides. *Unnerving.* Cocktail making. *Promising, but Riley made me promise not to drink and drive when she's with me.*

I almost give up until something jumps out at me. 'Theme park'. *Now that could work. It's fun and exciting. Isn't too girly. But it means she gets to see how brave I am. Winner!!*

Chapter Thirty

Gabe

"What brings you in? Haven't seen you in a while. Thought you'd moved on to that fancy new bike garage in town or some shit," Tate grumbles.

"Nah, no fucker is laying hands on my baby but you, old man," I reply as I give him a fist bump.

"Damn straight. Your ride is like a woman. Gotta handle it with love and respect or it'll be the death of ya," Tate croaks.

"You sound like shit old man," I tease. "Maybe it's time to lay off the cigars."

"Fuck that shit. The cancer will kill me long before my smokes do," he coughs. And I can't help but smirk at the irony of the stubborn bastard. Lung cancer and breathing machine, yet still smoking like a chimney.

"So let's see the beauty then," he says as he makes his way out to the parking lot.

"Damn, that's a big old scar," he says as he eyes up the scratch down the side of my otherwise pristine bike. "Don't worry girl, I'll have you looking perfect in no time."

He strokes my bike like it's an actual person. "Jimmy," he shouts, "take her 'round back."

I throw my keys to his son, who rides it around ready for Tate to start working on it. "Won't take me long. Go grab yourself a beer," Tate offers as he makes his way around the corner.

I head inside to the fridge ready to grab a beer as I always do, but stop in my tracks, remembering I'm meeting Riley soon. Instead, I grab a soda and begin looking around the shop.

"Anything I can help you with Sugar?" A leather clad biker looking chic asks.

"Nah, not really, just passing the time while Tate works on my bike."

"No worries Sugar, call if you need help."

"Actually," I say, a strange idea suddenly hitting me. "Do you sell girl's stuff?"

"What sorta girl's stuff? Like flowers and shit?" she asks as she turns up her nose.

"No, more like that," I say, motioning my finger up and down at what she's wearing.

"Oh, I get ya, sugar. Something for your Ol' Lady," she replies with a knowing grin. "Follow me."

My ol' lady? Is Riley my ol' lady? I guess she is kinda. I mean, I wouldn't be doing this shit for anyone else.

I follow the woman, who leads me to a small corner of the store stocked with leather jackets, helmets, and much more. "So is your old lady a proper woman or one of those pampered pussies?" she asks. *I like this woman already. I can definitely see why Tate hired her.*

"What's the difference?"

"Well we got practical stuff like this," she says, reaching for a nice looking plain black leather jacket. "Or this," she says in disgust as she reaches for a hideous pink leather jacket with stupid tassels hanging off the sleeves.

"Eww, definitely not that one," I say as I shudder in disgust.

"Thank fuck," she laughs.

My mind instantly goes to Kelly and all the times she would try to sit on my bike. *She'd definitely be one to pick that hideous pink abomination.*

"So what size is she, sugar?

My mind goes blank. *How am I supposed to know that?* "Uhmm,"

"Trixi," the woman yells, "get over here."

I see a young girl making her way over. "Yes mama," she replies as she reaches us.

"So is your Ol' Lady, bigger or smaller than my Trixi?"

I eye up the young woman, smiling away beside her. "'Bout the same height, but a 'lil curvier. My girl's got bigger, erm... assets" I say looking down at the girl who can't be any older than around fourteen.

"Lexi, be a doll and try on a few jackets," the older woman says before walking away.

I feel kind of awkward playing dress up with some random kid, especially when she's looking up at me with those innocent doe eyes.

She models two different jackets for me, both look almost identical, though.

"Which one would you choose?" I ask

"This one," she replies straight away as she reaches for the one in my left hand.

"You seem pretty sure about that," I say with a small laugh, "What makes this one so special?"

"It has pockets, duh," she replies, like it's the most obvious answer and I'm a complete fool for not knowing that.

"And pockets are important?"

"Trust me, your girl will love that it has pockets. And she'll love you for choosing it."

"Thanks!" A warm feeling settles over me. *I know this was the right thing to do. This is dating - Gabe style.*

"Does she need a helmet too?" the girl asks, bringing me back to reality.

"Erm, yeah."

I look at the helmets for a few moments, looking at the different types. I hear the girl rummaging around before pulling one out. "I'd go for this one," she says proudly.

"Why that one? Is it the newest?" I ask.

"No, silly," she laughs before turning the helmet to one side. I notice now it has some flowery swirls in gold. "It'll match the jacket."

She thrusts the helmet into my arms before asking. "Does she need anything else?"

"No, I think that's it," I say with a genuine smile.

I take it to the register, where Mama Biker is waiting. "Found everything you're looking for, Sugar?"

"I think so," I reply hesitantly, "but erm... is this helmet decent? Like road worthy? The girl is sweet and all but I don't wanna buy a piece of crap just because it looks pretty if you know what I mean."

"Don't you worry Sugar. Trixi may look like a dumb kid but her daddy has had her around bikes since she was in diapers. That girl knows more about bikes than most men do," she laughs. *Of course, she's Tate's daughter.*

She rings up the items and I pay her, ensuring that I round up the cost as a tip for the kid. "Tell Trixi thanks for her help." *I remember being a kid and what a difference a few dollars made.*

"The bike is near perfect again now," Tate says as he comes over and hands me the keys.

"Thanks old man," I reply. I look at my phone and realize it's almost ten o'clock already. *Shit!* I fire off a quick text to Riley letting her know I'm running late but will be with her in about half an hour.

Riley

P ulling out my phone again I check the time, 9:45 a.m.. I open up my messages, just in case he's messaged and I've somehow missed it

Yesterday 10:30 p.m.

Dark horse
> Yeah, I'll pick you up around 10 a.m.

10:37 p.m.

Me
> Awesome, can't wait to see you.

Today- 8 a.m.
> Morning sexy, what shall we do today?

9:20 a.m.
> Hey Sexy, sorry to bug you. Just wondering if you had any set plans in mind for today? So I know what to wear. Or maybe bring, if past history holds up haha.

9:40 a.m.

> Just me again. Just to say I've packed a couple of things just in case. If you've changed your mind or need to cancel today though just let me know.

Still no reply. *I should have known a real, official, planned date would be too much to ask for with him.* I'm about to text him and tell him that I've changed my mind, just to save face, when my phone buzzes in my hand.

Dark horse

> Sorry, I had to take my bike into the shop to get a few things fixed before I met you, and it ended up taking longer than expected. It'll be about half an hour. As for clothes, casual but hot!

I can't help but smirk at the last line. It's just so him. I look at my reflection for a moment, taking in my cute but casual black top, denim shorts, and sneakers. I've curled my hair and done my makeup a bit darker to give it a sexier feel, but I'm still kind of relaxed. Rummaging in my drawers, I pull out a pair of black fishnet tights to put under my shorts.

Checking myself out again, it's still not right. Sure the tights give it a sexier, edgy feel, and somehow make my legs appear longer and slimmer, but it's still not quite right.

"What's wrong with me?" I ask Harper who's reading on her bed.

"How long have you got?" she teases, putting her book down. "You snore like a fully grown man, you hog all the hot water, and you are always stealing my stash of goodies. And worst of all, you think pineapple tastes good on pizza," she says as she pretends to gag.

"Very funny, you sarcastic bitch." I laugh, at the same time as launching a pillow straight at her head, knocking her glasses off. "I mean, what's up with my outfit?"

Putting her glasses back on, she eyes me up and down. "You look good to me."

"I dunno, something isn't right. I wanna look hot, but something is missing," I complain as I twist side to side in the mirror trying to figure out what's wrong.

"Riley, you always look hot, you know you do. You could wear a paper bag and still have half the guys in school drooling."

"But Gabe's not just one of the guys from school, he's different–he's older and is used to girls throwing themselves at him," I admit. *I still don't get what he sees in boring old me.*

"Oh Rilez," Harper says as she throws her arms around me. "You really care about him, don't you?"

"Yes. I dunno how to explain it, you wouldn't understand, Harper. None of you see him the way I do. When we're alone it's so different. He makes me feel things I've never felt before. Yeah, he's a dick at times, but at other times, he's actually really sweet."

"Then let's make sure today's perfect then," she sighs as she steps closer, eyeing me up and down again, before heading towards her closet.

She bends down and begins rummaging around for something. "Here," she says as she pulls something out from the very back, "I bought them for Halloween the year we let Tucker talk us all into going out as superheroes," she laughs, handing me a pair of black knee high boots.

I slip them on and as soon as I see my reflection I know these are exactly what I was missing. "They are perfect," I gasp.

"Keep 'em if you want, they're a bit slutty for me," she laughs.

"Are you calling me a slut?" I gasp, grabbing my invisible pearls.

"Well if the boot fits," she jokes back.

I attempt to push her back onto the bed but she grabs hold of my shoulders and pulls me down with her. We begin poking and tickling each other while laughing and play fighting like we did when we were little kids. That is until a loud horn sounds outside and brings us back to reality.

"Shit," I laugh as I climb off the bed and begin straightening my outfit.

"Wait," she calls, before flattening down a piece of unruly hair at the side of my head. "There, perfect!" she smiles.

"Love you, sis," I say before turning to walk out the door. Butterflies form in my tummy as I make my way up the stairs, just as a second horn sounds.

Chapter Thirty-One

Gabe

I pull up outside of Riley's house and honk my horn. I wait a few minutes expecting her to come outside, but she doesn't. *Am I supposed to go to the door and get her? Is that a date thing to do?*

I climb off my bike and make my way towards the door, but as I get closer, I hear her dogs barking so I rush back to the safety of my bike. *Fuck that shit! I'm not messing with whatever dog that is. No way!*

I climb back onto my bike, honking my horn for a second time. The door flies open seconds later and my heart skips a beat. *Wow!!*

She's dressed in shorts, fishnets, and long boots and looks like the sexiest girl I've ever seen. My cock springs to attention, probably as quickly as it would have if she'd opened the door butt naked. *Fuck me, all I wanna do is drag her back inside, down to her bedroom, and lose myself in her.*

"Is everything okay?" she asks, looking at me with nervous eyes.

"You look… wow," I purr as all the blood rushes directly to my cock.

"You sure, it's not too…" Riley begins to say. But her words are cut short when I grab hold of her hand, pulling her closer, before moving her hand against the bulge in my jeans. "You look fucking hot. So hot in fact that I'm seriously considering scrapping this whole day and dragging you inside and fucking you senseless."

I release my hold on Riley's hand and step backwards, smirking as I see a mixture of emotions flash across her face.

Riley regains her composure, even though I can see by the blush on her cheeks that she's flustered. "Thanks. Harper gave me the boots," she says as she wags her foot in the air.

"I..I.. got something for you," I say as the blood finally begins to return to my brain.

"For me?" she gasps, sounding excited and surprised.

I climb off the bike, open the little basket, and remove the helmet and jacket I bought. "It's not wrapped or shit, but I got you these earlier."

Riley reaches for the jacket, running her hands across the cold, smooth material, before carefully putting it on. *I hope she likes it. Maybe this was a really stupid idea.*

She runs her hand across the front again, playing with the buttons before exclaiming, "It's got pockets!" I can't help but let out a loud chuckle.

"What's so funny?" she says as she looks over to me with a puzzled look.

"Nothing, Trixi said you would like the pockets," I say with a grin.

"Trixi?" Riley asks, her voice suddenly sounding much less excited. I don't miss the sad look now in her eyes. *Shit, she probably thinks Trixi is another cheap whore. I'm fucking this all up!*

"No, no, it's not like that," I add quickly. "Trixi is a kid."

"A kid? Who's kid?" Riley asks, looking even more puzzled.

Shit! Now she thinks I've got some secret kid somewhere. This is not going how I planned it. Taking a deep breath, I try again to explain.

"I went to get my bike fixed. Trixi is Tate, the owner's kid. She helped me pick out this jacket. She got excited over pockets too, but I didn't get why. She said it's a girl thing and you would understand," I say in a fluster. *Why am I so nervous? Does she believe me? Please believe me.*

A smirk forms on Riley's face as she watches me struggle to find the right words before she finally stops me. "Yeah, I get it. Pockets are definitely a girl's best friend," Riley says with a grin before leaning forward to hug me.

"I thought diamonds were a girl's best friend?" I joke, as I gently push her away. I tolerate them, but I'm not a huge fan of the long hugs.

"Nope, it's definitely pockets," Riley smirks.

"Rilez," a voice shouts. "You forgot your phone."

I see her sister standing at the doorway for a second before all I see is a huge mass of dark black fur bounding towards me. Instinctively I pull Riley in front of me to shield myself. As soon as I do, the dog leaps up and attacks, Riley squeals then.... *Laughs?*

"Oh, Honey," Riley laughs as the dog jumps up and tries to attack her face. *Why is she laughing? Is she scared? Is it a scared laugh? Do I drag the dog off of her? Do I smack it?"*

"Honey, stooop. I don't want kisses." Riley laughs again as she pushes the beast away.

"Honey! Enough!" Harper calls as she grabs hold of the collar and pulls the dog away.

"Thanks for your help there," Riley laughs as she wipes her cheek.

"Er, I thought about hitting it?" I admit

"Hit her, I'll hit you!" both girls exclaim in unison. *Wow, that's freaky.*

"Why did she attack you though?" I ask as I scratch my head in confusion. *Why would you keep a pet that is aggressive?*

"Attack?" both girls question again. *Seriously this horror movie, twin shit needs to stop.*

"You were just giving kisses, weren't you baby?" Riley coos bending down and bringing her face closer to the black haired beast.

The dog barks loudly in her face. Instinctively I try to grab her jacket to pull her back.

"Aww, is the big bad Gabey scared of mommy's little baby?" Riley coos. As she makes no attempt to move her face away from the gnashing teeth that dog probably has.

"Can we go?" I ask as I take a step back.

"Honey, bed bed," Riley commands, and instantly the dog retreats back towards the house. *Oh yeah, now the beast listens.*

Now that the dog is finally away, I pick up the helmet I dropped in the commotion and hand it back to Riley. "Look," Riley says towards Harper, "isn't it pretty?" she says proudly as she shows the pattern to her sister and carefully traces the gold pattern with her finger.

"So pretty," Harper confirms. *Yes! I did something right for once.*

"Gabe got it for me," Riley says excitedly, "and the jacket," she adds before spinning around to give her sister a full 360 view.

"Mmm," Harper says as she looks at me. "Nice to see you taking care of my little sister. Riley knows," she says turning her attention towards his sister, "that I don't like her riding on your metal death trap, but..." her attention and pointy finger are now aimed back towards me, "...since she won't listen, I'm trusting you to take care of her like precious cargo," she says in a very serious, commanding, will murder me kind of intimidating tone. "Because if you don't, you and this death trap will be making friends with my baseball bat."

Wow, and I thought Riley was the wild sister.

Unsure what to say, I simply nod. Thankfully, it must pacify her because she turns around without saying another word and walks back inside the house.

"I'm precious cargo, don't ya know," Riley says in a playful mocking voice. Before placing the helmet on her head. *That you are my little flame, that you are.*

Riley

Looking down at the way my leather blends in with his leather, I can't help but feel all fuzzy inside. *An hour ago, I was worrying he'd changed his mind about me and all this time he was out buying me proper gear.* A huge smile forms on my face, one I don't even try to hide, as I nuzzle my head against him as the bike speeds off.

Sure, flowers and chocolates are nice, but this is far more romantic. It wasn't some shitty ass, last minute generic gift picked up on a whim. This was thoughtful and special.

Gabe reaches back and gives my thigh a reassuring little squeeze as we stop at the red light and that simple touch alone causes heat and longing to form where our bodies meet.

We speed off, dipping in and out of traffic until we finally hit the open road. *This feels so freeing; it's almost like flying,* I think to myself as the wind whips beside me.

I rest my head against Gabe as my arms squeeze around his waist. *How is this beautiful, god of a man, mine?*

He places his hand on top of mine for a second and gives it a gentle tap before returning his hand back to the handlebars. *I wish we could stay like this forever.* I close my eyes and enjoy the moment until I feel us slowing down. Opening them and lifting my head, I see we are outside Six Flags.

"We're here," Gabe says excitedly as he parks.

"I love Six Flags!" I squeal. I attempt to climb off but my legs wobble. Gabe reaches his arm out to steady me.

"You'll get used to it," Gabe laughs as he runs his hands up and down my legs.

"They're all tingly," I laugh as I finally climb off as the pins and needles ease.

Gabe removes my helmet. "How do you look even hotter with this on?" he growls as he puts it away.

"So you're saying I'm hotter when you can't see my face?" I tease.

"No, but seeing you sitting on my bike, dressed like that, does things to me I cannot even describe," he says huskily, "and if we weren't in a parking lot surrounded by kids, I'd happily show you exactly what my mind is imagining doing to you right now."

My cheeks can't help but blush under his intense gaze. *Is it wrong that I want nothing more than for him to show me what he wants to do to me? Audience or no audience?*

We walk towards the entrance and I naturally head towards the line, but Gabe grabs me around the waist and pulls me in a different direction.

"I got us flash passes," he says, answering my unasked question.

We get led right towards the front. A couple of people are ahead of us but in no time at all we're at the front of the line. Gabe takes out his phone, scanning our passes. "Have a good day y'all," the young woman behind the glass smiles as she hands us our platinum passes.

"This must have cost loads, let me pay you back," I offer quickly.

"You can pay me back tonight," Gabe says cheekily as he gives my ass a playful slap. A woman in the line behind us scoffs and quietly remarks, "That's so inappropriate."

I turn to apologize, but Gabe being Gabe, beats me to it. "Not my fault that glasses over there clearly doesn't give you a good spanking," he snaps back.

"Gabe!" I whisper shout before mouthing the word sorry to the horrified looking couple behind us. "Come on," I say, pulling him away.

"What? Maybe if she got spanked once in a while that stick wouldn't be wedged so far up her ass," he scoffs, sounding like a petulant teenager who just got yelled at. I *swear to god I can't take this man anywhere.*

Chapter Thirty-Two

Gabe

My eyes go wide as I take in the sight. When I was researching it last night, it looked good but this is something else. A loud 'whoosh' sound echoes ahead and I duck causing Riley to laugh. "Don't worry it won't hit you," she teases, as she reaches for my hand and guides me back to my full height. I look up just as a spinning circle and dangling legs fly overhead again. "Woooah!," I shout.

"Oh my god! Is this your first time at Six Flags?" Riley gasps.

"Maybe," I admit shyly.

"Oh my god, a little Six Flags virgin. Let me be your guide, oh Innocent One," Riley says in a funny voice as she beams from ear to ear. "This is going to be so much fun!"

Pulling her close, I lean down and whisper, "Hmm, seems only fitting that you get to have some fun taking my virginity, since Baby, I had so much fun stealing yours."

A smirk forms on Riley's face as a flush creeps up her face. Just as a small hand beats against my chest. "Stop that," she groans.

"Stop what? Stop picturing how good it felt to be inside you? How tightly your pussy clenched my cock as you came all over it? Or stop..."

Riley thrusts her hand over my mouth to muffle my words. "Gabe!"

"What did I do?" I say, feigning innocence.

"You know exactly what you did," she says with raised eyebrows.

"How about we go somewhere else so I can feel what my words did to you instead?" I growl, suddenly having no desire to be at an amusement park.

"Come on," she says, completely ignoring my request as she tugs on the arm of my jacket, before running off like an excited toddler.

We line up for the first roller coaster and as we get near the front, I notice a sign saying you have to be so tall to ride it. "Oh no, look, no short asses allowed," I joke.

"I'm easily taller than that," Riley huffs and crosses her arms.

"I don't know... it does look kinda high, and you're pretty short," I say, trying my hardest to sound seriously concerned.

"Wait here," I hear her mutter as she leaves the line, marches over, and physically measures herself by standing with her back against the size chart.

"Told you. You're too short Riley," I gasp.

I can't help but laugh when she spins around with a shocked look on her face, that is until she sees that the line doesn't even come up to her shoulder.

"You're such a dick!" she spouts out when she realizes I was just teasing her.

She sculks back to me and stands beside me without saying another word. I look down a few minutes later and she's standing with her arms crossed with the cutest pout on her lips. I reach out, running my finger across her lip.

"Stop pouting," I say quietly.

"No," she scoffs defiantly.

"Stop acting like such a brat," I laugh. "I was only teasing you."

She looks up, rolls her eyes at me, then turns her back on me slightly. *Stubborn little shit! Her attitude reminds me of the way she was that first night in the shitty motel. I kinda love it.*

Throwing my arms around her shoulders from behind, I pull her against me. She tries to wiggle away, but she's locked in my grip.

Realizing she's trapped, she sighs and sinks into me. "That's better," I whisper. "Now I suggest you smile like a good girl and stop pouting like a little brat; otherwise, I may have my way with you right here until you smile and scream my name."

I feel her breath hitch against the hair on my arms before she turns to look up at me, desire clouding her eyes.

"You wouldn't dare?" she mouths.

I move one arm down around her waist, which to the outside world may look like I'm just giving her a tighter hug. But as I pull her hips closer, the wide eyed look she gives me lets me know that she knows exactly what I'm doing. "Try me," I whisper as I arch my hips ever so slightly to push myself against her ass. *Seriously, what I wouldn't give right now to pull her into one of these bathrooms or down a secluded corner and take advantage of that smart mouth of hers.*

"Next," the guy calls as he starts letting a few more people through to ride the rollercoaster. Riley shuffles closer and I have to tug down my shirt a little more to ensure no one gets an eyeful of the bulge in my pants.

We sit down on the ride and it begins moving, slowly at first. *This isn't so bad,* I think as we go over the first little dip, until we start climbing. Higher... and higher... and higher.

"Put your hands in the air," Riley says from beside me. I peer over and notice both she and the couple in front of us have their hands in a little surrender sign just a few inches above the safety bar. *Are they all crazy? I'm assuming the bars are there for a goddamn reason.*

"Trust me, hands up!" Riley says just as the coaster comes to a halt at the top of a steep hill. Reluctantly I comply, but just as I do, the rollercoaster flies downwards. "Fuuuuuuck!" I scream as we hurtle downwards and my arms take on a life of their own, flying high above my head.

The rollercoaster flies through the sky this way and that way, all the while my hands seem glued to the invisible ceiling. Suddenly out of nowhere, I feel fingers intertwined with mine. *Is she holding my hand? I don't remember the last time anyone held my hand. Memories of my mother flash through my mind like lightning.*

A split second later, we're stopping with a jolt. Our hands finally drop down to the bar but Riley doesn't release me. I stare at our hands for a long moment before she finally releases me. A wave of emptiness replaces the once warm feeling. "Sorry," she mumbles when she catches me staring.

We exit the ride in an awkward silence. Not wanting to ruin things, I point to another ride, one that looks kind of like a pirate ship, "Wanna go on that one?"

"Yeah, okay," she says with a grin.

As soon as it's our turn we find a seat and wait for it to finish filling up. The ride starts rocking us forward and back, getting higher and higher. It's not as fast or scary as the last ride, but still good fun. We both grip the silver bar with our hands side by side. Riley looks straight ahead letting out a small "woah" every now and then but I'm busy focusing on our hands. Our baby fingers are side by side, I move my finger slightly so that it overlaps hers but she doesn't seem to notice. *Why is this so fucking nerve racking? It's hand holding. Kids hold hands; heck, toddlers hold hands.*

I shuffle my hand over a few millimeters more so that now my baby finger and ring finger are resting on top of hers. *Come on Gabe, grow the fuck up. Your fingers have been around her throat and inside her pussy, you can put them on top of her hand.* I shuffle my fingers slightly closer. Suddenly her other hand reaches over, grabs mine, and places it fully on top of hers. I look over to see a small smile on her lips.

"At the risk of sounding like a pun, you looked like you needed a helping hand," she smirks.

The ride ends and I release her hand and make my way off, the next ride we go on kind of looks like a big circle filled with swings, except that it flies high into the sky.

This time as soon as we sit down, I reach out to grip Riley's hand. It's kind of clumsy at first, my big fingers kind of squishing her tiny ones. Riley wiggles her hand in mine until our fingers finally feel comfortable inside of each other, almost like they belong together. We spend the whole ride flying through the sky, hands firmly clasped together. I'm almost sad when the ride ends and we have to let go again.

"How about we grab a drink? My mouth is as dry as the desert after that," Riley says as she subconsciously pokes her tongue in and out like some sort of lizard.

"Good idea," I reply while trying not to laugh. Riley stretches out her hand to me, and I look at it dumbfounded for a moment.

"You know that our hands work when our feet are on the floor as well, right?" she teases.

"Yeah, of course," I mumble as I reach my hand out to meet hers. *Are we actually gonna do this? Be one of those cheesy couples that go for strolls holding hands?*

My question is answered when she locks her fingers into mine and begins walking and swinging both of our arms together. *Yep, I guess we are. It does feel kinda nice, though.*

And that's how the rest of the day goes. We walk around the whole place hand in hand. We grab food and drinks together. She buys photos of us squealing on one of the rides. Then we laugh and joke about who looks more terrified and before I know it, the park is getting emptier and emptier. I look at my watch and realize the park is going to be closing soon. *I'm not ready for today to end yet.*

"I think we should get going," I say, feeling a little sad.

"One last ride before we go," Riley says as she drags me towards an unusually childish looking ride.

"This one, really?" I ask as I see what looks like giant tea cups moving at about 0.1 miles an hour.

"Yeah, it's a tradition," she says with a cheesy grin.

"Fine." I acquiesce.

We make our way over, and unsurprisingly, there's no line. The ride has about ten cups, but only two others are already taken. We find a cup on the opposite side to the other two sets of people and sit down. The ride begins spinning slowly. *Why of all the rides does she want this snore fest?* I see Riley tugging and turning on the wheel in front, with an accomplished grin on her face.

"You gotta spin it to go faster," she laughs when she sees me eying her suspiciously. I do as she says, and the ride begins to spin a little faster but still at a snail's pace.

"Why this one? Of all the rides, why is this the one you needed to go on?" I ask as I continue spinning it.

"Dunno. Me and Harper have been coming since we were in preschool.

This was our favorite as kids and we just continued riding it for nostalgia sake as we got older, I guess," she shrugs.

"Wanna know something funny?" she asks with a little scoff. "I had my very first kiss on this ride." *What the fuck?* I feel the jealousy and frustration bubbling in my chest at the thought of Riley here with some other guy.

"Jason Phillips," she sighs as she places her hand on her chest.

"Who the fuck is Jason Phillips?" I snap. *Who the fuck is he? I know about Justin. And I assumed there had been other guys before, but did she love any of them?*

"My first crush," she replies with a faraway voice. *So she did love him then!*

"Who kissed who?" I snap, getting even more frustrated. *She's mine. Where's this Jason guy now? Do they still talk?*

"He kissed me. It was completely unforgettable," Riley smirks.

Not wanting to hear another word, I carefully unbuckle the loose belt and slide along the seat, right up against Riley. My body is snug up beside hers, and I tilt myself to face her. I place my hand on the nape of her neck, bring her to me, and kiss her hard. As she begins kissing me back, I gently pull her hair, forcing her to tilt her head so I deepen our kiss. I move one of my arms down her body, trailing my fingers lightly on the bare skin of her arm, causing goosebumps until it lands on her upper thigh. I give her a light squeeze, and she moans into my mouth in response. *I bet she can't even remember that fucker's name now!* I cup her mound with my hand, applying extra pressure to the area where her clit is. She grinds down on my hand and just as I hear her breathing really start to speed up, I end the kiss and pull my hand away.

"Bet that was a better kiss than Jason mother fucking Phillips," I say with a cheeky grin as I help her off the ride.

"Well, you can't get much worse than throwing up on the guy I guess," she laughs.

"What the fuck? You threw up on him?"

"Yup, but in my defense, I was only four. And my parents had stupidly let me eat two corndogs and then go on a ride." She says, holding her hands up in surrender.

"What the fuck? You were four? I need the whole story," I laugh. *I can't believe she made me jealous of some guy she kissed when she was four. She knew exactly what she was doing, too.*

"Well..." she says as we make our way out of the park, "it was a real Romeo and Juliet type of love affair. He was an older guy, almost five. It was true love. He'd share his juice boxes with me in school and I'd save him my last cookie. One day we found out he was going to a new school. Our parents decided to bring us all here together for a day of fun. Anyway, my dad was taking me and Harper on the teacups and offered to take Jason on with us. Everything was going fine until I started to feel nauseous. I told the group I felt sick and Jason said when he feels sick his mom kisses him better. He leaned over to kiss me better, and just as he did, I threw up all over his clothes.

I burst out laughing. "Oh my god Riley, that's the funniest shit I've ever heard."

"Don't laugh, it was really fucking traumatizing," she says, while laughing herself.

"Without a doubt, that's the best, bad first kiss story I've ever heard," I say, wiping a tear from my eye.

"Oh yeah, Mr. Smooth, I bet your first kiss was pretty shitty too," she huffs.

I think back to my first kiss. Twelve years old. Being basically molested by some woman old enough to be my mother while my scumbag of a father egged her on.

"Let's just say it wasn't as funny as yours," I say with a sad sigh. "Anyway, where shall we go next?" I ask, not wanting to ruin the best day in my whole life with memories of just how pathetic my childhood really was.

"I kind of don't wanna go home," Riley admits. "It's been so special today."

I don't want to leave either. She's right, today has been out of this world. I've gotten to be carefree and playful. I've gotten to enjoy myself and experience all sorts of things I never got the opportunity to while growing up. I don't want the day to end either.

"Do you have work tomorrow?" Riley asks and I can tell by the look on her face the cogs are turning.

"I don't have to," I reply. *Sure I was supposed to help with some stuff but I'm sure I could send Nate instead. I've covered for him plenty of times.*

"Good," Riley grins, "because I have an idea."

"Sounds good; let me just send Nate a message first," I say as I hand Riley her helmet.

I fire off a quick text asking Nate to cover my shifts all weekend and telling him I'm not sure when I'll be back but that I'll make it up to him.

"Okay, so where are we going then?" I ask as I shove the phone back into my pocket.

"There's a hotel just a few miles away. I can guide the way," Riley offers.

"I won't be able to hear you very well with our helmets on," I remind her.

Riley rubs her chin for a couple of seconds before she gets an idea. "I'll squeeze your thigh; whichever side you have to turn, I'll squeeze that thigh. It's not far away at all."

I don't quite believe it's going to work, but Riley seems determined, so I decide to give her the benefit of the doubt. We climb on the bike and begin driving. Sure enough a little squeeze to pull out left, a little squeeze to turn right, and in no time at all we were pulling up outside a big, white hotel. Thankfully and just in time, because the heavens open up with thick raindrops that begin pelting down on us. *Thank god we don't have to drive all the way home in this weather.*

I drop Riley off at the main doors, telling her to head inside out of the storm and that I'll follow her soon. I drive off, hoping to find somewhere safe and dry to park my bike.

Chapter Thirty-Three

Riley

"Evening ma'am, would it be possible to book a room for tonight, please?" I ask the older woman behind the desk.

"I'll deal with this Anne, you go grab a break," a younger guy says as he places a hand on his coworker's shoulder and guides her away from the desk.

"Hello, how can I help you today?" the guy says in a confident yet oddly sultry tone as his eyes scan down my body.

"Hey, so I was looking to grab a room for tonight please," I say as I tug my jacket closed, trying to cover myself up, realizing now my thin t-shirt is clinging to my damp skin.

"Sure thing, would that be a single room?" he asks as he begins typing away on his computer.

"A double room please," I request. Meanwhile, he continues typing.

I feel a hand graze across my ass as Gabe comes to stand beside me. I look up at my man who gives me a little wink in response. *God, he's so damn sexy.*

"Excuse me sir, you'll have to wait, I'm already with a customer," the guy says, sounding frustrated.

"Oh no, it's okay, we're together," I chuckle.

"Oh," the guy says as he looks from me to Gabe and back to me again. "So will your friend be needing a room tonight as well?" he asks, completely ignoring Gabe now and turning all his attention toward me.

Gabe's hand goes from a soft caress of my ass to a possessive grab. "No, the one room will be fine," he says in an authoritative tone, despite the fake politeness lacing it. *Why does it suddenly feel like I'm the wild giselle trapped between two hungry lions?*

"Of course, sir," the guy replies, sounding equally as fake.

He picks up two white cards from a stack beside him, swipes them along the side of his screen, and then slides them both towards me, letting his fingers graze mine for a second too long. "Room 302," he adds with a smile. *Seriously, does this guy have a death wish?*

I feel Gabe's grip tightening on me in a possessive manner as a frustrated growl leaves his mouth. I move my hand back quickly as I take the keycards. "Thanks," I say with an awkward smile.

Gabe takes the key cards from my hand and forcefully thrusts one back towards the clerk. "We'll only need one. She'll be with me the whole night," Gabe cheekily asserts himself.

"Perhaps she'll need one in case she decides to go for a little walk. We have entertainment and restaurants open until late." *I need to break whatever the fuck this is before a fight breaks out.*

"I'm here all night, so I'll be happy to assist you in any way you need," he continues, clearly with a death wish as he is completely ignoring Gabe once again while simultaneously turning his attention towards me.

I don't even need to look at Gabe's face to know the look that will be on it. That same look I've seen so many times before. The one that scares and excites me in equal measure.

Gabe flings his arms around me from behind as he pulls me tightly against him before leaning over the counter and menacingly whispers, "Don't you worry, by the time I'm done with her, she won't be able to stand, let alone walk off anywhere. I will make sure all her needs are met." At that, Gabe leans over and whispers more dirty words into my ear.

Heat pools at my core, and I know I should be pissed or at least embarrassed that he'd talk about me like this, especially in public to a stranger, yet all I feel is desire and longing.

I look back, just long enough to catch the shocked look on the other guy's face.

Gabe

Who the fuck does this punk think he is? Flirting with my girl right in front of me. Riley looks so uncomfortable, as she naturally leans herself closer to me. *Begging me to protect her.*

I throw my arm across her chest and pull her into my arms, wanting her to know that I'll always protect her. As soon as I do, she melts against me, resting her head against the cruck of my elbow. I notice the way the punk rolls his eyes, and it takes everything in me not to jump over this counter and beat the shit out of him here. But not wanting to risk ruining our special day, or worse, having Riley look at me with fear in her eyes, I decide against it.

Instead, I lean over the counter, right into this asshole's face, and can't stop myself from letting him know that I fully intend on keeping my girl satiated... *I need him to know she's mine and that he has no chance with her.* I don't miss the way Riley shifts as I speak, the way her thighs instinctively rub together with the sound of my voice. *My little slut likes it when my dirty thoughts leave my lips.*

So I lean in close to her ear and whisper loud enough for the asswipe to hear, "When we are finally alone, I'm going to fill all your holes so full that you won't need or want anything for at least a week." As I start to pull away, I nip her earlobe and place a soft kiss on her pulse point in her neck.

Her breath hitches, and I know full well that if I dipped my fingers into her panties, they would be soaking wet for me.

The shocked and furious expression on the punk's face does exactly what I intended though, so feeling triumphant, I lead her away.

I dare to turn my head to look behind me and see him shamelessly staring at her ass as he licks his lips hungrily. *Seriously, this fucker is begging to have his teeth knocked down his throat. If I wasn't fighting every natural instinct in my body, trying to be better for her, I'd turn around now and have him begging for mercy.*

We get into the elevator, the one that has a clear line of sight to the front desk and I waste no time pushing my girl against the glass as I kiss her roughly. *Watch that you asshole.*

As the elevator begins moving up, I move my lips down to her neck, eliciting a low moan from Riley's lips. I nip her neck, which causes her to throw her head back and arch her back to give me better access. And despite the urge to look at my girl as her desire grows, I look straight ahead, locking eyes with Mr. Wants to Steal My Girl, whose eyes are locked on us. I bring one hand down to cup her ass as I lift her leg up and rest it on my hip so I can step closer to thrust against her. Then using my other hand I flip him off with an smug grin.

"You're such a caveman," Riley says with a smirk as the elevator climbs higher and higher.

"What?" I ask, feigning innocence.

"You think I don't know all that was for him and not me? Talk about marking your territory," she laughs. *So she knows he was watching us? And yet still allowed me to use her as my own personal doll? Does she like the idea of people watching us? Or just the idea of me letting everyone know she's mine? Or perhaps both?*

"Just making sure he knows to keep his fucking eyes and thoughts off what's mine," I huff.

"You probably just gave him more for his spank bank," she laughs. *Fuck! I didn't even think about that. Will he be fantasizing about Riley later tonight? Imagining it was him she was with in the elevator?*

"Don't worry Caveman, he can think all he wants, only you get to feel what it's really like," she smirks. As her hand slides down to the bulge in my pants.

I'm tempted to take her right here in the glass elevator, but before I even have the chance to think about it, there's a loud 'bing' letting me know we've arrived on the third floor.

We find our door a few seconds later and head inside. It's not as nice as the last place we stayed, but still a huge improvement over the dingey motels we've been to in the past.

I remove my jacket as Riley makes her way toward the bed, "Gaaabe," she mutters as she catches sight of herself in the vanity mirror.

"You could have told me I looked a fucking mess." I see her trying to smooth down her wild hair. She's right; it kind of looks like a bird has made a nest in her hair. *How the fuck didn't I notice that before?*

"I'm jumping in the shower," she huffs and storms towards the bathroom. I remove my jeans, t-shirt, and boots while making my way towards the bathroom in nothing but my boxers, hoping to continue the fun from before. But as I enter the bathroom, the sight stops me in my tracks. I'm awestruck. Riley is breathtakingly naked behind the glass with her eyes closed and head thrown back as the water cascades down her long blond hair and all the way down her back. Her tits look amazing as her hard nipples poke toward the ceiling but it's her hair that I'm drawn to. The way she runs her hands through it as she tries to comb out the knots. *All I want to do is run my own hands through it.*

Coming out of my momentary paralysis, I walk over, remove my boxers, and then carefully slide the glass door open. Riley doesn't open her eyes to look at me but instead, she lets out a soft hum as she moves her head side to side, causing sprays of water to drip down her neck and between her breasts. I take a step forward and gently lick the droplets of water from her nipple. An action that causes Riley to jump. "Gabe," she moans. "I'm trying to..." she begins before I cut her off by placing my finger on her lips.

"Don't let me stop you; I just wanna watch." *Watch? Since when do I watch people wash their goddamn hair? Yet somehow, that's all I wanna do.*

She gives me a strange, crooked smile before she loads up her hands with liquid from the shampoo pump on the wall. I watch as she massages it into her hair, and all I want to do now is kiss her. I place my hands on either side of her jaw and kiss her. Soft at first before it turns more desperate. My hands find their way into the hair at the base of her neck as I continue kissing her and let my hands twist into her hair. Riley's hands find their way to mine as she begins massaging her soapy hand through my hair. Her nails dig into my scalp slightly as she tugs at the roots. I copy her actions, scrubbing and running my fingers through her hair as she lets out little hums of satisfaction. *How is something as boring and mundane as washing hair suddenly so tantalizing?*

I release her hair, pull her closer to me with one hand while I reach for the shower head with the other. Wasting no time, I use the shower to wash away the suds before spinning her around so the back of her head rests against my chest. Taking more soap in my hand, I carefully wash every inch of her body, down her perfect chest, the curves of her tummy and hips, and towards my favorite part. But rather than letting my fingers slip inside her like I know she wants me to, I let my fingers tease her opening for just a brief moment before they find their way back to the inside of her thighs. She parts her legs further for me, giving me better access but for once I don't take it. Instead, I place my free arm around her waist, hugging her tightly while peppering soft kisses behind her ear, down her neck and onto her shoulder, enjoying the feeling of peace and warmth as the hot water pounds down on us. *I could stay like this forever.*

Riley spins herself around so that she can rest her head against my chest and I hold her tightly against me, taking in the unfamiliar vanilla scent wafting from her head. We stay silently locked in our embrace until the water begins to run cold.

"I think it's time to get out." I laugh as the cold water begins to beat down on top of us.

"But I don't wanna let go," Riley whines, even as I feel the goosebumps appear on her skin.

Reluctantly, she releases her hold on me and reaches for the rolled up towels just outside of the shower, handing one to me first.

I use the large towel to wrap her in first before reaching for another one to wrap around my waist.

We make our way to the bedroom and climb straight into bed, not caring whether or not we're fully dry, just desperate for some heat, comfort, and rest after our hectic day.

"Thank you for today," Riley says as she looks up with the most beautiful, sleepy eyes.

"I'm glad you enjoyed it. I wasn't sure if..." I begin, but she cuts me off.

"It was perfect."

I run my hand along her jawline and into her hair, pulling her closer to me so that I can kiss her.

It starts off soft at first but her lips open. As my tongue darts in, a very small, soft moan leaves her lips. I reach my hand down, grabbing the back of her leg and pulling her leg on top of mine.

As our kisses grow in intensity, I find myself rolling on top of her to deepen it and to feel closer to her. *It's kind of nice to just kiss, without rushing straight for more. Who the fuck has my girl turned me into?*

"Mmm, I love... kissing you," Riley moans as she breaks away and hides her face in my chest.

"I like kissing you too," I laugh. *What a weird thing to say.*

Chapter Thirty-Four

Riley

I love kissing you? I mentally facepalm at my own awkwardness. I can't believe I almost blurted out those three words.

I love you! But do I? I know I care for him and that I don't want this, whatever it is, to end. But is it love? Real love? And more to the point, could he ever love me back?

"Riley? Did you hear me?" Gabe asks gently, tapping a finger on my shoulder.

"Sorry, what?" I ask as I shake my head and try to bring myself back to reality.

"I was asking if you wanted to watch TV or something?"

"Yeah, okay," I say as I shuffle out of the bed and reach for the remote that's placed on the bedside table.

I flick from channel to channel looking for something interesting to watch but nothing really sounds good. I continue looking until I hear a Taylor Swift song belting out.

"Oh my god! I used to love this song," I laugh as I begin singing along. "Don't tell me you don't know this one," I say when I see Gabe eyeing me up with a small grin.

"Not a clue what this is, but don't let me stop ya," he laughs.

"Taylor Swift! You don't know who Taylor Swift is?" I gasp.

"Think I've heard of her; no fucking idea what she sings though," he replies with a shrug.

"What?! Have you been living under a rock or something?" I say as I playfully hit him with my pillow. "She was the very first concert me and Harper went to. We begged our parents for weeks and weeks, to take us. Then we woke up at like 5 a.m. to go and spend a whole day waiting for a chance to see her."

"What time did it start? 5 a.m. is a crazy time for a concert." *He clearly does not believe that I would do that.*

"No silly, the concert was in the evening, seven or eight o'clock maybe, but we lined up all day to make sure we were near the front. We had floors!"

"What the fuck? You're telling me you stood outside in the cold for over twelve hours just to see some skinny blonde girl sing?" he says as he looks from me to the TV with a frown.

"Yes, it was amazing. We made friends in the line with other Swifties."

"Swifties?" he interrupts.

"Yeah, Swifties! It's what Taylor Swift fans are called, silly."

"More like crazies," he chides. "What did you do for all that time waiting?"

"We spent the day with my mum, that was before we realized how sick she was of course, and just had a great time. Pretty sure I still have a t-shirt somewhere from it," I say as I try to think of where it might be.

"It's a good thing you're cute, because you're fucking crazy!" he laughs.

"Aww, you think I'm cute?" I tease as I place my hands under my chin and try my best to look angelic.

"Well you look pretty damn cute when my dick pounds into that smart mouth of yours," he replies with a mischievous smirk.

"Seriously, is that all you think about?" I say as I playfully swat at his chest.

"Every damn second," he purrs as his eyes drop to my lips and he bites on his own.

"I thought I was horny, but you are insatiable." I say as I roll my eyes at him.

"Then maybe you should give me what I want," he suggests as he gently caresses my leg and leans toward me.

"Nope," I say as I shake my head slightly and tightly squeeze my thighs together to block his path. Gabe pouts like a child, so I lean forward and in my most seductive whisper, "I think you need to be punished first."

I see Gabe's eyes widen and fill with arousal, "Oh yeah, and how exactly are YOU going to punish ME?" he asks, his voice laced with longing.

"Well I was thinking..." I say as I stare deeply into his eyes, making him think he's about to get some sort of sexy prize.

"Taylor Swift marathon, and you don't get to touch me until you know at least one chorus of a song," I say with a laugh.

Gabe's whole face morphs from desire to confusion, then annoyance, before finally settling on a stubborn child pout.

"You are such a bitch," Gabe says in a playful yet grumpy way.

"I prefer the term brat, actually," I say as I poke out my tongue.

I turn up the TV, leaving Gabe to huff behind me and realize we're around halfway through the 'Top 10 Taylor Swift songs' so I make him watch them all. Every now and again he tries to talk to me or tries to distract me by kissing my neck or running his hand along my bare skin, and as much as I wanna give in, my stubbornness won't let me. So instead, each time I simply ask, "Do you know the words yet?" and smirk as he grumbles, "No."

I'm loving having the power over him for once, even if it's something as simple as this. It makes me feel oddly accomplished to know I'm in charge.

"I think I know this one," Gabe finally says.

"Oh yeah? Sing it then," I laugh.

"I'm not fucking singing," Gabe snaps. "That was never part of the deal."

"Fine, say the words then," I agree.

"And I get to fuck you if I do?" Gabe asks as he peppers kisses on my shoulder.

"Yep, get the words right and you can do anything you want to me," I smirk.

"Anything?" Gabe's eyes go as wide as saucers, probably thinking of some dirty thing he wants to do, and damn do I hope he gets the words right so that I can find out what that dirty mind is planning.

"Players, play, play, play," Gabe says in a very monotone voice.

"You can do better than that!" I laugh.

"Haters, hate, hate, hate," he says, this time in tune but still not quite singing.

"Something, something, shake it off, shake it off," he says with an 'I did it so now give me what I want' grin.

"Oooh, so close, but those are the wrong words," I tease, as I stand and pretend to leave.

Gabe lets a loud grumble out as he grabs my hand and pulls me backwards, causing me to fall back onto the bed. I let out a squeal of excitement and his hand flies up and covers my mouth.

"That's enough from you. I don't wanna hear another sound till you're screaming my name. For being a brat, I should really not let you cum," he snaps, in that powerful and bossy tone. The one that completely makes me melt.

He removes his hand and goes to stand, "whe..." I don't even have chance to get out one word before his hand is back over my mouth.

"I told you, Firecracker, I don't wanna hear another sound until you're screaming my name," he says as he gives my thigh a playful spank, while still covering my mouth and staring deep into my eyes.

I nod in response and get a small kiss on the neck as a reward. He stands up again and walks away. I don't say a single word but follow him with my eyes. He walks towards the end of the bed, bending down to where his discarded clothes are, and disappears from my eyeline for a moment. *What is he doing?*

He stands up a second later and I see he has something hidden behind his back. He looks down at me and must notice my confused expression as he steps closer and asks, "Do you trust me, baby?"

Do I trust him? Can I trust him? Should I trust him? My brain wonders for a moment as a mixture of fear and arousal surrounds me. But my mouth betrays me by mumbling a simple "yes."

A grin finds its way to Gabe's mouth as he slowly pulls a thick leather belt from behind his back. *Fuck! What did I agree to? Is he going to hurt me? Worse than the last time he punished me, up on the rooftop.*

My face must give away my thoughts as he quickly steps closer, and caresses my face with one hand while continuing to hold the belt with the other. "Don't worry Firefly, I'd never hurt you."

I nod my head in response, as despite the hard exterior he has, I know there's a softy inside him. When all is said and done I feel safer with him than any other boy I've ever dated.

"Tell me you trust me and I'll make sure you love every second. But if you can't, then we stop now," Gabe says as he grips my chin forcefully and forces me to look straight into his big beautiful green eyes.

"I trust you," I whisper slowly. *What am I getting myself into?*

I hear the belt drop to the floor as he uses the hand that was holding it to scoop around me and lift me higher up the bed as he kisses me.

"Close your eyes," he purrs as he loosens my towel, and exposes my naked body.

I do as he asks. I feel the bed dip as he moves and reaches down for what I can only assume is the belt.

"Keep your eyes closed, and trust me," he tells me again.

I try my best to do as I'm told, but my body and mind are on edge in anticipation as I feel the cold leather caress my legs and thigh as his hands and the leather stroke my skin.

I feel his hand grip my outer thigh as he forces me to turn slightly and pushes one leg over the other so that my ass is partially exposed. "Hmmm," he growls as he runs a hand over my bare ass.

"My belt is just begging to spank this."

What? My eyes fly open as I sling my leg back down so that I'm lying on my back and my poor ass is no longer exposed.

"I know I fucked up once before, baby..." he says as he places a soft kiss on my hip bone, "..but I promise I'll never hurt you again."

He has so much sincerity and guilt in his eyes that I decide to ignore my fears and trust him. I close my eyes again, let out a small breath and nod. Silently giving him permission to continue.

He lifts my leg again and moves it so that he has access to my ass again. He caresses it before giving me a small tap with his big strong calloused hand. I jump in surprise, but also in relief that it's his hand rather than the belt hitting me.

"Are you ready for the belt now?"

"I think so," I reply, still doing my best to keep my eyes closed.

A small, soft tap hits me, so soft in fact that I barely feel a thing.

"See, that's not so bad is it?" Gabe says cautiously. "I'm going to do it again," he says, just as another soft tap hits, this one slightly harder than the last, but still barely enough to leave a sting.

"Good girl," he purrs. "Now it's time to do it properly. One… two" he counts and the fear takes over causing me to screw my face in anticipation of a pain that I worry is coming.

"Fuck this," he says as he surprises me when he stops all together before standing up and walking away. "What are you doing?" I say opening my eyes again, this time sitting myself up so I can look at him.

"I can't do it; I need to punish you, but I don't want to hurt you," he says as he begins shuffling from foot to foot.

"I trust you. It's fine," I say as I attempt to pull him closer. "Tell that to your face, you're fucking scared of me," he says in a pained voice.

"I'm not scared of you Gabe. Sure, I'm a little worried that the belt is gonna hurt, but I'm not scared of you. Heck, I like it when you spank me and tell me I'm a bad girl. But I'm not sure about that." I say as my eyes dart to the belt lying on the floor.

"Oh," he says as he finally allows me to pull him towards me.

"So this…" he says as he pulls back his hand and swats my ass, causing me to let out a gasp of air, "… is okay?"

"Yep," I purr as I feel my arousal building.

"And this?" he asks as he swats my naked ass again, this time a little harder.

"Yeah," I moan.

"What about this?" he asks as he spanks me harder, causing me to fall against him slightly as I let out a moan.

I throw my arms around his neck and whisper, "Hmm, yeah, punish me."

"That gives me an idea," he says with a naughty grin as he pushes me backward onto the bed.

"Arms up," he demands and I comply. He picks up the belt and tightly loops it around my wrists before tying it to the bedpost.

Once he has me tied where he wants me, he forcefully spreads my thighs apart and places his head in between, wasting no time as his mouth and fingers bring me to orgasm, time and time again.

Next, he carefully loosens my restraint just enough so that he can roll me onto my front. He then grabs my hips and forces me to lift my ass until I'm basically on all fours.

"Yeah," he says as he gives my ass another playful spank.

"I've thought about having you like this since that first night. What did you call it? Cat in heat pose?" he teases. I can't help but smirk as I think back to that first night in the hotel after he rescued me from that concert with Justin. *Who'd have thought that would have changed the course of my life so massively?*

Another spank brings me back to reality. "Answer me," he demands. *Shit, I've no idea what he asked.*

"Yes?" I reply, hoping that's the right answer to whatever question he just asked.

"Yes?" he questions. *Shit, that obviously wasn't the answer he expected.*

"You weren't listening, were you?" he questions and I can hear a note of surprise in his voice.

"I was just thinking about that first time. How you came and took me away from Jus.."

"How dare you think of him? You need reminding of exactly who this ass belongs to?" he snaps as one harder slap attacks my bare ass.

"Dick," I mumble under my breath as I feel the heat and sting burn across my ass.

"As you wish," he chuckles and I'm glad to realize he's only pretending to be mad.

He grabs hold of both my hips and angles them upwards. I feel him move behind me just seconds before I feel him thrust inside me.

"Fuck me," I groan as I'm forced to suddenly stretch to accommodate his size.

"Anything you say, baby," he says as he wastes no time fucking me hard and fast until I'm a screaming mess barely able to hold up my own body weight.

He finally releases my hands and I flop down onto the bed feeling like my whole body is suddenly made of jello.

"That was...wow!" he pants from beside me.

I feel him pull me against him as he places kisses to the top of my head, but I'm too exhausted to move. I enjoy the warmth of his body against mine for just a moment before my eyes close and I drift off to sleep.

Chapter Thirty-Five

Gabe

I'm awoken by the incessant buzzing of my phone on the bedside table. I reach for it and feel Riley begin to stir in my arms. *Shhh, my little flame.*

Holding her close I begin to stroke her hair until I hear her breathing deepen again and the light sound of sleepy snores start once again.. *God I could listen to that sound forever if it meant I got to wake up every day to her body pressed against mine like this.*

My phone buzzes yet again so carefully I grab it, if for no other reason than to ensure it doesn't wake my girl up.

I spot a few messages from the Sinners group chat asking where I am and why I'm not at Saints for our usual monthly meeting. *Fuck was that tonight?* And then a few from Kelly, mostly begging to see me like the pathetic whore she is. I'm just about to delete the whole chat when another message buzzes through.

> Glory Hole
>
> Come on! It's been months since I've seen you. The rest of the guys are here. Come join us and I promise to make it worth your while.

If it were possible for my balls to crawl back into my body from disgust alone, they would. Even the idea of Kelly makes me want to chop my dick off.

> Me
>
> Not interested. Go find some other asshole to fill your hole, I'm done with you.

Her reply comes almost instantly. It's a selfie of her in nothing but a pair of pants with the words, 'Come see what you're missing, my body aches for you as much as I know yours aches for me.'

I feel the anger forming. *Why won't this bitch leave me alone?* I hit delete on the photo right away, not wanting Riley to ever see it and think the worst.

> Me
>
> Fuck off, Kelly. I wanna fuck you about as much as I wanna take a cheese grater to my cock right about now. Go find yourself some other asshole to fuck, as I can promise you now, hell will freeze over before my dick goes anywhere near any part of you ever again.

> **Glory Hole**
>
> Fuck you Gabe! You are a motherfucking asshole. I know you'll come crawling back to me. You always do! But don't even think about texting me next time you're bored and horny because I won't fucking answer.

Finally the bitch got the message. I'm about to put my phone away, happy to finally be done with her, that is until one last message comes through.

> **Glory Hole**
>
> You'll never find someone as hot as me again. Good luck with whatever skank you find next. I hope you end up sad and alone because no girl will want you. Enjoy sleeping alone with nothing but your hand for company.

I look down at the angel in my arms and a wicked idea runs through my mind. I carefully pull the blanket up just enough to ensure her breasts and everything else are covered and snap a picture. A picture of my beautiful semi naked girl, asleep in my bed, with her head nuzzled against my bare chest. I quickly access the picture, making sure there's absolutely nothing private of her on show, then hit send.

> **Glory Hole**
>
> Who the fuck is she??

I pause for a moment wondering what to reply. *I don't wanna tell Kelly her name, and her face isn't clear enough in the picture for Kelly to recognize her. I consider calling her my girlfriend, but we've not really had that chat yet and the word girlfriend still seems so foreign to me.* So instead I say the only thing that feels right.

> Me
> My salvation.

I then block and delete her number. Not wanting to ever hear from her again.

I snuggle back into my girl and drift off into a calm and peaceful slumber.

Riley

The light shines in through the curtains, pulling me out of my sleep. I reach over and grab my phone, realizing it's barely 6 a.m. *I'm never awake this early.*

I consider rolling back over and making the most of snuggling up to my man, but something tells me to get up instead. I carefully sneak out of bed realizing I'm butt ass naked other than a bunched up blanket beneath me. I look down at Gabe, placing a soft kiss on the top of his head as I carefully sneak out of the bed. I throw on my clean underwear and the baggy t-shirt I packed, and make myself a coffee. Coffee in hand, I slide the balcony door open quietly, taking one last glance behind me to ensure Gabe's still in bed, before I make my way outside to enjoy my morning coffee in peace.

I have never been one for lots of disruption when I wake up. I've always needed time alone to truly wake up and start the day. I slowly sip my drink, enjoying the quiet. No sound other than birds and the occasional voice on the ground below for company. That is until a loud bang from behind me startles me. I stand quickly and rush inside, unsure what I expect to find or do about it. What I least expect to find is Gabe thrashing around in bed. His arm swings out, knocking over the lamp on the table beside him. Then his other arm bangs against the headboard above him.

"Stop, no, stop," he cries out. I rush over to him, unsure what to do, but knowing I have to make it stop.

"Get the fuck off me!" he bellows as he continues to thrash around, fighting some invisible monster. *What the fuck do I do?*

"Gabe, wake up it's me, it's me, Riley," I say softly as I try to lightly shake him awake, but it's no use.

"Leave me alone," he bellows, barely coherently, as his arms and legs continue to kick out. I climb on top of him, placing one hand on either shoulder, and try to forcefully shake him awake.

Still asleep, his arms fly up as if to hit me and I panic. *Fuck, he thinks I'm the monster he's fighting.* Without thinking, I slap him hard. His eyes fly open and I see a mixture of anger and fear flash through them before they focus on me. They then morph into shock, embarrassment, confusion, and finally guilt.

"I'm sorry baby. I'm sorry, so sorry, did I hurt you?" he asks as he grips my face, turning it side to side, looking for evidence of marks I'm assuming. He runs his hands down my neck and over my arms, the whole time his eyes rapidly scan my chest and tummy.

"What the fuck did I do?" he whimpers as his hands and eyes continue their assessment of me.

"I'm fine, baby, I'm fine. You didn't do anything. You didn't hurt me," I tell him, the words coming out rapidly as I hope to calm him.

"I'm so sorry," he says again, this time sounding like he's holding back tears. He pulls me down against himself and holds me tight, like if he lets go I will somehow vanish.

I can feel his heart thumping out of his chest against my cheek as his rapid breathing continues. "It's fine baby; you're safe now," I try to say, despite the fact that my voice is muffled against his body. I try to pull away, just enough so that I can look at him, but his grip on me intensifies even further. I feel my shirt tighten against my body as his hands grip the fabric for dear life. He's holding onto me like I'm his only lifeboat, and he's lost at sea.

Realizing he needs me more now than anyone ever has before, I allow my body to entwine with his as I lay silently until he finally feels safe enough to let go.

"I'm so sorry," he whispers as he rolls me off him and attempts to leave.

"Wait!" I cry out as I lunge forward to grab onto him just as he's about to stand.

"Let go, Riley," he says sadly.

I wrap my arms around him as I bury my head against the back of his shoulder. "Don't go, please; don't leave me. Don't shut me out. Please!" I beg.

"I'm broken, baby. Broken beyond repair. You deserve so much more than I can give you," he says softly as his hands rest on top of mine.

"I don't want anything from you; I only want you." I reassure him, praying he hears the truth and honesty in my voice.

"But I'm broken; I'm damaged goods. You deserve perfect, and that's just not me!" he says in an oddly defeated tone like he's already given up on us. My heart breaks as a tear runs down my cheek and onto his shoulder. *I can't lose him, I just can't. Not like this. Not over some stupid dream. Not when we were so close to finally being together like I know we both want.*

Gabe must feel the tears continuing to fall as he pulls my hands apart so that he can move, but instead of running away, he drops to his knees in front of me. "Please don't cry. You deserve so much more than I can give you, baby. You deserve sunshine and flowers and fancy dates. You're good and kind like a mother fucking ray of sunshine brightening my pathetic life. Meanwhile I'm a goddamn blackhole of danger and destruction who will end up destroying yours. You're the light that illuminates my world and I'm just a black hole of darkness destroying yours."

"No!" I snap as my hands beat against him in frustration. "I don't want any of that bullshit; I just want YOU!"

"But..." Gabe begins, but I cut him off.

"No, you don't get to decide what I do and don't deserve. Who the fuck do you think you are?" I rant as the tears continue to flow.

"Maybe I don't want the perfect princess being rescued by the knight fairytale. Maybe I wanna be my own fucking warrior. Maybe, I don't want sunshine and rainbows, perhaps I want dark and dangerous and goddamn real. Did you ever think of that?" I snap as I push him away so that I can stand.

"You don't fucking know anything. You're a goddamn coward, Gabe." I shout. He reaches for me, but I slap his hand away.

"No. You make out that you're this badass scary, 'I'm not scared of anything' kind of guy. But you're a fucking coward. Scared of anything becoming real. Scared of being vulnerable. Scared of being open and letting anyone see the real you. You'll only get to push me away so many times before I'm gone, and you'll lose me forever. Last chance. If I walk out this door, I'm never coming back," I scream as I reach for the door handle.

Gabe pushes the door closed, pinning me in. "I'm broken..." Gabe tries to say again, but I'm too angry to listen.

"I..don't..fucking..care!" I scream, directly into his stupid, *yet devilishly handsome* face.

Gabe grabs me forcefully by the face and plunges his tongue deep inside my mouth. Our kiss is angry and depraved, our hands scratch and claw at each other as our mouths kiss and bite each other. And our hands waste no time before virtually ripping the clothes off each other. I feel Gabe's hands loop around the back of my thighs as he lifts me into the air and fucks me hard and fast against the wall. The whole time we're fucking it's angry and passionate, filled with a mixture of love, hate, longing, and desperation. When we're finally finished, we collapse into a sweaty mess on the floor.

Chapter Thirty-Six

Gabe

I roll over, leaving a panting and exhausted Riley on the floor, and force myself to stand. I make my way to the bathroom, in desperate need of a moment alone to gather my thoughts after everything that's happened in the last hour.

I head into the bathroom, shut the door behind me, close the lid to the toilet, and sit down. I rest my head in my hands while I take a few calming breaths and try to evaluate what the fuck I should do next.

Finally feeling a little more level headed, I exit the bathroom expecting to find Riley still lying where I left her on the floor. But when I open the door, she's nowhere to be seen. *Perhaps she's moved to the bed. The floor is uncomfortable as fuck*, I try to tell myself, despite the uneasiness washing over my body. I turn towards the bed praying to see her, but the bed is empty. *What the fuck?* I glance over to the chair, the one that had her clothes on it just moments ago, but those clothes are no longer there. *Fuck, fuck, fuck. She left! She ran away! I scared her away! I fucked shit up and lost the only truly good thing in my life.*

I rush towards the door, hoping to chase her down. After all, she's got no way to truly leave since we came on my bike. *But what if she ran down to that dickhead at reception and begged him to protect her. Maybe he'd take her home. Or hide her in some staff room that I can't gain access to.* The possibilities fly through my head at lightning speed, so fast in fact, that I almost don't see Riley. She is sitting, fully dressed, on the floor with her back against the door. *But why? Is she blocking my exit perhaps?*

I attempt to lift her up, but she kicks out. "No, you're not leaving me!" she screams as she continues to flail around in my arms.

I scoop her up like a child and hold her tightly against me. "I'm not going anywhere, baby," I say, with a promise, as I carefully carry her back into the main room and hold her tightly in my arms as I sit us both down on the bed.

"What was that?" she asks, voice barely louder than a whisper.

When I don't answer her, she clarifies, "The dream, the self doubt, the fear. What was all of that about?"

"My demons," I sigh, unsure what else to say and hoping that it will be enough for her. *I really don't want her to know that part of me. The part that will surely make her disgusted to be around me and will make her leave me, just like everyone else leaves me. I am gross; I am disgusting, but right now, at this moment, she doesn't see that part of me, and I want to keep it that way.*

She reaches up and grips my face, pulling me so that I have no choice but to stare directly into her eyes. "You can tell me...anything," she says softly, yet somehow with more intensity than ever before.

I feel a shift between us. I feel more connected to her in ways that I have never felt with anyone else. I want her to see me. I want her to know all about me.

Can I? Can I really tell her? Tell her all the fucked up shit that lives rent free in my mind? Can I trust her with my deepest, darkest secrets? Secrets I've never told another living soul?

As if she can hear my unspoken words, she answers. "You can trust me Gabe. I won't tell anyone, I promise."

I stay silent for a moment, still staring into her eyes, locked in some sort of battle of wills as neither of us wants to be the first person to break it.

"I can't. I wouldn't even know where to start," I admit, averting my eyes from her.

I see the sadness in her eyes as she looks away, clearly thinking I'm saying I don't want to tell her, rather that I truly have no idea where the fuck to start as my whole life has been such a disaster and that I no longer know what's normal and what isn't.

"But you can ask me anything, and I'll try to be as honest as possible," I add. *Am I making a huge mistake? What if she somehow uses this against me? What if I bare my soul to her and she then rejects me?* I look at her once more, seeing the kindness and sincerity behind those eyes, and decide that for her, I'm willing to risk complete and utter damnation.

"Okay," she says softly. As she climbs off my lap.

"I'm gonna need a beer first," I say as I walk over to the mini bar and pull out a can. *I know I said I'd do my best not to drink when I'm around her. But there's no way in hell I'm gonna survive this sober.*

"I'm ready," I say through anxious, gritted teeth as she joins me outside on the balcony.

"Who are the Jacksons?" she asks as she reaches out and places her hand on my lap.

"They were mine and Nate's foster parents after we got taken away," I say as I light a cigarette and take a long drag.

"Why did you get taken away?"

"Because my father was a sadistic mother fucker, who used to beat us, starve us, and abuse us in every vile way imaginable." I add as I try my hardest to stay calm and keep the emotion out of my voice. *The only way I'm gonna get through this is to be as factual, honest, and to the point as possible.*

"Every way imaginable? Does that mean..." she asks hesitantly, and I know exactly where her mind is trying hard not to go.

"Not Nate, no, never Nate," I reply, praying that she's able to read between the lines. I take a large gulp of my drink, praying for the usual calm it brings me as I try to distance myself from the situation. Not wanting to go down that particular memory lane.

"Oh," she says as she looks at me with a sympathetic look. One that hurts far more than any memory ever could.

"Next question. Please," I whisper, unable to take the pity a second longer.

"Okay, why did you come back? Why didn't you stay with the Jacksons like Nate did? You could have had a happier life like he had."

"I didn't know how to," I admit.

"What do you mean?" she asks as she looks at me with furrowed eyebrows and an inquisitive look.

"What you have to understand is that me and Nate are built very differently. My father was an absolute cunt to both of us. He hit Nate more times than I can count. But the way he tortured me was on a different level. He knew how much I loved my baby brother, and used that against me every single day. He would beat on Nate, make him cry, and cover him in bruises on a weekly basis. But those bruises would eventually heal. And once the attack was over, it would be calm for a few days. I never had that calm." I admit as I take another drag of my cigarette and chug some of my beer.

"You see, I lived with the constant threat looming over my head. The threat that if I didn't follow his every command, he'd hurt Nate, maybe even kill him. I lived with the fear that every time I walked out the door, even to follow his commands, I was leaving Nate alone and unprotected. I went to bed every single night fearful that if I slept too soundly, I may wake up next to a beaten and bloody Nate. So I was never safe." Riley reaches her hand up to cup my face but I pull away, knowing if I have to look at the sadness in her eyes, I'll never be strong enough to continue.

"And even after we were finally free from his grasp, I was never able to ease that tension in my body. I was never able to accept that another adult could be good. Never able to shake the fear I felt whenever one of them called Nate away from me or would come into the room to say goodnight."

My mind flashes back to one of the first weeks we lived with the Jacksons.

The sun is beaming down on me as I continue mowing the lawn in front of the house. Nate is with Mr. Jackson on the sidewalk just a few feet away. Mr. Jackson is trying to teach him to ride a small blue bicycle but Nates is too scared to ride alone. "Look at me Gabe, I'm doing it!" Nate squeals as he begins peddling as Mr. Jackson runs along behind him.

"Good job, bro!" I yelled back. For once feeling oddly peaceful.

"Mrs. Jackson, can I get a drink please?" I ask, trying my hardest to be good. Show them that I can be good.

"Of course, Gabe," Mrs. Jackson responds as she flashes me a smile.

I fill a glass full of water from the sink and am just about to take a sip when I hear a loud scream from Nate. Without thinking, I grab one of the big knives from the knife block beside the sink and rush outside. As I do, I see Nate lying on the hard concrete bleeding as Mr. Jackson crouches down in front of him.

"Get the fuck away from him!" I scream as I run towards Mr. Jackson with the knife in my hand. I throw my arms around my brother and hold the knife outstretched in warning towards Mr. Jackson's face. "Touch my brother again and I'll ram this knife so far down your throat you'll choke on your own fucking blood!" I scream as I desperately try to protect my brother from whatever this monster did in the thirty seconds my back was turned. I knew I shouldn't have left him alone. *Stupid, stupid Gabe. You're a failure. Never good enough to be able to keep him safe.* My mind taunts.

Mr. Jackson cowers in fear as Mrs. Jackson tries coming to her husband's aid.

"Gabe, give me the knife," she says but I hear the fear and quivering in her voice.

"Gabe, it's not like that; it's my fault, I..." Nate tries to defend the man who may be minutes from his death. I won't let Nate take the blame. He always tries to see the good in people.

"No, he hurt you. I know he did. And no one is going to hurt you. Never again. Not while I'm here," I tell him as I continue to wave the knife in the direction of our foster parents.

Riley's hand on my face breaks me out of my memories. "Where did you go?" she asks as she continues to stroke my face lovingly.

"I was just thinking about my time at the Jacksons."

"What about it?" she asks, looking confused.

"You asked why I didn't stay and well, I made everyone's life a living hell. I had to leave before they got rid of the both of us, and Nate lost his only hope at a real family." My heart aches as I think of the way it felt to leave him behind. And all the pain I've felt in those years since. But seeing the happy, loving person he became, I know I made the right choice.

"I'm sure you weren't that bad; they must have known taking in kids with childhood trauma wouldn't be all smooth sailing," she says as she tries to lighten the mood.

"You think I'm a dick now, I was worse as a kid. I threatened to stab my foster dad within the first few weeks."

"Everyone says stuff they don't mean when they're a kid," Riley interrupts.

"No Riley, you don't understand. I didn't just say, 'Oh I'm gonna stab you' in jest. I grabbed a knife and held it up to him and threatened to stab him with it," I admit. I see Riley's eyes widen as she swallows an invisible breath.

"I'm sure you had your reason," she adds, but it's clear from her tone and face that she doesn't truly believe that.

"Yeah, I misread a situation. He was teaching Nate to ride a bike, and I turned my back just as he decided Nate was doing well enough to let go. Nate panicked and ended up crashing. All I heard was a scream and as I ran out, I saw my foster father kneeling over a bleeding Nate. My first instinct was that he was trying to hurt him, or perhaps already had so I jumped in to save him without thinking."

"Oh, Gabe," Riley soothes as she leans down and kisses me softly. "That doesn't make you a monster; that makes you a protector. Sure, a kind of crazy one, but a protector nonetheless. You saw your brother in what you believed was danger, and since you'd never known anything other than danger, you naturally jumped to conclusions," she says as she grips my face and forces me to look at her again. "It's not your fault baby," she adds as she kisses me again.

How does she see me so completely? And not just the version of me that I show the world, but really and truly sees ME. The broken yet fragile me that I keep hidden deep within.

I don't know how long we sit outside going back and forth as Riley asks question after question about my past, my relationships, whether or not I have other family members, and so on.

"Okay, one last question and then we will head out for lunch as I'm starving," Riley whines at the same time as her stomach growls like there's a wild animal hiding inside. "What's the deal with you and Izzy? I still don't fully understand."

"What's there to understand?" I ask.

"Well, from what you've told me, everything you've ever done is basically to protect Nate and keep him safe, correct?"

"Yeah," I say slowly, not really understanding what she's getting at.

"Well I've heard Nate and Izzy tell their story many times. They talk about this whole epic romance they had, how they met as friends, and some fun things they did together. How they communicated through letters, letters that you helped Nate read and send. And how the three of you kind of grew up together. So Izzy seems like she was good. She's always been good for Nate. So why do you hate her so much?"

"There's always another side to every story, Cinders " I say, as I feel the anger and disappointment building up in me.

"So what's your side then?" Riley asks.

"She betrayed us. We trusted her; we were honest with her. The first person in our whole life we trusted, and she used that against us. Nate loved her. Heck, I think even I did in my own, protective big brother way, and she broke his heart.

"What do you mean?" Riley asks as she sits herself down on my lap to listen.

I tell her all about the first time they met, how I came home from school and Nate was missing. I spent hours circling the woods, shouting his name as I searched for him. My brain had me convinced my father had come home from work and hurt him. I describe how I hadn't been just looking for my brother playing, I was also looking for blood, signs of a struggle, or even a bloody and battered body discarded on the floor like trash. And how relieved I was when I finally found him sitting on her family's porch with a smile on his face. I explain how I begged Nate to stay away but how he disobeyed me every single time, which caused me stress constantly when I would arrive home and he was again gone.

I go on to explain how I slowly came to tolerate Izzy, and eventually even like her when I saw how happy she made Nate. I was truly grateful for her family showing him love and affection. Despite being jealous and envious, because I also longed to find what he had found in them, I was still happy for him.

I share how happy and fuzzy it made me feel as I got to watch them fall in love letter by letter. And how part of me wished the words I was reading, the ones saying how much she missed him and how much she couldn't wait to spend time with him were aimed at me. I admit that some of the words I wrote back to her about how great of a friend she was came from my own heart as well.

"But then she betrayed us both. We trusted her with a secret, a secret not another living soul knew about, and she ran to her grandparents. Because of her actions, our whole life was upended and thrown into a new level of chaos," I huff, "I'm thankful the Jacksons agreed to take us both in, even if for only a short time. We could have easily been separated and thrown into separate homes, never to see each other again. Or worse, we could have been put in another abusive home, one which we never survived."

"Oh baby," Riley replies sadly as she grips my hand reassuringly.

"What would have happened if my father had managed to talk those cops around, made them believe the house was fine? He would have killed one, if not both of us, for sure. Her loose lips could have been the end for us both." I feel the anger, fear, and hurt take over as I'm reminded of all those feelings.

"I understand but you have to forgive her; she was only a child. She didn't know what she was doing. I'm sure she was trying to help," Riley implores as she rests her head against my chest.

"It didn't feel like that, it still doesn't," I admit.

Riley buries her head into my chest and holds onto me tightly as she listens to me continue to explain how betrayed I felt when we got taken into care. What it felt like to be ripped away from the only bits of stability I knew. The anger that raged through me because I blamed Isabella for putting a wedge between me and Nate, and the loss I felt because up until we moved in with the Jacksons, he'd always depended on me. When we went there, it suddenly felt like he didn't need me anymore.

I feel silly as I hear how pathetic my own words sound now that I'm saying them out loud. Yet the whole time Riley nods along, not once laughing or making me feel guilty for my crazy thoughts or feelings.

"I guess when you had to move back here alone, it just made you blame her more for making you have to deal with all that shit alone," Riley adds. *Shit, does she truly agree and understand?*

"Wait, you agree with me? That it's all Isabella''s fault?" I gasp.

"Well, yes and no," Riley says with a shrug. "I know Izzy and she still feels guilty about everything that happened. She knows she had a role in what happened, but it was unintentional. Plus I know her, she's one of my best friends, and I know she'd never purposefully do anything to hurt either of you. Even now, when you still treat her like shit, she's always one of the first to defend you."

"Oh," *so she does think it's all in my head then.*

"But…" she adds with a pause, "I also understand why you'd see it the way you do. I know that for you, trust is a huge thing to give away, so in your mind for her to tell anyone else is a huge betrayal. I also kind of get why you blame her. But please, for me, I beg you to try to forgive her or at least tolerate her. Baby, you're just hurting everyone around you by holding on to your anger.

Imagine how nice it would be for the four of us to all be together. My best friend and your brother. It would be so nice. Please for me, will you try?" Riley begs as she runs her hands through my hair.

"For you, I'll try," I say. As much as I don't want to, I know she's right. I've seen small glimpses of the old Izzy I knew growing up. And I can see how if I let it, a friendship could easily form. Plus I hate that Riley feels the need to sneak around. I hear how she talks about her friends. And I hear how Nate talks about the group, the ones that became like a second family to him. And I can't help but secretly wish I could fit in with them all.

"That's all I ask baby. One day at a time." Riley sighs as she pulls me closer and kisses me softly.

Chapter Thirty-Seven

Riley

I climb off Gabe's bike, giving him one last kiss before I head inside. I hear the sound of his engine as he speeds away, and feel the sadness and longing in my chest already. *How can I miss him already? It's been like five seconds.*

"Harper," I call out as I run towards our bedroom.

"She's out with the girls," my mother shouts from the kitchen.

"Any idea where?" I ask as I walk into the kitchen and see my mother typing away on her computer at the dinner table.

"I'm guessing still at Izzy's. Didn't you spend the weekend there?" my mother quizzes.

"Oh yeah, of course," I lie, mentally thanking my sister for covering for me. "but I met up with Lexi earlier. She offered to help me study for my biology exam. You know she had to study all that stuff and I'm useless," I add.

My mother eyes me suspiciously for a moment before turning her attention back to her laptop.

"I thought she might be back by now, but obviously not," I say, changing the subject. "I think I may head over if that's okay."

My mother goes to say something, but a beep from her laptop stops her in her tracks. *Thank god for the charity auction.* "Yes, sure. I gotta get back. We've been having a few issues with the venue," my mother replies as she types away furiously.

I head to the fridge, grab myself a couple of snacks, and then head back out the door.

Izzy's house isn't far away, it's within walking distance, so I make the most of the afternoon sun as I make my way over.

I knock on the door before pushing it open slightly, "It's just me, Riley," I shout. Izzy's grandparents always leave their door unlocked and have told us to just walk in, but I still feel that I'm being a little rude when I do it.

"Hello, Mrs. Williams?" I call out as I push the door open slowly and step inside. "It's just Riley."

"Come on in, dear," a voice shouts in response.

I head inside and see Mrs. Williams coming out of the kitchen, carrying a plate. "The girls are all upstairs, make your way up. Take these with you though, dear," she says as she thrusts the plate of cookies into my hand.

"You're determined to make us all fat," I laugh. "If my butt gets any bigger it won't fit through the door."

"Boys like big butts, or so I hear," she replies with a cheeky grin.

"What's all this talk of butts?" Mr. Williams says as he appears, and attempts to steal a cookie.

"George," Mrs. Williams scolds as she slaps his hand away. "You know what the doctor said."

Mr. Williams rubs his hands while frowning. "But I don't want a piece of fruit," he grumbles.

"But it's better for your heart," she replies as she turns to grab an apple from the fruit bowl.

"Here," I whisper as I hand a cookie to him. He hides it behind his back like a naughty toddler, and at the same time, he reaches for the apple Mrs. Williams hands him a second later.

"I swear that man has a sugar radar," she laughs as Mr. Williams scurries away.

"And butts, someone said butts," he shouts back.

"Honestly, that man," she says, shaking her head. "He doesn't hear me bellowing his name to help me unload the dishwasher and doesn't hear the postman knocking at the door with the new cushions I ordered, yet he can hear the oven door opening or a rude comment from a mile away."

These two squabble, quite literally, like an old married couple. But it's clear to see they're still so madly in love. *I wonder if I'll ever have that.* I can't help but smirk as my mind tries to imagine Gabe as a little old man; he'd still be trying to bend me over the dining room table, even with two false hips.

"He's a boy. What do you expect?" I laugh.

"They never grow up dear; even in their eighties, they're still just giant babies... a few more years and they'll be back in diapers," she laughs.

"You're mean, but I so wanna be you when I grow up," I say with a laugh as I turn to leave.

I rush upstairs to Izzy's room and see her, Ava, and Harper all relaxing while watching a movie.

"There you fucking are," Ava gasps. "We were about one hour away from reporting you as a missing person," she teases.

"Seriously, where the heck have you been?" Harper asks.

"I've spent the whole weekend with Gabe. I've got so much to tell you all," I say as I kick my shoes off and throw myself on the bed.

"Thanks for covering for me though, girls."

"It's fine," Izzy replies with a smile.

"Don't worry, the girls had a lovely weekend, helped me de-weed the garden," Ava replies in a little old lady voice, the one I assume she used when she pretended to be Mrs. Williams.

"Go on, tell us all about it. Where did you go? What did you do? Was Gabe nice?" Izzy asks, seeming a little hesitant on the last question.

"He better have been, otherwise, his precious bike will have no tires left. I'm not afraid to go all Carrie Underwood on his ass!" Ava says.

"Honestly, it was the best weekend of my life," I sigh as some of the memories flood through my brain.

"Better than the time we found twenty dollars on the floor and spent it all on sweets?" Harper jokes.

"Definitely!" I laugh. "At least this one didn't end with me throwing up afterward."

Izzy grabs a cushion and lays down beside me, resting her head in her hands. "Tell us then, what did you do?"

"He took me to Six Flags..."

"I love that place," both Ava and Harper say at the same time.

"Never been," Izzy says softly.

"It's the best, you'd love it!" Ava replies.

"So what happened next?" Izzy asks as she looks at me with excited eyes.

"Well, we went to Six Flags; Gabe had planned it all. Oh yeah, and before we went, he went out and bought me my own leather jacket and helmet, just for me as he said he wants me to be safe and protected on his bike."

"Aww, that's so nice," Izzy replies.

"A helmet? And a jacket?" Ava questions, while pulling a 'that doesn't sound so great' face.

Who does she think she is snubbing my man's gift like that?

"Yeah, they were actually really nice." Harper interjects, and I can't help but feel grateful. "They weren't just boring, generic ones, they were actually super cute."

"I bet he put so much thought into it as well," Izzy interrupts.

Ava just shrugs in response. *Seriously, I love you girl, but fix your face before I fix it for you.*

"Okay so you went to Six Flags?" Harper says changing the subject.

"Yeah, we arrived and he'd pre-ordered us the Flash Pass tickets so we didn't even have to wait in the lines. We rode the roller coasters and the pirate ship followed by..."

I go into detail about all the rides and about how excited we both were. I explained that it was Gabe's first time there and that he was clearly nervous, but once we went on the first ride he was like an excited kid wanting to try each and every ride.

"And then we walked around the park holding hands for a while."

"Gabe held your hand? Really? " Izzy asks, sounding just as surprised, but excited as I was.

"I know, so unlike him but it just felt right," I reply with a huge grin.

"Really holding hands? What's so surprising about that?" Ava asks as she rolls her eyes. *Seriously if she doesn't fix her attitude, me and her are gonna be throwing hands in a minute.*

"If you don't wanna listen, then close your ears," I snap back.

"Oh, I wasn't trying to be a bitch, I was just asking." Ava replies looking a bit shocked.

"This is the man who won't even let his brother hug him, Ava. Gabe has hated physical touch for as long as I've known him. I tried to hug him once as a kid and he pushed me away so hard I ended up tearing my skirt as I fell. Another time my hand grazed his as we both reached for the ketchup and he reacted like my touch set his hand on fire, so believe me, this is huge." Izzy explains. *My heart breaks that she so clearly wants to be friends with him, but he's too angry to let her in. Maybe, just maybe, he will try now that we were able to talk and I asked him to see things differently.*

I feel a mixture of emotions as Izzy speaks. I feel grateful to Izzy for having my back, yet oddly sad that she clearly cares so much about Gabe, despite the fact Gabe acts like he hates her. I also feel pride that Gabe is letting me in and growing as a person, but at the same time, sadness that he finds something so simple, so difficult.

"Oh, yeah I guess," Ava replies with a shrug.

"What else did you do? You've been gone the whole weekend," Harper asks.

"We ended up staying at that hotel, you know the one Mom and Dad used to take us to," I say, turning towards my sister. "And then today we went for coffee and ended up catching a baseball game. Neither of us really understood the game, not properly, but we had fun stuffing our faces with hot dogs, and making up random names for the players to cheer for," I say with a giggle as I think back to it. "Oh and let me tell you something else that happened; it was so funny…"

I tell the group all about us going on the teacups; it gets a few confused faces from Ava and Izzy until I explain the significance of it being my and Harper's childhood tradition. I then tell them about the joke I played on Gabe and how he felt the need to prove he was a better kisser.

"Damn girl, that sounds kinda hot. Funny as fuck, but also hot as hell" Ava chimes in.

"You don't know the half of it," I say as I bite my lip and fan my face dramatically.

"Fucking tell us then," Ava wines as she playfully hits me with a cushion.

"Let's just put it this way, that man is a beast in bed,"

"Eww, I don't wanna know," Harper says as she covers her ears.

"Then go get me a drink, because I sure as shit do," Ava replies as she reaches for her empty glass and thrusts it towards my sister.

Harper pokes out her tongue but grabs hold of Ava's glass and makes her way out the door anyway.

"So tell us, is he big? Bad? Is he as much of a freak in the sheets as he seems?" Ava says, virtually bouncing in excitement.

"He's fucking wild!" I reply. "Take today for example, that man grabbed me by my throat, thrust me up.."

"By your throat?" Izzy gasps. "Are you okay?"

"This 'lil slut is more than okay, I'm guessing. That's hot!" Ava smirks.

"Damn right I am, so he had me pinned up the wall and he got out his belt."

"A belt?" Izzy gasps again.

"Maybe you should go help Harper," Ava says softly as she smiles at Izzy. *They've barely been best friends for a few months, but already Ava has taken it upon herself to be the protective big sister.*

"Erm, okay," Izzy replies before scurrying off with a shocked and confused face.

"Okay, so now her innocent little ears have left, tell me what the fuck happened next." Ava says, practically drooling in anticipation.

I give her a few snippets of some of the wild times we've had together, like the time he tied my arms up and fucked me. She didn't believe me when I described how this man gives me multiple orgasms in one night, and how much I love the way he can be both sweet and domineering in the same breath.

"Fuck me girl! No wonder you keep going back," Ava says, fanning herself. "Heck, if I wasn't already with Tucker, I'd be considering stealing him for myself."

"Keep your hands off my man, you couldn't handle him anyway," I joke back.

"Yeah, you're probably right," Ava laughs. "But I may have taken some mental notes to use next time I see Tucker. About time my man learned how to be a little more domineering anyway."

"Is it safe to come in?" Harper jokes as she and Izzy walk in.

"Yep, just talking about Gabe giving Riley a hand necklace," Ava replies with a cheeky grin.

"Aww, he got you a necklace, that's so cute," Izzy replies naively, which just causes both me and Ava to burst into hysterics.

"What's so funny?" Izzy asks, perplexed.

"You don't wanna know." Harper barely gets out because she is laughing so hard.

Chapter Thirty-Eight

Gabe

Reluctantly, I dropped Riley back at home about an hour ago, and now I'm just relaxing at home with a much needed beer.

"There you are," Nate says as he walks in the front door and sees me in the kitchen.

"Hey Nate, just making myself a sandwich, you want one?" I say with a smile, the same cheesy shit eating grin that's been glued to my face pretty much the whole weekend.

"Who are you and what have you done with my asshole of a brother?" Nate teases.

"Fuck you!" I laugh as I throw a cherry tomato straight at his head. It misses, and Nate bends and picks it up, then tosses it in the trash.

"Nah, seriously, it's nice to see you smiling for once." Nate beams as he reaches over and steals a tomato from my plate, popping it into his mouth. "So, where have you been all weekend?"

I grab another plate from the cupboard, cut my sandwich in half and place part of it on a plate for Nate. I then grab a Coke and another beer out of the fridge. " Well...." I begin.

Nate takes his sandwich and grabs two bags of chips for us while I tell him about going to see Tate and how his daughter Trixi helped me pick out proper biker gear for my little Wildfire.

"That's so sweet, yet so you," Nate says with a smile as we each find a seat outside, making the most of the warm night air.

"Where did you go next?" Nate questions.

"Well, I looked up some of those date ideas you suggested, but I'll be honest, most of them were boring as fuck. Picnics in the park, strolls on the beach, pottery making, it kinda seems like something a complete pussy would choose."

I see the expression on Nate's face and realize he and his precious princess have probably done all those things. "No offense," I add hesitantly.

"Some taken," Nate frowns, shaking his head.

"Oh shut up. Can you really see me packing a picnic and discussing the weather or nature? Or frolicking on a beach, picking up seashells?" I say with a raised eyebrow.

"Seriously, never use the word frolicking again," Nate chuckles.

"Point made," I laugh back.

"Where did you take her instead? Knife throwing? Fire breathing? Monster trucks?" Nate teases.

"Actually, you sarcastic dickhead, I took her to Six Flags."

"What? That sounds so cool," Nate comments, sounding like an excited child.

"Have you ever been?"

"No," Nate replies with a sad expression on his face.

"I'll take you soon, I promise. You'll love it." *Finally for once, there's a nice experience, something exciting I get to show him as his big brother.* "I'll speak to Riley, maybe we can go again in a few weeks."

"What?" Nate squeals as his eyes go as wide as saucers. "That would be amazing; I've always wanted to go. The rides look so exciting in the commercials."

My heart aches as I think back to our childhood; the way we'd see commercials with happy families and pretend it was us.

How we'd play in the lake and pretend we were at the beach, or we would take turns dragging each other around on an old blanket as fast as we could and pretend we were on our own version of a rollercoaster. *I'm going to take him for real. Prove to him that I can be a good brother after all.*

"I promise, I'll take us. We may need to take your car though."

"Of course. We won't exactly fit all three of us on your bike," Nate jokes.

"Actually…" I say, before taking a deep breath. *You're doing this for Riley and Nate,* I remind myself before I continue, "I was thinking maybe we could make it a foursome." *You can do this Gabe, it will be okay. You promised Riley you'd make the effort. Plus, you've got a lot of making up to do for the shitty way you've treated Nate since he got back with Isabella.*

"Foursome?" Nate says with a confused frown. "Who else is coming?"

"Perhaps... well maybe it wouldn't be the worst if... she's probably too much of a princess to risk messing up her hair but..."

Nate jumps off his chair and throws his arms around me in a tight hug, "Thank you!"

Nate releases me a couple of seconds later and gives me an 'oops, sorry' look as he does.

"Wait, you did mean..." Nate asks hesitantly as he sits back down.

"Yes, Princess fucking Isabella can come as well," I say as I roll my eyes and let out a breath. *I hope this works out! It could be a complete fucking disaster, but it could be alright.*

Nate beams from ear to ear like a kid on Christmas morning, and I must admit it feels nice to know that for once I'm the cause of someone else's happiness. *If anyone deserves some happiness in their life, it's him.*

"So what was it like? What did you do? Were the rides as fast and terrifying as they look on TV?" Nate asks excitedly.

I go into detail about the rides, about how I thought my heart was gonna fall out of my ass on the rollercoaster. I complained half heartedly about Riley making me go on some baby teacup ride and then tried to make me jealous.

"Yup, sounds like Riley, alright," he laughs.

I explained how we ended up staying in some hotel as the rain got too heavy to drive home in and then about how we went out for lunch and even visited a local stadium to watch a baseball game this afternoon before we drove back home.

"Wow, putting me to shame, Gabe," Nate laughs. "I'd best not tell Bella; she'll think she chose the wrong brother. Who knew you were such a romantic at heart?"

"What? I am not!" I exclaim, feeling oddly insulted.

Wait, am I? Am I romantic? I don't do all that flowers and chocolate bullshit, but I do like to make Riley happy, I guess.

"So you and Riley are getting pretty serious now. Never thought I'd see the day Gabriel Scott would settle down and get himself a girlfriend," Nate teases. But I can see from the huge grin on his face that he's proud of me.

"I'm just as surprised, heck probably more fucking surprised than you are about it," I reply honestly. "But there's something about her, she's just different. Different to anyone else I've ever met, I guess." *Why is it so hard to put into words what I see in her?*

"I'm so happy for you Gabe, I'm so glad you've finally let somebody in, plus Riley is amazing. I love her."

I must fire him a disapproving look because he quickly adds, "Like a friend; I love her like a friend. She's great for you, and I love seeing how happy she obviously makes you. You deserve it."

I deserve it? Is that a good thing? A compliment or an insult? Usually when someone says I deserve something, they're talking about a fiery death, or at least a shit ton of pain. But could it be just once that someone truly believes I deserve some happiness? That maybe I'm not beyond redemption, that I do deserve some goodness in my life after a lifetime of pain and trauma.

We sit in silent peace for a few minutes, just listening to the chirping sound of the grasshoppers around us, before I decide to speak.

"I told her about Dad," I say, my voice barely louder than a whisper.

"What?" Nate gasps as his head spins around to look at me.

"Yeah, today. I told her about Dad, and the Jacksons." I continue to stare ahead into the darkness surrounding the woodlands around us, just letting those words sink in.

"Fucking hell, Gabe, that's huge. What did she say? Are you okay?"

I think about it for a moment. *Am I okay? I opened my heart to another person and trusted them not to use my vulnerability as a weapon.*

"Yeah, I actually am." And for the first time I mean it. *I am okay. Like really and truly okay. Perhaps better than okay.*

I opened up to her about everything - things I thought would scare her away for good, yet she stayed. I gave her a glimpse of my demons, and rather than shy away in fear, she stood beside me ready to slay them for me.

"She didn't run," I say softly. "She stayed and listened."

"So what did you tell her?" Nate asks hesitantly.

"A lot, not quite everything, but more than I've ever told anyone else."

I see him wipe away a tear. *Shit! Is he upset? Did I betray his trust by telling our secrets? Maybe he didn't want anyone to know. I'm sure Izzy knows everything. But maybe he didn't want anyone else to know. Fuck! I screwed up. I betrayed him. Fuck, fuck, fuck. I can't do anything right!*

I see him go to stand and brace myself for the inevitable punch I expect to come. But instead he throws his arms around my neck, so tightly I swear he cuts off oxygen. "I'm so fucking proud of you, Gabe," he whimpers. "She really is the best thing that could have happened to you. And I'm so proud of you for letting her in, Gabriel."

Gabriel, that name. A name that is so rarely used by anyone. But one that holds so much emotion. The memories of my mother, the memories of a tiny little Nate looking up at me like I was his own personal superhero. That name, one that seems far too good to belong to someone like me. But one that fills me with so much love and warmth.

NATE

Gabriel. The name slips from my lips but feels so right. I can't stop the tears streaming down my face as I hug my brother, a hug that just a few months ago he would have rejected instantly, yet now, even though I can feel his body stiffening, he allows it.

I ease up the hug and see the way he finally releases the uneasy breath he is holding. *It breaks my heart that he's still so uneasy with a simple gesture, yet I'm so happy he's trying.*

If this were a movie, it would be the moment someone cracked open a bottle of champagne and sprayed it over us.

I still can't believe the difference I've seen in him since he met Riley. He's like an entirely different person.

I can't help but smile as I watch him retrieve his phone and type out a message, clearly intended for Riley, if the shit eating grin on his face is anything to go by. A few moments later, I hear his phone buzz, followed by an even bigger smirk as a carefree chuckle leaves his lips. I decide to fire off my own message to Riley, letting her know how grateful I am for taking the chance on my brother. I've never seen him happier.

"You want a beer?" Gabe mumbles as he makes his way inside, with his head still buried in his phone.

"Nah, don't drink. Remember?" I respond with a smile, shaking my head.

"Oh yeah, water I guess?" Gabe asks as he scratches his head.

"Nope, I'm fine. I need to get a shower anyway. I'm covered in mud from football with Tucker. Unless you wanna chat for a bit longer?" I add.

"Nah, I'm gonna go to bed," Gabe says with a mischievous grin as he walks back inside.

I look at my watch and see that it's barely even 7pm, but don't bother saying anything since I know today has been a lot for Gabe and that he probably needs some time alone to process it all. I don't wanna force him to run before he's able to walk.

Riley

I'm lying on Izzy's bed with the rest of the girls, watching a movie, when my phone buzzes.

My man
> This weekend was amazing. Can't stop thinking about how fucking sexy you looked with your legs pinned up on my shoulder. Looking forward to seeing what next weekend brings.

My heart pounds and my core flutters at his words.

Me
> Maybe four years of gymnastics comes in handy for something. I can't wait to explore just how flexible I am with you soon.

I'm about to send another cheeky message when a message from Nate pings through and dampens my fire.

Nate
> Hey Riley, I just wanted to say how grateful I am to you for taking the time to get to know the real Gabe. I've never seen my brother so happy or content, and that's all because of you.

My heart swells at the sweetness of Nate's message, but also makes me kind of feel like a giddy school girl knowing that the boy I am head over heels for feels the same about me.

> Me
>
> Awe, thanks Nate. I feel the same. Your brother has such a sweet side to him. I wish everyone else could see that side too.

Another message from Gabe appears.

> My Man
>
> Challenge accepted. I plan to have you in every position known to man while you scream my name.

I look around the room at my three closest friends and desperately wish I was alone right now.

> Me
>
> Maybe I'll pick up a kama sutra book on my way over *devil emoji*

I'm about to flirt more when another message from Nate appears.

> Nate
>
> You have no idea how happy that makes me to hear. Gabe probably won't admit it, but you're so important to him. Please don't break his heart. I know he pretends he doesn't care and he seems like he's made of stone at times, but when that man welcomes you into his life he will burn the world down for you.

Aww, what's he been telling Nate about me? Does he feel as strongly about me as I do about him? Heck, if even Nate is messaging to say how much I mean to Gabe, Gabe must be gushing about me to him.

I don't even have time to reply before another message from Gabe comes through.

My Man

> I plan to find moves with you not even the Kama Sutra has invented yet. Maybe I should ride over right now and we can get a head start. I'd love nothing more than to hear your beautiful moans before I fall asleep.

The contrast between the sweet and spiciness of the two conversations has my head spinning. I quickly reply to both and then hide my phone away.

To Nate:

> Don't worry. I have no intention of hurting Gabe or leaving him anytime soon. His stone heart is safe with me.

To My Man

> Can't wait to see what you come up with but I'm currently at Izzy's, surrounded by the girls and unless you want them to be the ones hearing me moan, I suggest you stop.

I hear my phone buzz beside me but I don't dare open it yet, as I know Gabe's hand will be just itching to punish me for being a brat, as he so kindly puts it.

Izzy's phone rings a moment later.

"Hey baby... yeah, I'm just here with the girls..." she begins.

"I know, Riley's just been telling us that she and Gabe went to Six Flags..." *Gabe told Nate, that's kinda cute.*

"What?" Izzy virtually screams into the phone. "Gabe said that? Are you sure he meant ME?" *Fuck, What has Gabe done now?*

"And he definitely meant me? Like he said my name specifically?"

"You okay?" I mouth as I rub her shoulder reassuringly, mentally preparing myself to comfort her for whatever mean thing Gabe has said or done to her. *He promised he'd try harder.*

Izzy nods her head in response but continues to look dumbfounded as she listens to whatever Nate is saying on the other end of the phone.

"No I do," she practically cries out. "Tell him thank you and that I can't wait."

Thank you? Can't wait?

"I love you too, baby, and I'm so friggin' excited!"

"What was all that about?" Ava asks before I have the chance.

"Gabe..." Izzy starts before she's interrupted by Ava.

"For fuck sake, what's he done now?" she huffs.

"He's... he's... invited me and Nate to go... to go out with him and Riley to Six Flags at some point soon."

"What?" I gasp. *What the fuck? This is huge!*

"If that's okay with you of course?" Izzy says as she looks at me with a nervous expression.

"That's amazing, I'm just shocked that's all," I tell her.

"Not as shocked as I am," Izzy replies as she hugs me. " I don't know what you did or said to him, but thank you!" Izzy says as she begins to cry.

"What are you thanking me for?" I say as I hug her back.

"I don't know, but I know I have you to thank for it. Gabe is different with you, even Nate has said the same. Nate says that Gabe's more like the brother he grew up with since he started dating you." *Really? Other people can see how much he's softened too? It's not just in my head.*

"Oh my god, we're going on a double date!" Izzy squeals excitedly.

"We could all go, make it a whole group event. I'm sure Tucker would come, and you could bring that guy from work you've been flirting with, Harper," Ava says excitedly as she gets ahead of herself.

"No," I reply, feeling oddly defensive. This is going to be hard enough for Gabe just with Izzy there. And it's such a huge step out of his comfort zone the last thing he needs is for us to bombard him with the whole gang.

"No?" Ava says, looking shocked and a bit angry. "You don't want us there? I thought we were best friends?" she adds, sounding hurt.

"No I do; of course I do. But Gabe...." I begin, unsure how to explain. Thankfully Izzy jumps to my rescue.

"We need this Ava. You have no idea how much of a risk and compromise Gabe is making by inviting me along. Getting Gabe Scott to be friendly is bigger than winning the lottery. Don't be mad, but I really need this. We all need this." *She cares about him too, and in her own way, she's just as protective of him as I am.*

"I guess that makes sense," Ava shrugs.

"Maybe another time," Harper adds with a smile before she hits play on the movie again.

I reach for my phone, ready to text Gabe and tell him how proud I am of him, but can't help but smirk as I see his response to my earlier message.

> **My Man**
>
> Do I have to remind you of what happened the last time you thought it was funny to act like a brat? You thought I punished you when you dared to look at someone else while you moaned my name? And that was just a fictional character. If I find out another person, girl, boy, friend or not, gets to hear you, I'll make sure your stubborn ass isn't able to sit down for a week!!

My whole body fills with arousal and anticipation as I imagine the look on his face and the tone of his voice as he says all that.

> **Me**
>
> Good thing you can't reach me then! But don't you worry, yours is the only name I plan on screaming, and when I go to bed tonight, you better believe it will be your fingers I'm imagining making me moan.

His response comes instantly. A picture of him in the shower with the caption, "That's good because I've already moaned yours."

Chapter Thirty-Nine

Riley

The last few weeks have been almost perfect. Our relationship has just gotten stronger and stronger. Gabe has joined the group a couple of times for parties or trips out with the boys. Although I can see he's still not completely settled within the group yet, he's much more settled and comfortable than he used to be, especially when it's just him and the boys. *Heck, the other night he even agreed to a double date with Nate and Izzy to some Italian restaurant in town as a 'trial' for today.*

"I'm nervous!" Izzy says as she shuffles from foot to foot while twirling her hair anxiously.

"It'll be fine," I say as I stroke her arm and try to reassure her.

"But what if he hates me? What if I say or do something wrong and ruin it all?" Izzy replies as she begins to chew on her nails.

"Izzy, relax," I say, pulling her hand away from her mouth. "Me and Nate will be right beside you."

Nate's car pulls up outside my house and Izzy instinctively walks towards the passenger seat, that is until she spots Gabe sitting there and stops in her tracks. He fires her his stereotypical, murderous gaze before flashing what can only be described as a painful looking forced smile.

"Hey Gabe," Izzy mumbles as she climbs in the backseat.

Gabe gives her a slight nod of recognition, but doesn't reply. Not wanting to draw too much attention to either of them, or add any more tension to the atmosphere that's already thick enough to cut with a knife, I decide to try and add a little humor.

"Damn it's hot today. Thank god for the air conditioning or I'd be nothing but a puddle by the time we arrive."

I see a smirk form on Gabe's face in the mirror and know he can't resist the urge to reply with a cocky comment,

"Well it wouldn't be the first time you've been wet for me, would it?"

I see Nate's eyes widen slightly before he playfully hits his brother in the arm. "You're so inappropriate," Nate grumbles as he rolls his eyes.

"I aim to please," Gabe replies with a smirk as he tips his imaginary hat.

We take off driving, there's the occasional comment from one of us but the air still has an uncomfortable feel to it. *This is gonna be a looong drive.*

"So Nate..." I begin as I lean forward to rest my head between the two seats, ".... have you ever been to Six Flags before?"

"Nope, kind of nervous but excited," he tells me with that boyish grin of his.

"Don't worry, your brother screamed like a little bitch the whole time, so I'm sure you'll be no worse than him," I tease.

"You screamed?" Nate gasps, before turning towards his brother.

"I didn't scream. I may have swore a little, but I definitely didn't scream," Gabe huffs.

"He did," I correct. "If I remember correctly you said... 'fuuuuuuuuuck!'"

"Exactly, I swore." Gabe gloats.

"I'd pay to have seen that!" Nate chuckles.

"And then he had to sit on a bench to recover as his legs had turned to jelly," I add as I playfully poke Gabe in the shoulder.

"No, my legs were just cramped as they were squished in the seat," Gabe says defensively.

"Yeah, yeah, whatever you say."

Nate starts laughing harder now, "Gabe's a little bitch boy," he sing-songs.

I sink back in my seat with a big smile on my face. I look over at Izzy, who is clearly also trying to hold in a laugh as we both listen to the boys squabbling in the front seat over who's gonna be the biggest wimp today. *Mission accomplished!*

The next hour or so of the journey is pretty good. The radio is playing some decent tunes, everyone is talking to each other and making plans about which rides we want to hit first, what we're going to eat, and just talking in general, which is actually so nice. *Maybe there is hope for us all to be close friends after all; I mean, best friends dating brothers is pretty much the dream right?!*

Nate suggests a game of I Spy to pass the time, but it quickly becomes apparent that when you stick these two together, the sibling competitiveness is just as strong with them as it is with me and Harper. *Especially when Gabe cheats by choosing M for moving vehicles.*

I look over at Izzy who's being unusually quiet beside me.

"Are you okay?" I mouth.

Izzy shakes her head slowly in response, before making a 'I feel sick' gesture.

"Any chance we can pull over at the next gas station? I feel kind of queasy," I lie. Izzy gives me a grateful half smile before closing her eyes and taking a small breath.

"'Course," Nate replies as he begins looking for a way to exit the highway.

"I'll pull in there," Nate pipes up when we spot a gas station a few minutes later.

The car is barely parked when Izzy flings the door open and runs away. I quickly follow behind her and find her throwing up just around the back of the building.

"Are you okay?" I ask as I grab hold of her hair.

"Sorry," Izzy says as she wipes her mouth with the back of her hands. "I sometimes get travel sickness on long journeys. I either have to sit in the front so I can see the road or lie down in the back. I don't think the nerves help either."

"What's there to be nervous about, you big idiot?" I say with a sympathetic smile.

"It's going so well; I don't wanna do anything to mess it up," Izzy admits.

"Leave it with me," I reply, before walking off towards the store.

I quickly buy a couple of bottles of water and a small bottle of mouthwash for Izzy. I hand the water and mouthwash to her, then together we walk back to the car.

"There you are!" Gabe sighs, as he and Nate lean against the outside of the car waiting.

"Yeah, sorry, I felt a little queasy. I needed to use the bathroom, and then I got us each a drink."

"You okay, do you have a temperature?" Gabe fusses as his hand reaches out and touches my forehead.

"No, no, I'm fine," I laugh as I brush his hand away. "I think it's the long drive."

"You were fine last time," Gabe points out. *Shit, he's right.*

"I know, but cars make me queasy sometimes," I lie.

I see from the look Nate is giving me and the way he's gently stroking Izzy's back that he knows full well I'm lying but thankfully he doesn't call me out on it.

"I fucking knew I should have brought my bike!" Gabe huffs as he slams his hand down on the roof of the car. *Fuck, now I'm the one ruining things, this is like walking on eggshells.*

"Dude!" Nate snaps.

"Sorry." Gabe grumbles. "But your car is making my girl sick." *My girl - swoon!* My heart flutters at his words. He's called me that a few times before but this is the first time he's called me his girl in front of anyone else. *Anyone else we know, at least, and he doesn't seem to even realize he said it.*

"Maybe we could switch it up? Either I get in the front with Gabe, or Gabe, you get into the back seat with me." I suggest.

"I don't mind sitting in the front," Izzy says at the same time as Nate answers, "Gabe, you get in the back."

"I'm not sitting in the fucking backseat; it's too fucking cramped!" Gabe snaps, sounding like a petulant child.

"Well you ain't fucking driving," Nate snaps back.

Fuck. This isn't going to end well. I look over at Izzy who gives me a 'what do we do' look as the two boys begin arguing over who should and shouldn't drive.

"I've been driving longer than you've been fucking."

"But I'm a much safer driver, plus I've not been drinking," Nate huffs back.

I look over at Izzy who looks like a deer in headlights.

"Neither have I!" Gabe retorts.

Nate gives him a dubious look to which Gabe replies, "Fucking smell my breath if you want, I've not had a single drop since last night, not even a beer for breakfast." *Does he usually have a beer for breakfast? Like I know he likes to drink, but does he do it every day when I'm not around?*

Gabe's comment is met by a look of disbelief from his brother, but I can see he's also kind of intrigued.

"Really?" Nate quizzes. "Not a single drink, not even a beer?"

Gabe replies by opening his mouth and breathing an exaggerated breath right into his brother's face, "See? Totally. Fucking. Sober! Although I really wish I wasn't if I'm expected to put up with your condescending ass all goddamn day," Gabe snaps before lighting up a cigarette and taking a long drag.

"When did you last drink?" Nate questions, but I can tell from his calmer, inquisitive tone that he's almost ready to give in.

"Fucking hell, you're worse than the police. I haven't had a single drop since around midnight, before I went to bed," Gabe says as he throws his hands in the air like he is being questioned by the police.

"How come?" Nate questions as he squints his eyes. "Don't get me wrong, I'm pleased, but you gotta admit, that's unlike you."

"Riley made me promise not to drink and drive whenever she rides with me," Gabe admits as he continues to smoke. *Wait, he actually listened? I know he's been better recently, but I didn't realize he was doing that just for me.*

"It's true, Nate," I whisper as I loop my hand around Gabe's waist, ready to defend my man. "He's not driven his bike once after drinking, at least not when I've been with him, not in months."

"Oh," comes Nate's genuinely surprised reply.

"Yep, she'll only agree to ride me if I agree to ride my bike sober," Gabe jokes as he squeezes my ass.

I roll my eyes in response. *I should have known he'd make a joke somehow.* "Gabe," I whine as I swat at his chest.

"What? It's true. First you ride the bike, then you ride the biker, those are the rules!" Gabe says with a mischievous grin.

"Eww, you're disgusting," Nate replies as he covers his ears.

Gabe

"Are we fucking leaving or what?" I grumble, holding out my hand. Nate reluctantly hands me the keys and then joins Princess fucking Isabella in the backseat. I can't help but give Riley a smug grin as I make my way to the driver's side.

I reposition my seat and the mirrors ready to drive off, and am just about to turn the key when Nate pipes up telling me, "You have to jiggle the ignition a little."

"I know." *I've only watched him drive this heap of junk every day for the last six months.*

I rev the engine and am about to pull out when again his voice sounds from behind me. "Make sure to check your mirrors."

"Yes I fucking know Nate," I huff. *Seriously, does he forget I was driving for dad long before I was old enough to have a license?*

I pull out and begin driving, and am just feeling my groove when yet again, like the annoying little shit he is, Nate's face appears between the chairs, "You might wanna switch…"

"Nate, sit the fuck back down, and shut your fucking mouth before I rip the fucking gear stick off and shove it down your goddamn throat!" I remain calm, but say it all through gritted teeth.

I almost burst out laughing as I watch him quietly slither back into his seat.

"You're such a dick," Riley whispers as she attempts to slap my thigh, but I grab her hand and pull it over, placing it directly on top of my cock before quietly replying, "But you love this dick."

My words are met with a little tap to the balls, before she pulls her hand away and furrows her eyes in mock annoyance. *That's it, keep pretending Firecracker, because I know if I was to brush my hand over your panties, they would give away just how much I know my words affect you.*

I look in the rearview mirror and see Isabella and Nate fast asleep. Isabella is curled into Nate's arms as he rests his head lovingly on top of hers and I can't help but feel a little envious, that it's not me and Riley curled up together instead.

As if reading my thoughts, Riley leans over to me and whispers, "I wish that was me curled up in your arms."

I reach my arm out and pull her towards me, before placing a soft kiss to the top of her head. "Later baby, later."

"So I was thinking..." Riley says, but her voice seems to fade into the distance as my brain hones in on the song playing on the radio. *No it can't be, not this song. Please.*

I continue listening as the song plays, and the memories of my mother singing this to me again and again play on repeat.

I can vaguely hear Riley's voice but it sounds a million miles away. "Gabe!" Riley calls, as she gives me a shove.

I blink back the tears and realize that the car has started to veer off toward the side of the road.. *Thank god there are hardly any cars around.*

I pull the car over, park it and climb out not even bothering to close the door as my feet take on a life of their own.

Chapter Forty

Riley

I'm telling Gabe about our plans for prom when I notice the car is starting to swerve.

"What are you doing?" I say turning to look at Gabe, expecting to see it's from him perving on me when I was removing my jacket or something, but although his eyes are facing forward, it's clear that his mind is elsewhere. *Is that a tear on his cheek? What's going on?*

"Gabe," I say again, leaning closer. I notice he does have a tear running down his face, but he seems completely lost in his own mind.

"Gabe!" I snap as I give him a forceful shove.

He blinks away the tears, causing them to slide down his face, as he straightens the car.

"Gabe, are you okay?" I say but he twists out of my reach.

"This song... I can't," he says before he pulls over, literally jumps out of the car and takes off running.

I stare at him in shock, the car door still wide open as he runs away and slumps down on a rock, head in his hands.

I turn my attention towards the stereo, trying to figure out what song could have possibly caused such a strong reaction.

The radio tells me it's a song called Gabriel by Lamb, but it's a song I've never heard before. I contemplate running after him, but as I watch him, sitting with his head in his hands, I can't help but think whatever it is, he needs time alone to process it. So instead, I sit silently for a moment, listening to the lyrics.

It tells the story of a woman who wants to fly away, leave, or die perhaps. But she's saved by an angel, an angel named Gabriel, who comes down to rescue her and keep her safe from harm.

As I listen to the words more, I can't help but wonder if the angel is perhaps a child. The lyrics could easily be a mother singing to her baby. *Is that what it is? Did Gabe's mom sing this to him?*

I turn back, hoping Nate may be awake to shed some light on the situation, but he's still fast asleep.

I carefully climb out of the car and make my way over to Gabe who doesn't even lift his head as he hears me coming.

I don't say a word; instead, I just sit down beside him and put my arms around him.

He leans his head against my shoulder and allows me to hold him but neither of us utters even one word.

"I'm sorry," Gabe apologizes after some time passes, and then removes his head from my shoulder and throws his walls back up as if nothing happened.

"Sorry for what?" I question, but he doesn't answer.

"Gabe, talk to me, please. I'm here to listen." Instead of engaging, he just reaches for my hand and pulls me back towards the car.

We climb back into our seats, and as I'm putting my seatbelt on, I look back towards Izzy and Nate again, wondering if perhaps the lack of motion in the car woke them, but I'm surprised to see they're both still fast asleep.

"Sorry I ruined things; that shit just hit me hard," Gabe confesses softly. He says it so quietly that if it weren't for the silence surrounding us I probably never would have heard.

"Your mom?" I ask quietly.

Gabe nods slightly but doesn't look at me. I squeeze his thigh in what I hope is reassuring, because I really am at a loss about what to do or say. My heart aches for Gabe and everything he has lost and has had to go through in his life. Gabe interlocks our hands and squeezes mine back, but doesn't say another word.

A couple of minutes later he finally speaks, again barely louder than a whisper. "She used to sing it to me."

"Who, your mom?"

Again he nods. "She used to sing it to me as a child, telling me I was her guardian angel. Sent to make her brave enough to survive my father's temper." There's a mixture of sadness and anger in his voice. *I hate that he had so much sadness around his parents.*

A mother who clearly adored him yet left him far too soon, and a father who deserved to be the one to die a long, slow, and painful death. I wonder what Gabe would have been like if it had been his father who died instead. *Would he be like Nate? Happy and carefree? Would he be kinder? With a more gentle soul? No,* he already has those traits. Maybe he'd have been entitled and selfish, a typical jock or bully who had no idea about kindness or trauma. Maybe he wouldn't have even given someone like me a second glance.

"I'm sure she loved you very much. I wish I could have met her," I comment, unsure what else to say or do to help him.

"I think she would have loved you, just as much as I do," Gabe sighs, sounding almost absentminded.

Wait! Did he just say he loved me? I look up at him expecting to see some reaction to coincide with his declaration, but nothing. He's just staring at the road as if nothing happened.

Am I imagining it? Maybe he said LIKE, she'd like me as much as he does? Yeah, that must have been it. That can't be how Gabe would say he loved me, surely. I mean he can't love me yet, can he?

My mind spirals as I think of our time together. *No, he can't be saying he loves me. But I did almost say it to him a couple of nights ago, so maybe this is love.* I've never felt this strongly about any other boyfriend. And I know that Gabe has never done the whole girlfriend thing before, so maybe this is love. *Fuck. This is amazing but also terrifying.*

"We're here," Gabe calls out, breaking me from my mental spiral.

Izzy wakes up almost instantly, which is unusual for her. Nate, on the other hand, is a little more groggy.

"Wake up sleepy head," Gabe says as he reaches back and shoves his brother's leg.

"I really need the bathroom," Izzy whines as we're climbing out of the car.

"It's over there," I say pointing towards the public restrooms just beside the waiting line. Izzy gives me a little wide eyed look so I offer to go with her.

"Get the tickets please. Here's my purse, we will be back in a sec," I say as I hand Gabe my purse, but he pushes it back towards me.

"Gaabe," I whine. "You paid last time. I refuse to allow you to pay again. It's my turn." I say as I stomp my feet, trying to show I'm standing my ground but he just smirks.

"Such a brat," he chuckles. "You can find a way to pay me back later; I intend on making sure you show your gratitude many times."

"Dude!" Nate grumbles as he covers his ears. "I don't need to hear that shit when I've just opened my eyes."

Gabe just chuckles and rolls his eyes in response.

"Come on," Izzy whispers as she tugs on my arm.

We head into the bathroom, but instead of going into the stall Izzy just stands there staring at me.

"I thought you wanted to pee," I ask, a little confused.

"No, I just wanted to get you alone," Izzy replies, sounding almost giddy.

"Okay? Why?" I ask before it dawns on me, "You weren't really asleep, were you?" I gasp.

"No I was, but I woke up after the car stopped. I was about to sit up to see where you had gone, but I'll be honest, I was half scared I would see one of you half naked on the hood of the car," she says and I can see a little blush creeping up her cheeks. "Then you got back in, and you and Gabe were talking and I kind of didn't wanna interrupt as it was clearly a super private conversation. I tried my hardest not to listen; I really did, but..." she says nervously.

"Did you hear what he said about his mother? About him wishing she had met me?" *Maybe she heard and can give me some clarity about what he said.*

She nods her head while smiling like the cat that got the cream.

"Did he say?" I ask nervously.

"Yup, I heard it with my own two ears," Izzy confirms.

"I fucking knew it! He basically said he loves me, right? I'm not losing my mind, please tell me I'm not losing my mind."

"Nope, you're not losing your mind Rilez, he basically said he loves you, although..." *Although? I don't like the sound of that.*

"I don't think HE registered that he said it himself."

"Oh," I say as I turn away, feeling kind of stupid. *Of course he didn't mean it. It was obviously just a stupid slip of the tongue, like when you call a teacher mom by mistake.*

"No Riley, I didn't mean it like that," Izzy says as she reaches out to grab my shoulder. "I'm not saying he doesn't love you, I truly believe he does. Gabe isn't the kind of guy to throw around that word to anyone. Heck, I've only heard him say it to Nate once or twice and even then it was more of a love ya bro, than a proper I love you kind of thing. What I meant was, I don't think Gabe even realized what he said, like his subconscious mind said it without his brain stopping him."

"Oh," I reply this time much happier; hell I feel almost giddy myself.

"We best head back," I say when I realize the boys are probably wondering where we got to.

We make our way back and find Nate and Gabe standing at the entrance, tickets in hand waiting. "Must have been a big shit Princess," Gabe teases, causing Izzy to blush and make herself seem even more guilty as she tries to rapidly explain that she only peed but there was a big line.

Gabe just smirks at her awkwardness as he loops his arm around me and leads us inside.

NATE

As disgusting as it is hearing my brother discussing not only his sex life, but that of one of my closest friends every two minutes, I'm loving getting to see the more playful side of him. A side of him that I thought was long gone, yet somehow Riley has done the impossible and brought it out of him.

I can't help but chuckle as I watch Riley drag him from ride to ride and he follows along like a love sick puppy. *I guess that must be what I look like with Bella.*

"He looks so happy, doesn't he?" Bella coos from beside me like a proud mother.

"I know. Who knew his face could actually smile without cracking?" I joke back.

"Don't be so mean," Bella gripes as she swats my chest, but I can see she's dying to laugh as well.

"That was amazing!" Riley says as she comes down from yet another rollercoaster.

"You really need to stop being such a pussy and join us," Gabe laughs.

"Nope," I say, shaking my head. "The queasy feeling from your last bright idea is only now starting to ease up."

"You'll join me, right Izzy?" Riley asks even though she's already linked arms and virtually dragging Bella towards the next ride.

Bella looks at me with guilty eyes. "You go, I'm fine waiting here," I tell her.

"Thank you baby," Bella calls, just as Riley pulls her into the next line.

"Come on Gabe!" Riley shouts as she beckons Gabe over.

"Nah, you go. I need a drink… I mean a soft drink," Gabe clarifies when Riley gives him a scolding look.

"Never thought I'd see the day Gabe Scott let a woman tell him what to do," I tease. "Could it be that a certain big brother of mine is whipped?"

"I'm not fucking whipped. No fucker tells me what to do." Gabe protests, just as Riley runs over and hands him her goddamn purse, which he takes without thinking.

"Yep, definitely not whipped," I laugh.

"Oh fuck off. Like you're not completely whipped, too. I've seen you running around like Isabella's little lapdog," Gabe huffs.

"Yup, the difference is that I'm not ashamed to admit it. I love my girl and would do absolutely anything to make her happy... What's your excuse?"

"Well... I... it's just," Gabe stutters.

"I'm just teasing you Gabe. It's nice to see you so happy and carefree. I really think Riley is great for you. You too seem so good together," I gush.

"We are good, at least I think we are," Gabe says, but I can hear a hint of uncertainty in his words.

Aww he's nervous. Who is this guy and what's he done with my overly confident brother?

The rest of the day goes by in a blur. We go on ride after ride, we eat far too much, and eventually we all decide it's time to make our way back home. Gabe tried suggesting we stay over at some local hotel, but the girls have to be up early tomorrow as they are planning on going dress shopping for prom.

We make our way back to the car, but this time I decide to drive since Gabe drove most of the way here. Plus it gives them a little alone time to nap in the back seat since poor Riley can barely keep her eyes open.

"Look, I got so many great pictures," Bella comments from beside me as she flicks through picture after picture of me and her posing, a couple of Riley and Gabe on different rides, or just cutesy candid shots. She'd tried asking Gabe to take a picture earlier in front of one of the rides, but he'd refused saying he doesn't take pictures.

"Look how cute this one is, Rilez," Bella states as she turns to show her a picture before realizing that both of them are fast asleep in the backseat.

"Ohh," she remarks out loud before turning the phone towards me instead. "Look how perfect this one is," she says with a grin. I can't help but agree. It's a picture of Gabe and Riley standing and waiting in line. Gabe is hugging her from behind and is kissing her neck, while Riley giggles and faces towards the camera.

"I'm going to get that printed for him," she states matter of factly as she continues to scroll through the rest of the pictures from today.

Chapter Forty-One

Gabe

"I thought you weren't drinking today?" Nate says, in a questioning, almost condescending way.

Fuck sake, get off my case will ya. "What?" I say as I retrieve my beer and close the fridge door.

Nate's eyes point to the beer in my hand before he shakes his head.

"Oh, fuck off Nate, it's one goddamn beer." I crack it open.

"I know, but you said…" Nate whines, before I cut him off.

"What I said was that I don't drink when I'm driving RILEY around. I said nothing at all about giving up drinking when she's not with me, did I?"

"That's true," Nate replies with a shrug.

"Plus, I've spent the whole goddamn day on my very best behavior. I didn't lose my shit when your little princess demanded we stop for ice cream. And I didn't lose my shit when you both refused to come on that huge ride with me. And I didn't even complain about the fact I had to listen to her fucking terrible singing… I mean come on, cats being strangled don't sound as bad as she did, but I didn't fucking say a word. So the least you can do in return is shut the fuck up and let me enjoy a goddamn beer in my own fucking house!" I snap back at my brother.

A guilty look crosses Nate's face. "I guess so," he mumbles. "Sorry. Thanks again for today."

"It's fine," I huff as I take a swig of my beer. *Damn, that tastes good!* I follow it up with another as I make my way outside, closely followed by Nate.

I sit myself down in my usual spot and Nate sits in his. I try to enjoy a moment of peace since my ears are still ringing from all the noise and chatter today, but I can't enjoy it because I can feel Nate's eyes boring into the side of my head. *Surely he's not still sulking over one beer?*

I look over at him, but he averts his eyes and looks away. But seconds later, I feel his eyes on me again. "What?" I snap as I whip my head back to look at him.

"No, nothing," Nate mumbles before looking down at his feet.

"Good," I reply as I stand up ready to grab another beer.

I pull two beers from the fridge this time, if for no other reason than sheer laziness and the fact I don't wanna spend my night walking back and forth from the kitchen to the backyard.

I sit back down, placing one beer on the grass while I enjoy the other. I hear Nate shuffling in his seat, seeming uneasy. "Seriously Nate, what the fuck is it?"

"Well, I wanted to talk to you about something...So I've been thinking..." *Fuck! Let's talk and I've been thinking, two of my least favorite phrases.*

I take a large swig of my beer, hoping to prepare myself for whatever he's about to say next. Yet nothing could have prepared me for his next sentence.

"I'm going to ask Bella to marry me!"

I spit my beer out in shock, spraying it all over the two of us. "What?" I splutter.

"What did you say?" I cough out.

"I wanna ask Bella to marry me," Nate replies matter of factly.

Why the fuck would he want to marry her? I know he's stupidly obsessed with her, always has been, but why would he want to commit to marriage.

My mind whips through all the unanswered questions. *Why the fuck would he settle down and marry his first girlfriend? Heck, she's the only person he's ever even fucked. Thousands of girls who would happily spread their legs for him, yet he's gonna marry the first girl? Imagine being stuck with the same pussy for life.* My mind shudders at the thought.

"Well? Aren't you going to say anything?" Nate asks, looking a mixture of sad and annoyed.

"Why?" I ask, unsure what else to say.

"Really Gabe? Why? That's all you have to say?" Nate huffs.

"Well, yeah," I shrug. "Wait..." I draw out as it finally dawns on me, "...is she pregnant?"

"What?" Nate says, his face morphing into shock and confusion. "What makes you think she's pregnant? Did Riley say something? Did SHE say something?"

Nate reaches out and takes the beer from my hand, taking a drink, before handing it back to me. "Why do you think she's pregnant?" he asks again.

"I dunno, I just couldn't think of any other reason why you'd marry a girl." *So if she's not pregnant, which she clearly isn't from Nate's shocked response, why the fuck else would he marry her?*

"You almost fucking killed me," Nate laughs, as he takes deep breaths. "I wanna marry her because I love her, you idiot. I love her more than anyone else in the world and I want to spend my whole life with her."

The shit-eating smile on his face as he says that takes me by surprise. *How is he so calm?* "Fucking idiot," he mutters under his breath, shaking his head as if I'm the stupid one for not knowing the answer.

"Oh," I reply. Because, *what else am I supposed to fucking say?*

"Do you have a ring and shit? I hear they're super expensive."

"No, to be honest, I haven't thought that far ahead yet, but I am starting to save up. I wanna make sure I get her the perfect ring." I look over at Nate and see that same, all too familiar, shit eating grin of his again. *Seriously, how is he not freaking out? I am and it's not even me proposing.*

"Well, if you need to borrow any money, let me know, I guess."

"You'd help me? You're not going to try and talk me out of it? Say something nasty or sarcastic in response?" he asks, sounding kind of dubious.

"I'm not saying I understand, because I'd rather pour paint in my eyes, than spend my life with little Miss Perfect. And I think marriage is a complete mistake in general, but I'm not gonna tell you you can't. You're your own man. Plus I'm hardly the person to judge anyone else's life choices, am I?" I reply as I take another swig of my beer and light my smoke.

"That means a lot bro," and I hear the sincerity in his words.

"I gotta help my baby brother right? Can't have him getting his heart broken because he proposed with a goddamn Dollar Tree ring, can I?" I laugh, trying to distract from all the sappiness of this conversation.

"Thanks, Gabe," Nate says as he wipes a goddamn tear from his eyes. *One day I'm taking that kid to the hospital just to make sure he does, in fact, have a dick. No normal man should be as emotional as he is.*

"You ain't gonna do it yet though, right?" I ask, holding my breath.

"I wanna speak to her grandparents first and get their permission, of course."

"Wait, ain't it supposed to be the girl's dad you ask?" *I'm sure that's how it works in the movies, not that I've ever paid much attention.*

"Well yeah, technically, but her parents are idiots who treat her like crap. They break her heart constantly so they don't deserve a say in her happiness. No, it's her grandparents' approval I really need. Without that Bella would never feel comfortable marrying me. So it's her grandparents I need to impress... I just hope they think I'm good enough for her." Nate voices out loud and I can hear the self doubt evident in his tone.

"They'd be fucking crazy not to love you. If they don't think you are good enough, that's on them, not you. No one would or could love Isabella as much as you do. Plus if they don't give their permission, they're old; they probably already have one foot in the grave, and I'm more than happy to give them an extra shove if you need me to," I add, only half joking.

"Gabe!" Nate snaps, while trying not to laugh. "That's not even a little funny. You touch her grandparents and I'll kill you," he adds with a forced frown.

"I'm just saying... you need help burying a body, I've got a shovel ready."

"You're such a dickhead," Nate responds, trying not to laugh. "You can't tell Riley though, or anyone else. This has gotta be our secret." Nate says while pointing a finger at me. *Damn, he really loves this girl.*

"Don't worry, I'm a master secret keeper," I joke, as I pretend to cross my heart. "I won't tell a single soul what happens behind these four walls." *As soon as the words leave my lips I regret them.*

Nate's face morphs from playful to sad in a microsecond, as like me, his mind instantly reminds him of all the many secrets these same walls held for us both growing up.

"I didn't mean..." I start, but the damage is already done.

"I know," Nate replies with a fake smile. "I think I'm gonna hit the hay anyway. I've gotta be up early in the morning."

He stands up and walks away, leaving me kicking myself, for yet again letting my stupid mouth spoil a moment where I was actually feeling close to my brother once again.

Why the fuck am I such a screw up? Even when I'm trying to be nice, or heartfelt or genuine, I'm still a thoughtless dick.

Why am I so shit with words? It's like no matter what I try to do or say, I screw it up. I bet if it was Tucker he was speaking to, he would have known the perfect thing to say in return.

Picking up my empty beer bottle I throw it at the nearest tree, not caring as I hear it smash.

Chapter Forty-Two

Riley

"Get up!" Ava hollers as she begins banging her hands on my bed.

"Fuck off," I grumble as I pull a pillow from under me and place it over my head. *I know we said we'd go dress shopping today, but it's like 5 a.m,, why is she here now?*

"Wake up Riley," Ava huffs as the bitch drags the quilt off me. I kick and punch the mattress in response. "Bitch!"

"Yup, and proud of it," she responds joyfully before she then insults me further by swiping my one remaining pillow from under my head.

"I fucking hate you," I say through gritted teeth.

"And I love you too, my little zombie." Ava jokes back in that mockingly joyful tone of hers.

"Coffee," I grumble as I finally sit up, knowing that the bitch isn't going to let up till I'm out of bed.

"Here you go Precious," she teases as she hands me my favorite iced coffee.

Thankfully she doesn't say another word till my drink is empty and I vaguely resemble a human again.

"Better?" she questions as I place my empty cup on the bedside table.

"Much," I respond, with a grateful sigh.

"It's safe to come in now!" she calls out, just as I hear Izzy and Harper come bounding down the stairs to me.

"I don't know how you do that," Harper laughs. "I'd one hundred percent have ended up with a black eye if I had tried half the shit you did," Harper laughs as she bends down and picks up my pillows and blanket from the floor and throws them back onto my bed.

"True, but she knows I'd hit her back twice as hard if she tried," Ava laughs back in response.

Both me and Izzy look at each other as if to say 'she's right,' before we just nod.

"What time is it anyway? It feels like it's pre-dawn." I complain with a yawn.

"It's almost twelve," Ava huffs. "We have already eaten breakfast and helped Izzy's Nana take some items down to Goodwill. So hurry the fuck up, we need to go prom dress shopping before there's nothing left in this god forsaken town." Ava says all of this with a frown. *She's so bossy!*

"Fine, give me thirty minutes." I sigh as I shuffle out of bed and towards the bathroom.

"You've got twenty," she shouts through the closed door.

I quickly brush my teeth and jump in the shower before there's a knock at the door. "What?" I shout back, refusing to get out of the nice steamy stream.

"Don't wash your hair, as we ain't got time," Ava shouts.

"Fine!" I snap back. *Seriously, why am I even friends with her?*

I jump out of the shower, quickly throw my hair in a messy bun, and put on just enough makeup so I no longer resemble the half dead. That done, I throw on a pair of jeans and a shirt, then make my way upstairs to find the girls waiting in the kitchen talking to my mom.

"Ready!"

"Eighteen minutes and...forty-five seconds," Ava says looking at her watch. "I'm impressed."

"It's a miracle!" my mom teases.

I just fire her a playful frown in response. "Hey you're supposed to be on my side; I'm your daughter not her."

"She brought cupcakes," my mom shrugs as she uses her finger to lap up the frosting.

We head into town and spend the next four hours going from shop to shop looking for something, anything that vaguely resembles a prom dress but unsurprisingly we have absolutely no luck.

"Arggggh!" Ava screams as yet again we walk out of another store empty handed.

"This is impossible," Harper huffs as she slumps against a nearby wall.

"I've got an idea," Izzy says reluctantly. "I'm going into the city next weekend. I'm supposed to be meeting my parents…"

"Okay?" I interrupt, not really understanding what she's getting at.

"Well, they'll probably only see me for like ten minutes before they get bored of me, that's if they don't cancel altogether, of course. So, if you girls come with me, we can do some shopping there for dresses," she adds, a hint of sadness evident in her voice.

Ava gives her a reassuring squeeze. We all know Izzy's parents are pretty shitty. They cancel on her and ignore her constantly. She pretends it doesn't bother her, but it's clear to see how upset it makes her.

"It's fine. They're just really busy with work," Izzy makes her usual excuses for them. "Anyway, why don't we make it a whole day thing? We could meet my parents early. I would love it if they both got to meet you all, especially since you're such a huge part of my life now. Then when that's done, we could head into the city and check out some boutiques. There's bound to be tons of elegant dresses for all occasions."

"That's perfect!" Ava squeals. "Let's do it!"

Izzy's phone rings and she retrieves it from her bag. Her giddy tone lets us know it's Nate on the other end of the phone.

"Nate wants to know if I want to meet him after work, do you mind?" Izzy whispers as she places her hand over the speaker of her phone.

"Go," Ava replies as she ushers her away with her hand.

Izzy finishes her conversation and hangs up the phone telling us that Nate is finishing work at six so we can leave and she'll see us tomorrow.

"You sure? You've got almost an hour. We can wait with you if you want." Harper offers.

"No, it's fine. I need to get a few items anyway - some more makeup, some conditioner, and a few other small items. By the time I'm done and I've walked over it will be almost six."

"We can wait and drive you over there," Ava offers, but again Izzy refuses, saying she'd like a walk since it's still pretty nice out.

"If you're sure," Ava confirms before we all make our way towards where the car is parked, leaving Izzy alone.

ISABELLA

I'm just about to leave the store when I spot it, a photo printing machine. *This is perfect!*

It's mine and Nate's anniversary next month and I want to make him a scrapbook of our time together.

I've already sorted out the pictures I want. It's just a case of printing them and buying the stickers and things to make it perfect.

I select the pictures- over fifty in total - and am about to hit print when I remember the pictures from six flags. I quickly scroll through, choosing my top five. That's when I spot it, the picture of Riley and Gabe, and an idea hits me.

I print and collect my photos, then head down to the aisle that sells photo frames. I spot a beautiful one for Riley. It's silver with a small black diamond heart at the bottom. It's quite simple but very Riley.

I spot the sign, '$7 each or 2 for $10' and inspiration hits. I grab a very simple, dark wood frame and decide to go and reprint the picture for Gabe. *Maybe this will be a good peace offering; show him that I'm not the wicked witch he seems to think I am.*

I carefully place the photo inside and am about to get a gift bag but it's almost six and I'm running late. Deciding Gabe won't care about a pretty bag, I just throw it into my backpack and rush off to meet Nate.

I arrive with minutes to spare, and as soon as I walk up the path a messy looking Nate runs over to greet me. "Sorry, are you okay to wait about ten minutes? I just wanna change my clothes. John's had me lugging sand most of the afternoon."

I take in his dusty appearance and have to agree. "Of course," I giggle before leaning up on my tiptoes to kiss him quickly before he darts off inside.

While I'm waiting, I spot Davis coming off the back of a big truck. "Hey," I wave as I make my way over. "How's the wife doing? Are you a daddy yet?"

"Sure am. Lilly was born three weeks ago, and she's absolutely perfect," he pats his pockets for a moment. "Shit, my phone must be inside, I'll have to show you a picture next time. It'll be worth it though I promise. She's the most adorable baby you'll ever see."

"That's fine, I look forward to it," I tell him with a smile.

"Have you seen Gabe, by the way?"

"Gabe?" Davis repeats, sounding surprised, "Don't you mean Nate?"

"No silly. I've already seen Nate. He's gone to change his clothes. I've got a gift for Gabe, though."

"Oh, I think he's in the office," Davis answers me as he points to a little hut looking building.

"Thanks." I make my way towards the building, removing the picture frame from my bag but as I get closer, I hear Gabe shouting at someone so I attempt to turn around and almost bump straight into the chest of another man.

I take in his appearance and a feeling of uneasiness washes over me. He's tall and slim, too slim. His head is shaved short enough that it almost looks like he's escaped from the army, except he doesn't have a friendly or reassuring face.

He's also covered in tattoos. Even with his work gear on I can see them peeking over his arms and hands and up his neck, and he even has a couple of small ones on his face.

"And what do we have here?" the man says in an intimidating tone.

"Oh, I'm sorry, I'm Izzy, Nate's girlfriend," I mumble. "I was looking for Gabe, but he seems a little busy." I turn to leave, but the guy rests his arm against the wall, blocking my exit.

"And what do you want with Gabe?"

"Erm, I just had something to give him," I say as I clutch the photo frame tighter. "But I'll come back another time. He seems a little busy."

"Nah, he's always like that, but don't worry, I'll take this..." he says, snatching the frame from my hands, "and make sure he gets it."

"It's fine, I'll give it to him another time." I say as I attempt to reach for it but he moves it high out of my reach.

"I'm going in there anyway so I'll give it to him for you," he says in a sweet tone, one that definitely doesn't match the look on his face.

"Please do. It's important," I add, unsure what else to say, but wanting to get out of this very small and tight space.

"It'll be my highest priority," he adds with a sinister smile, before finally moving his arm and allowing me to walk past him.

I rush away and as I do I spot Nate walking towards me.

"I don't like him. He's creepy," I shudder before throwing my arms around his waist and burying my head into his chest for reassurance.

Nate holds me tight and looks past me to the guy who's probably glaring in our direction. "That's Marko," Nate says, pulling away enough to throw his arm around my shoulders and lead me away.

"Does he work with you? I've never seen him before." I ask as I instinctively pull my body tightly against Nate's, needing the comfort and protection he always brings.

"No, not really. He hangs around John and Gabe mostly. He's not a nice guy though baby, keep clear of him. He gives me a very bad feeling."

Chapter Forty-Three

Gabe

"What do you want?" I snap, as I see Marko enter the office. *He knows that he's not supposed to be here, not during business hours.* And after spending the last hour arguing with some useless twat who can't even do a basic debt collecting job correctly, I have no patience left for whatever Marko wants from me. We despise each other at the best of times.

"Well?" I snap again when he doesn't answer me rightaway.

"John said you might need a hand. That someone needs to be taught a lesson," he replies, with a fake air of respect.

"Actually, yeah I do." I nod, for once grateful to see his ugly face. *I'll send him instead. I'm in no mood for this shit, not tonight. It's been an awful day, and all I wanna do is go see Riley and fuck my frustration away.*

"What do you need?" he asks, a glint of mischief and mayhem flashing across his face.

"McBride. That asshole owes us close to ten thousand, but he seems to have forgotten to pay his last three installments. I sent the new guys, Luke and Sam, to give him a warning yesterday, but they seem to think a few slashed tires were enough incentive. So, of course, there was no money when we tried to collect today. Think it's time to send in the big guns."

"Oh goodie, I have a new baseball bat that's just begging for some action."

"Fists only," I snap back. *He fucking knows how I roll - weapons are for pussies.* "If you can't win a fair fight, you shouldn't be in the fight at all."

"What the fuck? John never cares..."

"Well I'm not goddamn John, and I do care, so either fight fairly or I'll get one of the other guys to go. Do you fucking understand me?" I growl as I lose my temper further.

"Fine," Marko says through gritted teeth, "let me grab one of the other guys and the three of us will go together."

I reach for my phone, ready to call Phoenix or Michael, when I spot a bunch of messages from Riley.

17:30

> Hey babe, are you finishing work soon? Wanna meet for coffee? I'm near your work.

18:00

> I've gone home, but message me when you're done. Maybe we could go for a drive or something.

18:20

> Why aren't you replying? I'm home alone, Harper has gone out and my parents are at dinner. I'm bored and extremely horny. Come quick!

18:22

> Or do I have to find someone else to help me instead?

I can't help but smirk at my spoiled little brat and imagine the frustrated pout on her face as she sent that last message.

"You calling the guys or what?" Marko barks, breaking me out of my happy thoughts and instead making me think about bashing his fucking head against the wall.

I call Phoenix and tell him they all need to come over, knowing that they won't be long as they are probably at Saints' Bar, around the corner. As expected, he arrives less than ten minutes later followed by both Michael and Deeno.

"Here's the address. I expect a call when it's done," I instruct as I scribble down the location and hand it to Phoenix.

"You're not coming?" Phoenix questions.

"No, I got somewhere to be," I say, careful not to give anything else away.

"What the fuck is more important than this? You're just gonna leave us? This is like the fifth time you have disappeared off on us!" Marko complains as he bangs his fist on the table.

I reach out and grab him by the scruff of his collar. "What I do and where I go has abso-fucking-lutely nothing to do with you!" I growl before releasing him with enough of a shove that it causes him to stumble.

I see from his face he's desperate to punch me, and part of me wishes he would. Just to give me an excuse, any excuse to kick his ass.

There's zero love lost between the two of us. Marko has been desperate to take over my position as the boss for years, but we both know I'm basically family in John's eyes.

The only way he'd get my position is if I step down, and as much as I hate it, I have zero desire to do so. We'd both happily fight for the role of king of the pack but we know it would cause anarchy in the ranks if we did, so we don't.

"I am your fucking boss, and you will do as I fucking say," I bellow.

"But.." he begins.

"But what? There's four of you here, you're telling me the four of you aren't man enough to scare one jumped up little prick who owes us money? In that case, maybe I need to tell John we need to find some new blood if you're too much of a pussy to go alone."

"No, course not. I'm more than capable of getting shit done without you," Marko counters and he's so angry that I can see the veins in his neck are threatening to burst.

"Then get the fuck out of my sight then." I snap as I open the door and virtually kick them out.

The four of them scurry out of the office like the fucking cockroaches they are. Once they are gone, I lock up and leave myself. I fire a quick message to Riley letting her know that I'm on my way, determined to ensure she remembers exactly who owns each and every one of her orgasms.

I pull up outside her house, and notice all the lights seem to be out. I reach for my phone ready to text her, and see there's one waiting already. - 'The door's unlocked and I'm ready and waiting, come find me!!!'

I race inside not even caring if anyone else is home. As soon as I enter, I spot the stairs and am about to run up them when I see a piece of paper.

-Wrong stairs lover boy. Try again.

I turn around and spot another piece of paper stuck to a door.

I make my way towards it and there's another handwritten note.

Getting warmer lover boy, now come downstairs and

prepare for things to get hotter!

I fling open the door that appears to be leading down to a basement and make my way down. I almost turn back, thinking it's a joke until I spot another door. This one welcomes me to 'Riley and Harper's hideaway.'

I push the door open and spot my girl lying on the bed in a red lace bra and matching panties. *Fuck me! She definitely looks like fire.*

"You found me," her voice low and seductive.

I sprint over to her, seeming to make my way across the room in only a few steps. I kick off my shoes and whip off my jeans, wasting no time before claiming my prize.

We must pass out, as the next thing I know, I'm waking up as the heat radiates off my little hot water bottle. *How the fuck she can get so hot when she's asleep, I have no idea.*

Unsure where I left my phone and unable to see in the dark, I reach for what I think is my phone, but unfortunately it's Riley's.

As I do, I spot a message on the lock screen.

Twinnie

> really guys? in our room? I'm sleeping at Izzy's!

Feeling guilty but also confused about how her sister obviously managed to come in while we were sleeping, yet I didn't wake up. I decide to sneak out the open window, not wanting to risk bumping into any other family member.

My intention is to sneak out, have a cigarette, then sneak back in. I get out surprisingly easy and am just about to light up when all of a sudden everything goes dark.

Chapter Forty-Four

Gabe

Opening my eyes and feeling the fear and panic overtake my senses, I look around. My eyes struggle to focus at first, unable to see anything other than darkness. I blink a few times and can vaguely make out we're in a large room. A basement perhaps? *No, it's too large.* A warehouse? *No, I don't think so.* It's then that I hear the sound of a car pulling up as a glimmer of light illuminates the space. I turn my head in the direction it came from and see the wooden door more clearly. *A barn. Of course it fucking is.*

"Nice to see you're back with us," a sinister voice comes from behind me. *A voice that I know belongs to Marko, even though I can't yet see him as the barn is thrown into darkness again.*

"What the fuck do you think you're doing?" I bellow as I tug harder trying to free myself from the rope currently pinning me to a chair.

"Reminding you where the fuck you belong," Marko snaps back as he finally comes into focus, closely followed behind by Pheonix.

"Who the fuck do you think you are? Are you forgetting you work for ME!" I roar.

An evil cackle leaves his throat. "Work for you? YOU don't even fucking work for YOU recently!"

I see the way Marko's nostrils flare as the room becomes illuminated once more by the headlights from a truck as it pulls up just outside. "Maybe you forgot the motherfucking oath we all took to put the Sinners and the job before anyone else."

"And maybe YOU forgot who fucking made you all take that goddamn oath," I huff. *Seriously, who the fuck does this prick think he's talking to?*

Moments later I hear more voices outside. "Untie me now before I fucking kill you all. " I shout loud enough to be heard by whomever the footsteps belong to that I can hear closing in on me.

"Oh believe me, we all know exactly what you're capable of, don't we boys." Marko laughs as he looks past me towards his little fan group.

"Yep, we all know about Johnny Boy's precious prodigy," Micheal pipes up as he and two other guys in masks appear and take up their place beside Marko and Phoenix.

Micheal rips off his mask, "Only twelve years old and already killed his first man . . ." he mocks, as he repeats the words I know John has boasted about so many times. ". . . perhaps being back here will remind you of who exactly you are."

"Must be nice to have inherited the empire," Marko remarks venomously as he kicks my chair. *Oh, so that's what this is about. Marko is making his play to be head of the pack. He's fucking welcome to it. I never wanted any of it. But now is not the time to roll over or back down.*

"Oh dear, are we a little upset that Daddy never showed us enough love?" I mock. I see the anger rising on Marko's face, and decide to push him more. "No matter what you do, you'll never be his favorite, will you?"

His hand flies to the gun in his waistband as he thrusts it towards me. Both Michael and Phoenix reach out their hands to stop him.

"Don't do it," Phoenix whispers. "He's the only one who knows how it runs at the top."

I know he can't kill me, John would never allow it. As well as the promise to stick together, that stupid oath also guaranteed protection for our families. It was the only reason I agreed to it in the first place. As a small, malnourished thirteen year old, it was the only way I could guarantee Nate's protection from all the assholes my father pissed off throughout the years. If this jackass breaks that by killing me, his whole family and that of every other guy here will be in jeopardy.

"I'm calm, I'm calm!" Marko snaps as he pulls out of their grips and runs his hand through his hair.

"That's it, be a good boy and do as you're told," I mock.

"What I wouldn't give to blow your brains out right here!" Marko sneers through gritted teeth as he brings his face so close to mine that I'm almost knocked back unconscious by the stench of his breath.

"Then what the fuck is stopping you? Worried that John would have you dead and buried before the night was out?"

"Dead men don't have much power now do they? Not unless his ghost is gonna haunt me to death," He replies venomously.

"What the fuck are you talking about Marko? Seems like you've been sniffing a bit to much coke and it's fucked with your ability to string a coherent sentence together."

"Oh, you don't know, do you?" Marko says with a sinister grin. "Daddy's dead... or should I say another daddy is dead, since didn't your old man drop dead as well?"

I'm about to question him further when I see Phoenix move over toward a worn out tarp on the floor, one that until now I didn't even notice. As he pulls back the tarp I see it's hiding a body, and worse of all, it's John's cold, lifeless body.

"What the fuck have you done?" I bellow as I fight against my restraints. "He took you in when you were nothing but a punk kid living on the streets," I remind him as I turn my attention to Phoenix, knowing Marko is beyond reason. "And you," I say, turning my attention to Michael, who's been relatively quiet, "Who took you in when you had nothing? When you were nothing more than a junky kid, passing out blowjobs in return for the next high?"

Micheal dips his head in shame, or perhaps guilt. "We didn't plan it," he mumbles, his voice barely audible.

"No, it was you we wanted dead," Marko snaps. "John was only supposed to see the error of his ways and be brought here to agree to let me lead instead of you, realizing I was the real alpha of this pack," Marko explains as he takes out a joint and begins pacing back and forth.

"How was I supposed to know the old fucker would have a heart attack or something?"

I feel slightly better knowing John didn't suffer, but still, I plan to get my retribution for this. I may have had my ups and downs with John over the years, but he's the closest I've ever had to a parent; he took care of me when I had no idea how to take care of myself. He's been good to me, even if it's in an unconventional way.

"So now what? You're gonna kill me too? Take over the business? Then what?" I question as I turn my attention to Phoenix, having already resigned myself to my inevitable fate.

"Unfortunately, we need you. You're the only one that John trusted enough to show the inner workings to, the only one higher ups will work with without John," Micheal reveals, and I can tell by the look on his face he's furious about the fact that he needs me.

"So what? You're just gonna untie me, and you expect that we're all gonna be best fucking friends?" I question. *How the fuck did this happen? How the fuck am I going to get out of this? What about Nate? Riley? Even Isabella? Are they going to suffer because of me? I'm probably better off dead. I can barter their safety for my knowledge and life.*

"We may need you alive for now, but you've abandoned the Sinners Gabe; that can't go unpunished," Phoenix pipes up.

"Yes, and for some dirty little whore at that," Marko adds, "Hope her fucking pussy was worth it."

A sense of panic washes over me. *Shit, do they know about Riley? How much she means to me? How? I've been so careful to keep my two worlds apart.*

"Oh," Marko laughs, bringing his face just centimeters from mine, "You thought we didn't know about your little whore?"

"Leave her the fuck out of this!" I snap as I spit directly into his face. *How did they find out about her? Is she safe?*

"Cunt!" he shouts as he kicks my chair with so much force that I fall backward. As I do, one of the legs snaps off, making it easier for me to partially free myself.

"What I wouldn't give to kill you right now," Marko says through gritted teeth as he points his gun down towards me. My hands are still tied behind my back but my legs are now free so I take my chance and attempt to kick him away, but he's too quick. The sound of gunfire echoes around the room. I wait for the inevitable feeling of either pain or death to overcome me, but nothing happens.

"The next one won't be a warning," Phoenix shouts. I turn towards him and see he's holding his own gun high in the air.

"The bastard deserves it," Marko states coldly as he brings his boot down, and stamps directly on my abdomen, winding me.

I begin coughing and sputtering, trying not to throw up from the shock and pain.

"Man, you've no idea how long I've wanted to do that," he laughs as he attempts to do it again. This time I'm ready. Just as his foot comes down I roll over and his foot hits the chair, causing it to break, setting me free. *Bring it on asshole!*

Realization flashes across his face a second before my foot connects with his balls, bringing him to his knees. I waste no time climbing on top of him and punching and elbowing him as quickly and forcefully as I can. I enjoy watching the fear in his eyes as he realizes he's unable to break out from under me, despite all his attempts at thrashing around. I feel blow after blow connecting with my ribs and hips but barely register the pain, I'm too lost in the euphoria of the fight.

I suddenly feel arms attempting to pull me back and off him but I resist.

"Make the call now!!!" someone bellows as two sets of strong arms desperately attempt to drag me off a bloody and bruised Marko.

The sound of ringing fills the air for a moment, but unfortunately it's enough to distract me just long enough for Marko to escape from under me as Phoenix and Michael pull me off him.

"I believe you know my cousin Ryan," Marko says as he spits out a mouthful of blood and possibly a tooth.

The only man still wearing his stupid balaclava removes it and my eyes widen in shock. It's the wannabe rapist from Tucker's birthday. *He's Marko's cousin? How didn't I know that?*

I see the same sadistic smile lighting up the prick's face as the one I've seen on Marko's so many times before. *The family resemblance is fucking obvious now.* "I told you I'd get you back, didn't I?" he smirks.

"I'm gonna fucking kill you!" I bellow as I attempt to break free of the tight hold the others have on my arms.

"Fucking try it," he laughs as he presses a button and suddenly a projection of a familiar sight lights up a makeshift screen on the wall behind him.

My heart drops out of my ass as I see my beautiful girl, fast asleep in her bed. A masked man standing near her and holding a knife appears on the screen. *Please let this be fake, please!*

"Can you hear me?" Rapey Ryan says aloud.

The masked man nods his head before lifting his finger to his lips, telling us to be quiet. *Shit, it's real. These monsters have Riley.*

"Please!" I beg. "Kill me, but spare her."

Laughter erupts from the men around the room. "Seems our fierce leader has gone soft boys," Marko smirks before punching me square in the jaw. I try to fight back but the two men have a firm hold on me, plus my attention is still mostly on my sleeping beauty on the screen.

"Fucking bow!" Marko snaps. "Drop to your fucking knees and bow. Bow in front of everyone and let them know that you accept me as your fucking leader," Marko sneers as he manically bounces from foot to foot.

A growl of frustration leaves my mouth. "Never!"

"Seems he may need a little more motivation," Phoenix laughs beside me.

"Phase two," I hear Rapey Ryan say into his phone.

I watch as the masked figure flashes his knife at the camera, then walks over to Riley. He lifts the blanket and slowly runs the knife up her leg, "Gaaabe" Riley whines playfully before her snoring continues. *Seriously, how is she still asleep?*

Part of me wants her to wake up, fight, get away. But I know that will only make it worse. *These sadistic bastards would find it a game of cat and mouse then.*

So instead, I pray that, like the zombie sleeper I know she is, she stays asleep and oblivious to it all.

"Fine, fine," I concede as I reluctantly lower to my knees. "Stop it!" *Please stop! God if you're real, find a way to stop this.*

"Continue," Marko says as he snatches the phone out of his cousin's hand.

The masked man then moves the knife higher, up her thigh, and towards the hem of her shirt.

I want nothing more than to fight back, protest, and kill every last one of them. But if I do that I know Riley will be hurt so I have to fight every natural instinct I have.

"I bow, I bow, now stop!" I scream in a panic.

"Continue," Marko says into the phone as he looks down at me.

I watch in horror as the knife lifts the bottom of her shirt and makes its way towards her pussy as if in slow motion. But just before it reaches its destination the picture disappears.

I can't see Riley anymore as whatever was recording this has now been dropped to the floor. *Please be okay baby, please.*

"That's enough," a voice says from the screen. This is the first time I've heard the voice so I try desperately to pinpoint who it belongs to.

I can hear a hushed but frustrated conversation, but it's too low to hear what's being said or who the voices belong to.

"I didn't sign up for this shit." *Wait, I recognize that voice -Deeno.* The phone is lifted from the floor and I briefly get a glimpse of the figure leaving the bed. But I still don't know what happened in those soul destroying minutes when we were left blind. *I'm gonna make every single one of these cunts suffer for touching my girl. And if they've hurt her, I'll hurt them so bad they will be begging for death.*

I launch myself at the phone, tackling Marko to the floor as I do.

"Give me the fucking phone!" I bellow, but it's too late. The line's gone dead and the only connection I have to my girl has been stripped away from me.

Anger, panic, and fear overcome me as I begin to attack him. "Call them back! Call them back!" I scream in between punches.

The rest of the guys attempt to pull me off him but I'm too frenzied. Like a wild animal I suddenly seem to possess inhuman level strength.

"Call them back!" I snap again as I drag Marko off the ground and pin him against a wall.

"Never." Marko smirks as he spits out a mouthful of blood.

"I'm telling you..." I begin before I'm cut off.

"No, I'm telling YOU," Marko smirks with blood dripping from the side of his mouth, "I'm in charge now and you will do what the fuck I say, when the fuck I say it. Because I'm the fucking boss now."

"The hell you are," I reply before it suddenly hits me. I just agreed to this. In my panic, I agreed to this. I agreed to step down and let Marko take over as top dog. And in doing so, I signed my own death sentence. I can't do anything to him without the repercussions for not just myself, but my whole family as well. *He has me exactly where he wants me!*

If I try to break away, my whole family is in danger. That means my brother, Izzy, Riley, heck even their friends are fair game. If I disobey, I start a war I cannot fight alone.

Reluctantly, I step away and have no choice but to step in line.

"That's what I thought." Marko smirks as he straightens up and uses the sleeve of his hoodie to wipe away the blood from his mouth. *Keep smiling motherfucker, I'll fucking get you for this, mark my words.*

"Now fuck off bitch boy, I expect you to be available every day and all day. If I say jump, you ask how high!" he cackles.

"I'm gonna get you for this. Mark my words. I'm not backing down lightly," I vow under my breath.

"Oh you will back down; you'll step in line and lick my fucking boots if I tell you too," Marko laughs as he turns his back on me. I launch forward but am met with a bunch of angry looking faces, letting me know that at this moment, the whole gang is standing with Marko.

"Come on boys, I think we've all earned ourselves some booze, blow, and bitches," Phoenix smirks as he leads the guys out the door.

"Oh, and Gabe," Marko chimes, as he turns to look back at me. "I expect you first thing in the morning, ready to take up your new role as bitch boy. For now, I suggest you go bury your whore. That's if there's anything left to bury; maybe I should send Ryan around there first. He's always had a fascination with necrophilia, maybe I should let him test it out," Marko says with a sadistic laugh.

I run towards him, no longer caring about the rules, and simply wanting to murder him, but before I reach him the barn door is slammed shut and something is pushed through pinning the door shut.

I pound against the door, trying to escape, as I hear the truck start and then drive away. I run at the door, pounding against it with all my strength, once... twice... on the third time the door flies open, and I see a broken rake handle on the floor.

I run off in any direction, having no idea how to get home since it's been years since I was last here. Something in me must remember though, as I make it to the road relatively quickly and manage to hitch hike back to town and straight to Riley's.

When I arrive the front door is wide open, and with my heart in my throat, and fearing the worst I rush inside and straight towards her room. As soon as I enter I see she's lying motionless on the bed. *Fuck, fuck. FUCK. She's dead! They fucking killed her.*

I begin shaking her, not knowing what else to do. "What the..." Riley shouts and the sound of her voice and the relief I feel knowing she's alive opens the floodgates as the tears begin to pour down my face.

"You're alive!" I sob.

"Of course I'm alive," Riley says, sounding confused as she holds me as I sob like a fucking baby into her chest.

"Baby what happened; was it a nightmare?" she asks groggily.

"No... they were here... Sinners, they were here," I sob, even though I know I'm not making any sense.

"No one's here baby, it's just us," Riley tries to soothe. It would have almost worked, had I not spotted the discarded knife on the floor.

Bending down I pick it up. "Then what's this?" I say holding the knife in the air.

"No idea, I've never seen that before. Is it yours?" Riley questions as she rubs her eyes, as if she can't believe what she's seeing.

That's when it dawns on me. She really has no idea what the fuck happened tonight, how close she was to dying, or worse, all because of me.

"Err, yeah maybe," I mumble, because what the fuck else am I supposed to say? *Actually no, this belongs to one of the psychos that broke in tonight. Oh yeah, and each one is a thug for hire who'd think nothing of slitting your throat or raping you in your sleep. To top it all off, it's all my fault as I led them straight to you!*

I pull her body tightly against me as I snuggle down into the bed, terrified to let her go, knowing once I do, it will be forever.

"Gabe?" Riley attempts to ask, her voice confused and unsure.

"Shhh baby, it's fine. You're fine, go back to sleep my Angel," I whisper as I bury her head into my chest and I rest my own head against the top of hers.

I hold her in my arms one last time, memorizing everything about her. The way her skin feels pressed against mine. The faint smell of coconut that wafts from her hair. Heck, even the grunt-like sounds she makes when she snores. I lie awake holding her in my arms until I see the sun starting to rise outside the window. I pull out my phone and snap one more picture of her asleep in my arms, then place one final kiss on her temple, before I walk out of her life. Forever.

Acknowledgments

I apologize in advance that these are going to be lengthy, but as anyone who's ever had to have a conversation with me knows.... This girl can talk for all of England. I'd like to blame it on my neuro-spicy-ness but, nope, I'm just a 'lil whirlwind of craziness.

That said, this is my book. The book and main characters have been screaming to be written since the start of my first book, Forever Entwined. Those of you who have followed me on the many ups and downs of my writing journey will know that at one point I was adamant this book would never be written; but to those who pushed and pushed and begged and pleaded for me to write Gabe's story, thank you because without your love, support, friendship...and the occasional kick up the ass (yes, Jenn, I'm looking at you here) this book would have never become a reality. But I'm so grateful it did. It may have pushed me out of my comfort zone and forced me to tap into my inner smut slut, but throughout this story not only did Gabe heal and grow, but so did I.

To my children-

Jayden and Mason, you boys have been my biggest motivation throughout my journey and have pushed me to strive.

Thank you for the many times you helped me make up little book boxes or promo packs, and for even helping me carry them to the post office. And for the times when I was stuck with writer's block and you'd offer to play games to distract me or ask if I needed help with writing.... Thank god you have no idea what Mummy has written, though. Either way, I still appreciate all the hype you gave me over my 'pretty' covers and 'cool' bookmarks.

Kuristien Elizabeth-

My best friend. Partner in crime, sunflower, and soul sister. I don't know what I did to deserve you, but whatever it was, I will forever be thankful. You entered my life when I needed a friend the most, and you have taught me what it truly means to be seen by another. Your friendship, love, and understanding have been like a pillar of strength, guiding me to happiness even when I had no idea how to get there myself. You taught me to be stronger. You taught me 'the world breaks everyone, but afterward, some are stronger at the broken places.' I still can't believe our friendship began because of our mutual love for Anna Todd's After series and now Anna Todd holds copies of both of our books in her house. Who would have thought it, Girly?

Anna Todd-

Your books opened up a whole new world for me. Until *'After'* I had never had the desire to read a book, let alone write one. I stumbled upon your story one day by chance and was hooked from the first page. Until you, I assumed writers all had to be well educated with years of English qualifications under their belt, but you taught me that all you need is passion, desire, and an idea. Hardin is now and shall forever be my ultimate book boyfriend. He may be broken, but he is beautifully broken. Even now, I still fangirl like crazy every time we chat. And the day you messaged to say you were reading MY book. I nearly died of happiness and shock. You're such a beautiful person inside. You are now and will always be my ultimate author idol.

Jenn Maryk -

Words aren't enough to thank you for everything you've done for me. During my journey, you've been my friend, my PA, my editor, my walking spell checker. The bad cop to my good cop, and at times even my drill sergeant, bringing me back from the edge of despair when my own mind sends me on a mental spiral or when the stubbornness hits and I refuse to do as I'm told haha. I'm beyond grateful that I found you and Dusty, as you've made my journey so much easier and less stressful. At times, it definitely felt like this book was your book baby just as much as it was mine. Even if we did squabble daily over whether or not poor Gabe was a cinnamon roll (he's not by the way, and since it's my book and my character I get the final say... and yes, I'm poking my tongue out as I write this), but in all seriousness, you truly are an angel sent to help and support me, and I couldn't have done any of this without you. So thank you so much, Jenn for not only being my P.A. and editor, but for also being a true friend.

My author support -

H.L Swan, Dana Isaly, Melody Mode, Dusty Shirley, and so many more. Not only do I get to call all of you amazing women inspirations, but I'm lucky enough to call you friends. You've all helped and supported me in different ways, and after the disaster and black hole I was pushed into during book one, I'm so grateful to have had you ladies helping and supporting me, so I got to enjoy my journey during book two.

To my book besties team-

Thank you all for being there for me, supporting me, and listening to me. and stopping me from spiraling too badly when things went wrong. Through you, I have found my people and my community. I love and appreciate you all. Thank you for all of your help, love, and support. I don't know how you all put up with me and my million questions or end of the world panic attacks. I'm grateful to each and every one of you for taking the time to listen, support, and encourage me. You girls are all true friends. All our group chats, whether that be my alpha, beta, or little hype team, kept me going. You ladies inspired me to do better, to push myself further, and never once did you ridicule any of my crazy ideas, thoughts, or fears. You ladies are now and will forever be one of my favorite parts of my author journey. And a special thanks to Ashley, in particular to the many graphics she was inspired to make. Every time I woke up to a 'this may be weird but I had this idea' message, I spent the rest of the day beaming from ear to ear because I was so honored that anyone would take the time to make things or be inspired by my words.

About the Author

I am a UK based author who sees herself as a spicy, neurodivergent, crazy person. I love to read, spend time with my kids and family and spend far too much time scrolling on social media.

My two dogs, Kara and Skyler, are my shadows, and whether I'm reading, writing or just relaxing around the house, they will be beside me, making me laugh.

I love connecting with my readers and the people in the book community. If you are ever inclined, send me a message so that we can chat! You can find me mostly on Facebook (yeah, I know it's not most people's first choice, but I'm terrible with social media and just can't work most of them).

I also dabble with TikTok occasionally, although, I'll be honest, it's mostly to watch either dog videos or spicy BookTok videos when I'm supposed to be writing.

But feel free to come chat to me anytime.

linktr.ee/c.b_halliwell

Gabriel's Salvation is my second book and is book 1 of a trilogy.

If you'd like to know more about the Scott brothers, and get to know more about Nate, Izzy and the rest of the group, you can catch the heartwarming story of Nathaniel here .

Forever Entwined is an emotional friends to lovers, second chance, small town read that I promise won't disappoint and will definitely have you reaching for the tissues.

Printed in Great Britain
by Amazon